A Tennessee Folklore Sampler

Folk
Speak.

A Tennessee Folklore Sampler

Selections from the

TENNESSEE FOLKLORE SOCIETY BULLETIN

[1 9 3 5 – 2 0 0 9]

Edited by

TED OLSON AND ANTHONY P. CAVENDER

With a Foreword by WILLIAM FERRIS

THE UNIVERSITY OF TENNESSEE PRESS / KNOXVILLE

Published in Cooperation with the Tennessee Folklore Society

Copyright © 2009 by The University of Tennessee Press / Knoxville
All Rights Reserved. Manufactured in the United States of America.
First Edition.

The paper in this book meets the requirements of American National
Standards Institute / National Information Standards Organization
specification Z39.48-1992 (Permanence of Paper). It contains 30 percent
post-consumer waste and is certified by the Forest Stewardship Council.

Library of Congress Cataloging-in-Publication Data

A Tennessee folklore sampler: selections from the Tennessee folklore society
bulletin, 1935–2009 / edited by Ted Olson and Anthony P. Cavender, with a
foreword by William Ferris.
       p. cm.
Includes bibliographical references and index.
ISBN-13: 978-1-57233-668-1 (pbk.: alk. paper)
ISBN-10: 1-57233-668-4 (pbk.: alk. paper)
 1. Tennessee Folklore Society—History.
 2. Folklore—Tennessee—History.
 3. Tennessee—Folklore.
 4. Tennessee—Social life and customs.
 I. Olson, Ted.
 II. Cavender, Anthony P.

GR110.T4T457 2009
398.09768—dc22
2009015027

Contents

Illustrations

Foreword

I t is interesting to reflect on how folklore shapes the idea of a state and defines its identity both for its residents and for those who live outside the state. I grew up on a farm near Vicksburg, Mississippi, and have fond memories of George and Clara Rumage, an elderly couple in their seventies and sixties respectively, who moved from Tennessee and bought a farm adjacent to ours in 1927. My family affectionately referred to the Rumages as Aunt Clara and Uncle George. Uncle George was a timber man who bought and sold timber when he came to Mississippi and later grew sorghum cane, which he made into molasses each fall using a mule-powered machine to crush the cane.

As a child, I rode my horse three miles to their home each afternoon after school, gathered their eggs, and enjoyed a piece of Aunt Clara's delicious yellow cake with chocolate icing sprinkled with crushed pecans. Uncle George loved to tell me how he grew up in Hornbeak, Tennessee, fished on nearby Reelfoot Lake, and always voted for Estes Kefauver, a progressive Tennessee senator who was friends with his fellow Tennessee senator Albert Gore Sr. Because of my love for his stories, Uncle George considered me an honorary Tennessean, and to this day I associate the state with the colorful tales he shared with me.

The first question a southerner asks a stranger is "Where are you from?" We need to know the place a person calls home, the city or state with which he or she identifies. The state in which we grow up and/or live defines our identity and our voice both as southerners and as Americans in profoundly important ways. Today, we are increasingly drawn to local foods, economic resources, and culture as an anchor for our daily lives. We understand places through the stories, music, and material culture that celebrate them, and this is the world that folklorists know so well. Folklore studies of ballads, blues, gospel, folk tales, dogtrots, and baskets paint a rich portrait of Tennessee that allows us to understand the soul of the state. These are iconic worlds, close to the heart, that have mythic associations with the state.

The study of local folkways is an ancient, revered tradition in the American South. In the nineteenth century, Augustus Baldwin Longstreet celebrated his state's colorful worlds in *Georgia Scenes*, a collection of essays about horse trad-ers and storytellers. A century later, these stories inspired William Faulkner's fictional Yoknapatawpha County in Mississippi. Generations of southern writers, artists, and musicians have focused on the local, that highly personal place in which memories reside most deeply.

The publication of *A Tennessee Folklore Sampler* is a welcome resource for folklorists and a special treasure for citizens of Tennessee and the nation. Compiled and edited by Anthony Cavender and Ted Olson, the volume offers a rich sample of the state's folklore that has been documented and published in issues of the *Tennessee Folklore Society Bulletin* since the society was founded in 1934. Prominent members of the society over the years have included Eleanor Roosevelt, Estes Kefauver, Mrs. Cordell Hull, and Albert Gore Sr.

In their excellent introduction to this book, Cavender and Olson explore the history of the Tennessee Folklore Society and the evolution of Tennessee folklore studies, noting that few articles on black folklore appeared in the *Bulletin* prior to the 1970s. Materials in the volume cover the "three states of Tennessee" (East Tennessee, Middle Tennessee, and West Tennessee) and their respective capitols of Knoxville, Nashville, and Memphis. Linguist Michael Montgomery explores linguistic differences in these worlds in his fine article "Does Tennessee Have Three 'Grand' Dialects?" (1995). While music and folk tales have received extensive attention in the *Bulletin,* there has been far less attention given to material culture.

The articles included in the volume offer rich, colorful descriptions of Tennessee folkways. In his piece on "Illicit Whiskey Making" (1946), Charles S. Pendleton explains that when the mash ferments, it creates a "beer" that some locals drink. But Pendleton warns his readers that "to an outsider it is as vile a concoction as can be thrust down a throat."

Ben S. Austin writes about "The Vanishing Art of Cooking Table-Grade Sorghum Molasses" (1992) with mouth-watering prose. "When the bubbles are about the size of a silver dollar and burst in the middle, it is ready to be drawn off." At that point, all the reader needs "is a large pan of hot 'cathead' biscuits and a bowl of freshly churned sweet butter." Austin recalls a preacher who while speaking to a large congregation said he felt like the boy who fell into a barrel of molasses. "The youngster lifted his eyes to heaven and prayed, 'Lord, make my tongue equal to my opportunity.'" He warns the reader to avoid the dark "blackstrap" molasses in the supermarket because it is only good for "hoot and holler cake."

For the past seventy-five years, an important network of scholars based in major universities throughout Tennessee have devoted their careers to studying, writing, and teaching about the folklore of their state. David Evans (Memphis State University); Charles Wolfe (Middle Tennessee State University); Donald Davidson, George Pullen Jackson, and Bill Ivey (Vanderbilt University); John Work (Fisk University); Jim Akenson (Tennessee Technological University); and Tom Burton, Richard Blaustein, Ted Olson, and Anthony Cavender (East

Tennessee State University) are but a few of the folklorists who have deepened our knowledge of Tennessee folklore. These scholars and their academic institutions constitute a critical infrastructure that supports and affirms the state's folklore traditions.

In addition, individuals in institutions outside the academy have done outstanding work in preserving Tennessee's folklore traditions. These leaders include Judy Peiser (Center for Southern Folklore, Memphis), Charles Seeman (Country Music Foundation, Nashville), Bobby Fulcher (Tennessee State Parks, Nashville), and John Rice Irwin (Museum of Appalachia, Norris).

That the richest folklore traditions are often found in the poorest economic areas is a familiar pattern. In his study "Basketmakers of Cannon County: An Overview" (1986), Lawrence Alexander explains that the basketmakers "were subsistence farmers who occupied some of the poorest land in the county." And within the county, basketmakers were considered "the lowest level in the local social hierarchy." Tennessee's folklore thrives "on the edge," both geographically and economically, like weeds along the roadside. With the authority of their university positions, folklorists have long reached out to such worlds to affirm their value and to help preserve them.

The 1982 World's Fair, which was held in Knoxville, featured an important Folklife Festival that was organized by the Smithsonian Institution and the National Endowment for the Arts. The event drew visitors from around the world and provided an important stage for Tennessee's folk traditions. During the fair, John Rice Irwin showcased his fifty-two-acre Museum of Appalachia in nearby Norris, Tennessee. Irwin struck up a friendship with his fellow Tennessean Alex Haley and convinced Haley to build his impressive home and conference center just down the road. Joined by Lamar Alexander, Tom T. Hall, and Will Campbell, they formed the "Fellowship" and traveled in Hall's bus to communities throughout Tennessee to celebrate their folk traditions.

For music lovers, Nashville and Memphis are the heart of country music and blues, respectively. Nashville's Grand Ole Opry has supported generations of country music performers, and Memphis's Beale Street was home to W. C. Handy, B. B. King, and many other celebrated blues artists. Tennessee's leadership in these musical worlds is clearly unique.

Storytelling has an equally impressive presence in Tennessee. Both the International Storytelling Center and the National Storytelling Festival are located in Jonesborough. Each year thousands of fans come to hear storytellers from throughout the world tell their tales. The success of these programs grows out of studies folklorists have done on traditional storytelling in Tennessee.

A Tennessee Folklore Sampler features impressive articles by early scholars such as Donald Davidson, who was part of the celebrated Vanderbilt group know as the Fugitives. Davidson underscores both his interest in traditional Scottish ballads and his dislike for collectors such as Alan Lomax in "Current

Attitudes toward Folklore" (1940). A decade later, the distinguished folklorist Herbert Halpert published "Riddles from West Tennessee," which included the riddle "What goes up the chimney, but won't go down the chimney?" and its answer, "Smoke."

Important recent studies on Tennessee black folklore in the *Bulletin* include Elizabeth Peterson and Tom Rankin's "Free Hill: An Introduction" (1985), which describes an upland black community in Clay County, Tennessee, near the Tennessee-Kentucky border. Kip Lornell's "Successes of the 'Spirit'" (1991) traces the history of the Spirit of Memphis gospel quartet. And Bruce Nemerov's "John Wesley Work III: Field Recordings of Southern Black Folk Music, 1935–1942" (1987) traces the career of Work at Fisk University and his relationship with Alan Lomax. Nemerov later developed this article into a book, *Lost Delta Found: Rediscovering the Fisk University–Library of Congress Coahoma County Study, 1941–1942* (2005), and an accompanying CD of Work's recordings, *John W. Work III: Recording Black Culture* (2007).

While the essays in *A Tennessee Folklore Sampler* tell us much about the folklore of Tennessee, they also remind us that the folklore of the state's rich, diverse ethnic community is largely missing from the pages of the *Sampler*. The worlds of Tennessee's Jewish, Lebanese, Hispanic, Irish, Italian, German, Hmong, and Chinese communities, and of many other groups, await study. Future editions of this fine work will track the evolution of all families that call Tennessee home. Their respective cultures constitute the steadily broadening folklore worlds that enrich the state and make it a central part of the global South.

William Ferris
University of North Carolina at Chapel Hill

Acknowledgments

The idea for this anthology originated with the recently deceased Charles K. Wolfe, professor of English and folklore at Middle Tennessee State University, long-time editor of the *Tennessee Folklore Society Bulletin,* and nationally recognized scholar of traditional and popular music. The tremendous demands on his time as a prolific author, music producer, and consultant prompted Charles to turn the anthology project over to us. We hope that it successfully fulfills his vision.

The Department of Sociology and Anthropology at East Tennessee State University deserves special mention for its generous support of this project. Dorothy Harville, executive aide for the department, and departmental support staff Melody McPeak and Ankita Mithaiwala provided able assistance with manuscript preparation. We also thank the following individuals for their help with the identification and preparation of some of the historic photographs that appear in the anthology: Ned Irwin and John Fleenor, Archives of Appalachia, East Tennessee State University; Paul Wells, director, Center of Popular Music, Middle Tennessee State University; Lisa Pruitt, director, Gore Center, Middle Tennessee State University; James Akenson, Tennessee Technological University; Tom Rankin, director, Center for Documentary Studies, Duke University; and Sandy Conatser, Country Music Hall of Fame and Museum.

We express our genuine appreciation to the following members of the Tennessee Folklore Society who thoughtfully and enthusiastically responded to an invitation, extended to all society members, to participate in the process of selecting articles from the *Tennessee Folklore Society Bulletin* for inclusion in the anthology: Donald B. Ball, Thomas Burton, Robert Cogswell, Edwina Doran, Bobby Fulcher, Walter Haden, Benita Howell, Tess Lloyd, Ambrose Manning, Michael Montgomery, Robert Rennick, and Ken Townsend. We are, however, ultimately responsible for the anthology's content. Lastly, we would like to note that the essay in Appendix A, "A Brief History of the Tennessee Folklore Society," builds on a presentation by Bobby Fulcher delivered at the fiftieth annual meeting of the society in 1984.

Finally, the editors and the press gratefully acknowledge the financial support of the Tennessee Folklore Society in producing this volume.

A Note from the Tennessee State Folklorist

For seventy-five years, the *Tennessee Folklore Society Bulletin* has been a remarkable publication. But its circulation has been so limited that even many well-read Tennesseans will be surprised, in opening this anthology, to discover that the *Bulletin* exists, much less to learn that it may be the oldest state society folklore periodical in America. All of us associated with the society know that this sampling of riches from the *Bulletin*'s back issues will be a valuable and eye-opening addition to the available library of Tennesseana. We also hope that it will generate new appreciation and respect for the subject matter in which we share interest and that it will attract new members to our ranks.

These aspirations are far from new to the folklore cause. They've been continually voiced since the earliest years of the society and never fully met, due in large part to a subtext that ties together all of the topics and articles in this book. In the course of advocating for folk culture as state folklorist for over two decades, I've more than once noted in jest—and sometimes in frustration—that one of our state's major industries is being ashamed of ourselves. Tennessee has always been abundantly rich in folklore, reflecting, as this anthology attests, wide-ranging genres as well as geographic and cultural diversity. Folklore has long been close to the surface in Tennessee, closely interwoven with our identity. Yet rather than being regarded in an entirely positive light, that fact has often been taken by many, especially those in official and institutional capacities, as an index of our backwardness, as a perception by outsiders that should be corrected, as a blot to be expunged. In very real ways, pieces of Tennessee's traditional culture have been routinely targeted for condescension, criticism, and displacement under such assorted agendas as progress or modernization, scientific thought, social betterment, agricultural reform, education, cultural sophistication, artistic excellence, and civic boosterism. In their most benign varieties, less-than-supportive attitudes about Tennessee's folklore portray it as comprised of quaint but irrelevant oddities from the past, subsume it to superficial or stereotyped explanations, or simply dismiss it as trivial.

The authors in this anthology, like other members of the Tennessee Folklore Society throughout the organization's life, would probably all admit not only to some degree of unconventional and antiquarian intellectual interest but also, more importantly, to a fundamentally sympathetic view of folklore, folklife, and folk arts, and of the expressive and intangible material these overlapping areas encompass. Informal folk culture, passed down by word of mouth or customary example among various groups of people, indeed upholds myriad values, meanings, levels of truth, functions, and tenets of identity among those who share it. In regard to that which is passing, the society has always sought to document such culture and to preserve it in ways appropriate to changing times. The *Bulletin's* contributors have often characterized folklore as a living as well as dying thing, showing respect and validation for the communities and individuals that continue to give it life and acknowledging excellence among bearers of tradition and master folk artists. Many further recognize that the process underlying folklore is fundamental to human life and experience, continuing to sustain the culture of new immigrant groups in Tennessee and to generate new varieties of folklore in urban and other changing contexts.

One particularly commendable emphasis of the *Bulletin* throughout its history, which has kept it so strongly rooted to Tennessee people, has been the journal's welcoming policy toward publication of field collections and similar documentary reports. Its pages are refreshingly free of the conjectural constructs and double-talk that have passed for theory in many other publications in the field in recent decades. The society has made no apologies for its openness to presenting descriptive accounts and folklore texts framed in basic commentary. Those who are enticed by this anthology will discover in its pages how deep a record this policy has created. It underscores a belief in the inherent value of primary folklore materials. It also embodies the society's egalitarian spirit of inclusiveness.

That spirit is a guiding principle as the Tennessee Folklore Society now seeks to expand its membership and its outreach. Publication of the anthology comes at a time when the society is retooling for a new era, moving from a university affiliation into independent status as a contemporary nonprofit organization. Its membership has always included both academics and lay folklorists, but in coming years it seeks still broader representation by interested Tennesseans of all stripes, including teachers, arts and history programmers, traditional music and craft enthusiasts, community heritage advocates, and cultural activists of color and ethnicity. The society invites readers to join in building a stronger network in support of Tennessee's folk heritage.

Robert Cogswell
Folklife Program Director
Tennessee Arts Commission

The Tennessee
Folklore Society
A Short Remembrance

In 1966, my wife Betty, our three children, and I became Tennesseans. I was appointed assistant professor that year at what is now Belmont University in Nashville. That year, too, I heard Harry Harrison Kroll speak at a professional meeting in Jackson. I invited the novelist-folklorist to Belmont to hold a workshop in Tennessee traditions. At his invitation I soon became active in the Tennessee Folklore Society.

Unable to attend a 1968 meeting at Knoxville because of my class work at Vanderbilt, I received a call from TFS president Tom Burton. The news astounded me: I was now president-elect of the Tennessee Folklore Society.

It was at a music party at Tom Burton's home in Johnson City that I met Tom Morgan and sang harmony with him and his wife Mary. Tom Burton and his colleague Ambrose Manning helped me plan the program of the first TFS meeting I would be responsible for. At that fall 1970 meeting at East Tennessee State University, our performers included Doc Watson and his son Merle, Jeanette Carter of the Carter Fold, as well as surviving members of another pioneer group of RCA recording artists, the Fiddling' Powers Family. (If members of the Tenneva Ramblers had still been around Bristol, I don't doubt Burton and Manning would have managed to book them.) From West Tennessee's UT Martin, where I had taught since September 1967, I brought a twelve-passenger vanload of expert and, at that time, exotic folk dancers enrolled at UTM, bongo drums and all.

Soon Ambrose and Mary Manning invited me for a three-day stay at their Johnson City home. Long-time TFS secretary and *Bulletin* editor Ralph Hyde was entertaining me at his home a few miles out of Murfreesboro. The following October, Professor Hyde helped me arrange a program of folk talent that included not only Jeanette Carter but also Kentucky folk singer Yvonne Belmont Gregory, French folk singer Sonia Malkine, Grandpa Jones's "better-half" Ramona and their son Mark, a black spiritual duo, the Courthouse Gang bluegrass band from UT Martin, the Rutherford County Square Dancers, and an expert handsaw player.

Though I came to the Tennessee Folklore Society too late to know such pioneers in our field as former presidents Donald Davidson and Charles Faulkner Bryan and their musical production *Singin' Billy,* I found Vanderbilt graduate students were still discussing the ideas of these professors. Some English faculty and students recalled Davidson's seating himself on the edge of his classroom desk and punctuating his ballads course with traditional texts and tunes he accompanied on his guitar. Between 1969 and 1971, I became acquainted with TFS contributing members Professor Paul Brewster and Professor William Griffin, chatting with them in their offices on the nearby Peabody campus.

Now, forty years later, it is an honor to be working with TFS treasurer Tony Cavender, past-president Ted Olson, President Evan Hatch, past-president and *Tennessee Folklore Society Bulletin* editor Brent Cantrell, TFS secretary Tom Morgan, and each member of our organization's executive board. I thank Tony and Ted for editing this anthology of articles from the *Tennessee Folklore Society Bulletin* and the University of Tennessee Press for publishing this representative anthology.

I wish I could thank also my late, longtime friend Dr. Charles K. Wolfe for asking whether I would serve again as president of the society. And I wish I could let him know this second tenure is enough like our "junking" together for old 78s and then finding our way backstage at the Opry, that most of the work has been challenging but fun.

Walt Haden
Immediate Past President
Tennessee Folklore Society

Introduction

Today, people around the world think of the United States as a singular entity, and when Americans refer to their nation as a whole, they use singular verbs, such as in the sentence "The United States is a world power." Before the Civil War, however, Americans—and especially southerners —used plural verb forms when discussing their connection to a larger political unit. "The United States are a big country," they might have said. As would be revealed later in the "War between the States," antebellum southerners garnered their deepest sense of identity from their home communities, states, and regions, and their loyalties would only conditionally be directed toward their nation. Famously upon the outbreak of the Civil War, when faced with the choice of serving his nation or his "country," U.S. Army general Robert E. Lee decided that he could not turn against his home state of Virginia.

When the Confederacy surrendered at Appomattox Court House in 1865 and the northern states were reunited with those of the South, the nation moved closer to truly being the *United* States of America. And yet, while increasingly interdependent politically after the Civil War, U.S. society was far from homogeneous, and Americans remained a culturally diverse population. Even as the United States forged ahead at the vanguard of international modernization, many individuals and groups across the nation remained primarily dedicated to local communities and regional cultures, and as a result such people continued to practice cultural traditions strongly influenced by Old World folkways as well as by folkways associated with the early years of European settlement in the New World. This cultural conservatism was more evident in the southern states during the postwar industrialization than elsewhere across the United States. Tennessee in particular became nationally, even internationally, known for possessing a remarkable range of traditional culture. Indeed, generations of Tennesseans have proudly proclaimed some of their traditions as among their state's most significant cultural assets.

Granted their respect for traditional culture, Tennessee's residents have not always used the internationally accepted scholarly term—folklore—for such traditions. Nor have those residents necessarily valued more than a few manifestations of folklore or viewed the state's traditional culture from larger historical and socioeconomic perspectives. By the 1930s, in an effort to correct such oversights, a group of Tennesseans—recognizing the importance of helping Tennessee's citizenry gain a more reflexive and holistic understanding of their state's full range of cultural traditions and responding to the growing national interest in folklore (this was also the era of the Works Progress Administration's Federal Writers' Project, in which leading American authors wrote books that celebrated the traditional culture of specific states, including Tennessee)—formed the Tennessee Folklore Society, a statewide organization that was intended to foster wider appreciation for and preservation of the state's traditional culture.

The founders of the Tennessee Folklore Society, who included academics researching specific cultural traditions and nonacademics with a lay interest in folklore, implemented the publication of a periodical that was dedicated to chronicling and analyzing the cultural traditions across Tennessee. Titled simply the *Tennessee Folklore Society Bulletin*, this periodical was intended to be only one of that organization's activities. Never an artfully designed periodical, and never attaining widespread distribution or extensive readership, the *Bulletin* after three-quarters of a century endures as the nation's oldest continuously published periodical focused specifically on the folklore of one state. Having featured a range of scholarly articles on various topics relevant to Tennessee folklore as well as documentary pieces, book and recording reviews, and other folklore-related material, the *Bulletin* over the years has been widely read by scholars and students around the state and has been praised by folklorists across the United States. Taken together, the materials published in the *Bulletin* represent most, though not all, of the cultural traditions of Tennessee. Unfortunately, and perhaps inevitably, that representation has been incomplete, as several genres of folklore have either received marginal attention or have been overlooked entirely. Appendix A features an essay, "A Brief History of the Tennessee Folklore Society," intended to provide readers with a historical context for understanding the purpose of the society and the *Bulletin*.

The materials heretofore published in the *Tennessee Folklore Society Bulletin* illustrate the values and priorities of Tennesseans over the years and reflect larger trends in folklore research. For instance, the periodical reveals that throughout the twentieth century and into the twenty-first, numerous scholars and students residing around the state as well as others living across the United States have been interested primarily in particular aspects of Tennessee culture, the state's music traditions having been the folklore genre most often studied. Historically, the "discovery" of Tennessee folklore both within and outside the state was an outgrowth of the national interest in those manifestations of folklore that embodied the nation's social values of the late nineteenth and early twentieth centuries. That interest reflected the romanticized social attitude toward rural southerners associated then with many upper-class Americans. Believing that immigrants recently arrived in the United States were threatening to displace older, English-derived social values, such upper-class Americans assumed that revered Anglo-American values could still be found within the traditional culture of their rural southern white contemporaries. Accordingly, folklorists who shared that perspective visited Tennessee and other southern states in order to collect certain genres of traditional culture there. Several articles published in the *Journal of American Folklore* during the first decade of the twentieth century illustrate this tendency. As an extension of that trend, few articles about African American folklore appeared in the *Tennessee Folklore Society Bulletin* until the 1970s, in the aftermath of the civil rights movement. Through the 1960s, folklorists collecting in Tennessee—revealing older attitudes toward race relations—tended to overlook aspects of traditional black culture and instead focused on traditional white culture. (Interestingly, some of the most important collections of black folklore across the pre–civil rights era South resulted from the efforts of African American folklorists. While the best-known example of the latter activity was Zora Neale Hurston's fieldwork in Florida, also significant was the collecting work of a black Tennessean, John Work.)

Hence, when founded during the Great Depression, the Tennessee Folklore Society reflected the value system and interests of a particular Tennessee subculture. While the primary purpose of that organization was to encourage the collection, interpretation, and promotion of the state's traditions and to provide people from academic as well as nonacademic backgrounds with opportunities to share their research regarding the state's traditional culture, the Tennessee Folklore Society ultimately fostered an incomplete portrait of the state's cultural traditions.

Since the *Tennessee Folklore Society Bulletin* remains an ongoing commitment of the society, the periodical in the future has the opportunity to include within its pages new materials that redress past oversights in terms of coverage and balance. In compiling this anthology of representative materials from the *Tennessee Folklore Society Bulletin,* we acknowledge the fact that this book will necessarily reflect the limitations found in the *Bulletin* (through not fully representing the traditional cultures of some ethnic groups in Tennessee as well as generally underrepresenting the state's material culture traditions). That being said, it is our belief that this anthology will feature a collection of interesting essays originally published in the *Tennessee Folklore Society Bulletin,* and it is our hope that the anthology will draw renewed attention to the legacies of that periodical and the Tennessee Folklore Society in general. In addition to celebrating past achievements, this anthology is further intended to acknowledge the vital roles that the periodical and the organization can play in present-day and future Tennessee. Therefore, this anthology was planned as a fund-raising project of the Tennessee Folklore Society, with all royalties going directly into a fund maintained by the society to assist in its organizational work.

All of the people involved in the Tennessee Folklore Society share the strong conviction that folklore remains a vital field of study in a world seemingly overwhelmed by mass communication and popular culture. We collectively believe that a deepened understanding of the role of folklore in the lives of Tennesseans can only increase general awareness of the value of living in distinct communities within Tennessee. Additionally, we sense that such awareness—in keenly defining people's cultural identities by rooting those identities within familiar, meaningful soil—will enhance the ability of Tennesseans to feel grounded in an increasingly complex and decentralized world.

While over the years the editors of the *Tennessee Folklore Society Bulletin* included in that periodical numerous materials not specifically exploring the Volunteer State's cultural traditions, we have chosen to incorporate in *A Tennessee Folklore Sampler* only those articles that concentrate on the state's traditional culture since those traditions have long been the central focus of the Tennessee Folklore Society. An additional factor considered in the selection of articles from the *Bulletin* was the importance of representing the fullest possible range of folklore traditions from all sections of Tennessee. Accordingly, each section in this anthology is designed to offer a selection of articles exploring various manifestations of traditional culture within specific genres or subgenres of folklore from each of the "three states of Tennessee" (East Tennessee, Middle Tennessee, and West Tennessee). Given the scope of this project, our choices of articles were necessarily limited to what was published within the *Bulletin*.

After selecting a range of articles from the periodical, we addressed the task of how most effectively to organize those materials. The organizational strategy employed was largely determined by the quality and thematic focus of the materials themselves; hence, the subject headings for the various parts of this book are in no way arbitrary but result from the grouping together of similar articles from among the larger collection of articles deemed as the strongest work to have been published in the *Bulletin*. If, then, the parts of this book seem to favor certain genres of Tennessee folklore while focusing less on other genres, such imbalances in representation are those of the *Tennessee Folklore Society Bulletin* itself. Indeed, it is illuminating to identify patterns of interest and oversight among the contributors to that periodical since the 1930s. For example, the articles published in the *Bulletin* have concentrated on two of the three folklore supergenres—verbal folklore and customary folklife—while the third supergenre, material culture, has been largely neglected. This reflects longstanding biases among scholars and citizens within Tennessee toward certain cultural genres. Music, for example, has long received more attention from folklorists in Tennessee than other traditions, and that fact is discernable in the disproportionately large amount of space granted to covering music traditions in the *Bulletin*. The comparatively small number of articles on material traditions within that periodical is a symptom of national trends within the academic field of folklore, as material culture was not widely pursued as a focus of academic study in the United States until the past few decades.

To bring public attention to material culture, which was historically underexplored across Tennessee, this book's first part incorporates articles on such genres of material culture as handicrafts, boat building, and foodways. The next four parts survey scholarship on the state's customary folklife, including articles on folk medicine, folk beliefs and practices, customs, and play and recreation lore. Subsequent sections explore such genres of verbal folklore as folk speech, legends, folk ballad and song, and instrumental folk music/folk music collecting. The final part includes articles that represent the diverse folklife within specific Tennessee communities (and, as those particular articles illustrate, folk communities can be, and should be, defined after analyzing those communities for geographical, ethnic, racial, and/or occupational factors). The epilogue contains a single paper by Donald Davidson, "Current Attitudes toward Folklore," delivered at a meeting of the Tennessee Folklore Society in 1940. Davidson's paper is a provocative critique of the work of the society during its early years. More importantly, the paper addresses issues still debated in folklore circles today.

A few words of definition might be helpful to readers unfamiliar with the field of folklore. The term "folklore" refers to an individualized use of some tradition, whether it be a verbal or nonverbal manifestation of traditional communication employed by people interacting with other people in a specific social situation, a particular element of traditional knowledge used by one person to conduct an everyday task, or a particular action performed in a traditional manner for a traditional purpose (i.e., not for money or status). Many folklorists subdivide folklore into three main categories: verbal folklore, customary folklife, and material culture.

While it is likely and appropriate that *A Tennessee Folklore Sampler* will provide many older Tennesseans an opportunity to recall various facets of a disappeared or a disappearing way of life, another intention of this book is to help a new generation of Tennesseans better understand their home state's folk heritage. This book, therefore, is dedicated to all Tennesseans, past, present, and future.

PART ONE

Material Folk Culture

No aspect of folk culture in the South has captured the general public's interest more than moonshining. The Scots and Scots-Irish established the tradition of whiskey making in America, and they produced whiskey not only for recreational consumption but also, as described in part 2, for its putative medicinal properties. During the Prohibition era, one could earn a lot more money on a corn crop by making whiskey rather than selling it at the market. Charles S. Pendleton's article, "Illicit Whiskey Making," is informative about the whiskey-making process, but far more significant are his observations on the social world of this clandestine industry, particularly the relationships between the moonshiner, members of his community, and the revenuer.

Prior to World War II, most Tennesseans made a living farming. Cash was scarce and bartering was common. Many families supplemented their income through such activities as selling illegal whiskey, eggs, honey, wildcrafted medicinal plants, and handicrafts. In "Basketmakers of Cannon County: An Overview," Lawrence Alexander explores the economic and social dimensions of a cottage industry in Middle Tennessee that during its production peak in the 1930s was essential for the survival of some families. The basketmaking tradition continues today, and it and other aspects of traditional culture are celebrated during the annual White Oak Craft Fair held in Woodbury, Tennessee.

Molasses is a food distinctive to the South. Its consumption has fallen considerably over the years, but many older Tennesseans fondly recall, and many still enjoy, eating cathead biscuits slathered with molasses mixed with just the right amount of butter. Ben S. Austin's article, "The Vanishing Art of Cooking Table-Grade Sorghum Molasses," describes the traditional method of making molasses. He observes that the preparation of molasses was a communal event involving several family members or members of several families. In one sense, the event qualifies as a custom (see part 4 of this volume).

1

In many ways, material culture reflects humankind's adaptations to variable and sometimes challenging environmental conditions. The plasticity and inventiveness of human adaptation is illustrated well by the stumpjumper, a boat designed specifically for the swamp environment of Reelfoot Lake in West Tennessee. In "Dale Calhoun and the Reelfoot Lake Boat," Tennessee's state folklorist, Robert Cogswell, discusses the origin and evolution of the stumpjumper, its construction, and the efforts of an expert craftsman who at considerable personal sacrifice struggles to keep the stumpjumper tradition alive.

Illicit Whiskey Making
[1946]

Charles S. Pendleton

We approach the somewhat hush-hush topic of this paper in a chaste and subdued spirit. Personally we have never distilled whiskey, either within or outside the law. We have never visited a still in operation. Strictly *soto voce* to our intimate, scholarly, purely objective audience of folklorists, we wish we had; we should be more accurate as a student of an important and widespread social phenomenon if our acquaintance with it were direct instead of indirect. We are not even customers for the finished product. Some friends of ours are. We once by accident enjoyed (no, that's the wrong word for it) a wild night ride, with a really prominent citizen, with two glass jugs of "white mule" between our shrinking feet. Personally we have never tasted "white mule" and probably never shall. We are afraid of the stuff. Yet perhaps, indeed, we are only an unsophisticated victim of propaganda designed to spoil the market for poor-man's whiskey. Be that as it may, we are, in this paper, opening up a topic so widespread in Tennessee life and lore that no doubt it ought to be fully explored and recorded. Though illegitimate in itself, from a legalistic standpoint, it is a legitimate phase of social life. Perhaps other members of this Society can and will, from time to time, bring to publication a wide range of material that is beyond the grasp of the present paper.

In terms of the law and of highly organized society, illicit whiskey making is simply an avoidance of taxes. It is the making of untaxed liquor. The Federal Government, in its concept of raising money to pay National expenses, attaches a very heavy and profitable tax to liquor making, as it does to tobacco manufacturing and to other things. He who manufactures without paying the tax is breaking the law. Because the Government makes a strict and elaborate

3

▣ Still located near Gatlinburg, Tennessee, 1935. Joseph S. Hall Collection, Archives of Appalachia, East Tennessee State University

effort to enforce the law, he is in danger of arrest and prosecution. The penalty of conviction is rather severe, particularly beyond the first offense. Law enforcement is conducted, for the Government, by the Alcohol Tax Unit of the Bureau of Internal Revenue of the Treasury Department. Officers from this Unit, usually traveling in groups in a motor car, range widely through the country, then walk a long distance back into hills and hollows. They are not in uniform, but are well known and fully recognized in the countryside as officers. They are known as "revenuers"—a purely American colloquial term. They are, needless to say, unpopular; and this seems to be true even among persons who do not make liquor. In liquor makers' epithets they are classed with "varmints"—that is, with animals like skunks that one would not willingly associate with on any friendly terms whatever. This expressive word, "varmits," is (by the way) a king-word in a deep-country vocabulary. It is a variation of "vermin." It appears also in the form "varmint." It is very old; possibly as far back as two centuries ago (though a record in writing dates only from 1773) it was applied by frontiersmen to the Indians. Today it carries the same connotation that it did to the frontiersmen. Applied to the Alcohol Tax Unit officers it expresses a definite social attitude.

The revenuers, in their raiding, carry axes and other implements to destroy what they find. Their destruction is thorough. They make arrests if they can; but usually they cannot, for a countryman more than holds his own in a footrace, and particularly where he alone knows the paths.

Interesting examples of social cooperation exist among liquor-making people. Of these we cite two. Because Federal courts usually increase heavily the sentences they impose for successive convictions, one person frequently substitutes himself for another, up for trial, and accepts a sentence as if he were guilty, when really he is not. It would be interesting to know how many countrymen have "done time" in "Atlanta"—that is, the Federal prison there—vicariously in order to shield someone whose sentence would have been heavier. The local community seems to know the facts in such cases. Someone in it will remark casually that Bill Brown is "doing time" for Sam Smithers. What adjustments are made in recompense for such a sacrifice we do not know. There seems to be no social shame attached, in the community, to such a substitute.

Another example of cooperation consists in giving a warning. As a carload of officers, or a group on foot, passes by a home near which liquor is being made, some kind of effective warning to the workers at the still or stills will usually be sounded. In the country no one pays attention to a single shotgun shot, for a neighbor is probably merely getting a rabbit for dinner; but everyone pays attention to two shots, for this is a warning. There are other devices, of course. A telephone will carry a message to a point far ahead of the raiders. But in liquor-making country the people are too poor and too remote to have many telephones. In one region known to this writer, where two valleys join each other over a divide, there are good farms with telephones in the level-country outlets to each valley. These are miles apart, and there are no telephones in between. But when revenuers enter at either point, the other is immediately notified, and an alarm is started from there. An amusing story will serve to end this phase of our discussion. A young liquor maker who served as a lookout had an antiquated car with horn trouble. For a cause not easily perceivable his horn would on occasion blare continuously. On one short-notice occasion he drove, with his uproar, just ahead of the officers. They overtook him, stopped him, listened to his complaint, gathered around his car, peered under the hood—and were as helpless as he toward stopping the blare.

Officers raid fairly constantly. It is their purpose to prevent the manufacture of untaxed liquor. There are two ways to accomplish this. One is to imprison all the makers. The second, rather more practicable and effective, is to destroy the equipment. Liquor makers usually are poor; the complete loss of an outfit cannot be remedied by quick replacement.

In recent times, particularly in wartime, other factors have curbed liquor making. Sugar, a necessary ingredient, has been under strict ration controls. Copper for the worm of the still has been almost unobtainable; and to substitute galvanized iron produced a deadly liquor. There are other shortages. Even new, tight barrels are off the market. The employment of the airplane by officers for scouting also has been a blow to the industry. A wisp of smoke is readily visible to an observer high in the air. And no still can be operated without overhead camouflage to conceal it from above. Every now and then an innocent flyer, flying low, and perhaps lost and in distress, is horrified to be a target for well-aimed bullets fired from below. He does not know the background for his harrowing experience.

In any given area there are comparatively few places suitable for a location for a still. These are scouted eagerly by liquor makers. They also come to be known, in the course of time, to the Alcohol Tax Unit officers. The task of such officers is to some extent merely "walking a beat"— that is, to drop in at irregular intervals, upon each spot known to be a potential source of trouble. The strategy of illicit liquor making, on the other hand, is to be in and out again—in when the revenuers are not there and safely out when they are there. It is a game of hide-and-seek, with the bases around which the play occurs pretty firmly fixed. Of course there are exceptions, wholly new locations which remain secret a long time.

Everybody comes to know everybody before long. The officers know each liquor maker and each farm in their district who habitually makes whiskey. And the liquor people identify each officer. In the district there will be some farmers who are known to everyone never to make liquor. Sometimes—indeed, often—their farms are the largest in the area. Sometimes these contain spots for stills which are a liquor maker's dream of perfection. Yet because their owners never make liquor, the officers tend to inspect them not often or not at all. The countryside is extensive, and tramping hill and dale is hard work.

This situation brings about a three-way set up. A new character and a new place enter into the picture. There is also a complication in a certain law, designed to help revenuers which forfeits to the Government any farm used for making illicit liquor, as well as automobiles and implements. This law is, in general, not so effective as it would seem to be. A liquor maker who lost his farm might become a squatter on it afterward, with no taxes to pay. Social pressure would probably prevent anyone else from buying it from the Government and moving into the neighborhood. But the law hits hard a land-owner who is law abiding and responsible. If a still is surreptitiously placed on his farm, he is legally liable, even if, as is likely, the courts probably would not actually assess the penalty upon him. At least he would be embarrassed and troubled. Consequently this reputable farmer polices his acres on his own account. If he discovers a still thereon, he does not inform the revenuers. This would be poor neighborliness and poor social tactics if he did. Indeed, his barn might burn down, his spring be contaminated with a dead animal, or an auto tire be ruined—all with no traceable source. One keeps entirely free from cooperation with revenuers. But this farmer does talk firmly to one of his liquor-making neighbors. Anyone will do, for the word will be passed on. He says that unless everything is taken away before a certain time, set some two days ahead, he will come with his axe and smash it all. That is proper neighborliness. Silently, in the nighttime, everything will disappear.

This leads us to two remarks. Night is the time for all moving of equipment and materials for liquor making. This is not a daylight business. And, second, the labor involved is tremendous. Illicit liquor making is not a lazy man's job. Silently, in the dark, over steep hillsides and in underbrush, heavy packages such as hundred-pound sacks of sugar and of grain are carried, sometimes long distances. Even rocks to build a furnace may be lugged in sacks from distances up to half a mile if stone is not found at the place picked for the still. And the whiskey produced is carried out with the same labor. Wood for the fire may be at hand, or may be chopped at a distance and carried. The sound of wood chopping is not a welcome note at an illicit still. And wagon tracks, when possible, might indicate saved labor but would be a give-away to revenuers.

We might here touch a little on vocabulary. First, "moonshiner." The basis in fact for the term "moonshiner" should now be quite clear. And the meaning should have become realistic—associated with labor and quite stripped of any romantic aspects it may hitherto have had, such as basking lazily and perhaps with lovelorn or love-enthused heart, in the mellowing light of a humanity-influencing moon. There are such people, and the moon does seem to have on some folks such an effect. But the moonshiner's moon is different. It is like a farm lantern that lights a laborer to his heavy after-dark chores—except that, unlike a farm lantern, it is not also a beacon light to inform whosoever may happen to look its way that the chores are being done. A moonshiner works secretly, surreptitiously, and therefore at night, getting whatever light for his tasks he does get only from the moon, which is a telltale on nobody. In the illicit-liquor industry, "moonshiner" and its corollaries "moonshiners" and "moonshine" refer to the manufacturing end of the business, not to the sales end.

The term "bootlegger," on the contrary, refers to the sales end, as do its corollaries "bootlegging" and "bootleg." The stiff leather cuff of a high boot, the upper part of the boot into which trousers legs are tucked, makes a carry-all and place of concealment. What is carried is instantly within reach but hidden from observation. "Bootleg" has been applied, in American colloquial language, to a wide variety of objects carried in a boot-top—to gold, pistols, knives, liquor, and the like; and by extension it reaches out to cover a wide range of secreted articles and secretive business which only in a metaphorical sense have anything to do with boots. In this latter category comes the clandestine delivery of illicit liquor to furtive buyers. It also, by further extension, covers the manufacture. We have never heard, by the way, the term "moonshining" used to indicate the sale of liquor.

We were discussing the law-abiding land-owner on whose acres an illicit distillery is something secretly placed. Amusing stories have come to us about this kind of thing. One, worth giving here, came directly from a prosperous Nashville business man who owns a hilly farm in a wild section a long distance from his residence. Incidentally we may remark that an absentee-owned farm like this constitutes a moonshiner's paradise. This business man was subpoe-naed into Federal Court in Nashville one day to serve as a character witness for a young countrymen said by the bailiff to be on trial for moonshining. Being a kindly man he left his business, went to Court, took the witness stand, and testified that the youth had frequently worked for him on his farm, that he thought him of excellent character, and that he thought it unlikely that he would engage in illicit liquor making. Having testified, he started to leave the courtroom then changed his mind and sat down in the back row of spectators to listen a few minutes to the rest of the trial. From the testimony he soon learned two things. One was that the distillery in question did a really thriving business. The other thing was that it was located on his own farm.

Why moonshiners should locate their manufactories on the land of law-abiding neighbors is quite plain. There are two reasons. One is that the farm, because of its owner, is not regularly suspect to the revenuers, and therefore the still is less likely to be discovered than if it were on the land of a man known to make liquor. The second reason is that there is an advantage to the moonshiner if he can greatly widen the acreage the revenuers have to cover in their regular rounds of inspection. The wider the area, the less frequent the trips to any one spot within the area and, therefore, the better the chance to keep a given active still unvisited.

The chief menace to moonshining is the "revenuer." Second to the "reve-nuer" are not the preachers, teachers, reputable farmers, and other law-abiding elements of the neighborhood. These may not approve, but they seldom directly interfere. The menace comes from the "trash," the human riffraff of the near and the distant neighborhood. Such may do almost anything. They have utter irre-sponsibility. The country word is "mean."

At its best, moonshining is almost respectable. But we are told that now and in recent years it is much less endurable to respectable folk than in times past. We should be interested to know definitely about this—say, what changes in attitude have occurred, in a given community, and from what causes. Probably someone could gather quite definite information on this in specific communities.

At its worst, there is no respectability or responsibility at all, for human "trash" engages in it also and can align it with everything disreputable.

One reason that revenuers depend less on arrests than upon destruction of the equipment and the materials is that often the actual workers at a still are not its owners but only laborers paid a wage for working there. To some of the lower classes of country folk, labor at a still is not very different in character from other work, although the risk involved is recognized.

There are standards in moonshining. That is, there are men and communi-ties that take pride in enjoying a reputation for excellence. Long ago this writer learned incidentally from a city buyer of bootleg whiskey that the best liquor came from a certain-named county. The man referred to that county as if it were

◻ Law enforcement officials with confiscated stills in Washington County, Tennessee, ca. 1930s. Mildred Kozsuch Collection, Archives of Appalachia, East Tennessee State University.

a kind of sterling mark. From other buyers this writer has heard certain men referred to with praise. Further investigation would no doubt be interesting. Yet perhaps the results could not be fully published, because of the illegality of the manufacture. With reference to the county praised by the city buyer for its high standards, this writer had also an interesting verification from within the county, a statement made by a native which clearly indicated pride.

There is a region into which this writer is (if we may use schoolgirl language) "just dying to go." He feels that way because he has been told that it is absolutely closed to outsiders. Liquor is made there. But revenuers do not disturb; they simply do not enter. We inquired of the person who told us of this closed region what would happen if we really insisted—really went into it. He told us. But what he told us does not belong in our present paper.

Now a word about why people make illicit liquor. There seem to be two reasons. One, the stronger one, is economic. The other is rugged, irrepressible individualism. The first is an endeavor to make "cash money," at least a little real "cash money," out of one's ten acres of corn grown with toil on a barren rocky farm. The second is a belief that, law or no law, one has a right to use one's crop to the best advantage one can. The Government, in making repressive laws, is an interloper. It is to be evaded if it cannot be actively resisted. The desperate drive of poverty plus the still surviving independence of the pioneer forefathers is the combination that turns the meager corn crop into appreciable dollars, although to the financial detriment of rich old Uncle Sam.

A parallelism occurs to us. If one realizes that the issue is purely economic —avoidance of the payment of taxes—is there not, after all, a kinship between the illicit making of liquor and the juggling of accounts, suppression of facts about property, and conjuring up of exemptions which characterize the evasions of income tax and personality and realty taxes of a large proportion of all citizens? The Tennessee State Constitution to the contrary, is there anyone present who pays to the State a 3 percent tax on the cash he has on hand on January 10 of each year? The Good Book says, "Let him that is without guilt throw the first stone."

A while ago we spoke of the great labor involved in setting up and maintaining a still. We had a notion once that moonshining was romantic. We asked ourselves then what men talked about while they tended a still. We thought that maybe they sang "ballets" and behaved in other romantic folklorish ways. But now we have asked questions of people who knew. At a still, they say, you talk just as you do when you go about any other work. But you don't talk loudly; you don't shout; of course you don't sing. Do any of our readers know anything to the contrary?

There are two more topics in our paper—first, where a still is located and second (the climax of it all), exactly how whiskey is made.

For the location of a still, a long, dark, narrow hollow is more likely to be avoided than to be chosen by an experienced moonshiner. It looks suspicious. And it is a trap, with no good way of escape if the revenuers come. A more open place is better, if it is out of the way and if it has a good supply of wood and water. Rocks are desirable, but these can be carried in if necessary. Wood also can be carried in. But water cannot be. The essential thing, then, is a good supply of water. This can be piped some distance. It ought to be delivered at the still about four feet high.

When the location has been selected, the moonshiners begin to bring in the still. The equipment consists of about seven units. The work is done at night. On the first night perhaps only the boiler is brought in and some of the stone for the furnace.

On the next day the furnace is built. Equipped with a chimney for draft, it is made of stones plastered with mud. All the cracks are well daubed. The boiler is set into it. A furnace can be made in half a day if the materials are close at hand. It may require two days if they are not. The overhead camouflage, to guard against airplane observation, is also begun early.

Next the barrels are moved in—the mash barrels. They are set in a pattern. There are a good many of these. Bringing them in may require two nights.

After the barrels are in place, the boiler is filled with water and a fire is started in the furnace to heat this. Into each barrel is put about half a bushel of corn meal, or rye or barley—whichever is to be used. When the water boils, about twelve gallons of it is poured into each barrel, and after this another half bushel of meal. While this is going in it must be stirred all the time. After the meal is well scalded, the barrels are covered. They are left for two days.

Two days later the operators go back and fill the barrels about two-thirds full of water. With a mash stick and with their hands they break up all the lumps that may be in the meal. The barrels are then left for three days.

After three days the sugar is put in. Whatever amount of sugar is available, up to fifty pounds, is stirred into each barrel. Then the mash is capped. It is capped with a half gallon of barley or rye meal and a half gallon of corn, rye, or barley malt.

The mash now "works"—that is, ferments. It is left for from five to ten days to do so—whatever time is necessary for it to stop fermenting and to clear up. It is now "beer."

Hardened natives drink this beer. But to an outsider it is as vile a concoction as can be thrust down a throat. When the mash has become beer it is ready to run.

How much whiskey comes from a barrel of mash? Generally a barrel with twenty-five pounds of sugar in it produces three and a half gallons of whiskey. One gallon from every twelve pounds of sugar is the maximum expectation. Next comes the marketing. But that, it seems to us, is quite another story.

And so we close our account of a Tennessee institution. Yet this writer knows little, and our paper says little. Let the paper be nothing final in itself, but an invitation and a challenge. What misstatements does it make? What omissions does it have? Who knows more and can correct and add? Moonshining has been, and still is, a center for much Tennessee folk-life. Let us gather it all while we may.

Finally, we do hope that we haven't put naughty ideas into anyone's head. "Lead not to temptation," the Good Book says—or is it a Gospel hymn?

Basketmakers of Cannon County
An Overview
[1986]

Lawrence Alexander

W hite oak basketry is one of the European folk traditions brought to America by immigrants whose descendants settled in southern Appalachia. One of the regions best preserving this tradition is Cannon County, in Middle Tennessee, where women continue to make baskets in this traditional style. Here the basketmaking art is learned by imitation and practice as it is passed from one generation to another. Girls learn basketmaking from their mothers and other close kinswomen. Boys rarely make baskets, but men assist by gathering and splitting the white oak.

This study of Appalachian basketmaking draws upon data collected in 1979 and 1980 from Cannon County basketmakers and their families. It is based on interviews with members of more than 20 basketmaking households and other individuals associated with the industry. All of the informants were told that the interviews concerned a study of basketmaking in Cannon County, and all consented to the interviews. In order to protect their privacy, several of the basketmakers requested that their names and residences not be specified; for this reason, pseudonyms have been used when discussing specific informants. Generally, two to four interviews were required to establish rapport and were recorded in notebooks without the aid of a tape recorder.

In early interviews, the basketmakers provided information about (1) when, why, and how they learned to make baskets; (2) the means by which baskets were sold in the past as well as today; (3) manufacturing techniques; and (4) names and labels of specific baskets. The first two topics form the basis for this article, which seeks to provide a general outline of the Cannon County basketmaking tradition and its place in the social life of the basketmakers.

Geography

Most of the basketmaking families who participated in this study reside or have resided in an arc-shaped area ten miles long and six miles wide in central Tennessee. This arc is the physiographic transition between the Highland Rim of the Cumberland Plateau and the Nashville Basin, where there is an approximately 1,000-foot change in elevation in less than three miles. Low, rolling hills in the uplands and deep hollows that widen into valleys, with shallow meandering creeks, characterize the terrain.

This region was not attractive to the large-scale farmers who settled in the Nashville Basin during the early 1800s. The uplands on the edge of the Highland Rim are known as the "Barrens" for the heavily eroded and poor quality soil. Robert L. Mason describes the area geographically as follows:

> Here on the Rim the land is acid and infertile. The hills and hollows adjacent are rocky and steep, and respond sullenly to the plow and hoe. Vegetation, except woods and ragweeds, is scarce. (1946)

Most of the basketmakers still reside in this region of ridges and deep, wooded hollows. Today this area, like other regions of Tennessee with modern agricultural practices and fertilizer, is characterized by small, prosperous farms and timber-covered hill slopes. Small community grocers and gas stations are locked at five- to ten-mile intervals along the north-south and east-west roads that cross the area. The county seat, Woodbury, about 15 miles away, has a population of about 3,000. Nashville is 70 miles to the east.

Social Background

In the past, the basketmakers of Cannon County were subsistence farmers who occupied some of the poorest land in the county. Although this is no longer true today, these families were often extremely poor. As a result, some of the basketmakers were brought up on the income from baskets, and basketmaking helped to raise their children. A common expression is that "many of the people here were raised on baskets." For subsistence farmers or sharecroppers, cash was scarce. This was true especially during the Great Depression. Baskets were bartered for food and clothing at nearby rural grocery stores. Indeed, the number of baskets each family produced every week determined how much food they had to eat the following week.

Basketmakers recall that during the 1930s their families were looked down upon because they had to make baskets to survive. This stigma has gradually decreased, as many of the basketmaking families began to obtain a degree of financial solvency and were no longer dependent upon a minimal subsistence income. Nonetheless, condescension toward basketmaking families was still encountered in the 1980s. The basketmakers were considered by some to occupy the lowest level in the local social hierarchy. Some members of the rural community saw the basketmakers as lazy and given to lying around the house begetting children. An informant whose family did not make baskets stated it in the following way: "You could never get those basketmakers to work. All they did was sit around the house and make a basket or a chair whenever they needed some money." This viewpoint was not shared by the basketmakers themselves.

The Tradition

Five to seven families are still associated with basketmaking in Cannon County. All are related by ties of kinship and marriage. In one family, four brothers married four sisters, and two cousins married two sisters. In another large family there were several marriages between two first cousins. Other marriages between second and third cousins are known (Matthews 1965). Most of the basketmakers can recall their family's genealogies for three generations. Occasionally, four or five generations are remembered. Despite the importance of kinship ties, there is no great depth in genealogical knowledge.

An outline of two basketmakers' lives will illustrate how the tradition has been maintained. Hazel was born and raised in a family of five brothers and two sisters within five miles of where she presently resides. After her marriage to another area resident, the couple moved to Chicago, where they lived for over 25 years. She worked as a sales clerk and store manager, and her husband worked as a mechanic and later became a union representative. They have recently returned to Cannon County. Hazel has resumed the craft of basketmaking, and her husband works for the county.

Hazel's mother, grandmother, great grandmother, and their many sisters were all well-known basketmakers. One of Hazel's sisters and one sister-in-law currently make baskets. Her sister has returned to basketmaking during a recent layoff at a sewing factory where she had been employed. Neither of Hazel's two daughters who reside in the area can make baskets.

Another well-known basketmaker, Elsie, is a lifelong resident of the area who has never ventured more than 30 miles from her present residence. Elsie and her recently deceased husband built the three-room house where she currently lives. Her son now resides with his wife and child in a trailer next to Elsie's house. Elsie's husband had been a local farmer, part-time wage worker, and moonshine maker. Although her stepmother made baskets, Elsie was taught after her marriage to make baskets by her mother-in-law. Several of Elsie's sister-in-laws also have made baskets. She made baskets regularly for over 50 years but has recently had to quit because of ill health.

Through common residence and close kinship ties, most of the basket-making families have been lifelong acquaintances. One informant said: "When we grew up our best friends were always our cousins . . . because we felt more comfortable together. All of our families made baskets." When asked why all the basketmaking families tended to intermarry, one informant replied: "Those were the only people we really knew. Without cars . . . like they have now, people just didn't go anywhere. So how else could you meet someone else to marry?" Like other areas of rural Tennessee, many of the large families from an area are closely intermarried over several generations (Matthews 1965).

Thus common residence, a similar social background, and kinship ties helped create a feeling of cohesiveness among members of basketmaking families. This social unity is also recognized by nonbasketmakers. As a member of a nonbasketmaking family stated: "We did business with them just like everyone else, it is just that you would not be invited to Sunday dinner with them." This social cohesiveness of the basketmaking families is not as strong today. The basketmaking families in the eastern part of the county are distinguished as separate by other county residents.

Learning to Make Baskets

Most basketmakers claim that they and their sisters learned to make baskets from their mothers. Usually their grandmother also made baskets. Four cases were noted of women who learned the craft from their mothers-in-law. The reasons given by informants for learning from their mothers-in-law and not from their mothers are multiple. The mother of one of these basketmakers did not want her daughter "messing with baskets." One woman's father made baskets, but she learned the craft not from him but from her mother-in-law. One woman married into a basketmaking family from elsewhere and learned the craft after her marriage. And another woman learned basketmaking from her older sister because her mother was no longer physically able to make baskets.

Although basketmaking is considered a woman's task, men do the heavy work of locating and cutting white oak saplings in the woods, hauling them home, and splitting the saplings into eights. Men sometimes shave the hoops of the baskets or split the bolts of timber. Although male basketmakers are remembered, most men had little to do with basketmaking and regarded it as inappropriate for members of their sex. Today some men will help weave the basket,

◘ A basketmaker's workshop. Photo by Evan Hatch.
Courtesy of the Arts Center of Cannon County.

although few have the skill to make an entire basket from start to finish.

Most of the interviewed basketmakers learned to make baskets in childhood, many as soon as they were old enough to hold a basket. An older, more experienced basketmaker would start a basket and then turn it over to a child to complete the less demanding task of weaving the bottom. As each daughter in the family became old enough, she was handed a basket to weave. She learned the more specialized skills of shaping the basket and inserting the ribs through imitation and practiced under the supervision of her mother and older sisters.

Usually the basket production unit included all females residing in a household. In some families some of the girls were not interested and did not learn to make baskets. Sometimes after marriage, women quit making baskets because they no longer had to make them. Work groups were often formed, and women of more than one household, often close kinswomen, made baskets together. Today, the basket production unit is commonly a woman and other persons who maintain a close relationship with her. Among the older, less active families, the basketmaking roles are less sexually segregated, and often a woman and her husband work together. One woman and her daughter work together making baskets.

Basket Production

Basket production is a cottage industry whereby the women make baskets at their residence without adhering to any rigid production schedule (Boeke 1942). Most women integrate their basketmaking with housekeeping and raising children or grandchildren. One woman stated that "basketmaking was the only job [she] could get where I could stay at home, tend children, cook, and still make a little money." Other older women have returned to basketmaking after retirement or after working in a factory from ten to twenty years. One basketmaker stated, "I made baskets all my life when you couldn't get anything for 'em. Now I will make 'em when I can." The basketmakers point out that although their craft does not bring in as much money as factory work, it does allow them to stay at home, which is more desirable. One woman returned to basketmaking temporarily during a factory layoff. Thus basketmaking is an alternative to other jobs which allows much more freedom and flexibility. The quantity, kinds, and quality of baskets made are determined principally by the basketmaker's initiative.

Although baskets are made all year, production is greatest during winter, when people tend to spend more time at home. Baskets are made in front of a heater, often while the maker is watching television. The room where baskets are made is never carpeted, because the shavings are hard to clean from a carpet. During warm weather, basketmakers frequently sit beneath a large shade tree or on a front porch. Basket production often depends on how much spare time a basketmaker has or whether she "takes a notion" to make them.

The rate of basket production by an individual is largely determined by how much free time she has, her skill level, and the size of each basket. Generally, a basketmaker will prepare materials for several days' work and then begin making baskets. Often two or more baskets are worked on simultaneously until all are completed. A basketmaker, if the white oak has already been prepared, can produce two or three one-gallon baskets or two half-bushel baskets a day. One woman stated that her mother could make three large baskets in a day. Very large and very small baskets require the longest time to make. It often takes up to 10 hours to make a miniature basket. Show baskets, made with more material, which must be carefully smoothed, require two or more days to make.

During the period from 1920 to 1940, baskets were made by work groups of several women, and large numbers were produced. One family could produce 100 one-gallon baskets a week. Another informant stated that her mother and sisters could make a wagonload of baskets in two weeks.

Most of the basketmakers have the skill to produce any kind of basket, but they prefer to specialize in one or two kinds. Generally, medium-sized round and rectangular baskets which require moderate craftsmanship are the focus of production. These baskets are the most readily sold. The carefully wrought miniature baskets or show baskets are produced primarily for collectors and not sold as readily.

One woman and her family produce half-gallon and gallon rib baskets. Another woman produces only large market baskets. A third woman and her husband produce round bushel baskets and slat wood baskets. This decrease in specialization from the 1930 to 1940 period is the result of basketmakers adapting to the change in basket utilization and the preference of basket purchasers. When basket production was more specialized, baskets were produced specifically for domestic use. A particular range of basket types were suited for these activities. In the past, the basketmakers were more organized and integrated into a community where production roles were organized and specified to meet the market demands. Fewer peddlers sold baskets, and each peddler carried a range of basket types. Today, however, the baskets are produced as collectors' items. Consumers tend to emphasize more diverse basket shapes and finely made baskets. The basketmakers sell directly to peddlers who now sell baskets to a more diverse clientele. The traditional role of the rural grocer who warehoused baskets to be resold to peddlers has been replaced by a direct relationship between peddlers and basketmakers. These peddlers tend to purchase baskets they can most easily sell. The basketmakers now are also more segmented into smaller family groups with little community production organization. As a result, basket production has become more diversified.

According to informants, this form of specialization was more common fifty years ago than today. At that time entire families would specialize and produce only one basket type. The most common were egg, feed, and market baskets. Often a former basketmaker would be identified by her name and the kind of baskets she made. At that time, few people did not specialize in making a particular type of basket.

Some basketmakers do not specialize; they produce the entire range of basket shapes and sizes. When asked how they determined what kinds of baskets they were going to make, they generally replied that they just made what they felt like at the time or that they made the kind of baskets which would sell the quickest. Most often basketmakers produced four or five types of baskets regularly. Baskets are also made by special order for a customer who requests a particular kind. These women are generally more flexible, and they will make nontraditional styles and shapes of basket on request. One basketmaker stated: "If you can show me a picture of a basket, I can make it for you." These creative artisans are very proud of unique baskets they have made for special customers, and they will describe them in great detail.

In the past, most baskets were made for utilitarian proposes, and an emphasis was placed on making as many as quickly as possible. The size of the basket determined its price; there was little or no financial reward for producing a tighter or better quality basket. As a result, the baskets produced were "just thrown together" and were somewhat rough and unfinished. This utilitarian tradition continues today, and many baskets are produced just to a level of quality which allows them to be sold as rough baskets. These same basketmakers, however, also pride themselves on making good baskets which are "tight and strong and which will last for twenty-five years if kept dry."

Basketmakers' Criteria

Basketmakers evaluate basket on the bases of how tight the splints are, how strong it is, and by its finished shape. The weaving should be very tight, and the splints should not be compressed easily when a basket is squeezed on the rim or bulge of the basket. This tightness of weave is achieved by pulling the splits firmly snug when weaving the basket. After the basket has been allowed to dry for several days, the splints will have become loose, and additional splints will have to be added. A good basket also will have a strong, smoothly finished frame handle which fits the hand easily. A well-finished basket should be made with splints which are narrow, smooth, and free of fuzz or small oak shavings. The splints should be of equal width so that the basket attains an even appearance. The splints must be carefully tucked behind a rib when adding new splints so that no loose ends are exposed. The number of ribs used in basket construction and whether they are narrow and well rounded are also important criteria in determining the strength of the basket and how well woven it is. In addition to the tightness and finish, each basket should be symmetrical and well balanced, with body, handle, and frame being in proportion.

Each basketmaker has an established level of quality. Although she can make baskets of higher or lower quality, they will all be within that range. Basketmakers can readily recognize one another's product. When asked how, they reply, "We grew up together" or "She always makes the same kind of basket." It is very common for one basketmaker to examine another woman's basket and evaluate its quality. Each woman has an informal evaluation criteria of quality by which she associates the basket with the woman who made it. It appears that each basketmaker has a tacit set of criteria developed through a lifetime of experience which allows her to identify a basket's type, shape, and quality with known practicing basketmakers.

Selling Baskets

Several of the basketmakers have begun producing baskets of superior workmanship and excellent quality. They are very finely woven, take much longer to make, and are sold for a much higher price than ordinary baskets. Some women are acknowledged by other basketmakers as superior craftswomen. One informant, referring to her sister's baskets, stated, "She makes baskets for show and not for sale like we do." These basketmakers are extremely proud of their work and often compare their baskets to recognized masters of the art.

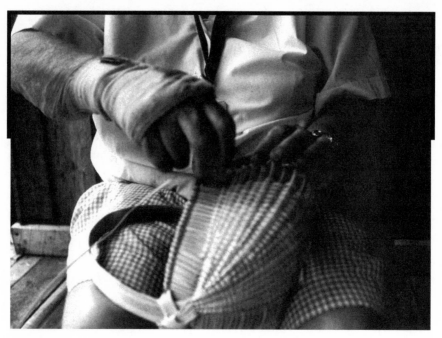

◘ The weaving hands of basketmaker Josie Jones. Photo by Jennifer Core. Courtesy of The Arts Center of Cannon County.

As the reputation of an excellent basketmaker spreads, she can receive a higher price for her efforts from basket collectors.

In addition to pride in their product, economic considerations are a primary motivation for contemporary artisans. Almost all of the baskets made are sold. Kinsmen and friends who want a basket must usually purchase it at the same price a collector or peddler would pay for it. Rarely, a basketmaker may keep one of her baskets because it has an experimental design or has acquired some emotional significance.

The basketmakers of Cannon County agreed that the art has declined from the peak production period of the 1930s. Mason has estimated that during that period there were about 50 families (approximately 400 to 500 persons) engaged in part- or full-time production of chairs and baskets (140). An elderly basketmaker, describing the period from approximately 1910 to 1940, stated that almost every household in the area was engaged in making baskets or chairs. Today approximately 30 households are engaged in basketmaking. An important contribution to the decline of basketmaking was the development of new employment opportunities in the area. A sewing factory, opened in 1947 in a nearby town, has attracted women who would otherwise have been making baskets. (Northcutt 1954, 79–80). Men have been employed at county and state jobs which were not available until after World War II. This income from public jobs has made basketry no longer a financial necessity.

◘ Cannon County baskets. Photo by Robert Cogswell. Courtesy of the Folklife Program, Tennessee Arts Commission.

According to several informants, 20 to 30 years ago the basketmaking tradition almost died out in the Cannon County area. During the 1950s and 1960s, crafts were de-emphasized nationally in favor of mass-produced, high-technology consumer goods. However, a craft revival began during the 1960s. A similar situation concerning Kentucky craftsmen has been described by Bernice Stevens (1962, 282). The popularity of the *Foxfire* books and other studies of traditional technology reflect this revival. During this time, many of the basketmaking women, who had entered the active work force during World War II, began to retire. After retirement, these women returned to making baskets and gardening as means to supplement their families' subsistence.

Basketmaking requires a great deal of hard work, and to many families it still retains the negative connotations of earlier years. For this reason, some women have not encouraged their daughters and nieces to take up the craft; other women, however, lament that their daughters are not interested in basketmaking. During the course of field work, I encountered only four women under 50 years of age who were engaged in making baskets. To be sure, many more younger women know how to weave baskets, but few will start and complete a basket. At the present time, two generations of women make baskets: The older generation is now 70 to 90 years old, and the younger generation is 50 to 70 years old. The older generation is represented by only a few active basketmakers. During the next 20 years, most of the middle-aged women will also cease making baskets, and the craft might well decline further. As fewer baskets are supplied, however, they will become more valuable. High prices and lack of other opportunities may induce many of the younger women to pursue their craft actively.

Basket production in Cannon County has always been a cottage industry. Baskets are sold to a wholesaler, who accumulates stock and sells baskets to consumers unknown to the basketmaker (Boeke 1942, 90). There is also some handicraft production whereby baskets are made to order and sold directly to the consumer. In the past, baskets were bartered or sold to the rural grocery store in the area. There they were stored all winter, and the store owner sold them to peddlers during the spring and summer. After purchasing a load of baskets and chairs, the peddler would travel throughout the eastern United States selling the baskets and chairs on the roadside and to stores along the way. The peddlers went north into Michigan, New York, and Illinois and south into Georgia. They traveled in wagons and later in trucks, sleeping beside the road.

Occasionally, a basketmaker would accumulate a truckload of baskets and chairs so that, selling them by the roadside, she and her husband could travel to Georgia, Kentucky, or Ohio. Basketmakers might also take a truckload of baskets into Nashville to be sold. One woman explained that the price paid for the basket could be doubled and that by selling the baskets themselves they could realize that additional profit.

During my research, three peddlers or dealers were purchasing large numbers of baskets from the artisans of Cannon County. One dealer sells a large number of baskets at weekend flea markets throughout the mid-South. Another dealer works for a traveling show that displays and sells crafts in large shopping malls throughout the Southeast. The third dealer sells baskets in craft shows but also sells them through a large mail order business. The mail order baskets are promoted in women's homemaking magazines as decorations for antique kitchens.

These dealers purchase baskets from the same families under a standing arrangement. The basketmakers can expect the peddler to arrive on a certain day to purchase their baskets. One peddler picks up baskets every two weeks while another makes weekly rounds. Because there is competition among the peddlers, if the baskets are not picked up regularly, they will be sold to someone else. Some peddlers attempt to convince the basketmakers to sell exclusively to them. Generally, the basketmaker knows that the peddlers will purchase their baskets on a regular basis, and they will not jeopardize their relationships by selling to individuals. As a result, strangers wishing to purchase a basket directly from its maker will often be told that there are none for sale, even though a large string of baskets is hanging in the back room.

Several women who produce high-quality baskets, however, sell from their residences to individuals exclusively. One woman has established a retail business and sells quality baskets for other basketmakers. She is becoming widely known among basket collectors for the high level of workmanship of her merchandise, and she can sell many more baskets than she can make. Occasionally basketmakers will be asked to give a demonstration at a craft show where they may also sell their baskets.

The price of baskets varies depending upon the level of craftsmanship and the relationship between buyers and sellers. Each basket peddler has a set price for a specified basket size. The prices will vary somewhat between basketmakers. One peddler, for example, is known to pay more for baskets than his competition.

When the baskets are resold, the prices will be increased from 20 to 300 percent. The price increase depends upon the type of market and the clientele to whom the baskets are sold. Many of these baskets will be sold to consumers through antique and specialized craft shops. Today baskets, like antiques, are purchased primarily by basket collectors for decorative rather than utilitarian purposes.

References Cited

Boeke, Joseph H. "The Structure of Netherlands Indian Economy." *International Secretariat.* New York: Institute of Pacific Relations, 1942.

Mason, Robert L. "The Life of the People of Cannon County, Tennessee." Diss., Peabody College, 1946.

Matthews, Elmora M. *Neighbor and Kin: Life in a Tennessee Ridge Community.* Nashville: Vanderbilt University Press, 1965.

Northcutt, Dixon L. "A Geographic Survey of Cannon County, Tennessee." Master's thesis, University of Tennessee, 1954.

Stevens, Bernice A. "The Revival of Handicrafts." *The Southern Appalachian Region: A Survey.* Ed. Thomas R. Ford. Lexington: University of Kentucky Press, 1962. 127–142.

The Vanishing Art of Cooking Table-Grade Sorghum Molasses [1992]

Ben S. Austin

The art of molasses cooking is unknown to most people in the United States. There are some areas in the South where high-quality sorghum molasses is still made, and the modern consumer can purchase small jars of the dark, rich syrup at many supermarkets. Quart and half-gallon tins of sorghum may be purchased at produce shops. Warren County, Tennessee, produces some of the best molasses, or "lasses," I know anything about, and the Amish settlement near Etheridge, Tennessee, in Lawrence County also turns out a fine product. My maternal grandfather, Frank Snell, made my all-time favorite, but he discontinued this aspect of his farm production when I was about ten. Some twenty years later, my father and I planted a sorghum patch in Glade Creek, on the Cumberland Plateau in White County, Tennessee. Dad bought an old horse-driven "Chattanooga"[1] mill, and we transported it to Glade Creek and set it up on my Uncle Ernest Ellis's farm. My grandfather agreed to accompany us to the mountain to show us how to cook molasses. So I have some first-hand experience with this whole process (see also Hemmerly 1983:406–410; Wigginton 1975:424–436).

Historical Background

Sorghum literally means "Syrian grass" (*Webster's Collegiate Dictionary*). It is one of the earliest known plants to have been cultivated and contributed significantly to the agrarian revolution. As nearly as I am able to determine, wild sorghum was first cultivated in Africa, where a strain, known as *durra*, is used extensively as fodder. Its use was also known in Assyria as early as 700 B.C. and in India as early as the first century A.D. It is not known whether the ancients in simple horticultural societies knew of the practice of making molasses, or sorghum syrup.[2] If they did not, they missed a treat. Its seeds were first brought to the United States on slave ships in the early 1700s and, because of its high yield in dry climates, became an important agricultural plant, particularly with the settlement of the territories west of the Mississippi River. The first sweet sorghum (*Sorghum bicolor saccharatum*), "Chinese Amber," was introduced in the United States in 1853 (Leonard and Martin 1963:681). There are several varieties of sorghum which yield fine table-grade molasses. My grandfather had a distinct preference for "Blue Ribbon," others prefer "Improved Orange," "Honey Drip," or other varieties. While sorghum is not, strictly speaking, a grain plant, it is classified in the cereal family along with millet and oats. Sorghum is similar in appearance to sugar cane, except it is not nearly as large in diameter. It grows to a height of 8 to 12 feet and, when mature, contains a rich sweet pap, or juice, which renders molasses when cooked properly.

The Production Process

There are several important stages in the process of making molasses from sorghum cane. The first step is to cut the cane. The leaves are field-stripped, the tops cut off, and the cane is hauled to the mill as soon as possible, since the juice will sour in the cane within two or three days.

The next step is to squeeze the juice from the cane.[3] In the old days, this was done with a horse-driven mill (in our case, the horse was Uncle Ernest's old mule, Janie). A long sturdy pole, called the "boom," is bolted to the top of the mill, and the long end of the pole is attached to the horse's harness.[4] The poor thing then walks around and around in a circle while the raw cane is fed into the mill. More recently, mechanical technology has introduced alternate means of powering the mill. Some mills today are run by self-contained gasoline engines. My grandfather Snell, in the last few years of operation, powered his mill with the old Farmall tractor.[5] A large leather belt some 30 or 40 feet long and 6 or 8 inches wide ran from the mill to the tractor's power take-off. The flattened dry cane, called "pummies," is then discarded or used as fodder or garden mulch.[6] As the juice comes out of the mill, it is strained through burlap and stored in a large barrel until it is cooked. This is the first of three strainings before the product is finished.[7]

The cooking process is the phase that requires the greatest skill and experience. First, you must have the proper kind of fireplace or furnace. It should be about 12 feet long and 4 ½ feet wide. It is usually built up to about 3 or 4 feet high. The fire is built the entire length of the fireplace and must be kept active for several hours. A good supply of hardwood is essential. Many molasses makers use sawmill slabs because of their low cost and easy accessibility.

The second thing you need is a good molasses pan or evaporator box. A molasses pan is a curious looking thing. Most pans are 10 to 12 feet long, about 4 ½ feet wide and 6 inches deep and are made of fairly heavy gauge stainless steel. There are several variations in the construction of the pan. The most primitive pans had no dividers. The raw juice was simply poured in the pan and cooked until it was done and drawn off. More modern pans have dividers that extend the entire width of the pan, creating four or five sections. Juice is poured through burlap into the first section and cooked for a while and manually scooped into the next section with a dipper. New juice is then poured into the first section. The pan we used had dividers that left a four- or five-inch space between the end of the divider and the side of the pan. The space is closed off with a wooden gate to prevent the gently boiling juice from flowing into the next section until it is ready.[8] When the juice in the first compartment has cooked just the right amount of time, the wooden gate is moved to the next section and new juice is poured in its place. Here it cooks some more and is released into the third section, and so on, until it reaches the other end of the pan, where it is drained off into buckets as molasses syrup.[9] As the juice makes its way down the slightly inclined pan, it changes to a dark amber color and becomes increasingly thicker.

◪ Evaporating the syrup on a farm in east Tennessee located near the Great Smoky Mountains National Park, 1935. Joseph S. Hall Collection, Archives of Appalachia, East Tennessee State University.

As the juice cooks, the pan must be scraped constantly to prevent sticking. A greenish foam, or skim, forms on the surface of the gently boiling syrup. The foam must be continuously "skimmed off" and discarded; otherwise, the molasses will have a bitter taste.

There is no substitute for experience in knowing exactly when the molasses has cooked the proper amount of time. Too much cooking will result in the syrup being too dark and too thick; too little cooking results in the syrup being "green" and likely to turn sour a short time later. Experts can determine if the syrup is done by examining the bubbles it makes. If the bubbles are too small, the syrup is still too thin. When the bubbles are about the size of a silver dollar and burst in the middle, it is ready to be drawn off. One of the more pleasant jobs in the cooking of molasses is the taste-test quality-control function. At just the right time it is drawn off into a large container, usually a lard stand, and allowed to cool. In the old days, molasses was kept in wooden barrels. On the back porch of our old farm house in the Blackman community in Rutherford County was a large molasses barrel. A tight-fitting lid was held in place by a large rock to keep children and other "varmits" out of the molasses. Most often, today, it will be placed in quart or half-gallon tins or glass jars.

After mastering the process described above, or purchasing molasses at the store, all one really needs is a large pan of hot "cathead" biscuits and a bowl of freshly churned sweet butter. Now, there is an art to knowing just how much butter to mix with the molasses; however, there is no way to tell anyone the secret formula, so the reader is left to his or her own tasteful discovery! I once heard a country preacher say, as he looked out upon a particularly large audience, that he felt a little like the boy who fell into the barrel of molasses. The youngster lifted his eyes to heaven and prayed, "Lord, make my tongue equal to my opportunity." The preacher had obviously tasted molasses. One warning to the novice is in order. Avoid the commercial grade, very dark "blackstrap" molasses sold in the "baking needs" section of the supermarket. This substance is good for baking "hoot and holler cake" and molasses cookies but is most unsatisfactory for direct consumption. Table grade molasses is about the color and consistency of dark honey.

Concluding Observations

As Hemmerly correctly observes (1983:408–409), molasses making is a vanishing art. Around the turn of the century over 16 million gallons of molasses were produced in the United States. By 1949, production had declined to about 6 million gallons (Kipps 1970). Today, except for a few large-scale commercial mills, most sorghum is produced in small family-farm settings, which make 50 to 75 gallons each year.

Cooking sorghum molasses is at least a two person operation—one to cook and one to skim. My personal experience is that three people can be kept fairly busy all day. Making sorghum molasses is extremely hard work requiring skill, artistry, and experience. The end product, however, is well worth the effort, and its passing is lamented by those of us who grew up with it.

Notes

1. Manufactured by the Chattanooga Plow Co., Chattanooga, Tennessee.
2. Sorghum molasses is not, technically, molasses, but syrup, since no sugar is extracted during the production process.
3. Some moonshiners in the mountains of North Carolina chose another use for sweet sorghum. They made "wildcat" rum from the fermented juice.
4. Some molasses makers run a lead line from the horse's harness to a limber pole attached to the short end of the broom to keep pressure on the horse so that it will walk in a circle.
5. The mill shown in the photograph is my father's old mill. [*Editors' note: This photo could not be located.*]
6. Dad told me once that Grandpa Austin laid the pummies in the row on top of his seed potatoes before covering them. This procedure aerated and fertilized the soil.
7. Photograph courtesy of the Tennessee State Library, Nashville. [*Editors' note: This photo could not be located.*]
8. One variation of this style is a solid divider, that is, one that extends the width of the pan, with small holes on alternating ends to allow the juice to flow from one section to another.
9. The finished molasses is strained a final time, usually through cheesecloth, before final storage.
10. Some people save the skimmings and cook them separately until they are very thick. They are then "pulled" to make molasses taffy.

References Cited

Hemmerly, Thomas E. "Traditional Method of Making Sorghum Molasses," *Economic Botany* 37, no. 4 (October–December 1983): 406–410.

Kipps, M. S. *Production of Field Crops: A Testbook Agronomy.* 4th ed. New York: McGraw-Hill, 1970.

Leonard, Warren H., and John H. Martin. *Cereal Crops.* New York: Macmillan, 1963.

Wigginton, Eliot, ed. *Foxfire 3.* Garden City: Doubleday, 1975.

Dale Calhoun and the Reelfoot Lake Boat
[1999]

Robert Cogswell

This article was originally compiled in January 1996 to accompany the nomination of Dale Calhoun for a National Heritage Fellowship. In July 1998, the National Endowment for the Arts announced that he would be among the recipients of the award for this year to be presented in Washington in October. Many other things have happened since this nominated text was written. Dale retired from the Tennessee Department of Corrections to devote full time to boat building. Dale and one of his boats appeared in the recent movie *U.S. Marshals.* More was written about him, and more video features were made, especially since the announcement of his honor. Through a special folk arts purchase award, the Tennessee Art Commission placed one of his boats in the permanent collection of the Tennessee State Museum. Now nationally honored for the tradition and career summarized here, Dale will continue to be one of Tennessee's most important folk cultural treasures.

Reelfoot Lake

Reelfoot Lake, in the northwest corner of Tennessee, was formed by the New Madrid earthquake, actually a series of geological upheavals during the winter of 1811–12. This seismic phenomenon caused the depression of a mature cypress forest into a lakebed and its subsequent flooding by disturbances in the course of the nearby Mississippi River. The lake and surrounding marshes, covering over 15,000 acres, afford a remarkable natural habitat known for its thousands of acres of "yankapin" (American lotus) growth, and in recent years for its large population of bald eagles. The human history of the lake has revolved largely around fishing and hunting, both for commercial and sport purposes.

Reelfoot's unique environment has been enriched by diverse folklife traditions. As a commercial fishery, Reelfoot is one of the few places where net fishing for crappie is legal and turtling is still done on a notable scale. Like commercial fishing, guiding has been a common traditional occupation around the lake, many generations deep in some families. Because of the nature of the lake, canepoles remain prominent in local sport fishing. One of the premier waterfowl hunting locales along the Mississippi flyway, Reelfoot has perhaps the most notable local tradition of duck-call making in the country. Boat docks and duckblinds are significant local folk architectural forms.

The Reelfoot Lake Boat or Stumpjumper

The most significant artifact in the lake's cultural heritage is the Reelfoot lake boat, long known in the vernacular as the "stumpjumper" for its durability in collisions with the cypress knees, stumps, logs, and other submerged obstacles that characterize the shallow lake. In hunting circles, they have also been commonly referred to as Reelfoot duck boats. Flat-bottomed with curved sides, pointed at both bow and stern, and usually built in lengths of 13 to 18 feet (15 ½ is standard), the boat is clearly akin to the Louisiana *pirogue,* but its many quirks make the stumpjumper a boat type all its own. It has most often been built out of local cypress (with white oak ribs), variously waterproofed with a painted canvas, sheet tin, or (currently) fiberglass outer layer. The stumpjumper design has evolved to accommodate both manual and motorized propulsion in ways that respond inventively to the lake's unique environmental conditions.

The origin of the stumpjumper is one of many points inconsistently reported in the writings about it. Some sources claim the boat was already in use on the lake "before the Civil War," conjoined with the cliché of "over 100 years ago . . ." in the first articles written in the 1950s. At the other extreme is the contention that the boat type dates from the 1907–8 period of the "Night Rider" vigilante war over Reelfoot fishing rights, although there does not seem to be any real basis for tying the boat's appearance to that historical episode. The later dating also ignores the only piece of hard chronological evidence related to early stumpjumpers. There is a firm patent date of 1884 for the bowfacing oar mechanism associated with the boat, which was registered by Fred Allen of Monmouth, Illinois, but according to one account invented earlier by a Hornbeak, Tennessee, man (Sanford, 1979). This would indicate that the local boat type existed by at least this date.

The Reelfoot boat-building tradition includes other boats historically and functionally related to the stumpjumper. The flat-bottomed, blunt-ended "jonboat," the most common traditional boat type throughout inland America, has always been built by local makers in varying sizes for use on the nearby Mississippi River. Over the past thirty years, cheap, mass-produced aluminum jonboats have become numerically dominant on the lake, but the lake boat designation for the stumpjumper seems to underscore the fact that handmade jonboats were not often used on the lake in earlier times. The "skiff"—with pointed bow, blunt stern, shallow draft, and slight keel—is the third commonly built local boat form. The larger "D-line skiff," usually 18–20 feet long, took its name and its pattern from a St. Louis boat company's once popular commercial craft. Its size and wide, stable deck made it the preferred boat for the handling of larger nets by pairs of commercial fishermen working together and for other heavy-duty work on the lake, such as hauling towlines of stumpjumpers for day excursions by sport fishermen in the early decades of the century, before the smaller boats were motorized. In keeping with the wider Reelfoot boat-building tradition, Dale Calhoun builds not only stumpjumpers but also occasional examples of jonboats and skiffs in various sizes and even other boat types, such as the pointed-bow, v-bottomed "outboard hull."

The stumpjumper may not have originated in their shop, but the Calhoun family has been the most important and prolific line of boat builders on the lake. Oral historical credit for building the first lake boats has been given to a man named Herman B. "Con" Young. Investigation of civil records has not yielded significant information about Young or the span of his career (Gammerdinger), but he reportedly worked in the Samburg area on the southeast bank of the lake and developed the design out of an earlier "3-plank boat" (Rawls). There were certainly other 19th-century boat builders on the lake as well, but they and their possible contribution to stumpjumper design have been forgotten.

The Calhoun family's association with boat building started during the 1910s, in the shop of Dale's great-grandfather Joseph Marion Calhoun (1852–1927). At some point during that period, Joe moved his family from Dyer County to the Obion County community of Shawtown, four miles southeast of Reelfoot Lake. Like most blacksmiths at that time, Joe was a versatile craftsman who practiced all sorts of woodwork and smithing. He made a few jonboats but was never a full-time boat builder. Joe's son (Dale's grandfather), Boone Calhoun (1889–1965), grew up in the Shawtown shop and took it over. John Milligan, a transient journeyman who had earlier worked for Con Young, introduced Boone to the making of stumpjumpers while he was employed as a hand in the Calhoun shop. Boone's son (Dale's father), W. W. "Bill" Calhoun (1913–1990), got involved in the boat-building operations as a teenager, and at

◘ Dale Calhoun with father Bill and son at the old Calhoun shop, early 1950s. Calhoun
family photo.

some point in the 1928–30 period, Boone established a new shop, specializing
in stumpjumpers, closer to the lake at Lassiter Corner.

During the following decade, the stumpjumper's unique inboard motor
and rudder system was developed. One account (Rawls) cites Claude Anders
of Union City, Tennessee, as being the first to mount a ¾- horsepower gasoline
motor, borrowed from a washing machine, into a stumpjumper. By 1938–40,
Calhoun boats were being motorized with regularity, and for a time this was
specialized work for Dale's maternal uncle Lewis "Booster" Walden, who had
a separate shop next to Boone's at Lassiter Corner. After Boone and Bill completed the hulls, the boats went next door for outfitting with motors and steer-
age by Walden, who later produced stumpjumpers independently as well. In
1944 the Calhouns moved their shop several miles closer to Tiptonville on
Lake Drive across the Lake County line. Just after World War II, Boone left the
shop to Bill and moved to Michigan to find factory work.

Although they are not well documented, there were other local craftsmen
still actively building stumpjumpers up to this point. A man named "Cap"
Bly was a prominent builder during the earlier decades of the century. Roland
Williams is remembered as operating a shop in Samburg into the 1940s. It might
be argued that building stumpjumpers remained an economically viable trade
in the community until about 1950, when demand dwindled, due in part to the
many boats already in use and to competition from cheaper, mass-produced
crafts. In the 1950s there were apparently even several failed attempts to manufacture molded fiberglass stumpjumpers (Champlin, 1979).

◘ Reelfoot Lake stumpjumper boat built by Dale Calhoun in dock at Samburg, Tennessee. Photo by Robert Cogswell. Courtesy of the Folklife Program, Tennessee Arts Commission.

Reelfoot boat building already faced declining circumstances as Dale Calhoun grew into the role of primary craftsman in the family shop during the 1950s. A few other craftsmen—such as Grady Taylor and Thomas Alexander (Gammerdinger)—would continue to try their hands at building stumpjumpers on occasion, but Dale rather early in his career emerged as the most significant bearer of this community tradition. Becoming the conservator of this heritage has had many implications for Dale, and he has accepted the mantle as much more than just a way to make a living. For decades, it has required him to work other "day jobs" while devoting regular weekend and off hours to the boat shop.

Dale Calhoun

Dale was born in 1935 and spent his boyhood around the boat shop. The details of the first boat he built, like other aspects of his story, have been variously reported, and Dale can't honestly recall his exact age (early adolescence, 11 to 14) or the years (some time in the late 1940s). But the gist of the story is that, to surprise his father and demonstrate his own skill, Dale worked furiously over a weekend to start and finish a boat on his own while Bill was away from home on a trip. By the mid-1950s, Dale was already being groomed to take over the shop and already receiving mention in the first articles being published about

□ Dale Calhoun at the remodeled shop on Lake Drive, late 1950s.
Calhoun family photo.

the stumpjumpers. During this period, Bill and Dale developed their technique of adding a fiberglass outer coating to the hulls.

Bill Calhoun also owned and managed a boat dock, and his activity in the shop decreased until his full retirement from boat building in 1974. In many respects Dale took charge of the operation at a much earlier point. In 1959, Dale bought the patent rights for the bow-facing oar mechanism from the Allen Company, which had for years been selling the devices to local boat makers from out of state. Having them cast for him by an Iowa foundry, Dale attempted to market the bow-facing oars separately, but outside of occasional sale as a curiosity, most of them have found use on his own boats. In 1960, Dale expanded and rebuilt the Lake Drive shop as a concrete slab-and-block structure.

□ Dale Calhoun at the Tennessee Program, Smithsonian Festival of
American Folklife, 1986. Photo by Robert Cogswell. Courtesy of the
Folklife Program, Tennessee Arts Commission.

Dale's commitment to sustaining this tradition was so clearly evident that
by the 1970s, before he reached the age of 40, he was regularly gaining attention as the only surviving master of a significant heritage craft. As the bibliography attests, feature journalism about him has increased continually since
that point, and he has also been the subject of occasional television features in
recent years (see Videography, below).

In 1981, the Tennessee State Parks Folklife Project (funded by the Folk Arts
Program of the National Endowment for the Arts) introduced Dale with a public
demonstration of his boat building at the first local folklife festival at Reelfoot
Lake State Park. His easy-going, friendly temperament made Dale a natural at
presenting his craft to event audiences, and he has since established an impressive
record of participation in folklife events at the local, regional, and national levels

(see Festivals and Demonstration Experiences, below). Dale's value in this respect to folk-arts efforts in Tennessee cannot be overstated, and those of us involved in folk-event production here feel enormously indebted to him. Practitioners of normally shopbound crafts are greatly inconvenienced to trot their operation out to a temporary setting. Dale has cheerfully done it—often sacrificing far more income from a weekend of lost work in his shop than he was compensated for— more times over the years than any of us can remember. Dale's excellence as a craftsman and demonstrator grow out of a love for what he does, great skill in doing it, and a relaxed nonchalance in sharing in with others.

In 1991, Dale moved his shop a short distance to a new building on the lakefront highway, across from the state park museum where exhibits inform tourists about stumpjumpers, the Calhoun family, and other aspects of the Reelfoot heritage. Mondays, Saturdays, and most late afternoons—whenever he is not at his job as a prison security captain at nearby Lake County Correctional Facility—Dale can be found at work in his shop, and visitors now regularly interrupt him there in much the same way they do at folk festivals. He always has time for them, and he conveys more than he or they often realize about traditional arts and Reelfoot folklife. Dale's approach to boat building has always been more pragmatic than purist, but that has in no way disqualified his craftsmanship as being deeply traditional. As appropriate power tools (especially saws) have become available, he has shown no resistance to using them, but he also holds to some hand-tool procedures many modern craftsmen would consider outmoded. He has restored, proudly shows off, and regularly uses a drill for oarlock fittings salvaged from his grandfather's shop. Dale adamantly insists that the "blueprints" for his stumpjumpers are "in his head." While he uses a few jigs and templates literally handed down in the family, a surprising number of the procedures and sizings he performs in building a boat are done entirely by "feel."

As Dale's reputation has spread in boating and sportmen's circle, and more recently, among "local color" and cultural tourism enthusiasts, the market for his work has changed and fluctuated considerably. The work of the Calhoun shop has always been driven by orders, and depending on current demand, Dale rarely completes more than a boat a week nowadays. There are no longer the kinds of local orders from rental docks and individual sportsmen that used to sustain heavy production. Since the late 1950s, the shop has increasingly received out-of-state orders from people who want a stumpjumper for use on "non-native" waters, and Dale has had to deal with the considerable trouble of shipping his boats. The boats' heightened significance simply as artifacts has also influenced changes in demand. In the 1960s, Dale was commissioned to build six stumpjumpers for use in an NBC documentary on Lewis and Clark by a production company who considered his handmade Reelfoot boats to be as close as they could get to authentic "period" props. More recently, his stumpjumpers have found homes in museum exhibits, at the Reelfoot State Park Ellington Museum, at the U.S. Fish and Wildlife Service's Reelfoot Visitor's Center in Walnut Log, at the Obion County Museum in Union City, and at the Tennessee Aquarium in Chattanooga.

Through a combination of circumstance, dedication, and intentional decision, Dale Calhoun practices his boat building within a very unusual niche. The niche has supported Dale's work as the only master preserving a unique family and community craft tradition. In some ways, however, the niche has inhibited prospects of his passing the tradition on to a future master. For decades, the level of production at the Calhoun shop has not justified the hiring of additional hands or the taking on of apprentices. At times, there is just barely enough demand for the work of one craftsman. In the two previous generations of Calhoun boat builders, this consideration probably had a great deal to do with the shop being turned over to the son earlier than might have been dictated by his father's age. In the 1960s and 1970s, Dale's two sons both spent time in the shop, but neither really "took to it." Dale's own intensity at the craft and its slim prospects for providing a viable livelihood may have played a part in one of them eventually turning to farming and the other becoming an electrician. Dale's current jokes about forcing the craft onto his youngest grandson reflect a real concern about what will happen to the shop and the tradition. He likely has quite a few years of boat building still ahead of him, and during that time, training a successor is definitely a goal Dale wants to realize.

Bibliography
Section A.
Reelfoot Lake: Other Traditions

Baird, Woody. "Turtle Trade Comes Out of Shell." *Tennessean,* June 26, 1995, 6B.

Caldwell, Russell H. *Reelfoot Lake: History-Duck Call Maker-Hunting Tales.* Union City, Tenn.: Caldwell's Office Outfitters, 1988.

———. *Reelfoot Lake: The Tourists' Guide.* Union City, Tenn.: Caldwell's Office Outfitters, 1988.

Harlan, Howard L., and Crew Anderson, *Duck Calls: An Enduring American Folk Art.* Nashville: Harlan-Anderson Publishing, 1988.

Leeper, John H. "Trammeling on Reelfoot Lake." *Memphis Commercial Appeal Mid-South Magazine,* November 12, 1978, 6–18.

Leonard, Llexie. *Reelfoot Lake Treasures.* Tiptonville, Tenn.: Lake County Banner, 1991.

Moss, Max. "Reelfoot's Fish Bring 'Reel' Profit." *Nashville Banner,* February 22, 1995, E-1, 3.

Nelson, Wilber A. "Reelfoot—An Earthquake Lake." *National Geographic* 45.1 (January 1924): 95–114.

Schoffman, Robert J. "Turtling for the Market at Reelfoot Lake." *Journal of the Tennessee Academy of Science* 24.2 (April 1949): 143–45.

Thomas, William. "Life on 'The Log.'" *Memphis Commercial Appeal Mid-South Magazine*, January 18, 1970, 4–6.

Section B.
Reelfoot Boat Building and Dale Calhoun

Andrews, James G. "The Reelfoot Boat-Builders." *Memphis Commercial Appeal Mid-South Magazine,* December 30, 1973, 4–6.

"Boat Builders to Show Work." *Lake County (Tenn.) Banner,* September 18, 1985, 12.

Bowden, Kevin. "Smithsonian to Host Area Craftsman: Festival Will Feature Calhoun's Stumpjumpers." *Union City (Tenn.) Daily Messenger,* June 18, 1986, 17.

———. "Boating Design Survives Times." *Union City (Tenn.) Daily Messenger,* February 23, 1988, 11.

Brannon, John. "Lake Boatbuilder to Show Off Skills." *Union City (Tenn.) Daily Messenger,* May 15, 1992, 1

———. "To Build a Boat." *Heartland Boating* 4.6 (August/September 1992): 30–31.

Caldwell, Russel H. "Boats by Calhoun." In *Reelfoot Lake: History-Duck Call Makers-Hunting Tales* (Union City, Tenn.: Caldwell's Office Outfitters, 1988), 68–71.

"Calhoun Takes 'Stump Jumper' to Smithsonian." *Correction Courier* (Tennessee Department of Corrections) 1.7 (Summer 1986): 9.

"Calhoun to Smithsonian Show." *Lake County (Tenn.) Banner,* May 21, 1986,:1.

Champlin, Tim. "The Reelfoot Lakeboat." *Inland Sea* (December 1977): 74–76.

———. "Tennessee's Unique Reelfoot Lakeboat." *Canoe* (March 1979): 22–23.

Christ, Mark. "Time, Not Stumps, May Stop Reelfoot Boats." *Memphis Commercial Appeal,* January 19, 1986, B3.

Clemons, Alan. "Hands of Time." *Huntsville (Ala.) Times,* February 1, 1998, C14.

Conover, Robin. "Calhoun's Reelfoot Lake Boats." *Tennessee Magazine* 35.3 (March 1991): 24–25.

Cook, Dan. "Calhoun 'Name' Goes with Reelfoot Boats." *Chattanooga Free Press,* September 25, 1994, G8.

Crawford, Byron. "Building on Tradition: Family Reels in Business with 'Stumpjumpers.'" *Louisville Courier-Journal,* April 3,1992, B1.

Creason, Joe. "The Boats That Go Hind-End Fore: The Can Dodge Reelfoot Lake's Snags." *Louisville Courier-Journal Magazine,* October 26, 1963, 35–38.

Dupree, Spence. "The Calhouns: Three Generations of Boatbuilding." *Jackson (Tenn.) Sun,* June 22, 1975, 6-C.

Ehresman, Jack. "Business Propped Up by Nature." *Peoria (Ill.) Journal Star,* July 3, 1993, C5.

Gammerdinger, Harry. "The Reelfoot Stumpjumper: Traditional Boat Building in Tennessee." In Robert E. Walls and George H. Schoemaker, ed., *The Old Traditional Way of Life: Essay in Honor of Warren E. Roberts* (Bloomington, Ind.: Trickster Press, 1989), 78–95.

Garth, Gray. "Reelfoot Revisited." *Field & Stream* 102.4 (August 1997): 68–71.

Green, Jean. "Handmade Reelfoot Lake Boats Still Popular After 100 Years." *Union City (Tenn.) Daily Messenger,* September 16, 1983, 1, 4.

"Joe Creason's Kentucky." *Louisville Courier-Journal,* July 16[?], 1965.

Johnson, Rheta Grimsley. "The Boat Builder Knows His Way around Reelfoot." *Memphis Commercial Appeal,* March 16, 1994, A13.

Jones, Evan. "Builder to Show at World's Fair." *Lake County (Tenn.) Banner,* February 11, 1982, 1.

"Lake Boats Go on TV." Unidentified clipping, 1964.

Laylock, George. "Reelfoot Boat." *Sports Afield Boatbuilding Annual,* 1957, 36–43.

Lebovitz. Richard. "The Reelfoot Lake Stumpjumper." *Ash Breeze: Journal of the Traditional Small Craft Association* 12.2 (Spring 1990): 6–7.

Mack, Tony. "Reelfoot Lake's Sleeper Bass." *BassMaster Fishing Annual,* 1976, 44–45, 94–95.

———. "3rd Generation Hand Crafting Stump Jumper." *Hall (Tenn.) Graphic,* May 6, 1977, 9.

Meeker, Francis. "Calhoun Family Boasts 100-Year-Old Talent." *Nashville Banner,* April 28, 1975.

Middleton, Harry. "Reelfoot: Tennessee's Earthquake Lake." *Southern Living* 21.2 (February 1986): 126–31.

Parker, Lin C. "Folk Life Demonstrations: Reeling in the Crowds." *Chattanooga News–Free Press,* May 27, 1992, A1.

Patton, Buck. "Family Tradition: Dale Calhoun Keeps Boats and Old Business Running." *Memphis Press-Scimitar,* March 25, 1982, C4.

———. "Family Tradition: Calhoun Boats Are Unique." *Union City (Tenn.) Messenger,* April 17, 1982, 1.

Pomeroy, Maurice. "The Stump Jumper of Reelfoot Lake." *Tennessee Conservationist* 40.9 (September 1974): 18–20.

Price, Steve. "The Stump Jumper of Reelfoot Lake." *Rod & Reel: The Journal of American Angling* (July/August 1981): 42–45.

Rankin, Bob. "New Style 'Bass Boat' Unique." *Cincinnati Enquirer,* February 13, 1977.

Rawls, Charles K. "Reelfoot Runabouts: Probably the Most Snag-proof Craft Afloat Are These Ingenious Boats from Tennessee." *Popular Boating,* March 1957, 34–35.

"Reelfoot Lake: Vacation Paradise." *Tennessee Thrusts* 2.2 (Spring 1974): 18–20.

"Reelfoot's No. 1 Stump-Jumper." *Southern Living* 12.7 (July 1979): 140–41.

"Reelfoot Stumpjumpers." *Southern Outdoors,* February 1993, 47.

Sanford, Vern. "Reelfoot: A Lake from a Quake." *Fisherman and Hunter's Guide,* September 1975, 42–45.

———. "Reelfoot's Unique Boat: 'The Stump Jumper.'" *Fisherman and Hunter's Guide,* March 1976, 50–53.

Smith, Mike. "Family Boat Building Almost as Old as Reelfoot." Unidentified clipping.

"Smithsonian Institution Honors LCRCF Captain." *Paragon* (Lake County Correctional Facility), June 1986, 3.

"Smithsonian Show Drew Long Lines." *Union City (Tenn.) Messenger,* July 1986.

"Southern Boat Builder: Calhoun." *Lake County (Tenn.) Banner,* July 8, 1976, 8.

Taylor, Jan. "Duck Boat Craftsmanship Is Guarded Family Secret." *Memphis Commercial Appeal.* Undated clipping, c. April 1964.

"This Boat Rows in Reverse." *Popular Science* 166.6 (June 1955): 121.

Todd, Roberta. "Builder to Fill World Fair Order for Reelfoot Lake 'Stumper Jumper.'" *Memphis Commercial Appeal,* February 2, 1982, B1.

Tuberville, Jake. "The Reelfoot Lake Boat: A Tennessee Original." *Tennessee Conservationist* 53.6 (November/December 1987): 3–5.

———. "A Well-Used Boat: The Reelfoot Lake StumpJumper." *Wooden Boat* 82 (May/June 1988): 19, 20, 23, 25.

Whittle, Donna. "Off to Washington! Old-Time Lake Craftsmen Travel with Nostalgic Talents." *Dyersburg (Tenn.) State Gazette,* June 24, 1986, 1.

Wilson, George. "Tennessee Tradition Set Adrift." *Crafts Report* 19.201 (December 1992):12.

Wilson, George Tipton. "Reelfoot Stumpjumpers: A Family Tradition." *Tennessee Conservationist* 61.5 (September/October 1995): 26–29.

Wilson, Taylor. "Carving Out a Family Tradition." *Jackson (Tenn.) Sun,* August 1, 1993, 6C.

Woolsey, F. W. "Reelfoot: The Place, the People." *Louisville Courier-Journal & Times Magazine,* July 6, 1969, 18–26.

Young Matt. "Reelfoot Lake Legacy." *Ducks Unlimited,* March/April 1995, 38–44.

Videography

WTVF-TV, Nashville, Tenn. Feature on the five oldest businesses in Tennessee, mid-1970s.

WHBQ-TV, Memphis, Tenn. "Channel 13, Eyewitness News feature, with Bill Anderson," mid-1980s.

WPSD-TV, Paducah, Ky. "People Beat with Sam Burrage," mid-1980s.

Community Cable Network, Tiptonville, Tenn. Feature program on Dale Calhoun by Coy Leake, c. 1990.

WBIR-TV, Knoxville, Tenn. "Reelfoot Lake Stump Jumper," Heartland Series, 1992.

Festivals and Demonstration Experiences

Reelfoot Lake Folklife Festival (Tiptonville, Tenn.), 1981–90
Folklife Festival, 1982 World's Fair (Knoxville, Tenn.), 1982
Tennessee Grassroots Days (Nashville), 1983, 1987, 1989
Northwest Tennessee Heritage Festival (Martin, Tenn.), 1985–86
Smithsonian Festival of American Folklife (Washington, D.C.), 1986
Forked Deer Festival (Jackson, Tenn.), 1987–89
Mid-South Music and Heritage Festival (Memphis), 1988–92
Tennessee Aquarium (Chattanooga), eight weekend appearances, 1992–93
National Folk Festival (Chattanooga), 1993

Further Reading in
Material Folk Culture

Alvic, Philis. *Weavers of the Southern Highlands.* 2003.

Ball, Donald B. "Observations on the Form and Function of Middle Tennessee Gravehouses." *Tennessee Anthropologist.* 1977.

Bullard, Helen. *Crafts and Craftsmen of the Tennessee Mountains.* 1976.

Cantrell, Brent. "Traditional Grave Structures on the Eastern Highland Rim." *Tennessee Folklore Society Bulletin.* 1981.

Dickinson, W. Calvin. *Upper Cumberland Historic Architecture.* 2002.

Eaton, Allen H. *Handicrafts of the Tennessee Mountains.* 1937. Reprint, 1973.

Glassie, Henry. *Pattern in the Material Folk Culture of the Eastern United States.* 1968.

Gundaker, Grey, and Judith McWillie. *No Space Hidden: The Spirit of African American Yard Work.* 2005.

Hill, Sarah H. *Weaving New Worlds: Southeastern Cherokee Women and Their Basketry.* 1997.

Howell, Benita. *Folklife along the Big South Fork of the Cumberland River.* 2003.

Irwin, John Rice. *Guns and Gunmaking Tools of Southern Appalachia.* 1980.

———. *A People and Their Quilts.* 1983.

Law, Rachel Nash, and Cynthia W. Taylor. *Appalachian White Oak Basketmaking: Handing Down the Basket.* 1991.

Moffett, Marian, and Lawrence Wodehouse. *East Tennessee Cantilever Barns.* 1993.

Murray-Wooley, Carolyn, and Karl B. Raitz. *Rock Fences of the Bluegrass.* 1992.

Ramsey, Bets, and Merikay Waldvogel. *The Quilts of Tennessee: Images of Domestic Life Prior to 1930.* 1986.

Rheder, John. *Appalachian Folkways.* 2004.

Riedl, Norbert, Donald B. Ball, and Anthony Cavender. *A Survey of Traditional Architecture and Related Material Folk Culture Patterns in the Normandy Reservoir, Coffee County, Tennessee.* 1976.

PART TWO

Folk Medicine

Folk medicine is commonly defined as traditional knowledge of the prevention, cause, and treatment of illness that is passed on informally from person to person and one generation to the next by word of mouth and imitation. The natural and supernatural folk medical beliefs and practices documented in Tennessee and elsewhere in the South are historically rooted in the countries from which the early settlers of the region came, notably, Scotland, England, Ireland, and Germany. The Native American influence is evident in the use of medicinal plants specific to the New World, such as sassafras, goldenseal, lobelia, boneset, horsemint, mayapple, and bloodroot. Often overlooked in discussions about the use of Native American–derived medicinal plants, however, is that the European settlers introduced many medicinal plants indigenous to the Old World, such as dandelion, plantain, ground ivy, mullein, balm of Gilead, red clover, catnip, and burdock. African-derived influences are evident, too, but this aspect has yet to be adequately investigated. Recent studies suggest, however, that the folk medical beliefs and practices of blacks and whites in Tennessee and other parts of the upland South are much more alike than different.

The conventional definition of folk medicine is useful in distinguishing it from official (or orthodox, scientific) and popular medicine in an abstract sense, and it appropriately recognizes the fact that many Tennesseans in the past, as in other parts of the country, were illiterate. It does not, however, acknowledge the fact that in the past there were literate people who obtained considerable healing knowledge from printed sources, including domestic medicine books, almanacs, patent medicine brochures, newspapers, and magazines. Domestic medicine books were especially influential, and there were many to choose from, including some written by Tennesseans, such as *Wright's Family Physician or System of Domestic Medicine* (1833) by Blount County physician Isaac Wright and *Domestic Medicine, or Poor Man's Friend in the*

Hours of Affliction, Pain, and Sickness (1830) by Knoxville physician John C. Gunn. Gunn's *Domestic Medicine* became a national bestseller and was reprinted 213 times by 1885. Gunn's intent was to "demystify" official medicine and make it accessible to lay people, especially those on the frontier in the nineteenth century who did not have access to a physician. Gunn's *Domestic Medicine* evinces a blending of state-of-the-art medical knowledge with bits of folk medical knowledge obtained from lay people, a common pattern in the practices of physicians in the South at the time. Domestic medicine books and encounters with physicians, however, introduced lay people to official medical theory and practice. The folk medicine record in Tennessee and elsewhere shows unequivocally that lay people at the time were treating illness in much the same manner as physicians through so-called heroic and sometimes fatal therapeutics such as bleeding, cupping, blistering, sweating, and the administration of powerful and highly toxic purgatives and emetics; furthermore, people continued using these methods long after they had been abandoned by official medicine following the emergence of germ theory.

The first selection, "Folk Remedies," by T. J. Farr, one of the founding members of the Tennessee Folklore Society, illustrates the essentially descriptive, item-listing approach that characterizes most of the early research on folk medicine and other genres of folklore. Farr's list also shows the early folklorists' skewed interest in the supernatural dimension. Most of the magical remedies are based on sympathetic magic (i.e., things that resemble each other also influence each other), such as placing an axe under the bed to "cut" (stop) a pain in the side and having three drops of blood to fall on the blade of a knife to "cut" (stop) a nosebleed. Another form of sympathetic magic, transference of an illness to an object, is noted in the cures for phthisic (asthma), stone bruises, warts, and rheumatism. Farr notes the presence of "thrash" (thrush) doctors. According to tradition, a seventh son or daughter, a person who never looked into the eyes of his father, and a woman whose married name was the same as her maiden name all had an inherent power to cure thrush by blowing into the mouth of the child. These healers were often called upon to cure other illnesses as well. Not mentioned by Farr are the supernatural methods employed by folk healers known as bloodstoppers, burn (or fire) doctors, goiter rubbers, and wart doctors.

Grady Long's essay, "Folk Medicine in McMinn, Polk, Bradley, and Meigs Counties, Tennessee, 1910–1927," focuses expressly on the naturalistic domain of folk medicine, mainly the use of medicinal plants, and he provides valuable contextual information lacking in earlier investigations on folk medicine. Long draws on his personal experience in recording remedies he regards as "tried and true," and most of the remedies he describes have been documented in numerous sources within and outside the South.

In stark contrast to today's world of mechanized farming and industrial food production, the agrarian life in the past involved a more direct association with and dependence on domesticated animals for food, labor, clothing, and protection. Maintaining the health of animals, therefore, was a top priority. Before the appearance of formally trained veterinarians, most farmers knew something about animal illnesses and how to treat them, or they consulted with informally trained folk veterinarians known as "cow doctors" and "horse doctors." Focusing on continuity and change in the folk veterinary beliefs and practices in Washington County, Tennessee, Rosemary Brookman's article, "Folk Veterinary Medicine in Upper East Tennessee," was a substantive contribution to a much neglected area of folklore at the time.

Folk Remedies
[1935]

T. J. Farr

To cure earache, blow tobacco smoke in the aching ear.

To cure chicken pox, have person with chicken pox lie down on the ground and run some chickens over him.

To prevent sunstroke, wear in the crown of the hat, a rattler cut from a rattle snake.

To stop a baby's slobbering, go to a brook and get a minnow and let the baby suck the minnow's tail.

To stop nosebleed, pick up a stone and let three drops of blood fall on the stone; then replace the stone in the original position.

To stop nosebleed, place a pair of pot hooks around the person's neck.

To stop nosebleed, let the blood drip on something bright.

To stop nosebleed, tie a red rag on the head.

To stop nosebleed, let the nose bleed on a knife blade; then stick the blade in the ground.

To stop nosebleed, drop a key down the back of the sufferer.

To prevent headache, carry in your pocket a bone out of a hogs-head.

To prevent headache, drink from a spring which flows toward the sunrise.

To prevent flu, keep sulfur in your shoes.

To cure sore throat, tie a dirty yarn sock around the neck and wear it until morning.

To cure sore throat, wear gold beads around the neck.

To cure frostbite, walk bare foot in the first snow three times around the house.

To cure the shingles, rub a black cat's tail over the body.

To remove a birth-mark, rub a dead person's hand over the birthmark.

To prevent drowning, a person should carry an egg in his pocket.

To cure toothache, place a bag of warm wood ashes on the side of the face where the tooth is aching.

To cure toothache, say a Bible verse every morning for three mornings before the sun rises.

To remove freckles, wash the face in stump water.

The child that wears a black silk cord around its neck will not have the croup.

If you wash your hands in the first snow, they will not chap during the winter.

When a baby is cutting teeth, tie a mole's foot around the baby's neck and it will not have a hard time cutting its teeth.

To remove freckles, go to a field of wheat the first morning in May before sun-up and bathe the face in the dew found on the wheat.

To cure sore eyes, use water made from snow that falls in April.

To cure thrash, the father before speaking or coughing, should blow into the child's mouth for three mornings.

The seventh child in a family can cure the thrash by blowing in the baby's mouth.

To cure thrash, take the baby to someone who has never seen its father and have that person blow into the child's mouth.

To cure phthisic [asthma], go to a tree and bore a hole in it even with the top of your head; put some of your hair in the hole and when the bark grows over the hole, you will be well of the disease.

To cure a pain in the side, put an axe under the bed of a person who is suffering, and it will take away the pain.

To prevent night sweats, sleep with a pan filled with water under the bed.

To cure a stone bruise, catch a toad frog and hold the stomach of the toad to the stone bruise until it dies. The fever from the stone bruise is said to go into the frog and kill it.

To cure rheumatism, bury the feet in the ground for two hours every day.

To cure rheumatism, carry a buckeye in your pocket.

To cure rheumatism, carry a potato in your pocket.

To cure rheumatism, rub the joints in the fat of a frog which has been cooked alive.

To cure rheumatism, go near a bee gum and permit the bees to sting you severely.

If a woman marries without changing her name, she can blow her breath into a baby's mouth and cure the thrash.

To remove a wart, pick the wart with a wooden shoe peg, letting the wart bleed on the peg. Drive the peg into a beech tree and the wart will disappear.

To remove a wart, get a dry bone and rub it over the wart, then throw the bone away without looking back.

To remove a wart, take a paper string and tie as many knots in it as there are warts on the person or animal. Then bury the string under the eve of the house, and the warts will disappear.

To remove a wart, take a black cat to the cemetery at midnight. When the devil comes to get his people, command the cat to follow the devil. Command the warts to follow the cat.

To remove a wart, pick up a beef bone and rub the warts with the side that was next to the ground; put the bone back just as you found it and your warts will go away.

To prevent cramps, put the soles of the shoes together and set them under the bed at night.

To remove a wart, place the index finger on the wart and repeat the names of three preachers.

To remove a wart, pick the wart and let it bleed on a thread. Bury the thread under the drip of the house and the wart will go off.

To remove a wart, cut a notch in a chestnut switch for each wart. Bury the switch and when the switch decays, the warts will disappear.

To remove a wart, pick the wart with a pin, hide the pin; when the pin rusts, the wart will disappear.

To remove a wart or mole, steal a dirty dish rag and rub it over the mole or wart and hide the dishrag. If no one finds it, the mole or wart will go away.

To remove a wart, get as many small stones as there are warts on a person, tie them up and throw them down on the ground, the person who picks them up gets the warts.

To remove a wart, pick the wart until it bleeds, wipe the blood on a grain of corn and let a chicken eat it.

To remove a wart, go to an old hollow stump that contains water and wash the hands or warts in the stump water. After doing this, walk home without looking back and the wart will go away.

To prevent blindness, wear earrings.

For epilepsy, catch a turtle-dove, cut its throat, and let the person affected drink its blood.

Cramps in your feet can always be prevented if you turn your shoes upside down at night.

If you burn a large frog to ashes, and mix the ashes with water, you will get an ointment that will kill hair wherever applied, and the hair will never grow back.

When you see a hog rubbing up against a fence, go and rub the wart in the same place, and the wart will disappear.

Folk Medicine in McMinn, Polk, Bradley, and Meigs Counties, Tennessee, 1910–1927
[1962]

Grady M. Long

In an earlier paper on folklore from the southeastern section of Tennessee, I avoided wherever possible mentioning remedies I had used or seen used during my youth. It is with the tried and true remedies that I wish to deal (for the greater part) in this paper. However, there are a few so bizarre or startling that I have included them as curiosities.

Roads in winter were often in such sorry condition that getting to the nearest doctor, save on horseback, was hazardous. And furthermore, when you reached his residence he might be out for the day or night, so for rather petty ailments there was always a remedy at hand. For cases that were major illnesses or accidents, there were also remedies that often helped a great deal until a doctor could be summoned.

Many who fretted and cried out every time they had to take a step with a stone bruise on their heel have reason to remember and call blessed anyone of several simple remedies. The leaves from a peach tree, bruised and dipped in boiling water and then cooled enough to apply to the aching heel, was a wonderful palliative. Plantain leaves often served for the same purpose, or leaves from a sweet potato vine.

And for boils, peach tree leaves were often pounded in a wooden mortar with a pestle until they were a juicy pulp; this pulp, placed in a clean bandage, was dipped in scalding water and applied to the boil at frequent intervals. Or better still was the old prickly pear cactus; with the spines removed and the outer skin stripped off, this made an extremely soothing and efficacious treatment for boils. As soon as one application dried out, a fresh one was put on. After two or three very hot applications of peach tree leaves, prickly pear, plantain leaves, or poultices made from flaxseed meal, the boil would come to a head, at which time the core would pop out easily.

If the bellyache failed to respond to a cup of "pennyrile" (pennyroyal) tea, rosemary tea, or ginger tea as the case might be, the next best bet was to chew a generous amount of sweet calamus root, which would soon dispel flatulence, uncomfortable distention, etc. If for any reason the pain continued and dysentery set in, then the really royal treatment was indicated: a few spoons of blackberry cordial at intervals of two to four hours.

If a chronic stomach condition caused you to have fever blisters, or ulcers inside your mouth and throat, you were purged with a generous dose of castor oil, followed by mild food and senna tea four or five times a day, and you chewed a few leaves of senna each day until the ulcers healed.

◘ Patent medicine almanacs were frequently consulted for information about health care.
  John A. Jones Collection, Archives of Appalachia, East Tennessee State University

Another much favored remedy for an upset stomach was to chew the bark of the slippery elm tree. Naturally I am referring to the inner bark, which was slick and of a yellowish hue. There were many people who insisted that any tree bark used medicinally should be peeled from the south side of a tree growing on the north side of a hill.

Often the hens were not laying, the butterfat content of the milk was low, and money was too scarce to use for even one bottle of the worm syrup most widely touted in the almanac. If you were pale, puffy eyed, and lethargic, you probably had worms—and even if you didn't, several cups of strong tea made from cassia bark (senna) and leaves never hurt anyone. Senna tea has long been recognized as an excellent vermifuge.

Earlier in this paper, I mentioned the use of pennyroyal or squaw mint for an upset stomach. Tea made from this low-growing, heavy-scented herb had manifold uses. It was excellent for producing a heavy sweat and breaking fevers. Women who were having painful and difficult menstruation drank copious quantities of "pennyrile" tea. And the plant itself, bruised until it gave off its strong minty odor, rubbed on the skin or strewn about the place, was an effective repellent against ticks, fleas, sand fleas, and other insects.

What boy or girl in the country in my youth did not have ringworm? I often wonder. In our garden or our mother's perennial border was the only cure we knew. Oil from the leaves and stems of cotton lavender, procured by bruising them and rubbing the affected portions of the body, put an end to ringworm after a few days of faithful application.

A standard remedy for colic and dysentery was kept side by side with the bottle of blackberry cordial. This was "vinegar wine," *not*, repeat *not*, wine vinegar. You took a pure vinegar (made from your own apples most likely), and in a generous amount of it you dissolved several handfuls of table salt (as much as would ferment and work clear—I do not remember the proportions) and left it to ferment. When the fermentation was completed and all the foam had been cleared away, the wine was bottled and corked and kept in an honored place alongside the blackberry cordial. Frequently it was kept under lock and key.

The back yard of many a farm house was bordered by the gray leaved prolific plant known as horehound. It, too, was an old and honored friend in hours of trouble. Tea made from the leaves, boiled down and laced with honey and brown sugar, was marvelous for coughs and bronchial ailments. The candy made in the farmhouse kitchen in no way resembled the pale substitute you can buy today. Large doses of horehound tea combined with honey were very effective as antispasmodics, and the strong tea without benefit of sugar was an excellent worm medicine.

Mention the word "goldenseal" in my presence and I can literally hear the piping, child-like voice of an old lady who lived near us who in time of need would call on my mother to lend her that greatest of home remedies. As she came breathlessly in at the door she would inquire, "Lucy, have you got nairy a spec of goldenseal? I'm plum out and Jim's taken with the night sweats." My mother always had plenty of goldenseal in a large tin box on a kitchen shelf. It was the "cure-all," good for man or beast. If you had cold sores, fever blisters, or some kind of sore or ulcer in your mouth or throat, you dabbed it with goldenseal or prepared a rinse or gargle. General ulcerations anywhere on the body were treated with goldenseal, and an enema was often used to soothe hemorrhoids. Larger doses were used as a laxative in cases of chronic constipation, and all liver troubles were treated either by taking a tea containing goldenseal by infusion or enema. A salve containing this prime "cure-all" was used to prevent "pitting" in severe cases of smallpox, and I was practically of voting age before I knew there was anything else to do for pyorrhea except use goldenseal and a black gum toothbrush! A cup of goldenseal tea just before bedtime was considered a sure cure for night sweats.

Queen of the meadow, or purple boneset, was another of the general "cure-all" familiar to most country families. For the ladies it was used as a tea to quiet their nerves after an especially harassing day. It has been said that Mithridates Eupator first used it as a remedy, hence its botanical classification as *Eupato-*

rium. To many it is also known as purple Joe Pye weed, and again the name comes from a user of long ago, an Indian who reputedly used the tea successfully as a cure for typhus. The fresh roots were gathered in autumn, cured, and carefully stored away. Many a sleepless night could easily be avoided by a cup of boneset tea. It was also an excellent tonic, an equally good astringent and antiseptic, and for gravel in the kidneys or any other kidney or bladder ailment it was virtually without peer. It was simply "good for what ailed you."

I have been a garden enthusiast for more than fifty years, and one of my earliest memories of a garden concerns one of the great household herbs that was once in virtually every garden. Ordinary garden sage was used for everything from seasoning for meats and dressings to a lotion for the breasts of mothers weaning their babies. In the latter case it was used as a tea to be drunk several times a day, and then some of the cold tea and wilted leaves were used as a poultice for the breasts to assist in drying up the flow of milk. Sage tea is an excellent nervine, and the past generation had the wits to stop their work and enjoy a cup when they began to feel frenzied, frustrated, and frantic. The cold tea was often the only antiseptic handy for cuts, sores, etc. It was also an effective hair tonic and was considered a sure cure for dandruff. For any eruption of the skin it was a "must," and several cups taken inwardly in such cases greatly facilitated a speedy cure. If you suffer from insomnia, don't take my word for it, but prepare yourself a good hot cup of sage tea just before you are ready to retire and see what happens. A little lemon juice and sugar makes it much more palatable.

Another palliative that was sipped many a time, while a group of tired women compared notes on their hardships, was clover blossom tea made from the blooms of ordinary red clover (*Trifolium pratense*) steeped (never boiled) in scalding water and sweetened with a little honey. There were many of the "old-timers" who firmly believed it would cure any and all diseases from pellagra to leprosy.

White clover blossoms were also treasured for their curative powers. Tea made by steeping the dried blossoms was used as a blood purifier, and the cold tea was frequently used as an antiseptic dressing. Often the tea combined with teas made from the roots of other plants was cooked into a salve with a sheep tallow base. This yellowish white salve would cure a chronic summer sore when all else had failed. I do not recall what any of the other plants were; I think one of them was burdock and another mullein, but I am not positive.

Another of the teas very common in my childhood was sassafras. I still notice sassafras on the shelves of local groceries and super markets. However, the pitiful dried-out shavings and match-stick lengths of "store bought" sassafras are a far cry from the healthy, freshly dug roots from which we made tea in my childhood. This was the great spring tonic and blood purifier, and certainly it was far more pleasant and palatable than the much-touted rival, sulfur and molasses.

□ Some once commonly used medicinal plants. From *The People's Common Sense Medical Adviser* by Dr. R. V. Pierce, 1895.

A weak solution of warm sassafras tea makes an eye wash far more soothing than many a highly recommended solution on the market today. And the freshly dug roots, scraped and scalded, made a very efficacious poultice for a sty. A few spoons of hot sassafras tea were frequently used as a soothing agent for babies who were having a serious bout with colic and spasms.

Speaking of colic brings to mind a household remedy so common in my life that I often wonder how families who didn't know about it managed to raise their children. There was a wide variety of soothing syrups on the market when I was growing up, but their greatest competitor was the catnip grown in the yard or garden. Many a man may thank his lucky stars that his wife, mother, or mother-in-law, knew about catnip tea and saved him from having to take his turn at walking the floor when his heir was bawling with the colic. A little honey in the water where the catnip is steeped will make the tea more palatable and most babies will take it very willingly.

A child in convulsions and no doctor available is a terrifying situation. Mothers in that era knew that a mild enema of catnip tea would often soothe and quiet the child. Frequently convulsions were brought on by worms, and catnip tea is probably one of the oldest of vermifuges known to man.

Another use of catnip tea was to increase urination and allay the pain of bladder and urinary infections; it is entirely possible that many cases of uremic poisoning may have been averted by this simple herb.

Blood-root.

Scull-cap

The great standard remedy for female troubles was Solomon's seal. Copious quantities of tea made from the roots of the plant were consumed by ladies of the past era. The roots pounded to a course meal and mixed with water also made very soothing poultices for wounds and chronic sores.

A strong solution of tea made from Solomon's seal used as a wash several times a day will stop the spread of poison ivy, and if used consistently will dry the existing rash. The tea was also considered very beneficial to tuberculosis patients as well as those suffering from an infection in the stomach or intestines which caused bleeding.

Mentioning poison ivy in the preceding paragraph reminds me of another standard remedy we used to cure poison ivy or poison oak, as well as other rashes we got from contacting poisonous plants. The inner bark of a white oak tree steeped for a long time in boiling water and mixed with slacked lime makes a positive cure. *Do not bandage*—simply bathe affected parts with the solution several times a day.

White oak bark had many other uses. A strong tea taken internally would expel pin worms, and furthermore it was considered beneficial in cases of hemorrhage, whether in lungs, stomach, or intestines. Many people firmly believed that faithfully used it would dissolve and remove gall and kidney stones. It is an excellent astringent and antiseptic for use in bathing chronic sores and ulcers. It alleviates aching legs where varicosities have created a problem. Hot towels wet with white oak tea and applied for half an hour will dispel that tired ache, and it is said that some of the tea taken internally is helpful in cases of severe varicosities.

Another tree bark (inner bark, of course) frequently used as a home remedy was that of the walnut tree. This bark boiled in honey and water for an hour made a tea that was unexcelled for ulcers in the mouth or throat. The granulated or pounded bark (about a teaspoonful) steeped in a cup of boiling water for about thirty minutes was a specific for diarrhea. You sipped two or three cups during the day and usually by the third cup your trouble was abating.

In the spring it was a common custom to go through the fields looking for the first tender greens for a "sallet." The long winter diet of dried or canned foods left one with an ardent "hankerin'" after something green. Poke, thistle, chickweed, and dandelions went into the mixture, and supreme among these for use as a "sallet" and blood purifier was yellow dock, or "narrie leaved" dock, as it was most often called. Tea made from the roots of this plant was used for about everything from leprosy to a tree falling on you!

A strong solution of the tea was effective as an astringent cleansing agent for all manner of wounds and skin eruptions. A weaker tea mixed with honey was taken as a blood purifier, and a salve was made by boiling the roots until they were pulp, then straining the liquid and combining it with balm of Gilead buds and sheep tallow and cooking these together until a "gooey" consistency was attained.

Yet another meadow herb used as an astringent and as the base for a good curative ointment was yarrow. Salve made from tallow and strong yarrow tea was excellent for ulcers, old sores, fistulas, etc. It was also very useful to stop the itching, burning rash of measles, and it was used on chicken pox and smallpox.

Not so commonly known, but sought out by the more primitive back-woodsmen, was wild alum root, cranesbill, or wild geranium, as it was variously known. The roots of this plant dried and powdered were used to stop bleeding. It was one of the best coagulative agents known to the country people.

In almost every kitchen, from the shaky lean-to up the fanciest one with a pump inside, one could usually find many strings of bright red cayenne pepper. A spoonful of crushed cayenne steeped in boiling water made a wonderful astringent and cleansing agent.

Cayenne pepper tea, weakened down with honeyed water, is rather tasty on a cold night when one has been chilled to the very marrow of his bones. It is certainly far more effective in warding off a cold than many other liquid potions one has had recommended for the same purpose. In my childhood, cayenne or "pepper tea" was used extensively to break fevers, and there were numerous stories of its great use in yellow fever epidemics. It has considerable efficacy as an antispasmodic, and the tea was often used as a quieting agent in cases of over excitement, etc.; there were claims that taken in capsules or eaten without mustard, vinegar, and other harmful ingredients it was beneficial for an ulcerated stomach.

As the basis for a liniment, cayenne pepper was without peer. Liniment was made by boiling the pepper in cider vinegar and bottling it unstrained. I do not recall the amount of salt added to each quart of vinegar, nor do I recall exactly the amount of pepper used. What I do recall is that the liniment burns like fire for a little while, but strangely enough it does not blister as will turpentine, kerosene, or numerous other concoctions used in homemade liniments. It was good for all sorts of congestions, sprains, bruises, cuts, sores, etc.

For spring fever and general sluggishness, hot pepper knew no peer, and it was freely used in sauces as a condiment and frequently even shredded and baked in cornbread. Which reminds me that when the hens were moulting and egg production was at a low ebb, plenty of red pepper in the chicken food and water was indicated. Frequently my mother baked batches of course cornbread filled with shredded pepper and fed it to the hens. Pepper tea boiled into a syrup with honey made a fine cough medicine, and if you had some slippery elm bark to boil with the tea, so much the better.

One of the most brilliant and long lasting of the wayside flowers is butterfly weed, due to its color more commonly known as "chigger weed." The root of this beautiful plant was dried and powdered to make tea, which was used to break up colds, grippe, etc. It knew no equal in giving relief from the agonizing pains of pleurisy. To many, the names I have mentioned above may be meaningless, for they may have known the plant as "pleurisy-root."

Toad flax, often called wild snapdragon, was common to almost every yard, garden, or neglected fence row. It is a prolific little plant, and the whole herb chopped and boiled in lard until it is crisp makes a wonderful ointment which is soothing and healing to ulcerous skin eruptions, summer sores, etc. It was a specific for bleeding hemorrhoids, cysts, and other rectal diseases.

An old garden favorite that often escaped to wayside streams and fence rows was tansy. Its fern-like foliage, bright golden blossoms, and vigorous habit made it popular, and it was practically indestructible. But who would want to be without such a boon to mankind? The crushed leaves strewn about will quickly dispatch fleas, ticks, and ants. Dried and used with sage, spices, etc., it was extremely useful in curing meats. Hot tansy tea would "pop out" the most stubborn cases of measles and chicken pox. It produces very free perspiration and was used to reduce fevers, break up colds and grippe, and give relief from all manner of illness.

Another wayside plant that was used as a sedative was snakeroot, frequently called bugbane or black cohosh. The roots were cured and used to make a tea, and with a good brandy base it was declared a sure cure for rheumatism. Two or three cups of the tea sipped daily were recommended to reduce swelling due to dropsy. Its quieting effects also rendered it a popular agent in the treatment of "asthmy" attacks.

Speaking of asthma brings to mind mullein. I have always regarded it as one of the really regal looking roadside plants. The individual florets are rather insignificant, but its tall spire rising from the silvery gray nest of furry leaves is very handsome, and thousands have been partially broken by lovelorn maidens and ardent swains who pointed the spires toward their true love's home. If the spire continued to grow, the love was mutual. But I digress, for it is with this lovely plant's medicinal qualities that I am concerned. The bruised or scalded leaves wrapped in gauze and placed on a stone bruise or feverish sore would soothe it in a matter of minutes. Mullein leaves dried and used as a tobacco or snuff were specified for asthmatic attacks.

Felons (in my childhood always designated "bone felon") were one of the most painful aggravations one could have. Toothaches were insignificant, stone bruises to be laughed off, and scalds and boils were but minute ailments compared to the felon. But if you only knew and started the remedy in time there was no need to suffer, for a poultice of chopped onions, changed frequently and applied with constant regularity for two days and nights, would dispel the inflammation and no splitting of the finger would be necessary.

People practically dead from uremic poison have been known to respond readily to one of the simplest of all home remedies: copious quantities of tea made from boiling watermelon seed. Watermelon seed tea was a standard treatment for all kidney and bladder diseases. Many an aching back has played second fiddle to tired legs and aching feet after a round of this efficacious remedy!

For all respiratory diseases and that dread specter pneumonia, there was little to be done save drink plenty of any one of half a dozen teas: sage, tansy, pepper, etc.; chew some slippery elm bark to keep the bowels open; and make yourself slippery with goose grease or hen oil to keep the pores open. Naturally you were well packed in a fifty pound feather bed and swathed in flannel cloths and weighted down with homemade "kiver lids"!

There were several other remedies I have heard discussed by my elders. They were already losing ground when I can first remember, but they must have been used at one time or another along Mouse Creek in McMinn County, for I've encountered their mention in that area more than once. The first mentioned is strictly Negro in origin. A slave of my great aunt firmly believed that had my Aunt Bell used charred owl eyes and sheep tallow as a pomade for her eyes, she would never have lost her sight!

The remedy for falling hair perhaps does not belong here, but it is so unique that I cannot resist listing it. Powder a cup of the kernels from peach seeds; boil these in a quart of your best cider vinegar until the mixture begins thickening like an oil. Bottle and use as a dressing for the scalp, brushing it in thoroughly each time you groom your hair. Extravagant claims were made for this tonic's effectiveness against baldness, thinning hair, etc.

In hinterland communities where roads were little more than poorly defined trails and the nearest doctor five or six hours away by horseback, croup took its toll among babies each winter. I have heard of more than one life being saved by the use of "chamber lye" (urine) or (even more effective) the naturally scalding urine from a mare.

Diphtheria also was a dread specter. But brimstone was believed to kill every species of fungus in man, beast, or plant, and it was the handy cure-all for diphtheria. A teaspoon of sulfur in a dram glass of water, mixed with the finger and used as a gargle in early stages, was considered a cure. If the patient was past gargling, the mixture was forced into the throat or sometimes poured over live coals on a shovel and the patient held over the fumes. It may have worked; people claimed that it did.

Folk Veterinary Medicine in Upper East Tennessee
[1977]

Rosemary Brookman

ince ancient times, the success of human societies has been intimately
tied to the health of their animals. While this is still somewhat true
today, most people in industrialized nations are very far from the centers of dairy and meat products that appear in markets in serving-size pieces,
ready to cook. The great chain of production—feeding, breeding, giving birth,
weaning, growing, and fattening—of meat animals and the equivalent pro-
cesses for dairy animals takes place far from urban man, and being out of sight
are also out of mind. The concomitant problems—getting and storing feed,
housing animals, and keeping them healthy and treating their illnesses—also
exist, as it were, in another world.

Almost all food products that appear in city markets are produced on
very modern, mechanized farms whose owners look to scientists and professionals for solving their problems and whose families are almost as dependent
on the supermarket for their goods as any city family. But the small, usually
diversified farmer who produces a large share of his family's food still exists
today and is still vivid in the minds of people who are not very removed in
time from the heyday of the small family farm, when Father was his own soil
and crop expert, stock breeder, and veterinarian. This paper examines some
of the veterinary practices that were used by farmers before they had access to
modern scientific theories and remedies for illnesses. Pseudonyms have been
used to maintain privacy.

The existing literature on traditional animal medicine is scanty, investigators for obvious reasons being more interested in collecting material dealing with human ailments and cures. All too often, collectors gather sayings such as "Killing a toad makes cows give bloody milk," neglecting completely to elicit information about what the farmer does about the bloody milk his cow is giving. While some collections have a scattering of animal cures in connection with other genres such as signs, human medicine, or farm lore, without recognizing animal medicine and beliefs as a genre in itself, animal medicine and often human medical practices are ignored almost totally in overviews and introductions to the field of folklore (for example, Clarke and Clarke 1965; Brunvand 1968). It is to regional collections that we look for data, and it is not frequently found.

Woodhull (in Dobie 1930) takes a look at some animal and human diseases and cures collected in Texas and includes a "Pharmocopedia Texana" that seems fairly extensive. Korson (1938), in his work on mining folklore of the Pennsylvania Dutch, gives a few examples of animal illnesses and cures. The Oral History Archives of East Tennessee State University has some items dealing with the topic recorded during taped interviews with local informants. One of the better collections for this purpose is Brown's collection, *North Carolina Folklore* (White and Baum 1952–61), which lists beliefs and practices concerning fowl, cattle, dogs, hogs, horses, and mules. The Brown collection contains in volume 7 a good compendium of beliefs and practices, and Randolph's (1964) work on Ozark folklore includes a section on crops and livestock and gives examples of several animal illnesses and treatments. However, none of these sources analyzes the social milieu of the practices or gives any information on who uses them and how they were learned. For the most part, the sources simply list beliefs and cures as if they were proverbs. For example, Randolph lists the belief (page 47) "If a cow loses her cud, give her a dishrag to chaw," but says he hasn't the vaguest idea of what this means. He does not seem to know that lost cud is a not uncommon folk illness in cows and has a variety for treatments and possible causes. As would be expected, the information gathered for this paper bears more resemblance to the North Carolina and Ozark collections than to the one from Texas.

In the present collection, a few of the remedies mentioned are procured from drugstores. Sweet spirits of nitre (ethyl nitrate) is a liquid whose only indication, according to the label, is for use on cold sores and is not to be taken internally. However, it is used for human as well as animal "kidney trouble." Blue stone (copper sulphate) is, according to the label, used for destroying algae in ponds and is a blue powder. It is, however, used for many medicinal purposes, mostly as a disinfectant when mixed with water. There are various kinds of "healing powders" which contain mixtures of medicinal substances, and Bag Balm is for chapped or sore udders. Red Liniment is available from the Watkins man, who sells Watkins products door to door. It is intended for use as a massage and body rub for aches and pains but is often used for chest colds, coughs, and colic in animals and people. Turpentine is widely used in the area as a general tonic and cure-all when one is ill.

Bowmantown, Sulphur Springs, and Fairview communities are located in Washington County, Tennessee, 100 miles northeast of Knoxville. Rural Washington County is made up of rich, rolling farmland, used principally for dairying and beef production on farms averaging about 125 acres. Since the Second World War, modern farming practices have been closely followed by most farmers, and the trend toward large size and specialization has helped the diversified family farm disappear, but some still do exist, although it seems doubtful if many of them will continue to be worked by the same family, if they are worked at all, when the present generation is gone.

These communities are small rural villages, with one or two groceries, gas stations, and churches to provide for the people of the area. While the Tennessee Valley Authority brought electricity to the main rural roads in the 1930s, many farms on secondary and tertiary roads did not have electricity until as late as 1950, certainly a factor in keeping the family farm alive and unaffected by modernization, and perhaps a factor in the relative cultural conservation of the area, as evidenced by the fact that many people still plant by the signs, a practice which Passin and Bennett (in Dundes 1965: 321) reported as disappearing in southern Illinois in the late 1940s.

The connection between the small family and traditional animal medical practices is central to the problem of maintaining the tradition; agribusiness type farming has no place for unscientific, unprofessional techniques. Only the small farmer who is not quite that concerned with the balance sheet and ledger will continue to use traditional ways.

In the discussion of old-time medicine, it must be borne in mind that remedies and treatments were dependent on what was at hand. Poor transportation as well as poor dissemination of modern techniques and ideas were responsible for making the farmer look to herbal cures, products easily obtainable from local stores or peddlers, or simply his own ingenuity in devising remedies. This factor was mentioned by informants; they were conscious of the makeshift nature of the remedies, but when they were thought to work often stuck to them even after more modern medicines were available. Interestingly, relatively few herbs are used to treat animals compared to the large herbal pharmacopoeia for humans ailments, and the two types of medicine, animal and human, are almost mutually exclusive in cures and treatments even for similar illnesses. Informants seemed amused when it was suggested that a particular animal cure could be used for people for similar illnesses, and vice versa, and doubted its efficacy.

Most informants when asked where they got their knowledge of these practices mentioned the importance of a local "cow doctor" or "horse doctor." These are men well known in the neighborhood for their knowledge of diseases and cures who would be consulted when necessary. A gradual evolution in the nature of the cow and horses doctor can be traced. George Elmer, born in the mountains of Greene County, Tennessee, in 1890, remembers a neighbor on Paint Creek who was known for his doctoring. When he moved to Washington County in the 1930s, Mr. Elmer relied on another neighbor, Sam Garst, dead now for thirty years, who also had a reputation in this line. These men were farmers whose years of experience made them effective doctors, and in those times they were the only animal doctors available. The next step is represented by William Payne, born in 1894 and quite modern for his generation. Mr. Payne is a self-taught veterinarian. He took up doctoring when he was in his thirties, worked with an older, more experienced man for a while, and learned the traditional remedies but never believed in the ones which were more magical than practical. When modern medicine became available he switched to it for the bulk of his practice, but used some older cures as well. Many veterinary medicines are available without a prescription, and Mr. Payne is able to have quite an up-to-date stock of materials. His modern techniques and cures were learned through observation and practices, supplemented by books. Mr. Payne still does some doctoring, and is widely known and called upon, but because of his age he doesn't get around much any more.

Martin Keys is a relatively young man, in his late forties, who is entirely modern in his veterinary practice and totally self-taught. He approached the field seriously and read extensively to learn modern methods, and while his skills and knowledge approach professional standards, he works for lower wages than a licensed veterinarian and is employed extensively in the area. Mr. Keys's clientele feel no compunction at his not having formal training and a university degree, probably because he is as effective as the university-trained field and keeps up with innovations. He is known in the community as a veterinarian, not merely as a cow doctor. Mr. Keys is familiar with the traditional practices, having grown up with them and encountered them in his work, but discounts their effectiveness for the most part, or at least prefers more effective modern cures.

The acme of this hierarchy is of course the university-trained, licensed veterinarian with the DVM degree, a thorough scientific background, and use of exclusively modern methods.

These four levels of professional style function simultaneously, each serving a particular, sometimes overlapping, clientele. Mr. Elmer and old-time subsistence farmers like him prefer to rely on themselves and their neighbors and not call in outsiders who would prescribe new cures and expect to be paid. Mr. Payne and Mr. Keys serve the ordinary small dairy or beef farmer and are more cognizant of the traditional cures than would be the modern licensed veterinarian, who is called in primarily by the up-to-date, business-conscious mechanized farmers, by newcomers in the area who look him up in the telephone book (Mr. Payne and Mr. Keys are not listed under "veterinarians"), or by smaller farmers when other help is unavailable. The modern veterinarian often has a telephone in his car and is easy to get in touch with even while on his rounds. These styles are adaptive; they were and are the most appropriate responses for the time and need, and each type has its adherents still. Relying on experienced neighbors was the most sensible thing when that was all there was to rely on, full-time veterinarians being quite unknown or totally unavailable and books or the information in them equally so. The self-taught, unlicensed but serious professional was the reasonable response to the growth and dissemination of modern practices and the continued unavailability of the licensed veterinarian, who became part of the local scene only after the Second World War.

As far as the bearing of the tradition is concerned, it is men who, as the principal keepers of the animals, are responsible for their well-being, and without a doubt, the older the informant, the more traditional his repertoire of cures or his knowledge of the tradition. The younger the informant, the more likely it is that the cures are just memories, never acted upon, but it must be borne in mind that most informants in their seventies or eighties are retired from farming, and though they once used these cures, they have no opportunity to do so now. They may believe the old-time cures are more effective than modern ways and may have passed the cures to their children, who, more often than not, have moved to town and left farm life behind. However, there are some cures which are amazingly persistent, even if not especially effective, such as throwing salt in the eye of an animal with pink eye, which everyone has heard of and which even a young farmer will do if not specifically cautioned against it by an authority. Perhaps the commonness of the disease, its contagious nature, and slowness of other, more modern cures makes it worthwhile to the farmer to try this traditional one. All the cures cited in this paper have at least one practitioner, although in the case of some of the beliefs and preventative measures these were memories of parents' and grandparents' repertoires. The information concerning diseases and cures elicited from the informants was very similar from person to person, the only exception being Mr. Elmer, perhaps due to his being raised in the mountains of Green County, a different ecological zone than the valley farming of Washington County with a concomitant, and different, lifestyle and tradition.

Categorizing the diseases and cures may be done in several ways. A distinction can be made between actual diseases and diseases which were called "fictitious" by some of the informants. For example, *sore tongue,* a not too common disease in cattle, is thought to be caused by worms in the tongue. The tongue swells up and has pimples on it which are thought to contain worms.

The cure is to scrape the tongue very hard with a knife and pack it with salt and pepper or turpentine. Martin Keys calls this a "fictitious" disease, perhaps originating in the pimples cows may get on their tongues from licking salt blocks. *Hollow tail* is a disease reported by some informants to be quite common in cattle, caused by a worm in the tail. It is treated by making a slit in the tail where the worm appears to be (shown by the tail being limp in that spot) and packing the opening with salt or salt and pepper or turpentine and wrapping it was a cloth. However, some informants and modern medical authority consider hollow tail to have no basis in fact. Some feel that it stems from undernourished or poorly nourished animals who seem unhealthy, and the old-time farmer, not knowing the cause, felt the animals must be treated for something, so he blamed it on hollow tail. Those who believe in hollow tail defend it stoutly against non-believers, and other informants simply weren't sure whether it was real or not. Hollow tail is a very common fictional folk disease with a great many believers.

Several old-time diseases which were thought to be a specific ailment are in fact considered today by modern veterinarians and farmers to be symptoms of malnourishment or illness and not diseases in themselves. It should be remembered that scientific animal feeding did not come to this area until three or four decades ago, and before then animals were not fed the scientifically determined, balanced rations fed now. An unbalanced diet will produce symptoms of illness, but better practices were simply not known or impossible to follow. An example of this treatment of symptom rather than cause is the disease *hide-bound,* whose adherents can't pinpoint a cause but say the hide of the animal (generally cows but sometimes horses) gets very stiff and "grows into the bone." The cure is to work on the hide and move it around, and you can hear it pop and crackle while you do this. Modern veterinarians say this condition is due to malnourishment and the real cure is improved feeding, but its believers disagree and say they have seen it in well-fed animals.

Another case of treatment of the symptom is *lost cud.* A cow who stops her almost constant chewing is said to have lost her cud, and this is seen as a problem in itself, while modern authorities would say it is a symptom of some other illness and that cows tend to stop chewing when they are sick. The old-time treatment is to take a greasy dish rag or a nubbin of peach leaves and push it down the cow's throat. One informant remembers her father asking her to stick the dishrag down the cow's throat when she was a young child because her arm was skinny and could reach down there. The cow may belch up this mass and chew on it, the value being to get her belching again (belching is essential in ruminants) and maybe she will feel better.

Womb calves are thought to be cancerous growths in the reproductive organs of a cow which cause sterility and should be removed. What they actually are, according to modern authority, is a natural part of the apparatus which holds the membranes surrounding the unborn calf to the mother cow and should not be removed as their removal will cause sterility. This is a good example of complete confusion over the physiological nature of the animal.

An allied ailment is sterility caused by a cow being *closed up*, meaning that the entrance to the cervix was closed due to injury in calving, perhaps, and semen from the bull cannot go through to impregnate the cow. Old-timers would "open up" the cow by hand, which is actually impossible as the cervix opening is very small and much narrower than a finger. Modern informants believe it is very unusual for a cow's cervix to be damaged in this way and this treatment wouldn't help. More than likely, sterility is caused by removal of the womb calves.

Cows about to calve may be fed English rosin to prevent complications, and after a cow freshens (has her calf) it is of some concern that the afterbirth be expelled promptly. The afterbirth is called the "cleanings," and the cow is said "to clean herself." Cows are given a cup of salt, or salt water, or the brine from cured meat, or salt is sprinkled on the calf which the cow will lick off. This is quite unnecessary as a routine, as most cows will expel the afterbirth with no trouble and these aids wouldn't help anyway, according to modern authority.

A very common ailment in young calves is *scours,* or diarrhea, which can cause dehydration and death in serious cases. There are as many cures for scours as there are farmers, among them giving flour and soot or eggs and flour mixed in the feed, feeding cheese, red clay, nutmeg, or parched flour, or drenching (pouring down throat) with Coca-Cola, vinegar, vanilla flavoring, coffee diluted stock dip, ginger tea, and Karo syrup. Martin Keys feels that the reason for many of these cures is that the dark substances give a normal color to the manure, while the other ingredients have binding effect, or, like coffee, are stimulants.

Lactating cows sometimes suffer from *milk fever,* in which the cow gets sickly and the teats collapse, the inner walls of the teats sticking to each other. This disease is currently thought to be caused by malnourishment, especially telling when the cow begins to lactate. The old-time remedy is to put hollow quills up the teats and pump the bag full of air, leaving them this way for fourteen hours. This has the effect of making the cow retain her milk and not expel valuable nutrients. The modern treatment is to give glucose subcutaneously.

Another problem cows in milk may have is *mastitis,* which some informants believe comes from cows resting on anthills and getting bitten by the ants. The cow gets sickly and gives stringy milk. Vinegar or salt in hot water is used to take down the swelling and the bag is rubbed with Bag Balm.

Some other ailments in cattle are *bloat, packed stomach, lice,* and *sore foot. Bloat* is a serious and not uncommon sickness arising from the peculiar ruminant digestive system. It is essential for cattle to belch every so often, and when a cow cannot belch enough to relieve itself, it can swell up and may actually burst. This swelling can be caused by eating grain if they can get a chance especially in the early morning when the dew is on it, or gorging with grain. Cattle will literally kill themselves eating grain if they can do so. The old-time remedies for bloat are drenches of Watkins Red Liniment mixed in water, kerosene in milk, mineral oil to loosen the bowels, coal oil in milk or water, linseed oil, or lamp oil, or putting a stick in the animal's mouth to be chewed and, hopefully, help it belch, or running a hose to the stomach to get the air out. Exciting the cow may cause it to defecate and belch, and so dogs were set on it to chase it around. The modern treatment, more direct and efficient than the last, is to puncture the animal's hide and paunch with a trocar to allow the gas to escape.

Packed stomach might be caused by the cow eating too much cottonseed meal, for instance, before feed was mixed mechanically. The cow won't eat, can't defecate, and goes dry. The cure is to give a quart of linseed oil as a drench.

Lice in hogs and cattle are treated with burnt cylinder oil, tobacco juice, diluted stock dip, or a meat skin rubbed on the back. One informant said her father would rub ashes on the animal's backs on Ash Wednesday as a preventative.

Sore foot, similar to *scratches* in horses, is present when the hoof develops sore places or infections. It is treated with carbolic acid as a wash or with blue stone powder (copper sulphate) and tied with a bandage.

Cattle are the most important animals on East Tennessee farms, but horses and mules once occupied an equally important place. But the day of the horse and mule is over; tractors began replacing them in the 1920s, until now it is almost impossible to find a working horse or mule in the area, although horses are of course kept for pleasure and one does see an occasional mule. Horses and mules seem to be plagued by fewer diseases than cattle, and mules are acknowledged to be tougher and less prone to sickness than horses.

Bots are worms in the stomach, caused by ingesting fly eggs, which hatch into larvae and burrow into the stomach lining. The animal gets very sickly. Elder leaf tea or tobacco juice is used as a drench. Mr. Keys recommends a dose of molasses which dislodges the worms, and then a drench of worm medicine to finish them off. George Elmer, when a young boy, saw a man rub a silver dollar on the underside of the lips of a horse sick with bots. Mr. Elmer says he didn't know what to think, but it seemed to work.

A horse develops *sweeny* by being worked unevenly or having the yoke pulled unevenly. As Mr. Elmer puts it, "One shoulder perishes and the horse takes to hopping." A poke root or penny is put into a slit made in the weak shoulder, left until the wound festers, and then cleaned out. Or the shoulder can be pumped up with air or simply massaged. Mr. Keys recommends just letting the horse rest.

Kidney trouble is the euphemism used for the inability to urinate, a not uncommon problem in horses. Remedies vary from the practical to the magical. Sweet spirits of nitre can be used as a drench. Mr. Elmer advocates holding a cup of turpentine under the horse's navel for four or five minutes, while another informant says to pour turpentine on the horse's back. Kidney trouble in cattle is treated with pumpkin seed tea.

Greasy heel and *scratches* are similar problems, being infections in the foot and hoof caused by working in mud for long periods or, when horses were used for transportation, being ridden on muddy roads and not having their feet cleaned properly afterward. Carbolic acid, muriatic acid, or "healing powders" were mentioned for use on *greasy heel,* and a red oak bark poultice or mixed fruit acid and alcohol swab was used for *scratches.*

A horse that has been worked too hard may get the heaves, the symptoms of which are shortness of breath and general debility. Mr. Elmer recommends a little dynamite crumble in the feed as a temporary help, though there is no permanent cure.

Colic is gassiness and coughing caused by eating clover with the frost on it. It is treated with a drench of powdered alum or ginger in water.

Mr. Payne treated what he called a bloody wart or cancer in a horse with a paste of powdered arsenic in castor oil. He rubbed it on daily for three days, skipped three days, and rubbed it in again daily for three days more. Another informant recalled that galls, growths on the shoulder or on the back caused by heat, sweat, and falling hair, were treated by putting a dip of mud from the bottom of a pond on them, which would have a cooling and soothing effect. Fistulas, swellings usually on the shoulder, were treated with a poke root plaster or blister. Poke root poultices were also used for poll evil, which is bruises on the top of the horse's head caused by the bridle.

Sprains were bathed in elder leaf tea, and bleeding wounds were packed with spider webs, or the sixth verse of the sixteenth chapter of Ezekiel ("And when I pass by thee, and saw thee polluted in thine own blood, I said unto thee when thou wast in thy blood, live; yea, I said unto thee, when thou wast in thy blood, live.") can be read to stop the flow of blood.

Chickens have few diseases and are not worth spending much money on to treat them when they do get sick. Coccidiosis, a pulmonary disease, is treated by putting blue stone in the drinking water. Neck moult is said to be caused by hens laying too much; they lose the feathers from their necks and get sickly. A cure is to put lights in the chicken house to extend the day-light hours, which has an effect on the laying capacity of the hens. The local Watkins man, who sells Watkins products door to door, recommends using Watkins's Red Liniment for roup in chickens, three teaspoons in a gallon of drinking water. Roup is a virus disease which gives chickens lesions on the face and causes them to make a sound like "roup." This same Red Liniment is the one used for bloat in cattle, and is also used for colic and colds in humans, even though there is nothing on the label for the bottle that would indicate these uses, it being intended as a massage for aches and pains.

The only disease in hogs that was reported was *quinsy,* a sore throat and fever, which was treated by pouring lamp oil on the animal's head.

The following are some techniques used that are preventative rather than curative in nature: pennyroyal leaves can be rubbed on a dog to keep off fleas or rubbed on a horse to keep away flies. The herb dog fennel is poisonous to the eyes of small animals if they walk through it and can be used to repel dogs. A horseshoe kept in the fire in a fireplace will prevent hawks from snatching chickens; the hawk will come close but then be forced to fly away. Rub cattle's backs with turpentine or salt to prevent warbles, the maggot of the botfly which burrows out of the animal's body through its back. To dry up mare's milk, heat a shovel in the fireplace and milk the mare onto the hot shovel. Feed dried wintergreen to horses for a tonic and to cows when they seem sickly or wormy. Several informants had heard that if you cut off a pig's tail, it will save five to ten bushels of corn, and the same was said about horns on cattle, the assumption being that it took extra feed to grow these useless appendages on the animal and it was economical to do away from them.

Attention was paid to the astrological sign on the calendar for certain events dealing with farm animals. Like most collections of sign lore, the various prescriptions were inconsistent and contradictory (Passin and Bennett in Dundes 1965:322). The two important events are castration and weaning. It was advised to castrate a pig or calf when the sign is below the knee, or in the feet, or in the new moon, and not to castrate in the head or heart. Weaning was advocated when the pointers are down and the signs below the legs, in the feet or knees, or in the head, and is bad in the heart or head. If weaned in the wrong sign, either the calf or the cow will bawl itself to death.

References

Brunvand, Jan. *The Study of American Folklore.* New York: W. W. Norton, 1968.

Clarke, Kenneth W., and Mary W. Clarke. *A Folklore Reader.* New York: A. S. Barnes & Company, 1965.

Dobie, J. Frank. Man, *Bird and Beast.* Dallas: Southern Methodist University Press, 1930.

Dundes, Alan. *The Study of Folklore.* Englewood Cliffs, N.J.: Prentice-Hall, 1965.

Korson, George. *Minstrels of The Mine Patch.* Philadelphia: University of Pennsylvania Press, 1938.

Randolph, Vance. *Ozark Magic and Folklore.* New York: Dover Publications, 1964.

White, Newman Ivey, and Paul F. Baum, gen. eds. *The Frank C. Brown Collection of North Carolina Folklore,* 7 vols. Durham, N.C.: Duke University Press, 1952–61.

Further Reading
in Folk Medicine

Bolyard, Judith. *Medicinal Plants and Home Remedies of Appalachia.* 1981.
Brady, Erica. *Healing Logics: Culture and Medicine in Modern Belief Systems.* 2001.
Cavender, Anthony. *Folk Medicine in Southern Appalachia.* 2003.
Crellin, John, and Jane Philpott. *Herbal Medicine Past and Present.* Vol. 1, *Trying to Give Ease.* 1990.
———. *Herbal Medicine Past and Present.* Vol. 2, *A Reference Guide to Medicinal Plants.* 1990.
Evans, E. Raymond, Clive Kileff, and Karen Shelley. *Herbal Medicine: A Living Force in the Appalachians.* 1982.
Hand, Wayland D. *Magical Medicine: The Folkloric Component of Medicine in the Folk Belief, Custom, and Ritual of the Peoples of Europe and America.* 1980.
Kirkland, James, Holly F. Matthews, C. W. Sullivan, and Karen Baldwin. *Herbal and Magical Medicine: Traditional Healing Today.* 1992.
Lornell, Kip. "Sod Rogers: Tipton County Herbalist." *Tennessee Folklore Society Bulletin.* 1982.
Lumpkin, Ben Gray. "Remedies." *Tennessee Folklore Society Bulletin.* 1976.
O'Dell, Ruth. "Before You Call the Doctor." *Tennessee Folklore Society Bulletin.* 1951.
Pruitt, Virginia. "The Bold Hives in Tennessee." *Tennessee Folklore Society Bulletin.* 1964.
Redfield, W. Adelbert. "Superstitions and Folk Beliefs." *Tennessee Folklore Society Bulletin.* 1937.
Rogers, E. G. *Early Folk Medical Practices in Tennessee.* 1941.
Snow, Loudell. *Walkin' Over Medicine.* 1993.
Wigginton, Eliot. *The Foxfire Book.* 1972.

PART THREE

Folk Beliefs and Practices

As used here, a folk belief, or what some call a superstition, is a notion or idea concerning various phenomena that is generally accepted as valid even though there is no scientific evidence that it is. Today most folklorists classify folk beliefs into two broad categories: magical and empirical. Magical beliefs are associated with the supernatural realm and include omens, taboos, divination, charms, and concepts of witchcraft and sorcery. Empirical beliefs are based on experience and observation of the natural world and include, for example, knowledge of predicting the weather, how to grow crops, and how to treat illness. The distinction between magical and empirical beliefs, however, is often unclear. Planting by the signs of the zodiac, for example, is viewed by some as magical thinking, but others contend that the movements of the celestial bodies have an influence on the natural world. The midwife of old who placed an axe under the bed of a woman giving birth to "cut" (diminish or stop) labor pains, and the folk healer who removed warts by rubbing them with a dishrag or bean leaf, did so because of past experience, either their own or that of others, that these administrations worked.

The problem of discerning a clear boundary between magical and empirical knowledge is academic; more important is the realization, as illustrated in the articles in this section, that many Tennesseans in the past made no clear delineation between the secular-empirical and magical-religious realms. Psychologically, magical beliefs and practices instill a sense of control over one's existence and thus reduce the anxiety associated with the potentially dangerous moments of human existence, such birth, sickness, and death. It must be kept in mind, however, that many magical beliefs induce anxiety and fear as well.

"A Collection of Middle Tennessee Superstitions" by Neal Frazier, illustrates the essentially descriptive approach of early investigators and, more important, the variety of magical and empirical folk beliefs once prevalent

71

throughout the South. Most of the magical beliefs reported by Frazier are concerned with the prevention of misfortune and prediction of future events.

E. G. Rogers's article, "Switching for Water," shares information he gathered from residents of Middle and East Tennessee in the late 1950s on traditional methods and techniques of locating water sources by "switching" (also known as "dowsing" and "water witching"). Many people today would no doubt agree with the perspective of those interviewed by Rogers that there is nothing mysterious or magical about water witching; it works because it is based on the "laws of nature."

The articles by Joseph S. Hall and Anna Lett provide additional information on supernatural beliefs and practices once common throughout America. Hall's informants were older whites who lived within or near the Great Smoky Mountains National Park. Lett's key informant was a black woman, Mama Mollie, a fortune teller in Jackson, Tennessee. Comparing Mama Mollie's knowledge of magic and conjuring (witchcraft) with the material provided by Hall's informants is instructive. First, it is immediately evident that both whites and blacks believed in witchcraft. Second, there are strong similarities in the supernatural beliefs and practices of the two groups. It is difficult, if not impossible in most cases, to say with certainty that this or that particular belief is African or European in origin. It seems apparent that both groups influenced each other.

A Collection of Middle Tennessee Superstitions [1936]

Neal Frazier

Planting, Harvesting, Animal Husbandry, etc.

Plant anything whose root you wish to use for food in the dark of the moon.

Plant anything whose bloom or fruit you wish to use (all flowers) in the light of the moon.

Plant peas or beans when the sign of the zodiac is in the twin.

Corn planted in the dark of the moon will make a heavy ear and little stalk; if planted in the light of the moon, it will make a tall stalk and a little ear.

Kill hogs in the dark of the moon and the meat will "swivel" away and make more lard; kill in light and it will be spongy and grease won't come out.

Plant watermelon seed the first day of May before sun up.

Take Irish potatoes and onions up before "dog days" [*Editors' note: July 3 to August 13.*] or they will rot.

Lay a rail fence in the light of the moon. If it is laid in the dark of the moon the bottom rail will sink in the ground.

When setting out a tree, keep the side to the north that originally grew in that direction.

If a cow's bag goes bad when she comes fresh, get a rock and rub the bag and then put the rock back exactly as you found it with the same side up.

To teach a cow to drink slop, put salty slop on her side in fly time and she will get a taste of it when she knocks the flies off with her tongue and will learn in this way to drink slop.

Keep a billy goat at the stable to keep away distemper from horses.

Never set out plants when the wind is in the north.

Never set a hen when the wind is in the north. The chickens will "holler their heads off."

Always set a hen after supper so the chickens will go quietly to sleep.

Weather Signs

If it thunders in February, it will frost in May.

When rocks sweat, it is a sign of rain.

When you see the stars "ready to cry," it is a sign of rain.

When the peafowls give a shrill cry it is a sign of rain.

Pay the preacher in time of drought and it will rain.

Heavy fogs in August mean heavy snows in winter.

Heavy shuck on corn, thick fur on animals, abundant crop of nuts, all indicate hard winter.

When the fire crackles so that it sounds like the crunching of snow underfoot, it is a sign of snow.

The first twelve days of the year forecast the weather for the twelve months of the year.

If it is hazy around the horizon, it will rain within thirty-six hours.

If it rains the first day of the month, it will rain the first fifteen days of the month.

Rain before seven, quit before eleven.

Sunshiny shower, won't last half an hour.

Lightning in the north is a sign of dry weather.

If pigs squeal at night, it's a sign of cold weather.

Rainbow at night, the shepherd's delight;

Rainbow in morning, the shepherd's warning.

Evening red and morning grey, sets the traveler on his way;

Evening grey and morning red, lets the rain fall on his head.

A red sun has water in its eyes.

A new moon with crescent up indicates rainy weather. Crescent turned down indicates dry weather.

If it is dry or wet when "dog days" start, the weather will remain that way for forty days.

A hog carrying straw or shucks in his mouth is a sign of cold weather.

Death

Don't sew white goods with black thread; the person for whom the garment is being made will die.

When a red-headed woodpecker pecks on your house, he is driving nails in your coffin.

Put a poker (or shovel) in the fire when a screech owl "hollers," else someone will die.

Never make a garment for someone who is sick in bed. He will never get up to wear it.

It is a bad sign to see a sick person picking at the cover.

It is a bad sign to burn the garment of a person who is sick in bed.

When you hear a cow low at midnight, it is a sure sign of death.

When you hear a tinkling sound in the ear, it is the death bell and is a sure sign that you will hear of a death in a few days. The side on which you hear it indicates the direction in which the death will occur in the community.

Cover the mirror when there is a death in the house. If the casket is reflected in the mirror there will be another death in that house within a year.

If a hen crows, it is a sign of death in the family.

If you count the cars behind a hearse, the youngest member of the family will die.

If you sneeze with food in your mouth, some member of the family will die.

Sneeze twice before breakfast on Monday and you will hear of a death before Sunday.

If you cut off your fingernails while sick, you are more than likely to die before you get out of bed.

Bad Luck

It is bad luck to burn or scorch a new garment before you put it on.

It is bad luck to turn back after starting on a journey.

It is bad luck to walk on walls.

If a rabbit crosses your path to the right, it is good luck; if to the left, bad luck.

If a rabbit crosses your path, make a cross and spit in it to break the evil charm.

It is bad luck to have a moon vine growing on the house.

Wear a rabbit's foot to avoid bad luck, the left hind foot of a rabbit caught in a graveyard in the dark of the moon.

It is bad luck to go under a ladder.

It is bad luck to step over anyone who is lying on the floor. He won't grow any more.

Never cut out a garment on Friday unless you can finish it that day.

Never start a journey on Friday.

Never start a new piece of work on Friday.

A whistling woman and a crowing hen never come to a very good end.

It is bad luck to stumble upon going upstairs.

To remove bad luck from turning back from a journey, make a cross mark on the road and spit in it.

It is bad luck to bring an axe in the house on your shoulder.

It is bad luck to light three cigarettes on one match.

It is bad luck to borrow a knife open and return it closed, or vice versa.

It is bad luck to seat thirteen at the table.

It is bad luck to burn wood from a tree that has been struck by lightning.

It is bad luck to burn sassafras wood.

It is bad luck to carry a chair on your back.

It is bad luck to burn brush on Sunday.

It is bad luck to turn back without making a remark about it.

It is bad luck to kill a dove, since it is regarded as a sacred bird.

It is bad luck to spill salt, but its effect can be counteracted by throwing some over the left shoulder.

It is bad luck to walk with one shoe off and one shoe on.

It is bad luck to walk backward.

It is bad luck to see a full moon over the left shoulder.

It is bad luck for a cat to walk under a ladder.

To kill a cat means seven years of bad luck.

If you watch your kin folks out of sight, the next time you see them they will have blood on them.

In preparing a fish net for a fishing trip, it is bad luck to step across the net.

Some consider it bad luck to have a black cat cross one's path. This is especially true among Negroes.

To cry in your sleep is bad luck the next day.

If you drop a book pick it up and kiss it, or have some one else pick it up. If you don't, you will have bad luck.

It is bad luck to rock a chair no one is sitting in.

It is bad luck to address a letter before it is written.

It is bad luck to a person if anyone steps across his feet. To undo the mischief step back immediately.

Two dollar bills are unlucky. Tear off a corner to break the spell.

Walking with one shoe off and one shoe on causes bad luck, one year for each step.

If a new moon is seen through brush one will have bad luck till the next new moon, unless he breaks a twig from the brush and sleeps with it under his pillow.

It is bad luck to walk by and shut an open gate.

It is bad luck to walk in another's tracks. To counteract the bad luck, retrace every track backward.

Good Luck Signs

Spit on a horseshoe, throw it over left shoulder and have good luck. If you look back it will bring bad luck.

If you find a horseshoe with open end pointed toward you, it will bring good luck; if pointed away from you, it will bring bad luck.

Hang horseshoe over the door for good luck.

See a pin and pick it up, all the day you'll have good luck.

See a pin and pass it by, to good luck you'll say goodbye.

A whistling woman and bleating sheep, the best property a man can keep.

See a load of hay, make a wish and look away, and it will come to you.

See the new moon clear and any wish you make will come true.

See the new moon obstructed from view by timber and you will have bad luck.

A dime with a hole in it, tied around the ankle, brings good luck.

If one's right eye itches, he will surely cry unless he tells someone else; then the person told will cry. If the left eye itches, he will have good luck and be pleased. The person told will likewise have good luck.

Love and Marriage

On Halloween night, peel an apple and toss the peeling over the left shoulder. The letter formed is the initial of the girl's future husband.

When sleeping in a new room, name the four corners for four lovers. The corner one looks at on first waking bears the name of one's future husband.

Star light, star bright,
First star I've seen tonight
Wish I may wish I might
Dream of my true love tonight.

Counting apple seeds:

One I love, two I love
Three I love I say.
Four I love with all my heart
Five I cast away.
Six he loves, seven she loves
Eight they both love.
Nine he comes, ten he tarries,
Eleven he courts, twelve he marries.

Counting buttons to find out the profession of future husband:

> Rich man, poor man, beggar man, thief
> Doctor, lawyer, merchant, chief.

Change the name and not the letter, change for worse and not the better.

If you take the last biscuit, you will be an old maid.

Count seven stars seven consecutive nights then put a mirror under the pillow and in your dream you will see the face of your future husband.

Look in a well on May 1st morning and see the face of your sweetheart.

Put a wish bone over the door. The first to enter is your future husband.

If someone sweeps under your feet you won't marry.

Name a fire after your lover; if it burns, he loves you. If it goes out, he doesn't.

When you see a red bird, start saying ABCs. The letter you are saying when he flies is the first letter of your sweetheart's name. You will marry him some day unless the bird lights on a fence. You can make a wish and throw a kiss at him before he flies. It will come true.

Place a four-leaf clover in your left shoe; the first man who takes your hand will be your husband some day.

Walk as many railroad rails as you are years old without losing your balance. Look behind you when you are done, and the person you are to marry will be there.

On the first day of May find a snail. Place it in a pan of meal and leave it over night. The next day the snail will be gone and the initial of your future husband will be written in the meal.

A bridegroom should carry his bride over the threshold of their home.

The bride should wear

> Something old, something new
> Something borrowed, something blue.

On New Year's night, place a gold band ring in a glass of water, go into a dark cellar, and see your husband's picture in the bottom of the glass.

Go into a dark cellar and look into a mirror. Your husband will be looking over your shoulder.

To try your fortune: Go by yourself to a peach tree and say:

> "New Moon, true moon, pray tell unto me
> Where my true love shall be,
> If I'm to marry close at hand, let me
> Hear a dog bark; if I'm not to marry at all,
> Let me hear my coffin knock."

On Tuesday night say:

"Now I lay down in white
On this blessed Tuesday night
Pray tell unto me
Who my true love shall be.
If I'm to have him let him come to me laughing;
If not let him go away crying."

Signs of Visitors

If a rooster comes around to the front of the house and crows three times, it is
   a sign company is coming.
Oh, my nose, my nose it itches, somebody's coming with a hole in his britches.
If left side of nose itches, a man is coming; if right side, a woman.
If you drop a knife, a woman is coming; if you drop a fork, a man is coming.
If you drop a dish rag, a slovenly person is coming.
If you take a piece of bread, when you already have one on your plate, someone
   is coming hungry.
If you drop a dish rag and it is folded when it falls someone is coming but not
   for a meal; if it falls open, someone is coming to eat with you.

Friendship

If you give a friend a knife, it will cut the friendship in two. This may be avoided
   by paying a penny for the knife.
Wash together, friend forever, wipe together, fight forever.
If you walk with a friend and come to a tree, both must go around it on the
   same side, else their friendship will be severed.
If you buy a present made of leather and give it to a friend, you will be enemies
   the rest of your life.
Kill the first snake you see every year, and you have killed all your enemies.

Babies

Take a new born baby upstairs or to a high place to make it "high-minded."
Never toss a baby up in the air. If you do it will make it feeble-minded.
Rub a minnow on the gums of a baby who is teething to make the teeth come
   through.

Dreams

If you dream of snakes, you have an enemy.

If you dream of marriage, it is a sign of death.

If you tell a dream before breakfast, it will come true.

Witches and Conjures

Keep knife and fork under pillow to keep witches away.

If one awakes with badly tangled hair in the morning, the witches have tangled it.

If one awakes very tired in the morning, the witches have ridden him in the night.

Negroes make a chalk mark around a place and conjure anybody who crosses over that mark against their will.

If you kill a snake, its mate will come and harm you.

If you awake in the morning with blue spots on your body, it is because the witches have pinched you.

Disappointments

Sitting on a truck means a disappointment.

An extra fork instead of a knife means a disappointment in the near future.

Miscellaneous

Eat chicken gizzards and you will become beautiful.

If you don't put your tongue in a place where a tooth has been pulled, a gold tooth will come in its place.

The jay bird goes to hell on Friday to have his head combed.

The jay bird goes to hell on Friday and stays till Monday.

To make meat tender, put a piece of coal in the vessel where it is cooking.

To make meat tender, stick a nail in it while it is roasting.

If cold chills run down your back, a possum is running across your grave (the place where you will be buried).

If your left foot itches under the bottom, you are going to the graveyard.

If your right foot itches, you are going to walk on strange territory.

If you ear burns, somebody is talking about you.

If the palm of your hand itches, you will get new money.

Use forked willow, peach tree, or hazel wand to find water. The power to do this belongs only to certain persons.

If you put salt on a bird's tail, you may easily catch him.

If you lose a marble, pitch another into the air in the general direction of the lost one and away, "Marble, go find your brother." You will find the two marbles close together.

To find a lost article, spit in the palm of your hand, slap the spittle with the index finger, and whichever way the spittle flies is the direction of the lost article.

To find which way cows went ask the "Daddy Long Legs," or "Grand-daddy." He will point toward them.

Put a horse hair in water and it will turn to a snake.

Nail on boards in light of moon and they will cup up on the roof.

Pretty is as pretty does.

Little head, little wit; big head, not a bit.

Kill the first snake you see that season and it will rid you of your enemies.

If your initials spell a word you will be rich.

Yell "money, money," when a star falls, and you will be rich.

If you walk across the floor with one shoe off and one on, people will tell lies on you.

If you sing before breakfast you will surely cry before supper.

Keep a black cat in the house and there will be old maids in the family.

If it rains all day Christmas, there will be a full graveyard that year.

If you hear an owl "holler," pull off one of year shoes and turn it upside down and the owl will hush.

If a turtle bites you, it won't turn loose till the sun goes down

To kill black locusts, cut them in the dark of the moon in August.

Singing in bed at night means that you will dream about the devil.

If a turtle bites you, he won't turn loose till it thunders.

If a foot is amputated, bury it in the right position, else the person will feel his toes cramp.

Switching for Water
[1955]

E. G. Rogers

I t is perhaps as axiomatic to say that there is a "water-witch" in every family as to say that any animal born with its eyes closed may go mad. The literal meaning of this may account for the frequency with which the peachtree switch is used in seeking for the hidden, underground stream as well as in the correction of the truant child. The practice of "switching" for water is a rather frequent skill with a believing number of individuals.

The selection of a desirable location for a well was once considered most essential to family health. As much attention later came to be given to this as was formerly given to the matter of selecting a well-protected spring near which the pioneer home was to be built on the hillside. And so there is still quite a number of individuals, both men and women, whose services are sought when a spot is to be chosen for the location of a well.

Areas Sampled

The practices and illustrations treated here were gathered from Sumner, Smith, Putnam, and White counties of the Middle Tennessee area and from Bradley, Polk, McMinn, Meigs, and Monroe counties of East Tennessee. There are a few multiple occurrences reported from without these areas by persons now living within the areas. A further sampling will reveal that certain modifications of the practice are rather general and widespread.

Kind and Nature of the Wood Used

The majority of persons claiming to possess the power of "waterwitching" suggest that the forked twig be cut from any kind of growing tree which produces a fruit bearing a stone. The order of preference therefore seems to be a peachtree, plum, dogwood, and apple. However, other kinds of woods are chosen depending upon the particular locality and the traditional practice within that locality. Recently a farmer demonstrated his ability to locate the mysterious stream by trimming down a blackgum fork from an overhanging limb. He observed meanwhile that peachtree usually works much better. One person suggested the use of willow. Others suggest that any kind of wood will do just so it is pliable and flexible. One person, however, was willing to demonstrate just how he would prepare the forked prong but would make no effort to locate an underground stream with it since, for him, the wood had to be peachtree.

How the Switch Is Prepared

A branch with forked prongs is cut so as to leave some four to six inches to that part beyond the conjunction of the prongs. The length of the entire switch should be from eighteen to twenty inches. A shorter switch will work, even as short as one with eight-inch prongs, but with proportionate difficulty. The branches are cut to an even length and are trimmed free of other branches. A few persons use a single switch cut some four to six inches shorter. The branches must be green and freshly cut.

Who May Switch for Water

This is a moot question. Most persons seek for an elderly person. This preference may involve the factor of experience, or it may indicate that many younger persons do not wish their friends to know that they lean toward any practice which cannot or has not been adequately and scientifically explained. As one young lady in a college class remarked, "I have tried it, and I know it works. It works for me. But please don't tell the class. They would not believe it if they saw it." There are some who connect "waterwitching" with "power doctors," and yet the greater majority do not try to explain it at all—they just go ahead using their knowledge or skill in helping a neighbor locate a spot to dig his well where a sufficient supply of water may be found. There are many for whom it "just will not work." Others say they could not do it until a practiced person taught them.

Holding the Switch

The free ends of the forked prongs are held with the wrists upward and the thumbs pointing horizontally outward so that the loose ends of the prongs will extend three or four inches beyond the thumbs. The switch is thus rigidly held so that the larger end of the fork will extend upward and slightly forward. Another method is to hold it in a somewhat similar position except that the palms of the hands are downward. Still a third way is used by those who prefer the single straight switch. The switch in this case is held by the smaller end in a single hand allowing the switch to extend forward horizontally while it is held between the extended forefinger and thumb.

Illustrations of Use and Practice

The individual with a switch so prepared and so held then starts walking slowly in the vicinity of the desired well's location. The presence and location of water is determined by "the pull" on the switch downward. The stronger the stream the more forceful the downward pull.

The following account is given by Mrs. Margaret Lowe of Athens, McMinn County, as told to her by her grandfather, the Rev. R. B. Rose, of how water-witching was practiced by his brother. "He used a peachtree 'witching stick' cut in the usual manner of a fork. The stick begins to turn downward when one is over water, and points straight down at the place where the water is nearest the surface."

"Then," says Mrs. Lowe, "after listening to my grandfather explain about his brother, I decided to try it for myself. After he had prepared the switch and showed me how to hold it, I decided to prove for myself whether waterwitching will work. My brother led me around with my eyes closed so that I could not come upon a predetermined spot or location. The switch pointed downward at an exact spot where it had pointed before. At one time I decided not to let the stick turn in my hands. I held it as tightly as possible. Again there was a definite pull on the stick. And the tighter I held, the harder was the pull. I did not move my hands, but one of the branches broke off at a joint. And I have learned for myself that waterwitching is possible. I know, for it worked for me."

Says Janette Cheek of Benton, Polk County, "We had a well dug last summer by a man called General Moates. He used a 'witching stick' to locate the well. He asked whether he might dig the well in the most likely place according to their findings. When we agreed they began walking over the back yard in a crisscross manner much like the spoke in a wheel to establish the closest proximity of water. At the spot where the stick showed the greatest downward pull, they began to dig. Water was found within six inches of the depth which had been predetermined."

Bill Akins of McMinn County tells of a Mr. Kennedy, a farmer of the Pond Hill community, who decided to locate a well convenient to his dairy barn. With his peachtree switch, he started walking within the vicinity of the spot where he wished to have a well dug. In a very favorable location the twig began to pull toward the ground. He hired a well-digger and water was found at the spot which the twig had indicated. His neighbors, however, doubted.

Norma Jean Kyle of Meigs County quotes a Mr. Jones as saying that the pull for him was often so strong that the bark would twist in his hands. According to him, this method never fails to strike water. Paul Conner of Englewood reports this definition of waterwitching as given to him by Jake Perry: "Waterwitching, as I understand it, is the passing art of finding an underground stream with a forked, freshly cut, peachtree branch." Jane Ann Vineyard of Sweetwater, Monroe County, reports a Mr. George A. Roy of the Christianburg community who has been waterwitching for his neighbors for the past forty years. Mr. Roy holds the switch so that it turns toward him as it points downward for the "pull."

Mr. Smith of Cookeville, Putnam County, reports that he switches with one hand by gripping the small end of the switch between the thumb and forefinger, letting the end of the switch rest against the palm. The switch is extended in a horizontal position and forward as he starts walking. When water is found, the loose end of the switch will start vibrating vertically. This will continue for a longer or shorter time depending on the strength of the stream. Horizontal vibrations indicate depth.

How Depth Is Determined

Mr. Smith, just referred to above, says that each complete horizontal vibration indicates one foot in depth to which the well must be dug. When the exact depth is reached, the switch will again vibrate vertically.

Mrs. L. Dosser of Calhoun reports a Mr. Potter who determines depth by using a single straight switch, although he used the forked switch to locate the stream. He counts the total number of vibrations as the number of feet in depth to which the well must be dug.

Clifford O'Dell of Monroe County reports an eighty-year-old water wizard as practicing a unique way of determining the depth of the stream. He judges the depth of the water by the number of buds or branches on the switch being used. This number is multiplied by two in determining depth.

In the Janette Cheek account the depth was determined by holding a straight peachtree switch over the spot where water had been located. The number of vibrations before the switch came to a stop was forty-two. Water was found at forty-two and one-half feet. Mrs. Lowe says that the distance from the first indication of "pull" to the downward point is the distance one will have to dig to reach water.

Switching for Other Substances

The "divining rod" used in locating minerals, the Geiger Counter for uranium, and the "salt test" for the presence for oil in the West are common knowledge. There are a few persons, however, who also claim that they have the power of determining the location of other substances in the same manner as they switch for water. A Mr. Pole Parker on the headwaters of Dixon Creek in Smith County has the reputation of being able to locate gold or other metals through the use of a similar switch. It is related of him that by such means he once located a five-dollar gold piece which had been lost in a corn crib.

Witchlore and Ghostlore in the Great Smokies
[1970]

Joseph S. Hall

I t is my intent to tell something of the few surviving beliefs in an age and in a place that is slowly becoming sophisticated and educated. If the subject seems slightly unattractive, one may remember that ghosts are not so highly regarded in the Smoky Mountains either. For example, a mountain man met a ghost going down the road as he was coming up the road. Some distance after passing, the ha'nt shrilled out, "I'm not no friend to ye." The mountain man, now safely away, answered, "I'm mighty damn proud [glad] of it."

Amid the scenic splendor of the mountains known as the Great Smokies, which crown the state line between Tennessee and North Carolina and are now a national park, archaic folkways and speech, folk tales and ballads were handed down from the remote past of these people until the national park was formed in the 1930s.

The notion of old-fashioned mountaineers speaking Elizabethan English has been a romantic one beguiling press and public alike since late in the last century. Actually, Smokies people were far from being direct descendants of the Elizabethans, having come from all of the British Isles as well as other countries in Europe, notably France and Germany, representing many different periods and routes of immigration to the mountains, and having no doubt undergone a good deal of intermixing with various types of Americans before and during their life in the Smokies. However, poignant old ballads, weaving. and cooking have lent glamour to a people who, being social and economic underdogs, needed this flattering attention for their self-esteem.

In the light of these folk survivals, it is not surprising that other remnants of the lore and ways of the remote, misty past lingered in the mountains until recent years, and even until today in the region surrounding the park. The survivals which I wish to describe and illustrate briefly are witchlore and ghostlore.

While I found no evidence that witchcraft was actually practiced in the four counties of my studies, and no one indicated that anybody tried to hex anyone else by incantations, figurines, or potions, there appears to have been a fairly widespread belief that certain people were witches and that a number of people suffered from their wily works. If one has friends in the mountains, one may hear today accounts of the evils supposedly caused by witches in the past and the counter measures taken.

As to ghostlore, some middle-aged and elderly people still enjoy the eerie excitement of relating encounters that they or others (almost always others) had with apparitions of various kinds. These narratives are locally called "ha'nt" (haint) tales, but many people are convinced that the strange incidents they relate actually happened.

When several clues to belief in witches came to light, I interviewed some fifteen people, who included Smokies friends and other informants. The interviews took place for the most part in 1956. Two were held in 1959, but one woman became rather reticent, thinking possibly that I knew too much about witchlore for comfort. Many of the accounts were recorded on tape which will eventually go into the collections of Columbia University, the Library of Congress, and the National Park Services.

Evils Caused by Witches. Lewis Clabo of Gatlinburg, Tennessee, a native mountain man and former school teacher, defined a witch for me. He said simply, "A witch is the devil." When I asked Mrs. Polly Grooms of Newport, Tennessee, what evil things a witch could do, she stated:

1. Witches could tire you out by riding you all night on a broom. She said, "When people got up in the morning, they would say, 'I'm so weak. That old witch has rode me on a broom all night.'"
2. They could give you the jerks and make you cry out in your sleep at night.
3. They could make a cow give bloody milk.
4. They could refuse to loan or give you anything. ("Loaning you something would break their power.")
5. They could cause clabbered milk. (Mrs. Delia Cahorn of Cades Cove, still living in the park, said, "They was an old man Hicks was said to be a witch and who caused clabbered and bloody milk.")
6. They could keep a cow from giving milk.
7. They could keep milk from churning.
8. They could transform you into a cat, a dog, a hog, or any other animals. They could transform you into a horse and ride you. (Jarvis

Ownboy of Low Gap, near Gatlinburg, Tennessee, said, "Demon
Thomas witched Gramma into a horse and rode her all night. She
said, 'He rode me all night last night. I was a horse.'")
9. They could cause unexplainable noises and strange and terrifying
lights in the night.
10. They could cause serious illness or death of an animal or a human
being.

Probably other nasty tricks will come to light in future interviews if those
with knowledge of the old lore continue to live a few years longer.

As for the reasons why witches cast their spells, the informants were uniformly
reticent or uninformed, with the exception of two people who said that witches
tried to buy something like a cow or a pig at a lower price than the prevailing price
and they cast a spell causing the farm animals to weaken, or threatening that the
animal would lose its ears, eyes, and tails. In most cases, we may believe, a person's
suspicions that he was being bewitched were based on vague fears of the intentions
of another person. In some cases, people on long and lonely night rides or walking
through dark forests or uninhabited mountain areas at night saw witches when
their emotions were greatly heightened by fear of the dark or by guilt or both.
Some cases seemed to grow out of family or even interstate rivalries.

There may be a little indication of the spirited state rivalry between Tennesseans and North Carolinians who live near the common border of these two
states. One woman in Sevier County, Tennessee, spoke disparagingly of witches
across the state line: "Times were hard during my mother's life in North Carolina. The witches over there in North Carolina would witch everything you had."
There is a suggestion in her account, too, of bewitching livestock so that the
witch could purchase it at a low price.

Identification of People as Witches. Six people were named directly or indirectly as witches, but usually in a reserved manner as follows. Incidentally,
both men and women were called "witches."

An old lady, a Gunter, was accused of being a witch (Lewis Hopkins,
XVIII, 13).1

"They was old man Hicks—his beard would come down that fur—was
said to be a witch and who caused clabbered and bloody milk" (Mrs.
Delia Cahorn, XVII, 47).2

"They said Granpap's sister Squad McGaha was a witch" (Oliver Hicks,
XVII, 34).3

External objects, in one case a hair or conjure ball, in another a red
handkerchief worn on the head, help identify women as being witches.

"Russ Maynor's mother was said to be a witch. Wads of hair were found in
her straw bed when she died" (Mrs. Polly Grooms, XVIII, 3–4).4 She was

referring to the hair or conjure balls thrown at intended victims to bring sickness or death. (See Vance Randolph, *Ozark Superstitions,* Columbia University Press, 1947, 211: The hair ball is "just a little bunch of black hair mixed with beeswax and rolled into a hard pellet. The old woman tossed this thing at the persons she wished to eliminate." See also Wayland Hand, *North Carolina Superstitions,* VII, 101.)[5]

The old woman (previously named in the narrator's account) wore an old red handkerchief.

The cousin and a great aunt ("Granpap's sister") were named or referred to in two cases.

Staring or rolling eyes characterized two witches, according to Mrs. Polly Grooms: "I had a cousin to witch people. He stood over my bed all night. My mother said his eyes didn't move" (XVIII, 3).[6]

"We young'uns would cry when Mother would take us to her house. She would roll her eyes around and look at us as if she could run plumb through us."[7] There is undoubtedly an association with the evil eye here, and rolling, fiery eyes are characteristic of many devilish ghosts or animals, told of in mountain tales.

Having been in the presence of a witch during the day could frighten children at night: "My bother would cry out at night and jump up and down and get the jirks like he was scared to death. 'O Daddy, she's agettin' me,' he said. Mother would say, 'Get that Testament, Joe, and put it under his head. That old lady might have witched him.'" (Mrs. Polly Grooms, XVIII, 4–5).[8]

Other forms assumed by witches will appear below.

How a Person Became a Witch. Having learned that witches are devils, that a number of people were called or thought to be witches, and what witches could do, I asked Mrs. Grooms, of Newport, Tennessee, if she could tell me how a person became a witch. She said:

> My uncle that lost his mind and died, said to witch, you had to belong to the devil. You had to put one hand under your foot and another hand on top of your head, and you had to say that what was between 'em belonged to the devil. You put a handkerchief on the ground and then said, 'there will be three drops of blood fall from the elements upon the handkerchief.' Then you could witch people.[9]

As to the blood falling from heaven onto a handkerchief, one is reminded of the witch mentioned above who wore a red handkerchief on her head (the color is probably significant); and one recalls the necromancer Dr. Faustus in Marlowe's famous play who, in futilely imploring God's mercy in his last horror-filled hours, says:

The stars move still, time runs, the clock will strike,
Oh, I'll leap up to my God! Who pulls me down?
See, see where Christ's blood streams in the firmament!

In the play, the blood across the sky is Christ's, presumably the blood of Christ on the cross, yet the association of blood with the sky is not only dramatic but is interesting in connection with Mrs. Grooms's present statement; and the identification of the witch by her wearing of an "old red handkerchief" may offer an intriguing lead for further investigation.

"Was a person stuck with being a witch for good?" I asked. Mrs. Grooms replied, "My uncle went to a witch doctor who said he could get over it [i.e., being a witch] if he would take baths. But he was in bad shape. The witching made him lose his mind. They couldn't get him to take a bath or change clothes. He hit my daddy on the head with a banjo."

Counter Measures. Measures to counteract a witch's spell were mentioned by all informants. In general they consisted of:

1. Using hard objects, chiefly iron, steel, silver, or flint in some way, involving for example, putting a horseshoe or flint in the fire to keep hawks out of the chickens; the familiar practices of shooting a silver bullet into a picture of the witch, or driving a nail into a beech tree on which a likeness of the witch had been drawn.
2. Using fire in some way, often in conjunction with hard objects but also in combination apparently with other methods.
3. Drawing blood from the witch.
4. Handling the witch roughly.
5. Cutting a limb off an animal thought to be a witch; cutting a portion of an animal's ear and heating it in the fire.
6. Putting a Bible under one's pillow at night.
7. Saying the "three highest words" of the Bible.
8. Hanging a broom across the door.
9. Sprinkling salt around the house.
10. Tying up three apple seeds in a dishrag and putting the dishrag with the seeds under the stove.
11. Stirring bewitched milk with a holly twig as the milk is being heated.
12. Following the advice of a witch doctor.

Salt, Broom, and Apple Seeds. General protection against witches was afforded the home by sprinkling salt around it or making a ring of salt around it ("Witches won't step over it"), or by placing a broom across the door way ("No witches won't step over it"). The latter practice was alluded to in the common expression, "They jumped the broom" for "They got married," meaning that a broom was laid across the doorway before the bride and groom entered the house so as to keep out witches. A third measure was as follows: "Tie up three apple seeds in a dishrag. Put the dish [rag] under the stove and don't remove it for three days. That would keep the witches out of the house."

Use of Iron, Steel, etc. Iron, steel, silver, and flint were effective. To keep cows or their milk from being bewitched, put a dime in the churn ("That silver runs her spirit off"). Or put a horse's bridle on the churn. This measure is probably intended to restrain the witch in her mad ride. To keep hawks out of the chickens, put a horseshoe or a flint in the fireplace. (The hawks are likely witches in bird form. Compare the expression used for rain falling while the sun shines: "The devil is beating his wife and all her feathers are coming over.") To make a witch stop causing an animal or a person to weaken or die, "draw the witch's picture on a beech tree and drive a nail part way and hit that nail nine times every mornin' before the sun riz" (Fred Metcalf, XVIII, 6). Mrs. Sarah Cole of the Glades, near Gatlinburg, formerly of the Sugarlands (now in the park), said, "A witch had my uncle near dead. He could just barely sit up. A witch doctor drawed a picture of the witch and nailed it back of the door, driv a nail in her heart, and then she died."

Lead. The direct application of lead against witches was obviously ineffective in two stories. Here is one:

> Joe Gunter went to take care of a women's house till she went after her grandson. They said about dark witches like black cats went up in the loft, and he said he shot at one and they went ZIP! and on up in the loft. And the old women had some tobacco hung up there, and the next mornin' they wasn't a piece of tobacco as big as your three fingers and when daylight the witches all come down lookin' like black cats and left (Phoebe Ramsay, Tape 12).

Incidentally, also a bullet shot at ghosts never seems to be zeroed in properly, for it fails to hit their marks in the local stories.

Heat. Making things too hot for witches was suggested above in the counter measure of putting a horseshoe or flint in the fireplace to keep hawks out of the chickens. These examples of heat applications have to do with keeping witches from reducing or contaminating the milk supply.

> "Nancy Baxter's grandchildren came in and said, 'Grandmother, why have you got the milk in the oven in a bottle?' She said, 'Someone's witching' my cow and they tell me if I boil it the cow will give more milk and I can make more butter.'"

Heat was combined with stirring the milk with a holly brush in this incident, which brought exposure of the witch. "Gran Tritt said her cow couldn't give no milk hardly. Someone said for her to put the milk in the fire [i.e., fireplace] and whip it with a holly brush till it boiled away. Granny said Seb Webb jumped in (into the house) and said, 'If you don't take it off I'll die.'"

Another case of the use of heat, combined with iron and steel, is shown in the following account, also resulting in injury to the witch and her exorcism. Lewis Hopkins, formerly of Big Creek just beyond the park bounds, told this unusual tale:

My grandmother's folk had a cow and she give bloody milk. An old lady, a Phillips, was accused of being a witch. So they got to talkin' to Sam Evans who said he was a witch doctor and knowed about witches. The witch doctor told the folks to put a baker lid [i.e., the lid of a Dutch oven] in the fire. So they pecked on it with a reap hook [like a scythe or sickle]. So this old women Phillips come to this old man Evans and raised a fuss with him about tellin' him what to do. They got into a fight and this old man pulled her dress up and they saw the pecks where they was a reap hook a-hackin' her. [But] she jumped out and got away from him."

Drawing Blood. In one narrative "drawing blood" was the counter measure used to deprive a witch of her power.

Squad McGaha was a witch, so I've always been told. She witched Granpap McGaha when he was a small kid. They told Granpap how to get the witch off her was to draw blood from her so he clumb up on top of the house and tore a board off, got him a rock, and when she went to bed that night he slipped up there and dropped that rock in on her head and just skinned the side of her face all over, and the witch came off of them then.

Incidentally "rocking" (that is, throwing rocks at) was mentioned in two tales as the treatment for cows thought to be boogers or ghosts.

Putting a piece of a cow's ear in the fire suggests that drawing blood was combined with heat in one instance. Mrs. Sarah Cole said, "The witches over there in North Carolina would witch anything you had." If your cow has been bewitched, she said, "Cut a piece of the brute's ear off and wrap it up in cloth or anything and put it to hot ashes to break the spell."

The next tale is somewhat more remote and advanced but also involves, apparently, drawing blood and cutting off a limb of the witch in animal form. It occurs as Tale No. 97, "The Cat-Witch," in Richard Dorson's *Negro Folktales in Michigan* (Harvard University Press, 1956), 146–147.

An old half-nigger, Old Nigger Jane, claimed she was witched into a black cat and traveled miles and miles and miles. A black cat came to her that she thought was Nigger Bill. When it come meowin', she was in the door pawin' to get in. She was cuttin' meat when she heard Bill a-comin'. She just hacked the paw off with a meat knife, and the paw had a ring on it, and she knowed Nigger Bill's ring and she tuck the ring off the paw and took it to Bill, who played sick that morning after losin' his paw. He was still in bed when she got there with the ring.

There are almost no Negroes in the mountains, and the association of this story with Negroes is curious, especially considering that five of 29 variants are Negro in source.

Witches or Devils in Squirrel Form. In the last tale, the witch is Squad McGaha, again at her evil enterprises. She refuses her sister's request for some apples and makes a "wish" on her—that is, bewitches her with unfortunate results, her spell bringing an attack by devils or witches in the form of ground squirrels. In the preceding incidents and tales, witches or devils had the form of hawks, a horse (causing Granny's nightmare), cats, and cows. Here, beside this novel shape of the witches or devils, is the motif in which the witch refuses to give a loan or gift. Such a loan or gift would cause her to lose her power.

Squad McGaha witched her sister [Nance]. Her sister came to her mother and told her she wanted some apples, and Squad didn't want her to have the apples. [Her] mother told her to go on and get her apples anyway. [Nance] went on to the apple orchard and picked her up a sack of apples and started back. [Nance] started back to the house and she felt something in front of her dress. She looked around, and there was a ring of ground squirrels plumb across [the field] to the fence holdin' to her dress tails. She broke to run and run to the house and fell at the door dead.

With this baleful tale, I think we better go back to our dream of Elizabethan English for comfort from witches' woeful workings in the Smokies.

Ghostlore

Close to the evils and uncanny happenings caused by witches are the occurrences, mostly unpleasant, involving ghosts, specters, skeletons, animal spooks, luminous shapes, lights, and weird noises.

The spirits of the innocent, the wronged, and those dead before their time of course exist in Smokies' accounts of incidents and in tales. In one familiar story, the ghost of a man murdered for his money sees that those responsible are punished. In another story, somewhat in the specters' mass tradition, a brave young man, for the promise of reward, dares to spend the night in a haunted churchhouse, with an absorbing evening spent among the spirits of departed church members and rattling bone assemblies usually called skeletons who make things interesting for the young man, to call attention to the neglected state of the church.

Then there is the pathetic ghost who goes around at night disturbing people's sleep by asking over and over in a moaning voice, "Where will I put it?" to finally get the disgusted reply of one of the sleepless humans, "By gosh, put it where you got it." This slightly mixed-up spook finally earns his rest by restoring to its proper place whatever he had heedlessly removed.

Also there is the pitiable spirit of a man who committed suicide by drowning and sloshed through the creek every night returning to assert ownership of his home that had passed into the hands of others.

Lonesome and friendless is the spook who follows a man, doing neither good nor evil: "I heard my first man's daddy say that, when he was goin' down the road toward Knoxville, there was another man with him" (Mrs. Sarah Cole, XVII, 85).

Sometimes a solitary human rider in the night finds that he has unexpected spectral company sharing the rear seat of his horse with him.

Ghosts have to be humored. If you agree with them, you will be rewarded. But if you argue with them, the result may be fatal. According to Mrs. Polly Grooms, ghosts return if they have money hidden. If you say the "three highest words" in the Bible, "In the name of the Father, the Son, and the Holy Ghost, what do you want?" they will tell you where to find the money. Another informant related: "A feller over here said his father and mother saw one of them things—ha'nts. Quite a few people tried to follow it, disagreed with it, and got killed. One old lady tried to follow him, treated him nice, agreed with him, and he led her to a big stump where there was a pot of gold buried under it" (Lewis Clabo, XVII, 69).

But the large majority of human and animal spooks, vague shapes and lights seem to be sinister and malign. A ghostly catalogue from the Smokies would include a frightening array of apparitions ranging from near-human specters through human shapes clad in white, people with hands whose bones you can see through the flesh at night, a colorful variety of headless people on foot or horseback, mysterious wolves and panthers which hunters' dogs shy from following, calves with ears sticking straight up and with eyes big as pint cups and red as balls of fire or luminous calves seen on a dark forest pathway with rolling shining eyes, lights which sail over lonely travelers on remote mountain trails to haunt the conscience-stricken souls of those carrying illicit liquor to sell in a neighboring settlement, lights in the form of fish, and noises like a ton of exploding dynamite heard by booze-haulers.

When do people meet up with these unearthly, unsavory characters? Some of the circumstances have been indicated above. Usually the unpleasant or unfortunate encounter takes place in a house or church said to be haunted, on a lonely stretch of road on a dark night, or on a solitary night ride, and often in the midst of activities that make the conscience tender, such as cursing, playing cards, or carrying a load of mountain moonshine on a dark or moonshiny night. Remote schoolhouses (often churches) and graveyards offer excellent opportunities for ghostly encounters.

What do people do when they seem them? If you talk to the human spooks, they won't answer. If you try to shoot them, you always miss. If you are brave, you "rock" (throw rocks at) spectral calves. Generally, people find it pleasanter to be someplace else as fast as possible. And they run for their lives to cross water "to get shet of the ha'nt," or they run though doors, breaking them down in their haste, and pitch themselves onto the floor of a warm, friendly lighted room.

A woman danced along the road following a man riding home from the mill. He thought she was a witch. She might as easily have been called a spook. He ran into his house, got a gun, shot at her, missed as usual, and she caused his death.

Sometimes the spook is clad eerily in white. In this case the ha'nt seemed bent on thievery at a man's mail box: "My son was a-coming out to his brother's at the Sugarlands. They was man at the mail box dressed in white. My son spoke to him. The man didn't answer. He shot at it. [My son] left on the horse, and when he crossed the branch at about a mile it left him" (Mrs. Sarah Cole, XVIII, 82).

Long before I looked into the witch and ghostlore of this area, prompted by folklorist Wayland Hand's inspiring example in the whole field of superstitions, I heard hunters in their accounts of bear hunts mention that their dogs wouldn't run wolves or panthers. The awe with which this supposed farce was uttered was always a little puzzling, and it was not until I read Barbara Woods's fascinating *Devil in Dog Form* that I realized that the wolves must have the traits of the diabolical canine, and that panthers must have some of the characteristics of witches' cats.

A Cosby Creek informant, Sam Stiles, related this suggestive incident:

> We lived over there about two miles from here, when I was a kid like. We built a new house. We used a door peg. We had a couple of dogs, and we cooked in the fireplace. This here door would fly open every day. The peg would jump out in the middle of the floor. The dogs couldn't find nothin'. There were wolves howled on that mountain. Then the old man hunted a whole lot. There was wolves in there. The hound wouldn't follow him at all. He went up there and found a gang of wolves eatin' a bunch of sheep (XVII, 54).

There seems an unmistakable implication that evil spirits had made the door peg jump out onto the floor and were one of the same as the wolves. This is surely the devil in wolf form, and one remembers in this connection that horses balk and shy away in the presence of ghosts.

One of the most curious tales in the collection is the one told above about how Squad McGaha witched her sister, hurling the curse that the devil would get her if she insisted on taking the apples against the witch's wish. Ground squirrels tug at her dress as she tries to get to the house. As she reaches the door she falls dead. These squirrels are surely the devil in animal form once more.

There is the story of the man who spends all night in church for $500. The mayor and the deacons make this offer because the church has fallen into disrepair and is believed to be ha'nted. The windows are broken. Cobwebs gather, and weird shapes are thought to be seen when moonlight shines through the windows. A stranger in town, a brave young "feller," accepts the offer. That night in the shabby old building he is surrounded by the spirits of the departed brethren, some of them cut open and bleeding. When things go too far for comfort for him among this mad crew, he thinks it is time to go. As he starts for the door he is surrounded by a ring of skeletons. Knowing he will have to play it cool before things get too hot, he stealthily picks up a couple of heavy wooden collection bowls with which to fight his way out. Just then an idea strikes him. He pushes the bowls out in front of him and says, "Here, we're gonna take up collection!" When he says that, every skeleton is gone, and he walks out of the church safe. He gets his $500. The plight of the church is now realized and everyone pitches in to help remodel and support the church, which shows that after dishing it out long enough, the ghosts get it in the end.

Notes

1. That is, interview of Lewis Hopkins by this author, Field Notes, XVII (1956), p. 13.
2. Field Notes, XVII (1956), p. 47.
3. Field Notes, XVII (1956), p. 34.
4. Field Notes, XVII (1959), p. 3–4.
5. *Popular Beliefs and Superstitions from North Carolina in the Frank C. Brown Collection of North Carolina Folklore,* VII (Durham: Duke University Press, 1964).
6. Field Notes, XVIII (1959), p. 3.
7. Ibid.
8. Ibid., pp. 4–5.
9. Ibid., p. 3.

Some West Tennessee Superstitions about Conjurers, Witches, Ghosts, and the Devil
[1970]

Anna Lett

The supernatural has held man's interest from the beginning of time and therefore holds an important place in folk literature. In this paper, I report some of the magical practices and witchcraft as related to me by an old Negro fortune teller and sorceress named Mama Mollie in Jackson, Tennessee. I first learned of Mama Mollie during the Thanksgiving holidays when I was taken to her house to have my fortune told. After the old woman had prophesied about my future, I asked her if I might come back to see her for a lesson in magical practices. When I returned to see her, she spent nearly two hours telling me about conjuring, casting spells, preventatives of witchcraft, warding off spirits, and other magical practices. Although Mama Mollie vowed she is not a witch and gets her clairvoyant abilities from a divine source, she knew a great deal about witches and witchcraft. I have attempted to relate these practices of magic and witchcraft exactly as Mama Mollie told them to me.

Conjurers.

A man "conger" (conjurer) can teach a woman, but a man cannot teach a man, and a woman cannot teach a woman. Charmers cannot charm for themselves. It is better for a man to charm for a woman, and vice versa.

A Negro cannot conjure a white man.

Charming causes the charmer to be ill. Most claim to get pains.

Negroes conjure a person by taking little coils of hair and scattering them around the spring from which that person gets water.

A hair tied to a string and placed prominently around a spring will conjure the spring and work harm on anyone drinking the water.

A spring can also be conjured and the water made unfit to drink by placing a circle of lime around it.

Places along streams where women wash clothes may be polluted by conjury, that is, by a conjurer throwing various roots into the stream, thus forcing washwomen to go elsewhere.

A circle of lime around a house will conjure an entire household.

Salt and sulfur sprinkled over beds and tables as a means of conjury is supposed to reform a person of his bad habits.

Sowing salt in an enemy's yard and repeating a rhymed incantation is an effective death charm.

A spell is usually worked by a conjure ball buried in the victim's path. Bent pins and human hair are the commonest ingredients, but snake tongues, lizard tails, ground puppy claws, and other ingredients are also used.

A man fixed up a conjure bag and left it in the path of another man. The second one found it and walked around; otherwise he would have been under the other's control.

Many think that by throwing some needles and horsehair on the doorstep they can put a spell on the person living there without the help of a conjure man.

If you carry a lock of hair of a person, you will have power or control over that person.

A person possessing a nail or some hairs of a person may punish that person through the possession of them.

To cast a conjure spell on another person, take a lock of hair, fingernails, and toenails, blow the breath into them nine times, and throw them away where you will never pass them again. The first person to pass that way is grabbed by the conjure.

Make a little wax figure, put some of his hair, paring off his nails, and any small possession of his in the wax and burn it. This is a death charm.

Wet a rag in your enemy's blood. Put it behind a rock in the chimney. When it rots your enemy will die.

If a dime that is worn to keep spells off should turn black, it is a sign that someone is trying to "throw" the person.

When a snake is found in bed, it is a sign that that person is conjured.

To point an index or dog finger of the right hand at a person will give that person bad luck.

To work evil upon someone, get the person's picture.

Take seven hairs from a blood snake, seven scales from a rattlesnake, seven bits of feathers from an owl, add a hair from the head of the person you desire, and a bit of nail paring, and cook these for seven minutes over a hot fire in the first rain water caught in April. Sprinkle the concoction on the clothes of the person to be charmed. It cannot fail.

To conjure a well, throw in some graveyard dirt.

A conjurer said he could take a stick and three grains of coffee and put a spell on people.

One day a man with a wagon of wood mired down. He thought a spell had been put on the wagon. He took an axe and drove it into one of the logs. He heard another man coming on a galloping horse, and it was the conjure man. As he passed the wagon, the axe flew out, the mud dried up, and the man in the wagon drove away.

I knew of a family who were known as conjurers. One time a man went to steal a chicken there, and the old man came out and stopped him, and conjured him just as he put his hand up, and the man stood there all night, until the spell was broke.

To take off spells, dig under the person's steps that casted the spell.

To cast off a spell, put something under your enemy's doorstep for him to walk over and catch the spell.

A person who has been conjured by another person can go to his home and spit on the doorstep; then he will be able to get revenge.

A conjurer's spells may be broken if a charm is hidden where he will step over it.

To take a conjure off, take a lock of hair, fingernails, and toenails, blow breath into them nine times, and throw them away where you'll not pass any more. The first one that passes that way is a victim to the conjure, which releases you and jumps up and gets him.

The bone of a dead person is proof against conjure.

To prevent conjuring, tie a piece of silver with a hole in it to the right leg.

To keep spells off, wear a dime around your ankle.

To prevent conjuring, wear a dime in the shoe.

Horseshoes nailed to the door will also keep off conjuring influences.

To keep off spells, keep a "ruffled" chicken in the yard to scratch away the "goofer" or conjure bags.

Rabbit feet worn around your neck will keep off spells.

If a snake track is seen across a person's track, one must stoop down and rub it out with his cheek to break the spell.

To remove a conjure spell, take a cabbage leaf with a little green lizard hidden inside. The person who is getting rid of the conjure takes the patient and holds the cabbage leaf to his leg, slits the leg with a knife, at the same time releasing the lizard. The patient is cured, for a lizard has jumped out.

Carry red pepper in the pocket to prevent conjuring.

To take off spells, bring the drinking water across a running stream.

If you are conjured, take nine new needles, put them in a dipper of water, boil until all the water is gone. This will take off the conjure.

To take off spells, read the Bible and do something for the service of Christ.

If a person has been conjured, he may draw a picture of the person conjuring him, put it up, and shoot it. If it is the fight person that person will die.

In order to put the enemy out of business, draw a picture, naming it for the person corresponding to the marked coin, fasten the picture to a tree and shoot it with quicksilver. Through this process, any enemy can be found out and quickly removed.

Witches.

To become a witch, the candidate goes to the Devil to the top of the highest hill at sunrise nine successive days and curses God. The Devil then places one hand on the candidate's head and one on his feet and receives the promise that all between his hands shall be devoted to his services.

If you put one hand on the top of your head and the other hand on the bottom of your foot, and, while in this position, swear by all good and evil that you will forsake all that is good and uphold the Devil in all his works, you will become a wizard.

If an old woman has only one tooth in her head, she is a witch.

A woman who has long straight hair that curls at the ends like a drake's tail can practice magic.

A seventh daughter, born on Christmas Day, possesses mysterious powers.

A red-haired Negro is a witch. If he gives you a rabbit's foot, you have an all-powerful talisman against evil, and for good luck.

The power of a witch or wizard to banish at will is obtained from some bone of a black cat.

Black cats are witches.

When you see cats' eyes shine at night, you see witches' eyes.

To become a witch, eat grasshoppers or crickets.

Anyone who refuses to step over a broom is a witch.

Lay a broom down in the doorway when you see company coming. If the person steps over it, he or she is not a witch, but if they pick it up they are.

Among the Cherokee, twins are preferably chosen for a career as witches.

If a warm current of air is felt, witches are passing.

If the wind makes a weird noise about the house, witches are near and some mischief is abrew.

Witches do all their traveling in bad weather.

A phosphorescent glow often seen on the ground at night in the summer is sometimes called witches' eyes.

If you are awake at eleven, you will see witches and black cats at twelve.

When one has sores in corners of his mouth it is a sign witches have had him bridled.

The twitching of the eye is a sign that one is bewitched.

If your shoestring comes untied, the witches are after you.

If a knot comes in the thread while you are sewing, the witches are after you.

If a fire you are attempting to make goes out, you are bewitched.

If you are going to wash dishes and you boil your water to wash them, the old saying is that the witches will ride you.

If you are shown a piece of hair near the door and you do not pick it up, the witches will overtake you soon.

If a witch goes to church, she will sit with her back toward the minister.

Do not eat too much grease, or you will be bewitched.

The howling of dogs shows the presence of witches.

The charms of witches are made from the entrails of cocks sacrificed to demons, certain horrible worms, various unspecified herbs, dead men's nails, the hair, brains, and teeth of boys who were buried unbaptized, with other incantations—over a fire of oak logs in a vessel made out of the skull of a decapitated thief. This was used to inflict death or disease on the bodies of the faithful.

It is unwise to keep egg shells, because witches go to sea in them.

If a spider is consumed falling into a lamp, witches are near.

By rubbing her hand on a gun, a witch can put a spell on it so that its shot will not hit anything.

You bewitch someone by pointing any sharp instrument at him.

At this point, Mama Mollie seemed to be waning a bit, so I decided it was time to go elsewhere for information. I next visited the home of an old friend of my grandmother's, Mrs. Maybelle Searcy. My grandmother had told me that Mrs. Searcy in years gone by had sat by the hour and told the neighborhood children all about witches, the Devil, ghosts, and Halloween. Mrs. Searcy seemed, according to my grandmother, to be the authority of her time on such subjects. Old Mrs. Searcy was only too glad to give me an audience after I explained my project to her. Many of the beliefs that she passed on to me were quite similar to, or at least seemed possibly to have come from the same source as, those told to me by Mama Mollie.

The perfume of the offal of a black dog and his blood besmeared on the posts and walls of the house prevent a witch's entrance.

To keep witches away from the house, hang a horseshoe over the door.

Hang a horseshoe covered with tinfoil over the door for even greater protection against witches.

I knew a lady who lived alone with her daughter in a sparsely settled district. Every night she sprinkled a trail of sand around the house, keeping absolute silence while she did so. No person with malevolent intentions could cross the sand line, according to her. I noticed that she also kept a large dog, however. Perhaps her magic was not so potent as she hoped!

If a tenpenny nail and some hair are placed under the steps, witches cannot come into the house.

An old woman said to be a witch told a family that before they moved into their new house they had better take a twenty-five cent piece and place it on the sill at each corner of the house. The people gave the old woman the coins to be placed under the house. No notice was taken of the matter until after the family had moved, settled down, and a member of the family took sick. The old witch woman was sent for and asked to account for the sickness. She said that someone must have removed the money. A search was made and no money was found. This caused the family to discontinue their belief in witches.

If you want to keep witches away, lay a straw broom in the doorway.

To break the charm of a witch, spit on the brush of a broom, once for the witch and once for each member of her family. Brush it down the rear of the fireplace; then place the broom across the front door. Finally, send for her. She can do no further harm unless you give her or lend her salt or something else.

By hanging a sieve on the door of your home you could be assured that a witch could not enter while you were asleep, because she had to go through every hole in the sieve.

As a protection against witches, hang a sieve on the door. Fill the tiny openings in the sieve with dirt. The witch cannot enter without getting the dirt out of each hole and going through it. If you hang a bread sifter on a door knob at night, you will find witches in it the next morning.

If you are troubled by witches, it is a good plan to sleep with a meal sifter over the face. When the witches come to worry you, they are compelled to pass back and forth through every mesh. By this time you will have had sufficient sleep and can get up.

If anybody comes to your house and acts crazy, go out to your front door and scatter salt, for he's a witch and it will keep the charm away.

A girl died in my old home town, and an old Negro man said it was a witch and put salt under all the stones and put it in the barrel of his gun and shot it off to scare them away.

Mr. E. R. heard about a witch doctor that treated a young girl who was deranged. He scattered salt in the spring and put salt and powder in his gun and shot under the house and around the spring. He said that this would cure her because witches couldn't stand salt and powder.

Burn salt in the fireplace to drive away witches, or to keep them from coming down the chimney.

The smoke of sulfur and frankincense and hallowed water scares witches.

Boil sweet milk on the fire, and stir it with a fork, if you want to drive the witches away.

To remove a witch's hold on a person, cut the witch out of the victim's leg.

The hair was tied in little plaits and balls to keep witches off.

If you are afflicted with witches, a hoodoo ball made of gum, and purchased with a piece of silver, will scare away the witches.

To ward off witches' spells, an old Negro man used to carry a small bundle of roots wrapped with several kinds of hair. He wouldn't go out a gate if a cross was made in front of it.

To keep a witch from bothering you, wear two hats.

Wear your coat turned inside out to keep witches from riding you. You can also wear your shirt wrong side out to keep a witch from bothering you.

Never go to bed with your shoes higher than your head, for if you do, the witches will be after you for three months.

To avoid being bewitched, never lie on your back while asleep.

If a knife is placed under the pillow, witches can do no harm to the one in bed.

Ghosts.

If you see a ghost coming toward you at night, say, "What in the name of the Lord do you want with me?" and it will go away.

To keep away spooks, make a new door facing out of new wood.

Put salt on the fire to keep ghosts away.

If a person murders another, he may guard himself against the ghost of the victim following him by placing ten tenpenny nails in the pocket of the victim.

A hot stream of air in a swamp reveals that haints are near.

The common attendant of haints is a little white dog.

If a picture falls, the house is haunted.

The Devil.

If a person draws a circle on the ground and counts five stars and five bricks while standing in the circle, and then runs around the house five times, he can then look under the house and see the Devil.

Take a black cat and carry it alive down to a spring of running water; next take a pot and fill it with water and put it over a fire to boil. When the water begins to boil, put the black cat in it alive and let the cat boil until all the meat has been boiled from its bones. When this has been done, pour the contents of the pot into the spring, and the bones of the cat will go up the stream instead of down the stream. The person who has done this will begin to see the Devil and all of his imps.

The fiddle and the banjo are instruments of the Devil. They are without exception laid aside when the musician has been changed from nature to grace.

Sneeze on Sunday, and the Devil will be with you all the week.

If you cut your nails on Sunday, you will be ruled by the Devil all the week.

Negroes believe that a person who has sold himself to the Devil can walk right out of the jail behind the jailor and never be caught because he has sold himself to the Devil and can do anything mean.

Further Reading in Folk Beliefs and Practices

Browne, Ray B. *Popular Beliefs and Practices from Alabama*. 1958.

Faulkner, Charles H., and Carol K. Buckles, eds. *Glimpses of Southern Appalachian Folk Culture*. 1978.

Hand, Wayland D., ed. *Frank C. Brown Collection of North Carolina Folklore*. Vol. 6. 1952.

Hyatt, Harry M. *Hoodoo, Conjuration, Witchcraft, Rootwork: Beliefs Accepted by Many Negroes and White Persons, These Being Orally Recorded Among Blacks and Whites*. 1970.

Kittredge, Lyman. *Witchcraft in Old and New England*. 1956.

Puckett, Newbell Niles. *Folk Beliefs of the Southern Negro*. 1926.

Randolph, Vance. *Ozark Superstitions*. 1947.

Thomas, Daniel L., and Lucy B. Thomas. *Kentucky Superstitions*. 1920.

Vogt, Evon Z., and Ray Hyman. *Water Witching U.S.A.* 1959.

PART FOUR

Customs

C ustom is broadly defined as a traditional behavior shared by members of a social group that serves as a mechanism for strengthening group cohesiveness and providing a sense of group identity. Like folk beliefs, some customs are performed to control one's fortune in life. Customs are commonly associated with the rites of passage: dressing newborns in pink if they are girls and blue if boys, the groom carrying his bride across the threshold, and holding a wake for the dead. Some customs are calendrical, such as shooting fireworks and eating black-eyed peas and hog jowl on New Year's Day, displaying a carved pumpkin and trick or treating on Halloween, and decorating a tree and hanging mistletoe during Christmas season. Customs are practiced individually or communally. All the articles in this section illustrate the communal aspect of customs.

The contemporary wedding custom of tying cans to the back of the newlyweds' car is likely a vestige of a much older and no longer practiced custom known as the shivaree. The term "shivaree" is derived from the French term *charivari* which means "a noisy mock serenade." The shivaree was introduced by the French who settled Louisiana and it subsequently became a popular wedding custom west of the Mississippi. The origin of the shivaree is also linked to the English *skimmington* (or *skimelton*). Centuries ago a *skimmington* was performed to publicly shame a man guilty of wife beating or a woman who committed adultery. Effigies of the offender were made and paraded about the community, and people gathered around the offender's house where they made noise with pots and pans and shouted insults. In America, the *skimmington* evolved over time into a custom with the more positive intention of celebrating a wedding. As described in "The Shivaree" by Frances Boshears, in Scott County and Morgan County, members of a community would gather around the house of the newlyweds and make merry by banging spoons and sticks on pots, pans, washtubs, and shovels, ringing bells, and singing. The noise would continue until the newlyweds invited the revelers into their house for food and drink. Sometimes the groom placed the bride into a cart and wheeled her around the courthouse square. Boshears notes that "you were considered unpopular" if you were not shivareed. The shivaree, also known as a "belling" in some parts of the South, often involved elements of hazing, such as dunking the groom in water and painting the bride with mercurochrome.

There are numerous customs associated with Easter, but one that is probably specific to Tennessee is the egg fight held in Peters Hollow near the community of Stoney Creek in Carter County. The first egg fight occurred in 1823, when residents of Iron Mountain challenged residents of Peters Hollow to a contest to determine who had the toughest egg. The "egg fight" does not, as the name suggests, involve contestants throwing eggs at one another, but tapping one boiled egg on another until one of the eggs cracks. Ultimately, one person ends up with the winning egg. In "Historic Egg Fight," Allison Yeager observes that the egg fight, which has taken place now for over 170 years, is a homecoming occasion; many participants who relocated to other states travel long distances to attend the event. The egg fight is not only an occasion for participants to connect with kindred and place but also a lot of fun. Yeager quotes one participant who said, "We like it better than Christmas."

In "Social Activities Associated with Two Rural Cemeteries in Coffee County, Tennessee," Donald B. Ball describes a custom known throughout the South as Decoration Day or Memorial Day. The custom arose out of a practical need to clean and maintain the grounds of family cemeteries. Decoration Day, like the egg fight, also serves as an occasion for a family reunion; relatives from near and far gather to share a good meal and catch up on family news. Ball observes that Decoration Day in Coffee County, and no doubt elsewhere as well, serves "primarily [as] a homecoming for the living and only secondarily as a day of remembrance for the dead."

The American love of fireworks is evident in the millions of dollars spent each year on them, particularly during the Fourth of July and New Year's Day. Before the emergence of the fireworks industry, guns and cannons were fired and, in some cases, communities would have an anvil shoot. Anvil shooting has a long history, and in the past it was performed during Christmas Eve, Armistice Day, and Election Day and in some communities was part of a shivaree. Today, an anvil shoot is associated with a variety of events, including the Fourth of July, New Year's Day, the opening of fiddling contests, and a variety of community festivals. As described in Bill Harrison and Charles K. Wolfe's article, "Shooting the Anvil," people enjoy the thrill of the thunderous sound produced by an anvil shoot. "The result," they observe, "is an earth-shaking roar that can be heard up to fifteen miles away. . . . The shock wave from a blast can flutter a man's pants legs at thirty feet away." At some events, an anvil shooting contest is held and the winner is determined by who is able to produce the best ring of an anvil. It is of interest to note that the authors speculate that this custom was introduced by German settlers.

The Shivaree
[1953]

Frances Boshears

A neighbor had some bees. The bees swarmed, that is, left the hive, and the neighbor got them into another hive by beating on a dish pan at the entrance of the other hive. I had watched him "settle the bees," as he called it, just a few days before, so when I heard a lot of noise made by the beating on pans, ringing of cowbells, and rattling of tin cans, I told my father: "Mr. Potter's bees have swarmed again."

My father then told me that they were "shivareeing" a neighboring couple that had just married. He explained that it was a custom in this section of East Tennessee to gather at the home of newly married couples to serenade or "shivaree" them. The friends of both the bride and groom met at a designated place, brought every conceivable noise maker, surrounded the home, and began making all the noise they possibly could. The couple either invited the friends into the house and served refreshments, or if they failed to do this, the groom was "taken for a ride" on a rail and thrown into the nearest creek or pond. This was done regardless of the season of the year or kind of weather.

So I was a very small child, about five years of age, when I had my first experience with shivareeing. I was allowed to join in the fun of this first one that I can remember. I still remember that I carried a tin pie pan and beat on it with a stick, and also that they treated us with candy and fruit.

As I grew older, I participated in many such serenades and discovered that it was an event that all newly married couples looked forward to because it was proof that you were well liked by the people of your community. It usually turned into a neighborhood party with lots of fun for all.

I remember when Jim and Bess, a couple of this community in Scott County, Tennessee, were married. We gathered in the usual manner with all of our noise making. After allowing us to have our fun for quite some time, they greeted us at the door and invited us into the house. Such a display of refreshments as they had for us! There was a much greater quantity of food than we would have at a wedding reception today. They had anticipated the event and prepared for it in advance.

Another experience that I remember very distinctly happened in Morgan County, Tennessee. This occurred when I was a senior in high school. One of the lady teachers in our school married one of the most prominent businessmen in the town.

A large group of people gathered together, including a number of high school students. We had pans, horns, cow bells, and a two-wheel cart. We made plenty of noise, because no one can do this better than a teen-age group.

When the couple appeared on the scene, the groom was made to put the bride in the cart and push her around the courthouse square. The town was the county seat of Morgan County, and as is typical in such towns, the main streets of the town formed a square around the courthouse. I suppose I might add that after the bride was taken out of the cart, the high school students put my boyfriend and me into the cart and pushed us around the square. No doubt that is why I remember this shivaree so vividly.

After the ride, we were all taken to the drug store and dutifully treated to ice cream, candy, and drinks.

People from all walks of life took part in the shivaree, as well as being "shivareed" themselves. You were considered unpopular if you were not.

Rather than be classed in the unpopular group, I had better tell next of my own shivaree. It happened in a kind of freakish way. It was the custom to "get them" right away, but we were away for quite some time after our marriage. Afterward we returned to the community, and my husband and I went to a basketball game. Some of our friends came to us and told us about the marriage of two of our friends. They said they were going to "get them" that night after the game, and asked us to join them. My husband was from another state and knew nothing about this custom. Naturally, he was eager to join the group to see what it was all about. I suspected, however, that we would probably be included, even though it had been quite some time since we had been married.

This was, of course, exactly what happened. When we gathered at the house and had been invited in, the first thing that was said was, "Now we have two couples instead of one." Naturally we helped to treat the crowd too rather than ride the rail or be dipped into the river.

The shivaree sounds all fun, and it generally was, but one in our community almost ended in tragedy. A crowd went to serenade a couple. Just as soon as they started their noise making, the man came to the door, shotgun in hand, and fired into the group. Fortunately they were scattered and far enough away so that no one was injured. He evidently didn't want to be disturbed. This event was the cause of the shivaree gradually becoming a custom of the past.

Historic Egg Fight
[1969]

Allison Yeager

U p a "holler" in East Tennessee on an Easter Sunday afternoon in 1968, dust rose from the narrow gravel road, cars inched slowly through the crowd, and men on horseback surveyed the action from an advantageous height while women still wearing Easter morning corsages visited with other women wearing kitchen aprons.

Beside the winding road a small stream gurgled over stones on its way to rendezvous with Stoney Creek in the valley. Dogwood blossoms whitened the hillsides, and creeping moss in colorful clusters brightened every yard of the little houses perched on the hillsides of Peters Hollow.

The occasion was the more-than-a-century-old contest between the hardy Anglo-Saxon peoples of Iron Mountain and Peters Hollow. A thousand people came and went through the afternoon of egg fighting.

The first such event took place in 1823 on the homestead of Mike Peters in the quaint, natural depression in the mountain. The men of Iron Mountain on the Holston Mountain side of Stoney Creek Valley had challenged the men of Peters Hollow to an egg fight on Easter Sunday morning. The contest starts after the morning church service on an already busy day of sunrise services, family reunions, and visits with friends.

The egg fight is a friendly game during which the contestants, carrying ample supplies of boiled, gaily colored eggs, mill through yards and up and down the hills challenging each other with the age-old cry, "I fight ye," or "Come hit me." The challenger holds his fighter egg between thumb, forefinger, and middle finger and taps lightly the egg cupped in the challenged person's palm. The egg which breaks is eliminated from the fight and given to the one who

◘ An egg-fighting circle, ca. 1980s. Participants have brought their eggs in preparation for the fight conducted between pairs of individuals within each circle. Photo by Eveleigh Stewart and courtesy of the *Elizabethton Star*.

◘ An egg fight in process, ca. 1980s. Photo by Eveleigh Stewart and courtesy of the *Elizabethton Star*.

broke it. The unbroken fighter egg is carried on to fight another. The fighter egg remaining unbroken after all the battles is declared the winner. Bantam chicken and guinea eggs are excluded from the contest.

In the early days, the owners of champion eggs claimed their hens were the "hard-scrabble" variety, getting their food by scratching in the dirt, not from eating mash.

◘ Winners of an egg fight holding their awards, ca. 1980s. Photo courtesy of the Elizabethton Star.

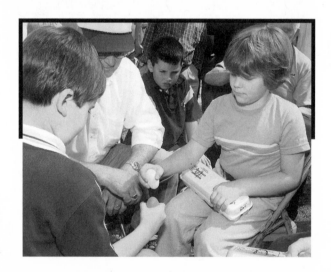

◘ Two young participants
engaged in a fight, ca.
1980s. Photo courtesy
of the *Elizabethton Star.*

In 1958 a little yellow hen became famous for her hard-shelled eggs then strangely refused to lay any eggs at all. She came to a tragic end by accidentally hanging herself in a tree.

Fred W. Behren of the *Elizabethton Star* wrote of the 1960 winner, Paul Peters, who had only ten dozen eggs for the fight and whose winning blue egg cracked about eight dozen eggs of opponents: "'God Almighty, you can't break the thing!' said Freeman Taylor, constable on Stoney Creek and runner-up in the egg fight last year. The blue egg of Paul Peters had practically drilled a hold in his own hard-shelled blue egg."

The 1967 champion was Robert Greer of Rome Hollow. Of his sixty colored eggs, a little brown toughie won. One year, a Blue Buster owned by a little boy, Deward Taylor, finished off 800 challengers to become the winner. Some contestants through the years started with as many as 800 eggs. One brought his collection in a wheelbarrow!

Two of the oldest participants in this unusual bit of Americana were Lee Taylor, who died in 1967 at the age of eighty-seven, and Spitter Jake Taylor, eighty-eight, who was ill and could not attend the 1968 event. Spitter Jake's father before him was a contestant also.

The 1968 winner of the Peters Hollow fight was Mrs. Ruth Peters Jones of Kennburg. Mrs. Peters, runner-up for five years, determined to be the first women winner and was. She fed her game hen crushed oyster shells.

Among those attending in 1968 were public officials, representatives of law enforcement and the legal profession, leaders of the valley's industries and unions, the Elizabethton Chamber of Commerce, and relatives of residents coming from as near as Virginia and as far as Chicago, Illinois, and Texas.

How did this seemingly strange custom come about? Easter had its own traditions, and this one goes back farther than any. Thomas Hyde, Orientalist, professor, and writer (1636–1703) wrote in *Oriental Sports* that the children of the early Christians in Mesopotamia bought eggs, stained them red in memory of the blood of Christ, and played this very game with the exact rules as those used today in East Tennessee. The game was later played in England and called "An Egg at Easter." The same game, with variations, was also played and called "Cock o' Two Eggs."

Children in Mexico battle with eggs a week before Lent each year, and in Holland and other European countries the egg breaking is done by players in two straight lines using matching colored eggs but otherwise following the ancient rules.

Frank Thone, an anthropologist, says, "Most of us have forgotten the symbolism once taught us at Sunday School: that the egg, capable of producing a living chick when its seemingly lifeless shell was cracked, is a sign and token of 'resurrection, and life everlasting,' breaking the seal of the sepulcher."

Around Stoney Creek are hollows: Peters, Rome, Liberty, Grindstaff, Estep, Hurley, Muddy, and Dry. The beautiful valley itself and these hollows have a unique, love-instilling power. Men born there drive one hundred and twenty miles round trip to work rather than move away. One young man said of the egg fight, "It's our best time of the year. We like it better than Christmas."

The eggs from the fight are not wasted. As many as can be used are given to a children's home. The rest are pickled and canned by the women of the hills and valley.

The knowledge of the egg game is known over the area. A physician in nearby Johnson City, Dr. H. B. Cupp, recalled Easter egg fighting as a childhood fun time for him and his childhood playmates.

Stoney Creek Valley has a road winding beside the creek and crossing its clear waters. Churches line this thoroughfare only a stone's throw from one another, yet no stones are thrown. Each church holds services and is well attended, yet all the inhabitants are held together by the love of the valley, its beauty, its traditions, its people.

In 1969, in this space-minded America, a religious custom of the ancient world survives. In this tiny valley where early American music is still sung, where hill homes are simple, people are friendly, and tables are loaded with hearty fare, this simple amusement may hopefully be a symbol of new life for America and for the world.

Social Activities Associated with Two Rural Cemeteries in Coffee County, Tennessee [1975]

Donald B. Ball

U surping the simplistic definition of "folk" as applied by Henry Glassie to indicate that which is "traditional" in terms of material culture, the practice in the southern United States of relatives of the community's deceased converging at the local cemeteries at a set time of the year may be termed a "folk" activity.[1] The occurrence of such events (termed "cemetery scraping") during the month of August has been included in the annual round of rural activities in eastern Louisiana,[2] and a less formal arrangement consisting of young men representing several families in the community volunteering to "clean the cemetery" has been observed in an unspecified summer month in Knox County, Kentucky.[3] The social events involving the two cemeteries in Coffee County, Tennessee, presently under discussion, although not concerned with the actual cleaning of the cemeteries, are held on the last Saturday in July (for the Robinson Cemetery) and the second Saturday in August (for the Shady Grove Cemetery). Significantly, all of these activities take place during the summer months and, being calendrical in occurrence, conform to a type of social interaction which is dependent upon a stabilized and orderly sequence of agricultural events.[4] The correlation of this orderly sequence and the date selected for the gathering at the Robinson Cemetery was expressed by one informant as that time of the year when farmers had "crops laid by"—that is, the period between cultivation/planting and harvesting.[5]

◘ Crowd gathered at Shady Grove Cemetery Decoration Day, Coffee County, Tennessee, August 10, 1974. Photo courtesy of Donald Ball.

The Robinson Cemetery lies at an elevation of 1,370 feet above sea level in a relatively hilly section of northwest Coffee County and is immediately adjacent to neighboring Cannon County.[6] Its earliest dated gravestone is inscribed "1883." Since that date a total of forty-eight marked graves (and several unmarked graves) have come to occupy the cemetery.[7] The use of the cemetery is predominantly reserved for the Robinson family and its branches. The Shady Grove Cemetery, located about thirteen miles to the east, lies at an elevation of 1,075 feet above sea level in the relatively flat northeast corner of Coffee County.[8] Its earliest dated gravestone is marked "1860." The cemetery at present contains over 430 known interments.[9] As opposed to the Robinson Cemetery, the Shady Grove Cemetery is considered to be non-restrictive and is available for use of all families in the community. The points of similarity between these cemeteries are: both are well maintained and fenced, both are still in active use and offer free burial plots to the families which use them, and the ground surface of individual graves in each has been leveled to facilitate maintenance.[10]

The first occurrence of the afterward annual family meetings at the Robinson Cemetery took place in 1908 and was attended by about forty people. At that time the first gravestones, in some cases a quarter of a century overdue, were erected. Through the intervening years the cemetery has been maintained by various family members and is presently cared for solely by one elderly gentleman who receives only small annual donations for his efforts.

◘ Lunch time at the Robinson Cemetery Decoration Day, Coffee County, Tennessee, July 27, 1974. Photo courtesy of Donald Ball.

In the course of his fieldwork the author arrived at the Robinson Cemetery in late morning on July 27, 1974, to find that a number of the participants had already preceded him and had, in fact, been congregating since ten o'clock. The weather on this day was mild with a light shower in the afternoon. Maximum attendance was noticed shortly after twelve noon, at which time approximately eighty persons were present. During this time about twenty-five to thirty cars and trucks, all carrying local license plates, were crowded onto the small area utilized for parking adjacent to the cemetery and along the nearby narrow gravel road. Two informants had differing opinions concerning the size of the crowd as compared to previous years—one felt that there was a tendency for the crowd to become slightly smaller each year since (apparently) the mid-1960s, while the other felt the crowd was as large "as always." Both, however, were pleased with the turnout and felt that, at least for that day, the event was well attended.

This annual gathering was alternately called both "Decoration Day" and "Memorial Day."[11] During the day, flowers (mostly plastic) were placed on twelve graves and earlier in the morning a brief sermon had been presented by a mid-aged friend of the family. One informant stated that she always made a practice of arriving late because she frankly thought these annual sermons to be too boring to suit her.

The actual conduct of the day's activities gave more the impression of a homecoming or family reunion than of any event so solemn sounding as a

"Decoration Day." Before lunch, conversation groups tended to cluster in various family and age sets with discussions ranging from state politics to crops. The mid-day meal was provided by lunch consisting of fried chicken, potato salad, bread, iced tea, cold drinks, and so forth and was spread on a large, permanently installed, wooden table in one corner of the cemetery. This year, as in years past, more food was brought than was consumed. Lunch was served on paper plates, and the low, flat gravestones served as convenient seats for youngster and adults alike. Following lunch, various conversational groups reconvened and an impromptu "baseball" game was begun with several youngsters dashing across a number of graves chasing the ball. The crowd had completely dispersed by 3:00 P.M., and the grounds were left in meticulous order.

The earliest recollection among the informants questioned of any annual event involving the Shady Grove Cemetery occurred in 1912. One informant believed, however, on the basis of comments made by her parents (now deceased) that annual gatherings were held at the cemetery before 1900. These early gatherings were devoted to "graveyard workin,'" and lunch was spread picnic style at the cemetery for the benefit of the men actually performing the work of cutting trees and brush and repairing the splitrail fence which formerly stood around the grounds.

Since earlier days, the chronology of local practices involving the cemetery become blurred, although it appears that during the 1930s the present practice of hiring labor for maintaining the cemetery began. The hiring of labor necessitated in turn the beginning of the now well-organized commercial aspects of the present "Shady Grove Annual Picnic." This commercialization through the years enabled the community, through a board of trustees, to establish in the spring of 1974 an endowment fund via the purchase of some $10,000 worth of interest-bearing bonds from a local bank. Hence, the activities of the picnic are composed of both longstanding social interactions combined with the newer commercial aspects. Fieldwork here was conducted on August 10, 1974. The weather on this day was generally hot and humid with no rain.

The annual "picnic" is now held at the Shady Grove Community Center, a former schoolhouse, located one-half mile from the cemetery. During the course of the day money is raised from the sale of refreshments (mainly cold drinks and hamburgers) beginning early in the morning and continuing into the evening. The funds thus received are supplemented by bingo and through the sale of chances on a handmade quilt for twenty-five cents and a calf for one dollar each. In previous years a cakewalk and auction were held in the schoolhouse during the evening, although this was limited only to the auction in 1974. The material sold at the auction is donated and consisted of clothes, household items, and some antiques.

As with the case of the annual gathering at the Robinson Cemetery, conversation groups tended to cluster largely in terms of kinship and age. None of those long familiar with the picnic doubted that its attendance of at least 300 persons and over 100 automobiles and trucks and out-of-state persons (to the knowledge of the author) represented Florida, Idaho, Indiana, and Ohio.

The age range of persons present extended from babes-in-arms to well over eighty years. Seating, particularly for the elderly, was provided in the form of a number of old church pews placed under the available shade trees. Entertainment through the day consisted of horseshoes, amplified tape recorded music (gospel and bluegrass), and, in the evening, a live country music band. Following the auction in the evening most people had left by about 11:00 P.M.

Although over seventy-five graves in the cemetery were decorated (again, with predominantly plastic flowers), the cemetery was not a major topic of conversion and no memorial service of any type was given for the deceased. The activities of the day were viewed by the participants as primarily a homecoming for the living and only secondarily as a day of remembrance for the dead.

In tracing briefly the history of the activities associated with each cemetery, a minimal pattern begins to emerge. Each began as a day set aside for the maintenance of the cemetery per se and only incidentally as a social event. Although a study of the sub-regional economics of Coffee County is beyond the scope of the present work, it would appear, at least subjectively, that a changing farm economy has caused a movement of people away from the hilly areas such as those surrounding the Robinson Cemetery and the increasing use of the Shady Grove Cemetery have likewise influenced the social activities involving them. The increasing demographic isolation of the Robinson Cemetery has not been conducive for any degree of rapid alteration of the Decoration Day concept—the donations, however small, which are given to the gentleman presently involved with the actual maintenance work may be roughly equated with the initial hiring of paid labor to maintain the Shady Grove Cemetery begun in the 1930s. Hence, while demographic pressure is not to be considered the sole reason for social change, in the present cases, of the modification of rural practices involving annual activities at a local cemetery, it would appear to exert a large degree of influence.

Interestingly, this process of evolving customs need not be traced over a long period. In the course of conversation with one informant, the observation was made somewhat cynically that Shady Grove no longer had an annual picnic—1974 marked the first year at which no lunches were spread out in the course of the day's activities by at least a few participating families. The absence of lunches was caused not by lack of interest on the part of the families which traditionally prepared and brought them but by the request of the local directors of the event. In carrying out this decision, the stretched wire-mesh tables located on the grounds and normally used for serving the lunches were removed in preparation for the "picnic."

In conclusion, the activities here discussed are presented as variants of a rural activity having wide distribution through the southeastern United States.

The fact that such gatherings are perpetuated indicates a continuing cohesiveness and sense of identification by the groups involved.[12] These activities, however, are as subject to change as any other work of man and, if to be understood in terms of both change and tradition, they must be studied while at least a few suitable informants are available. To observe only the outward form of any activity is to negate its function in the eyes of its participants and render fieldwork meaningless.

Notes and References Cited

1. Henry Glassie, *Pattern in the Material Folk Culture of the Eastern United States* (Philadelphia: University of Pennsylvania Press, 1968), 4.
2. Milton Newton Jr., "The Annual Round in the Upland South: The Synchronization of Man and Nature Through Culture," *Pioneer America* 3 (1971), No. 2, p. 68. See also Fred A. Tarpley, "Southern Cemeteries: Neglected Archives for the Folklorist," *Southern Folklore Quarterly* 27 (1963), No. 4, p. 329.
3. John Fetterman, *Stinking Creek* (New York: E. P. Dutton and Co., 1970), 123–25.
4. See Aram A. Yengoyan, "Ritual and Exchange in Aboriginal Australia: An Adaptive Interpretation of Male Initiation Rites," in Edwin N. Wilmsen, ed., *Social Exchange and Interaction,* Anthropological Papers No. 46 (Ann Arbor: Museum of Anthropology, University of Michigan, 1972), 6.
5. Rather than acknowledge singularly items relevant to the oral history or attitude toward the cemetery gathering, the author will acknowledge collectively, and gratefully, the following residents of Coffee, Davidson, and Rutherford Counties, Tennessee, for their assistance and hospitality during fieldwork at both gathering: Mrs. Gertrude Brown, Mrs. Lois Holt, Mrs. John Lewis, Mr. and Mrs. Claude L. McFarland, Mr. Rollyn McMahan, and Miss Sue Robinson. All of these persons were over sixty years of age and have attended, at least sporadically, their respective gatherings for a number of years.
6. USGS/TVA 7.5" Quadrangle "Beech Grove, Tenn." (1953).
7. Verna Thomas Jernigan and Sarah Marsh Shapard, *Tombstone Inscriptions of Coffee County, Tennessee* (Tullahoma: privately published by authors, c. 1972), 571–73.
8. USGS/TVA 7.5" Quadrangle "Morrison, Tenn." (1956).
9. Jernigan and Shapard, 579–606.
10. An interesting contrast to the recent practice of leveling graves was observed by the author during an August 1974 visit to the cemetery associated with the relatively close Gilley Hill Methodist Church in southern Cannon County. In this cemetery approximately twenty graves gave the

appearance of recent re-mounding during the cemetery's 1974 Decoration Day observances, thus giving some evidence for a local esthetic of the proper appearance of a grave. Speculatively, such mounds may well be a carry-over of the practice of placing "body-stones" over graves beginning in 18th-century England. Kenneth Lindley, *Of Graves and Epitaphs* (London: Hutchinson, 1965), 39–40.

11. While the historic origins of Decoration Day observances are beyond the scope of the present paper, future research may well show that such practices, as hinted at by Tarpley, 328–29, are Protestant modifications of the annually observed Roman Catholic All Saints' Day (November 1) and All Souls' Day (November 2). A short discussion of the evolution of these days into the Christian cycle from the pre-Christian feast day called Hallowmas is noted in George C. Homans, *English Villagers of the Thirteenth Century* (New York: Harper and Row, 1970), 355–56. A more contemporary description of the Catholic observance of these two days is recorded in Horace Miner, *St. Denis: A French-Canadian Parish* (Chicago: University of Chicago Press, 1963), 154–55.

12. A similar function has been assigned to university homecomings and alumni associations. See Robert Jermone Smith, "Festivals and Celebrations," in Richard M. Dorson, ed., *Folklore and Folklife: An Introduction* (Chicago: University of Chicago Press, 1972), 167–68.

Shooting the Anvil
[1977]

Bill Harrison and Charles K. Wolfe

I t is easier to describe the preparations for an anvil shoot than to define the shoot itself. One large (150 pound) blacksmith's anvil is filled with black powder, a second anvil is placed on top of the powder, and the charge is set off. The resulting roar can be heard for miles around; the earth literally shakes; shock waves flutter an onlooker's clothes; the top anvil flies high into the air. For many people who have not been in battle, the anvil shoot is the loudest, most devastating sound they have ever heard. Yet it is an authentic sound from America's past, and the excitement of an anvil shoot was very much a part of the holiday life of turn-of-the-century America. But little is really known about the history of this impressive custom. The present study is an attempt to remedy this by collating documented references to anvil shooting's history to the differences in technique used at various times and places and to the different occasions on which the anvil has been shot. Both authors have for some years been fascinated with the provenance of anvil shooting. Bill Harrison, who has recently revived the custom of anvil shooting at fiddling contests throughout the South, is himself one of the very few practitioners of the art left and has been instrumental in locating informants and information about the subject. The material that follows is the result of a joint collation and evaluation of the leads that these informants have provided.

While anvil shooting is remembered by many older people today, we have been unable to find any serious attempts to collate information about it or to study it as a well-defined folk custom. The standard dictionaries of language and folklore, as well as standard encyclopedias, do not list entries for "anvil shooting"; indexes and bibliographies of folk studies have yielded no references to the subject. Research on the topic in the Library of Congress has failed to uncover any references to it. Aside from our own delving into the history of the custom, the only research on the subject currently under way has been done by Ruby E. Hammersly of New Pine Creek, Oregon. Mrs. Hammersly, who remembers the anvil shoot from her own childhood, has done extensive interviewing and corresponding with natives of the West Coast who remember aspects of the anvil shoot. She has also discovered numerous references to anvil shooting in printed sources about the West. We are indebted to her for bringing to our attention many of the references listed in our notes—especially those references to anvil shooting in Oregon and Washington. However, virtually all the other references in this study come from personal communication with informants in the Upper South.

For approximately twenty years, Bill Harrison has been shooting the anvil at various celebrations throughout the South. Harrison, a retired civil servant, learned his anvil shooting skills from an old blacksmith named Jakie Hathcoat who lived a few miles north of Athens, Alabama, near the Tennessee-Alabama line. At the time (late 1950s) Hathcoat was seventy and had not shot the anvil for years until Harrison prevailed upon him to demonstrate how it was done.

Coauthor Harrison was born in 1920 in Salem, Alabama, a small hill community northeast of Athens. Although anvil shooting had died out in the community proper before he was born, the anvils were still shot throughout the 1920s farther back in the hills. "They would shoot the anvils on Christmas Eve, and I recall hearing the distant thunder of the shoots when I was five or six, and asking my father what it was. When he told me, I was intensely curious about it and desperately wanted to see it performed."

One of the most famous anvil shooters in the Athens community at that time was an old man named Spot Starkey (Perry Woodson Starkey, 1863–1926). A brief sketch of his life suggests the kind of men that were attracted to anvil shooting as a sport. Starkey was described by his grandson as "a tobacco-chewing blacksmith, circuit-riding Methodist preacher, fiddler, and anvil shooter. He loved to preach, play in the local fiddlers' contests, and work in the blacksmith shop." His daughter clarified this: "He loved his family, the Methodist church, his fiddle, and anvils, in that order." Starkey was the last man to shoot the anvil in Salem; he never failed to shoot the anvil every Christmas Eve as long as he lived there. Starkey last shot the anvils in Salem in 1916; that next year he moved to Athens and there did not shoot the anvil again until the end of World War I. Starkey's grandson recalled: "It was then that I helped my grandfather shoot the anvils in front of the blacksmith shop. I was nine years old. We couldn't get black gunpowder in bulk due to the scarcity caused by the war. So we emptied the black powder from shotgun shells to use. This powder wasn't too good; [it was] too coarse and it took us three tries to get off a shot. Finally my grandfather dampened a newspaper and put it over the charge between the anvils and touched it off with a big, red-hot iron rod heated in his forge. It went off with a big boom, which tickled him very much."[1]

Methodology

The exact procedure Harrison uses in shooting the anvil is derived from a combination of traditional lore and his own trial and error. He starts with two anvils of approximately the same weight; at present he is using a 180-pound anvil for the base and a 150-pound anvil for the top. Both of Harrison's anvils are made of steel; cast iron anvils, or those with part of the body made of cast iron, have been known to break off or even fly apart during the explosion, creating a serious danger to spectators. Harrison turns the bottom anvil upside down on a level, open area of ground and fills the cavity (the one made by casting the anvil) full of black powder. Good results are obtained by using a #4 "F grain" black powder—a very finely ground black powder, generally considered the best available. (The finer the powder, the faster the burn and the bigger the explosion.)

After the anvil base has been filled with powder—Bill's anvil generally takes about half a pound of powder—a heavy piece of flat metal is placed over the charge. This is to prevent air from getting into the powder; again, the less air that gets into the powder charge, the bigger the explosion. The use of a piece of heavy flat metal as a damper is an innovation that Harrison himself made in refining his craft. Next a dynamite fuse is inserted under the damper plate into the powder, and then the second anvil is placed right side up on top of the plate. The assembly is now ready for firing.

Bill uses a standard dynamite fuse, tar coated with a powder core, that is about 18 inches long. Since these fuses burn at the rate of approximately one foot per minute, this gives everyone ample time to back off—usually to a radius of at least fifty feet. One of the possible dangers in the fuse system is the chance that the fuse can go out. This generally happens when the tar coating melts and creates a blob of molten tar, which keeps the powder core from igniting. An old coal miner some years ago showed Harrison how to counteract this effect. Now Bill splits the end of the fuse, inserts the head of a kitchen match, and then lights the fuse. The head of the kitchen match explodes and ignites the powder core of the fuse, assuring instant ignition. The result is an earth-shaking roar that can be heard up to fifteen miles away; the top anvil is often thrown as high as twenty feet into the air. The trajectory of the top anvil is nearly always straight up, and in some cases it falls back directly on the bottom anvil. The shock wave from a blast can flutter a man's pants legs at thirty feet away.

Harrison has refined his method over the years until it is as safe as he can make it and as satisfying (in terms of a loud explosion) as he wants it. But his methodology differs in some important respects from some of the older

◘ Co-author Bill Harrison priming an anvil for a shoot, ca. 1975. Photo courtesy of the Center for Popular Music, Middle Tennessee State University.

traditional methods we have been able to document. One of the major differences is in the firing system. Numerous accounts from the nineteenth century describe shooters detonating the powder charge by lighting a powder trail with a red-hot poker or stick. In such methods, the anvil bottom would be filled with powder, as usual, and a powder trail would be scattered from the charge of powder in the base cavity to the edge of the anvil. The other anvil would then be placed on top, and the shooter would apply a long metal rod, heated to a cherry red in a fire, to the powder trail. This way of setting off the charge is very similar to the "touch hole" method of firing a cannon. How long these rods were would presumably depend on the amount of the powder charge and/or the courage (or sobriety) of the shooter. We have documentation of the use of iron rods 10 feet long (Indiana, 1890s),[2] 16 feet long by ½ inch thick (Washington state, pre–World War I),[3] and 15 feet long by ½ to ¼ inch thick (Oregon 1890s).[4] An informant from Middle Tennessee reported that about the turn of the century he witnessed yet another method: "Actually, what I saw used as a small lad . . . was a piece of iron rod wired to the longest cain [sic] they could get—that powder trail left out to the edge bears no resemblance whatever to a time fuse."[5] Detonation occurred after the iron rod, heated red hot, was thrust into the powder trail. One informant recalls that the charge was somehow ignited by batteries,[6] though it is difficult to see how this would have caused the necessary spark to set off the powder. And on at least one auspicious occasion coauthor Harrison was party to an attempt to ignite a charge on which a fuse was unavailable by building a dry-grass fire around the anvil; this method was successful, if rough on nerves.

There are also different methods of forming the powder chamber. One common alternative to the damper plate is the use of the "torus ring": this was described by a correspondent from California writing in the *American West Magazine* in 1968.

> The blacksmith takes a short length of round iron rod, say, an inch or so in diameter, heats it red hot, and hammer-welds it into a torus, or ring, about the size of a large doughnut. He files a narrow groove across one face of the torus, so that a "touch hole" extending from the space inside it to the space outside it is formed. The ring is laid on the smooth face of an anvil with the groove at the bottom, filled level full with fine black powder, and the second anvil is placed with its smooth side down on top of the filled ring. A small pile of powder is tamped against the outside, right opposite the touch hole, then a suitable long fuse is tucked into the pile and the assembly is ready to fire.[7]

The use of a "round band" to hold the powder was also reported from an informant in Oregon describing a turn-of-the-century anvil shoot.[8] Different damping devices have also been used to keep air from the powder chamber; an 1890s account from Indiana describes the use of damp cardboard,[9] while a similar account from turn-of-the-century Oregon describes an old leather shoe tongue being used.[10] Without some sort of damping element over the powder chamber to make it tight, a virtually forceless "flash-out" will result and the top anvil will hardly move.

The object of anvil shooting is traditionally two-fold: to create a loud, satisfying boom and to propel the top anvil as high into the air as possible. But in at least one case, we have found that the anvil shooter was expected to propel the top anvil only a foot or so in order that it would always fall back on the first, "causing a big noise of explosion followed by the ring of the anvil as it came down again on the bottom anvil" (Oregon, 1892).[11] And a modern Mississippi anvil shooter asserts that, in anvil shooting competitions, "The sport doesn't involve how much noise can be made . . . or how high the top anvil will go." The exploding powder "causes the bottom anvil to ring, and the trick to winning is having a better ring."[12] Another account mentions that once in Massachusetts a railroad coupling pin was inserted into the powder and fired from an anvil.[13]

Some people interviewed also thought that at times the bottom anvil was left right side up, and the powder packed into the "rod" hole, a trough an inch or so wide and several inches deep that was on top of the anvil.[14] Others recalled packing the "hardy hole" on the face of the anvil with powder. The description quoted above explaining the use of the torus also mentions that the bottom anvil was left right side up, and the top anvil inverted, in order to get the two smooth surfaces necessary for a tight powder chamber. This difference in methodology is also complicated by the fact that different types and sizes of anvils have different features and dimensions.[15]

Occasions for Anvil Shooting

During the last ten years, the anvil shoot has often been used to open fiddling contests and folk music festivals in Georgia, Alabama, Tennessee, and Kentucky. It is at present unclear just how far back this association of anvil shooting with music per se goes. Fiddling contests and square dances and other music-making occasions have often been associated in the mid-South with traditional holidays, such as the Fourth of July, Labor Day, and election days. We have been able to document cases of anvil shooting to celebrate a number of these more traditional holidays, including the Fourth of July, Christmas, elections, weddings, and Armistice Day. We have also found some evidence of anvil shooting on other occasions not related to traditional frontier celebrations.

Anvil shooting was used to celebrate the Fourth of July well before the Civil War. Herman Francis Reinhart, describing his experiences making a trip west by wagon train in 1851, remarks at one point: "That afternoon we lay over on the Sweetwater River and celebrated the Fourth of July with Anvils and guns and rested our stock."[16] In *Love Song of the Plains,* author Mari S. Sandoz describes a Fourth of July picnic in 1854 held at the then-new city of Omaha, on what was later to be called Capitol Hill:

> After a couple of preliminary speeches, the two blacksmith anvils were set up on a bare knoll, one with a fused bag of blasting powder laid in the worn little hollow, the other anvil upside down on top of it, and the fuse lighted to the mock alarm and squeals from the girls and some of the women as they stuffed their fingers into their ears. The men ran, the black fuse gave one last sputter, followed by a great bang as the anvils flew apart, one going high and dropping, end over end, and rolling, while a stinking cloud of blue smoke spread off over the bottoms. It wasn't a cannon, but as a makeshift it was really more fun.[17]

This passage suggests some of the social context surrounding the shooting, that is, that it was part of a traditional Fourth celebration, with political speeches. If the speeches were really "preliminary" to the shoot, it also suggests that the practice was looked on as something special in the lives of the frontier community. In other instances, the anvil shoot was not part of a formal celebration but was invested with a certain type of symbolism. In two accounts from the Midwest, in Indiana and Illinois, both dating from about the turn of the century, we find the anvil being shot at midnight between July 3 and July 4, presumably as a device to initiate the Independence Day celebrations.[18] The account from Fairbury, Illinois, undated, describes a midnight anvil shoot as part of a larger midnight celebration: "For all the good Americans of Fairbury, the celebration began at midnight with firecrackers, rockets, torpedoes, small cannon and 'anvils.'" Similar accounts dating from 1900–1910 describe a slightly different practice in the far West (Oregon and California); there the anvil was shot at "4 a.m." on the morning of the Fourth.[19] Presumably this was about dawn and served to wake the people up to their Independence Celebration. Another account from Massachusetts describes boys firing anvils during the early morning hours of the Fourth and disturbing hotel guests.[20] One of the most curious instances of number symbolism attaching itself to the anvil shoot comes from an interview of Ruby E. Hammersly with William Arzner of Lakeview, Oregon, whose father and uncles (first-generation German immigrants) would fire the anvils thirteen times for the celebration in days prior to World War I.[21] Though the informant does not specifically state it, the number thirteen presumably was derived from the thirteen stripes on the flag. As recently as July 1968, the popular magazine American West ran instructions on how to shoot an anvil if one wished to do so "in celebration of an old-time Fourth of July."[22] One of the very few anvil shooters still practicing today, Holt Hill of Spankum Hollow, Tennessee (Moore County, near Lynchburg), still customarily fires the anvil on Independence Day at nearby Tullahoma, Tennessee.

If accounts from the West and Midwest emphasize the anvil shoot to celebrate the Fourth of July, several accounts from the South describe the custom in conjunction with Armistice Day. One came from the late President Lyndon B. Johnson; speaking to NASA officials at Huntsville, Alabama's, Redstone Arsenal in 1964, the president said: "In this century in which we live, all my life we have been either preparing for war or fighting a war or protecting ourselves from war. When I grew up as a kid, one of my first real memories was hearing the powder go off on an anvil on Armistice Day."[23] A more specific occasion was recalled by Mr. J. B. Bender: "The date, November 11, 1918; the place, the public square of Shelbyville, Tennessee, where as a lad of fifteen I witnessed the celebration of the end of World War I. And the principal and most obvious mode of celebration was anvil shooting. They must have had several pairs of anvils as it seems that the thunderous noise, loud or louder than a cannon, reverberated every few seconds."[24] It is unclear whether the anvil shooting in Shelbyville was continued as a regular Armistice Day custom or whether it was just a one-shot (no pun intended) affair. However, numerous people have

◘ The firing of an anvil, unknown locale, ca. 1970s. Photo courtesy of the Center for Popular Music, Middle Tennessee State University.

recalled to us how small towns across the South celebrated the end of World War I by firing anvils.

Another form of multiple anvil shooting involved shooting the anvils in rounds, where a blacksmith in one community would shoot an anvil and then wait for an answering shot from a nearby community. (The sound of an anvil shot would, depending on weather conditions, carry as far as fifteen miles, or even further.) Such rounds were occasionally set up as part of the Christmas celebrations in rural Middle Tennessee at the turn of the century. Mr. J. E. Coleman described in a letter such a Christmas celebration:

In our community, anvil shooting was generally indulged in Christmas Eve night. Sixty years ago blacksmith shops were located roughly within ten miles of each other; naturally that is where you would find two anvils. Always, out in back of the shop was the place where wagon tires were heated for shrinking on the wheels; this operation required a clear spot in which to build a sizeable fire safely. Weather being cold, a good bon-fire was also a part of the anvil shoot and so to this spot they brought. The smaller one is turned upside down, using the largest one on top—we had a big 250-pound "Peter Wright" which always went on the top. You get a good bon-fire going; the iron-rod wired to the long cain-pole is fixed and placed in it to get red-hot and along about eight o'clock you touch off the first shot. Everyone has to get well back because a big one will bounce a 250-pound anvil ten to twelve feet in the air . . . Then everyone gathers round the fire rather quiet-like to listen; pretty soon, there comes the answering shot from the blacksmith shop in the next community. Then, another wait for the shot from the shop up the other way. Then it was your time again. As I recall, the shots were roughly about 30 minutes apart and an "anvil shoot" never involved more than four to six shots.[25]

In interviewing numerous older blacksmiths throughout the mid-South, we have found that in this region, Christmas Eve was by far the most common time for shooting anvils. (It is probably related to the southern custom of celebrating Christmas Eve with firecrackers.) C. H. McKennon's book *Iron Men* also refers to Christmas anvil shooting in Ft. Smith, Arkansas, in 1891, though not in rounds.[26]

Anvil shooting also had a political dimension and was on occasion used to celebrate the election of favorite sons to political office. Persistent stories about Davy Crockett tell about how, in a West Tennessee frontier village, he was afforded the honor of touching the red-hot poker to the loaded anvil to celebrate his election to the U.S. Congress. A blacksmith from Fayetteville, Tennessee, witnessed a similar political anvil shoot in 1893, when Cleveland was elected president and the Democratic Party made a major sweep in Congress, thus controlling both houses and the presidency for the first time since the Civil War. Celebrations were held across the South, and in Fayetteville, Tennessee, the anvil was shot in batteries. Brave wielders of red-hot pokers set off charges by order of a tipsy, self-appointed commander.[27]

Shooting the anvil might well have been a way to frighten Indians on the frontier. One of our informants, a New England resident, stated that he had been told by older natives in his area that the anvil shoot was used to simulate cannon fire in poorly fortified frontier settlements. The Indians, thinking the settlement would have a cannon, would be less inclined to attack. (This is the origin of Harrison's alternate name for the anvil shoot, the "pore man's cannon.") We have been unable to find much documentary evidence to support theory, but the account of the 1854 July Fourth picnic at Omaha cited earlier does mention an Indian response to the shooting:

> After the echoes of the salute to Independence Day were gone, one of the men started the real spread-eagle oration of the day, but he hadn't gone very far when the report of the anvils along the river brought results—a lot of Indians running into sight along the bluffs, whooping and yelling at what seemed a cannon on their land.[28]

Note, however, that the Indian response is hardly one of fear; the sound of the anvil shoot here causes them to attack.

There were a number of other occasions for firing anvils. In Valdosta, Georgia, it was the custom to commemorate the "lost cause" by setting off mournful anvil blasts on Confederate Reunion Days.[29] Other uses were less serious. In Warm Springs, Georgia, a group of young sports who called themselves the Cherokee Hell Raisers were fond of disrupting Negro baptisms with surprise anvil shoots; however, in an exemplary display of bipartisanship, they also routinely broke up meetings of the local Ku Klux Klan in the 1920s.[30] In southern Missouri, anvil shoots were sometimes performed during the course of a shivaree in honor of newly married couples; sometimes the anvils were discharged only a few yards from the couple's bedroom window.[31] We have even found one oral report of anvil shooting contests held on the town square at Jasper, Tennessee, in the Sequatchie Valley, in the early 1930s; the contestants would line up their anvils and see which man could shoot his anvil the highest. In the 1960s, an anvil shoot was scheduled at the army's Redstone Arsenal in Huntsville, Alabama, to honor space expert Dr. Werner von Braun. This curious juxtaposition of modern and primitive aerodynamics never came off, though, as the security officers at the arsenal vetoed the plan as simply too dangerous in the confines of such an installation.

In addition to the fiddling contest, another festival that includes anvil shooting today is the Civil War reenactments that are often held in national parks and battlefields. At such a reenactment in Lexington, Kentucky, in July 1971, small (three to five pounds) anvils were shot from mortars to initiate the mock battle. After the reenactment itself, the cannoneers competed in an anvil shooting contest with the same small, "work-bench" anvils. A series of concentric flour circles were drawn on the ground with the anvil assembly in the center. One aim of the competition was to see whose anvil would fall closest to the center of this target; hitting the circle immediately around the bottom anvil, or hitting the bottom anvil itself with the top one, gained the contestant the maximum points. Some of the cannoneers at the Lexington ceremony were so skilled that they were able to bring the top anvil down directly on the bottom one. (These small anvils were shot very much like the bigger ones, with powder being placed in the bottom inverted anvil, a damper plate placed, a fuse inserted, and the top anvil positioned.) The contest also involved shooting for height. Contestants would fire different rounds, each round using a prescribed amount of powder, such as two ounces, five ounces, eight ounces, etc. Nearby telephone poles were used as informal gauges, with some shots going as high as the length of two telephone poles. Our informant who witnessed these contests said that many of the cannoneers were seemingly quite familiar with this brand of "baby anvil" shooting.[32]

Origins of Anvil Shooting

In pioneer communities, anvil shooting was often associated with blacksmiths and the smith's art, and many of the informants for this study have been black-smiths or former blacksmiths. It is perhaps significant that in earlier cultures smiths have often attributed to them supernatural powers. The fact that so many of our people could remember anvil shoots so vividly after fifty or sixty years suggests that at least a vestige of this awe was preserved through the anvil shoot.

Many of the blacksmiths we interviewed were second- or third-generation German immigrants, and nearly all of them were taught anvil shooting by their fathers. For instance, two old German blacksmiths were interviewed in Loretta, Tennessee, a community settled in the late 1800s by largely German immigrants; both of these smiths, now in their eighties, were taught their art by their fathers, first-generation Germans. An interview with William Arzner quoted earlier describes a family of anvil-shooting smiths who were first-generation German immigrants.[33] It is generally accepted that the southern custom of shooting firecrackers at Christmas Eve is of German origin, and we have seen that anvil shooting was commonly practiced on Christmas Eve.

In 1971 Ruby E. Hammersly interviewed Anton Erlebach, who immigrated to the Tiller, Oregon, area about 1906 from Bohemia, Austria. He was asked if he remembered anything like anvil shooting in the old country. "As a child of under ten years, he remembers that his father, at certain holiday celebrations, would perform some kind of feat wherein he used black powder which he lighted with a long pole, and which produced an awfully big noise that echoed over the mountains of his native Austria. He has no memory of anvils being used, but he thinks it possible that they were."[34]

Erlebach's statement, along with the testimony of other first-generation German immigrants who apparently came to the country well versed in anvil-shooting skill, is circumstantial evidence, to be sure, but it strongly suggests some sort of Germanic origin for the practice. Beyond this, though, there is simply not enough evidence to conjecture further. Hopefully future research into European folk celebratory customs will clarify the extent to which American anvil shooting was borrowed from the old world. Wherever it came from, it seems to have spread pretty well over the United States during the western expansion of the nineteenth century; we have documentation on shoots all the way from Massachusetts to Alabama, and from the Midwest to the California coast.

Conclusions

With anvil shooting as much a part of folk wisdom as it is, it seems strange that so little has been written about it. Like other aspects of folklife, some neglect can be attributed to collectors' continuing preoccupation with folk literature. Other reasons may have to do with the fact that, in many parts of the country, the custom has virtually died out, and in many places two or three generations have grown up not even knowing what an anvil shoot was. As far as we can determine, only three people are actively practicing heavy anvil shooting in the South today: Bill Harrison of Madison, Alabama; Holt Hill in Moore County, Tennessee; and Buddy Tate in Elizabeth, Mississippi. Yet just the activities of these three shooters have created a wave of publicity and interest in anvil shooting. Indeed, modern anvil shooting is creating its own bits of lore and legend. We have heard numerous versions of the tale of "the man who rode an anvil," about a man who got drunk and decided to ride the top anvil on an anvil shoot. The story is apparently rooted in an actual event that occurred in the 1920s in northern Alabama, but it has acquired all kinds of variations when told and retold around the annual fiddling conventions at Athens, Alabama. In some cases, the man loses both arms, in some cases an arm and a leg, in some cases both eyes and both eardrums; in no version does his effrontery remain unpunished.

All of which brings us to one of the most salient characteristics of anvil shooting: the fact that it is highly dangerous. No one should attempt to shoot an anvil without having had personal, detailed instruction from one who has done it. A half pound of black powder has the potential for causing a great deal of injury in a crowd of incautious onlookers or to a careless shooter. One 1927 newspaper clipping in our files announces the funeral of Steven M. Harris, killed while shooting anvils for the Fourth of July celebration; after the first anvil had been fired, "the second blast caused the accident, somehow hurling the long heated firing rod into Mr. Harris as he ignited the powder."[35] Many other people we talked to had tales of maiming and even death to accompany their information about the custom itself. Certainly we would not wish that anyone attempt to shoot an anvil simply on the basis of reading this article.

More research is needed to determine the origin of the anvil shoot, to explore its dissemination throughout the land, and to document more fully the exact functions it has played and continues to play in the lives of the people. We have hoped here to demonstrate that anvil shooting is a legitimate folk art with a long and distinguished pedigree, and that it is much more widely known by people around the country than the meager published data on it would indicate. However, this study must be considered a preliminary report, and the authors welcome any further information about one of the most assertive sounds from America's past: the anvil shoot.

Notes and References Cited

1. Material on Spot Starkey is drawn from interviews with Ross Starkey, Huntsville, Alabama, February 1977; grandson Maurice Nichols, Athens, Alabama, September 1976; daughter Mrs. Ora Nichols, Athens, Alabama, September 1976; and Lynn Beasley, Salem, Alabama, early 1960s.
2. Letter from the late Dorothy Marlatt, Rensselaer, Indiana, to Ruby E. Hammersly, describing interview with an unidentified eighty-year-old blacksmith in 1971.
3. Interview with the late James H. Evans, near Milo, Oregon.
4. Statement of Charles Mansall Hall, Douglas County, Oregon, October 3, 1938; furnished courtesy of George B. Abdill, director of the Douglas County Museum, Roseburg, Douglas County, Oregon.
5. Letter from J. E. Coleman, Nashville, Tennessee, November 16, 1964.
6. Interview of William J. Lawson by Ruby Hammersly, 1970; Mr. Lawson was raised in the Midwest and later moved to the Los Angeles area.
7. "The Truth About Anvils," *American West* 5, no. 6 (November 1968): 58. An earlier article on anvil shooting had appeared in the July 1968 issue of the magazine, but we have been unable to locate a copy of the earlier issue.
8. Charles Mansall Hall.
9. Letter from Dorothy Marlatt. Note also that this method of damping was described by the relatives of Spot Starkey; cf. above.
10. James H. Evans.
11. Interview of Washington Hughes, retired railroad conductor in his seventies, Roseburg, Oregon, by Ruby Hammersly, ca. 1974.
12. "Anvil Shootin," *Delta Democrat-Times* (Greenville, Mississippi), November 21, 1976, 1.
13. Charles O. Dean, "Under the Spreading Chestnut Tree . . . ," *Good Old Days,* July 1969, 34.
14. Letter from J. B. Bender, Nashville, Tennessee, to Bill Harrison, November 17, 1964.
15. For a history of anvils as they developed in America, see Clarence T. Hubbard, "Anvils in America," *Antiques Journal* 25, no. 8 (August 1970): 26–28. Hubbard dates the first American anvils from the sixteenth century, when they were copied after anvils brought from Europe. Also see Alex W. Bealer, *The Art of Blacksmithing* (New York: Funk and Wagnalls, 1969).

16. Herman Francis Reinhart, *The Golden Frontier* (Austin: University of Texas Press, 1962), 18; this is a printing of an earlier account by Reinhart of his pioneer experiences going west by wagon train in 1851. Another account of firing anvils in the Old West is found in Effie O. Read, *White Pine Lang Syne: A True History of White Pine County, Nevada* (Denver: Big Mountain Press, 1965), 189, where the author describes a Fourth of July anvil firing in 1883 in Taylor, Nevada (citation courtesy of Prof. Kenneth Clarke).

17. Mari S. Sandoz, *Love Song of the Plains* (New York: Harper, 1961), 147–48.

18. Letter from Dorothy Marlatt, Indiana; Alma Lewis-James, *Stuffed Clubs and Antimacassars* (Fairbury, Ill.: Privately printed, n.d.), 105.

19. Interview of Mrs. Dave Darst, Lake City Oregon, by Mrs. Ruby Hammersly, ca. 1974; Charles Mansall Hall.

20. Charles O. Dean.

21. Interview of William Arzner, Lakeview, Oregon, by Ruby Hammersly, ca. 1974.

22. "Truth About Anvils."

23. Excerpt from President Lyndon B. Johnson's remarks to NASA officials, August 1, 1964, Huntsville, Alabama, transcript MS, 17–18 (authors' files).

24. Letter from J. B. Bender.

25. J. E. Coleman. The "Peter Wright" model anvil referred to is a very old model anvil whose manufacture was discontinued many years ago. Co-author Harrison has such a model anvil and has been able to trace it back several generations.

26. C. H. McKennon, *Iron Men* (New York: Doubleday, 1967), 114. McKennon is a newspaperman from Tulsa, and his book is based on extensive research and based on actual pioneer people.

27. Interview with the late E. B. Noles by Bill Harrison, at Noles's blacksmith shop in Fayetteville, Tennessee, 1963. Noles was in his late seventies at the time.

28. Sandoz, *Love Song of the Plains,* 149.

29. Interview with T. C. Floyd, 1966, Huntsville, Alabama, by Bill Harrison. (Mr. Floyd was a former resident of Warm Springs, Georgia.)

30. T. C. Floyd.

31. Interview with Robert King, Walnut Grove, Missouri, August 1976, by Charles K. Wolfe. King was in his early seventies at the time.

32. Interview with Michael McMullen, Murfreesboro, Tennessee, January 1977, by Charles K. Wolfe.

33. William Arzner.

34. Letter from Ruby E. Hammersly, January 20, 1971.

35. "Killed on 4th, Steve Harris Laid to Rest," *Cheny (Oreg.) Free Press,* July 7, 1927, 1.

Further Reading
in Customs

Brown, Roger L. *Ghost Dancing on the Cracker Circuit: The Culture of Festivals in the American South.* 1997.

Cohen, Hennig, and Tristram P. Coffin. *The Folklore of American Holidays.* 1987.

Faulkner, Charles H., and Carol K. Buckles, eds. *Glimpses of Southern Appalachian Folk Culture.* 1978.

Hatch, Jane M. *The American Book of Days.* 1978.

Rehder, John B. *Appalachian Folkways.* 2004.

PART FIVE

Play and Recreation Lore

For purposes of definition, play involves the interactions of young people with other people (whether younger or older) in ritualized ways that involve both verbal and nonverbal components. Anything but frivolous to young people, play activities are integral to the process of learning about how to interact with others and how to abide by rules. Furthermore, some forms of play enable children to develop motor and mental skills. In contrast, recreation involves various activities of adults that provide diversion from hard work and the psychological stresses of everyday life. Indeed, during earlier times, particularly in rural settings, Tennesseans valued recreation activities not only because they offered temporary escape from work but also because they provided people with an opportunity for social interaction with other family or community members.

In the essay "'Let's Go Hunting': A Nursery Song and Its Background," West Livaudais examines the historical and cultural context for a nursery song recorded in the early 1960s by a college student who lived in Memphis. The song had circulated within several generations of the student's family on both sides of the Mississippi River, but Livaudais traces "Let's Go Hunting" back to England and Scotland and dates the earliest version of the song to at least the mid-seventeenth century. The seemingly absurd story told in the lyrics of this song—like other nursery songs through the ages—no doubt encouraged the psychological development of young listeners by engaging their imaginations.

Martha Freedle's essay, "Children's Games and Amusements in Sumner County in the Good Ol' Days," surveys the manifestations of a major genre of children's folkore in one West Tennessee county. Because of changes to the social, geographical, and material environment in which young people are raised, the genre of traditional children's games is today virtually extinct. While it is limited in terms of scope of coverage, Freedle's essay effectively categorizes the basic forms of children's games popular among many Tennessee children in an earlier era. Freedle implies that while much has been gained during the "progress" of the last century, much has been lost. While they may have displaced traditional children's games, computer games and other technology-based entertainments do not replace all of the functions of their predecessors, particularly social interaction.

The other essay in this part explores one form of adult recreation: cockfighting. Charles R. Gunter Jr. provides a well-rounded discussion of this ancient and controversial "sport," providing description of the birds' training process and the contest rules, as well as a succinct review of the ethical and legal dimensions associated with cockfighting. Because it has long been an illegal activity that has occurred in the geographical isolation of such rural regions as East Tennessee, cockfighting is necessarily strongly traditional in nature because it endures outside of the control of an official organization that would regulate the way it is practiced.

Children's Games and Amusements in Sumner County in the Good Ol' Days [1961]

Martha Freedle

I n my discussion of children's games and amusements that were popular two or three generations ago in the community in which I live, I have arranged my findings in the following groups: (1) amusements involving homemade toys and resources at hand, (2) amusements centered around community resources, (3) games played at school, and (4) night-time games and amusements enjoyed with the family and friends.

Amusements Involving Homemade Toys and Resources at Hand

Most children are fairly resourceful and have little difficulty in finding something with which they can amuse themselves. This was especially true sixty or seventy years ago. If there were no toys, they made them. I base these conclusions on the following facts related to me by my mother, Mrs. Mark Freedle.

Little girls enjoyed playing with dolls then, just as little girls enjoy them today; but their dolls were not "store-bought." Many of them were made of cornstalks. The body, arms, and legs of the doll were made from the dry stalk; the head was made of the pith from the stalk; and the hair was fashioned from the corn silks. The appendages were attached by making small slits in the body at the appropriate places and slipping the various parts into positions. The hair was inserted by means of a sharp instrument such as a pin or scissors. The dolls were given names such as Mehetabelle, Angeline, and Sophronia and were put to bed in beds made of cornstalks and covered with patchwork quilts made by the hands of their ingenious owners. If one did not wish to take the time to make a cornstalk doll, she might cut a doll, or a row of dolls, from used brown wrapping paper which had been stored away for further use. Some little girls became quite adept at cutting such dolls. If a tablecloth was desired for a tea party, it too might be cut from used brown wrapping paper or a newspaper which had been thriftily laid by. Time might be taken, if the need was not too urgent, to cut scallops or zigzags along the edge to make the cloth more decorative. Teacups also might be cut from paper and folded into shape. Any other article that could not be made but that was needed in order to proceed with the playtime activity was quickly and effectively produced by the employment of one's imagination.

Boys also were quite good at making articles with which to amuse themselves. One article that was almost a necessity was a slingshot. It must have resembled the one that David used to slay Goliath. Constructed of a piece of leather that might once have been a rein or a line used to guide or control a horse or mule, the sling, containing a small stone or pebble picked up from a creek bed, was slung around and around the head until a certain speed was attained; and then by a jerk the stone was propelled into the air. Another "weapon" that might be made, whether skillfully or rather carelessly, was a bow and arrow. Hickory was the usual choice of wood for its construction; the ends of the bow were held together by heavy string which had been frugally collected and stuffed into one's pocket to be used for just such an emergency. A sharp point was sometimes desired for the arrow, and this was supplied by wrapping a piece of tin around one end of the arrow and beating it into shape. The piece of tin so used was usually a part of a can that had once contained snuff. Another article of amusement that was homemade was the kite. Perhaps it would not be recognized as such by a youngster today, but it would fly nevertheless. My uncles made the frame of their kites of dry weed stems. The frame was covered with brown wrapping paper, which was held in place by means of paste made of flour and water. The tail of the kite might easily be many colors of the rainbow, the pieces for its construction having been obtained from the "rag barrel," which stood in one corner of my grandmother's attic. All that was needed at this stage of the process was plenty of string. Many an hour was whiled away by the neighborhood boys with a homemade slingshot, a bow and arrow, or a kite such as I have described.

Other homemade articles of play and amusement were enjoyed by both the boys and girls. One such article was a whistle; it might be made from a squash stem or a willow twig. Besides the material for its construction and a knife for shaping the whistle and providing air holes, the only other thing necessary was a bit of knowledge and skill in the manipulation of the knife. Perhaps one's desire to tower above those around him brought about the making of the next device, a pair of stilts. To fashion the stilts two long poles, appropriate pieces of wood for footrests, a hammer, and some nails were needed. A footrest was nailed securely on each pole a certain number of inches or feet from the bottom of the pole, the number of inches or feet depending on how high one wished to tower above his associates. Some skill was necessary to gain a foothold on each of the footrests, hold on to the poles, and maintain sufficient balance to walk about, looking down on those below.

Articles that had to be made were not the only sources through which one could derive amusement at home. Often one had only to look about him and use his ingenuity. A barrel hoop lying around the back lot, when set upright and given a push with a stick lying nearby, would challenge one's agility and alertness to keep it moving. And when there were two or more hoops, sticks, and playful children, an exciting race might ensue with the loser being called "a rotten egg." Another type of race might be held with the participants riding stick horses. A stick horse might be any stick of considerable length, diameter, and strength which was lying about. A race was not a necessity for a stick horse to be enjoyed, of course. A "long ranger" might spend a very enjoyable hour or two surveying his domain on his trusty steed or chasing outlaws across the imaginary plains. When one grew tired of these activities, he might persuade a brother or sister to push him around the yard or lot in the wheelbarrow. Of course, he was more likely to get his ride if he agreed to take his turn at the handles and give the other the benefit of jolting along in the wheelbarrow, too. Another enjoyable activity that called for little resourcefulness was riding the drag in the field while one's father or older brother handled the team. There were bumps every now and then, to be sure, and sometimes one had to grab hold of father or brother to keep from losing his balance. Riding or driving the mules to water at noon was another activity on the farm to which some youngsters looked forward. This was one of my mother's delights when she was a small girl. She was handed the lines, after the mules were unhitched from the play, and permitted to drive them to the branch for water. She could not always get the mules to go in the direction she chose; and several times, instead of backing up and turning around after drinking, as she tried to get them to do, they led her on across the branch, shoes and all. Then they turned and came back across with her trailing along, still holding on to the lines. In spite of the unplanned wadings she took, driving the mules to the branch for water was a privilege that she would not relinquish. Other possibilities for amusement were explored by farm boys, such as my uncles as they grew older and looked for more excitement than could be found in playing with inanimate objects such as barrel hoops, stick horses, and wheelbarrows. They might be found in the pasture riding the cows, twisting their tails to make them "buck." Another adventurous stunt that they tried occasionally was to jump from the barn loft down to the back of an unsuspecting, rather startled cow that was standing idly by, minding her own business and chewing her cud. Yes, there was ample opportunity for fun and excitement at home if one only took the time to look about him and find it.

Amusements Centered Around Community Resources

There were also opportunities for deriving pleasure and amusement from the resources of the community. I gathered information about the following activities from Mrs. Grubbs, a neighbor, who during her childhood lived in the Brooks community.

In those days wooded areas were more plentiful than they are today, and another outlet for the energy of both boys and girls was climbing saplings and swinging through the air to the ground. Swinging on grapevines also was a thrilling adventure unless, unfortunately, the grapevine broke while the swinger was in mid-air.

An enjoyable afternoon could be had by a group of girls who met to stroll along the roads and hillsides in the spring to pick flowers. One might find them seated on a grassy spot, making clover chains or picking the petals from a field daisy, to answer the age-old question, saying, "He loves me; he loves me not." When these activities lost their attractiveness for the time being, the girls might stroll on to a grove of trees, collect some good-sized leaves, and busy themselves with making leafs hats or belts. The leaves were attached to each other by "pinning" them with bits of dry stems. On their homeward way the girls would gather honeysuckle or wild roses to make bouquet for the family to enjoy.

The branches, creeks, and ponds in the community afforded opportunity for fun during many months of the years. In the spring and summer many delightful hours were spent wading and swimming. In the fall, during the rainy season, branches and creeks often rose from their banks and spread out over neighboring fields, affording the opportunity of boat riding in a homemade boat, if one had an indulgent uncle or older brother who was inclined to spend an afternoon rowing a boat to give pleasure to a group of youngsters. And with the approach of winter the children began to anticipate the freezing over of the branches and ponds to a sufficient depth for skating. One could easily while away an entire afternoon, gliding and scooting back and forth across the surface of a frozen pond or branch. If the winter was severe, the sole of many a shoe become thinner and thinner as a result of encounters with the ice.

The opportunities for hunting in the community were numerous, but no gun was used. Hunting for arrowheads was a pleasant pastime; and a group of youngsters might be seen on a sunny morning scattering over a hillside, hurrying to see who could find the largest number of arrowheads to add to his collection. In the fall, after Jack Frost had made several visits, the hunting season really began. Hickory nuts, chestnuts, paw paws, and persimmons were to be had for the taking. Saturdays were awaited with eagerness. Instead of going to school one could join a group of friends and spend the morning or afternoon in search of nuts and fruit. If one was lucky, he might, on a chilly night, be permitted to join a group of grown-ups on a 'possum hunt. It mattered little if he scratched his hands and face on briars, fell into the creek, shivered until his teeth rattled, or got so sleepy that he fell asleep standing up. To follow the dogs and get the 'possum was the object, and he was one of the group. Nothing else mattered. Of course, it was always good to get home, get to bed, and surrender in blissful sleep to that weariness that had saturated his body and mind; but it was a grand feeling to be able to say to the other youngster the next day, "I bet I did something last night you didn't do. I went 'possum huntin.'"

Games Played at School

The games played at school were entered into with enthusiasm, and everybody took an active part, as a rule. There was very little clannish play, if any.

One of the games played at Brooks School and described Mrs. Grubbs of Portland was "Marching Round the Levee." This was a singing game, and it was usually played by the smaller children. To play the game, all of the players except one formed a circle and joined hands. The remaining player, who might be either a boy or a girl, took his place in the center of the circle. As the other players sang the first stanza of the song, they marched around the player in the center.

First stanza: We're marching round the levee
                   We're marching round the levee
                   We're marching round the levee
                   Since we have gained this day.

As they sang the second stanza, the player in the center of the circle moved in and out, going under the raised arms of the players forming the circle.

Second stanza: Go in and out the window,
                  Go in and out the window,
                  Go in and out the window,
                  Since we have gained this day.

As the third, forth, fifth, and sixth stanzas were sung, the player in the center of the circle continued to perform the actions indicated by the words.

Third stanza:	Come back in here, my dear, Come back in here, my dear, Come back in here, my dear, Since we have gained this day.
Forth stanza:	Go forth and face you lover, Go forth and face you lover, Go forth and face you lover, Since we have gained this day.
Fifth stanza:	I'll kneel because I love you, I'll kneel because I love you, I'll kneel because I love you, Since we have gained this day.
Sixth stanza:	One sweet kiss and I'll leave you, One sweet kiss and I'll leave you, One sweet kiss and I'll leave you, Since we have gained this day.

Mrs. Swann, another resident of Portland, told me of a singing game called "Froggy in the Middle" and described it as it was played at Portland School, which was located where the First Baptist Church stands today. One of the players was the "froggy." He took his place in the center of a good-sized circle, marked off with a stick, and the other players joined hands and marched around the circle with their eyes closed, singing these words:

Froggy's in the middle and can't get out;
Take a little stick and stir him about.

While they sang, "Froggy" ran out of the circle and hid nearby. Then the players opened their eyes and shouted, "Where's Froggy?" After they had separated to look for "Froggy," he jumped from his hiding place and tried to catch one of the players before he could get back inside the circle. If a player was caught, he had to be "Froggy" for the next game.

Another singing game, which was described by my aunt Miss Arrie Lane, as it was played at Concord School, was "Chickama Chickama Craney Crow." One player was the "old hen," two were "thieves," and the remaining players were the "chickens." There was a spot designated as the well and a spot designated as the hiding place of the thieves. As the game began, the "thieves" went to their hiding place and the "old hen" gathered her "chickens" about her. Then the "old hen" moved toward the well, singing:

Chickama Chickama Craney Crow went to the well to wash her toe.
When she got back, one of her black-eyed chickens was gone.

While the "old hen" was on her way to the well, the "thieves" stole one of her "chickens"; but they had to steal it without her seeing them. The game continued until the "thieves" had stolen all the "chickens."

"Kitty Wants a Corner" was also played at Concord School by my aunt and her schoolmates. One player was the "Kitty." Each of the players was stationed at a definite place—a tree, a large rock, a corner of the schoolhouse, or some similar spot. "Kitty" went up to one of the players and said, "Kitty wants a corner." The player answered, "Kitty can't have it." While this conversation was taking place, two of the players would attempt to exchange places. "Kitty" would try to get to one of the places before the other player. If "Kitty" got there first, the player who lost out was the "Kitty" for the next game.

"Snap" was one of the games played at Hopewell School and described to me by Mrs. Crafton, also of Portland. Two players stood facing each other with their hands raised and their fingers interlocked. One player was chosen to be the "snapper." The other players stood nearby. The "snapper" ran up to one of the group, snapped her finger, and said, "I snap you." When the player caught the "snapper," those two took the places of the two who had faced each other and another played became the "snapper."

Mrs. Crafton also told me a game that was played to determine who would be leader in a game. It was called "William William Trembletoe." The players seated themselves in a circle. Each player placed the index finger of his right hand on his knee, doubling the other fingers under in a partial fist. Then one of the players, pointing to a player's finger each time he said a word—expect in the case of the word *out* when he spelled the word and pointed for each letter —repeated this rhyme:

> William William Trembletoe, he's a good fisherman,
> Catches fish and puts them in a dish,
> Catches hens and puts them in pens.
> Some lay eggs; and some none.
> Wire briar limber rock, three geese in a flock,
> One flew east; one flew west;
> And one flew over the cuckoo's nest.
> O-U-T spells out goes he,
> You old dirty dishrag you.

The player to whose finger he pointed while saying the last word was disqualified. He continued to repeat the rhyme until all of the players except one were disqualified. That one became the leader.

"Blind Man's Bluff," as it was played at Portland School, was described to me by Mrs. L. D. Austin. One of the players was blindfolded with a handkerchief and turned around three times. While he was being turned around, the other players moved about in a given area. When he had completed his third turn, all players had to stop where they were and remain there. The blind-folded player then tried to find one of the other players. When he found a player, he was allowed to touch the player's face and head; and he tried to guess who the player was. If he guessed correctly, that player was blindfolded for the next game.

One of my mother's favorite games was "Anti-over." She described it as it was played at Portland School. A ball was necessary, and the ball used was a small hard rubber one which was wrapped in a string to give it size. Thus it was called a "string ball." The players divided into two equal groups. One group went around to one side of the school building, and the other group went to the opposite side of the building. The group with the ball, group one, shouted, "Anti-over" and someone threw the ball over the building. If a player caught the ball either as a fly or on the first bounce, he and his group tried to slip around the building and hit one or more players of the first group with the ball before they could move to the opposite side of the building. The players hit by the ball had to remain on that side, thus becoming members of group two. The group which had the larger number of players when the game ended won.

A popular game that called for a bit of daring on the part of its partici-pants was "Pop the Whip." This is the way it was described by my mother, Mrs. Grubbs, and Mrs. Crafton. Anyone who wanted to take part lined up and joined hands with those standing next to him. The one who wanted the biggest thrill took places near the end of the line. After all players were in line, they ran forward. Suddenly the leader stopped and swung forward the person next to him, who in turn swung the person next to him; thus the swinging continued on down the line. By the time the pressure reached the end of the line, the last two or three players were moving rather fast and received quite a jolt. The last player in the line was lucky if he managed to remain on his feet.

The remaining games that I shall mention were described to me by Mrs. Grubbs as they were played at Brooks School. "Statue" was enjoyed by the girls. The players stood about in a circle, each one being several feet away from the one on either side of her. The leader approached the first player, swung her around several times, turned her loose, and then shouted, "Stop!" At the signal the player had to stop and maintain the position she happened to be in at the time. The leader then moved to the second player and on around the circle until each player had been swung and command to stop. If any player failed to hold her pose, she had to drop out of the game. The leader then selected the girl with the most pleasing pose, or perhaps the most ridiculous pose, as the "statue." If another game was played, the "statue" become the leader.

"Draw Base" was played with a "string ball." The players divided into two equal sides and stood about ten or twelve feet apart. A member of team one threw the ball, trying to hit a member of team two. If he succeeded, the player who was hit became a member of team one. Then a member on team two threw the ball and tried to hit a member of team one. The team with the larger number of players at the end of the game was the winner.

"Town Ball" was similar to today's baseball and softball, but there are striking differences. The ball used was a "string ball"; and the bat was a flat homemade bat, which an older boy had trimmed and shaped out of a piece of wood that had been discarded as useless by an adult. There was no limit to the number of players so long as there was an equal number on the two sides. Two captains would choose the players for their teams. There was a home plate, a pitcher's base, and a first, second, and third base; but the only defensive players who played on base were the pitchers and the hindcatcher, whose position was behind home plate, of course. The other defensive players all played in the field, some playing farther out than others. The captains guessed a number between one and twenty-five to decide which team would be "in town" first. The players batted in the order in which they had been chosen. The batter was not required to run the first time he hit the ball; he might wait until the second hit or even the third. However, he was required to run on the third hit, even if it was a foul. Three strikes meant an out. If the player struck the ball and begun to run the bases, a defensive player had to hit him with the ball while he was off base to put him out. The only way to score was to make a home run, which counted one point. But a player could become eligible to bat again by reaching home plate after advancing from base to base on hits by his teammates. If a player advanced to first base on a hit he made, then he had to try to make second the next time the ball was struck by one of his team, whether the batter chose to run or not. When three offensive players were put out, the defensive team was "in town." There were no innings as such. The bell for "books" determined how long the ball game would last.

Night-time Games and Amusements with the Family and Friends

My mother and my aunt described to me winter evenings around the family fireside which were spent playing quiet games. One of the games was "Hull-gull." It could be played by using grains of corn, acorns, peas, or beans. Each of the players was given the same number of the object that was being used. The leader picked up an undisclosed number, shook them about in his closed hands, and said to the player on his right, "Hull-gull." The player replied, "Handful." The leader then asked, "How many?" The player replied by naming a number. If he happened to name the exact number of the object that the leader held in his hands, the leader had to relinquish to the player the object to make the number that the leader had in his hands. For example, if the leader held eight grains of corn and the player guessed five, the player gave the leader three grains. Or if the leader held eight grains and the player guessed eleven, the player still had to give up three grains. Then the player became the leader, and the game continued around the circle. The player who was able to get the largest number of the object was the winner.

Another fireside game was "Jiggama Hornacup." This game was played by two participants. One would bend over, hiding his face in his hands. The other would tap him on the back with his fists, saying this rhyme: "Jiggama jiggama hornacup, how many fingers do I hold up?" He then held some, all, or none of his fingers, as he chose. The other would guess a number. If he guessed two and the player had held up two fingers, the player holding up his fingers would continue with the rhyme: "Jiggama jiggama hornacup, two you said, and two there were. Jiggama jiggama hornacup." Then he would hide his eyes and guess number of fingers the other held up. However, if the player hiding his eyes had guessed four fingers and there were two, the other player would say: "Jiggama jiggama hornacup, four you said, and two there were. Jiggama jiggama hornacup." Then the player guessing continued to guess until he guessed the correct number.

A fireside game that the boys especially enjoyed was "Club Fist." The children formed a circle, sitting very close together. Then they stacked their left fists on someone's knee. One player would say to the person whose fist was on top, "Knock it off or take it off?" If the player chose not to have his fist bruised, he answered, "Take it off," and then he removed his fist. If he answered "Knock it off," the other players took turns hammering at his fist with their fists until they removed his fist from the stack. This continued until all fists had been removed. Then one of the players said, "The first one who shows his teeth gets three slaps, three pinches, and three hair pulls." Each tried to make the others laugh. Someone finally laughed, of course, and took his punishment.

If one of the children had spend-the-night company, the group might play "Pretty Bird in My Cup." The players seated themselves in a circle. The leader silently chose the color of a bird and moved around the circle, with a thimble filled with water concealed in his hand, saying to each player, "Pretty bird is my cup. What color is yours?" The player named the color of a bird. If he named the same color the leader had chosen, the leader threw the water from the thimble in the player's face. Then that player became the leader. And thus the play continued until bedtime.

A present-day youngster might be completely at a loss about finding amusement if time could be turned back and he could be placed in such a playtime environment as my investigations have revealed. There would be no electric trains, robots, jet planes, doll house complete with furniture, talking dolls, roaring lions, or other of the many elaborate toys available today. The youngster would probably be extremely unhappy and would let it be known that each day he endured a miserable existence. His viewpoint would clash resoundingly with that of his grandmother, because in her thoughts the days about which I have spoken were truly "the good ol' days."

Informants Interviewed

Mrs. Mark Freedle, Portland, Tennessee. June 25, 1959; July 2, 1959.
Mrs. Nancy Grubbs, Portland, Tennessee. July 2, 1959.
Mrs. N. F. Swann, Portland, Tennessee. July 6, 1959.
Miss Arrie Lane, Portland, Tennessee. July 9, 1959.
Mrs. George Crafton, Portland, Tennessee. July 9, 1959.
Mrs. L. D. Austin, Portland, Tennessee. July 10, 1959.

"Let's Go Hunting"
A Nursery Song and
Its Background
[1964]

West Livaudais

S ally Mixon, a sophomore at Southwestern (now Rhodes College) at Memphis during the session of 1962–63, made for me a tape-recording of a song which she calls "Let's Go Hunting." Obviously a nursery song, it tells in simple dialogue an intentionally absurd story of a crow hunt in which the crow is treated as if he were big game. After he is killed he is hoisted, evidently with much difficulty, into a cart, carried home, boiled, and eaten with gusto. Miss Mixon, who lives in Memphis, learned the song from her grandmother, Sallie Newbern Cotter, of Marianna, Arkansas. The song, which has been handed down in the family from time out of mind, reads as follows (with repetitions deleted after the first stanza):

1. Let's go hunting, said Rickety-Rockety;
   Let's go hunting, said Robbety-Bobbety;
   Let's go hunting, said Johnny Malone;
   Let's go hunting, said everyone.
2. What shall we shoot at? Etc.
3. Shoot at a crow . . .
4. Bang! Bang!
5. Dead! Dead!
6. How do we get him home? . . .

7. Borrow a cart . . .
8. How'll we get him in? . . .
9. Up! Up!
10. Take off the wheels . . .
11. Push! Push!
12. How shall we cook him? . . .
13. Boil him in a pot . . .
14. How he's done . . .
15. Let's eat him . . .
16. Smack! Smack!

Reference to standard collection of folk song indicates that collectors have not often found the song in this country, through it is common in Britain. Surprisingly, it does not appear in Randolph's *Ozark Folksongs* or in Arthur Palmer Hudson's *Folksongs of Mississippi,* and even more surprisingly only a fragment is found in *North Carolina Folklore.* Henry M. Belden's interesting bibliographical comment and references in *NCF,* however, show that originally the bird hunted was the wren, not the crow, and that the song grew out of folk beliefs many centuries old. These facts, added to the fullness of the Mixon Cotter nursery version, warrant a survey of the background of the song.

According to *The Golden Bough,* the wren was regarded as king of birds by the ancient Greek and Romans, as well as by most modern peoples of Western Europe.[1] An explanation of this ancient notion comes from an unexpected quarter, the United States. According to Elizabeth Wheeler Hubbard of Massachusetts, an old fable tells of a contest among birds to see which could fly highest. The wren perched on the eagle's head and was declared the winner and the king of the birds.[2] In modern times the wren has been involved in Christian folklore, but at what time the myths arose we can only surmise. William Henderson, in his field researches in the northern countries of England during the mid-nineteenth century, found that the robin and the wren were invested with something of a sacred nature, the former because of its association with the crucified Savior, and "the wren" says he, "generously shares in the reverence paid to the robin,"[3] as it shown in this well-known rime from the north:

The robin and the wren
Are God Almighty's cock and hen;
Him that harries their nest,
Never shall his soul have rest.[4]

He cites a passage in the *Pastorals* of George Smith, 1770, to illustrate the superstitions associated with the two birds:

I found a robin's nest within our shed,
And in the barn a wren her young ones bred;

I never take away their nest, nor try
To catch the old ones, lest a friend should die;
Dick took a wren's nest from his cottage side,
Are era a twelve-month passed his mother died.[5]

From other British collections of folk beliefs made in the nineteenth century it would be possible to list a considerable number of quotations of the same purport. But three more examples will here suffice: from Sussex—"Robins and wrens are God Almighty's friends," from Essex—

Hurt a robin or a wren,
Never prosper, boy nor man.[6]

And in Scotland the wren was called the "Lady of Heaven's hen."[7]

Despite the veneration of the wren, it was customary in many parts of Britain and Ireland to kill the little birds, usually on St. Stephen's Day, December 26. In some cases it was servants or peasants who did the killing; in others, young people and children; and in still others, mummers (who conceivably might also be servants or peasants and/or young people). The pattern was on this order: The celebrants killed a wren and mounted it, wings extended, on the top of a long pole (or suspended it by the legs in the center of two hoops set at right angles to one another,[8] or mounted it in a furze bush or holly branch).[9] They then went from house to house chanting a rime and asking gifts of food or money from the householders. In some localities the celebrants concluded the day by carrying the bird to the churchyard and burying it with chanting, signing, and dancing.[10] This custom has persisted into the mid-twentieth in at least one locality, the Isle of Man.[11]

Most of the nineteenth-century English commentators seemed to feel that there was some inconsistency between the veneration of the wren and the killing of the bird on St. Stephen's Day—a feeling which was probably the result of Victorian hypersensibility; the word "cruel" is occasionally used in reference to the Christmastide custom. But it is unlikely that the folk themselves were aware of inconsistency or considered the wren-killing sacrilegious or cruel— as it shown in the song sung by the merry-making in Essex as they went from house to house:

The wren, the wren, the King of the birds,
St. Stephen's Day was caught in the furze;
Although he be little, his honor is great,
And so, good people, pray give us a treat.[12]

There was a time, however, when in certain parts of Ireland the wren is said to have been hunted with malice. During an era of religious conflict the bird was allegedly considered anti-Catholic. Aubrey (1696) says that while an armed conflict in Ireland was in progress a Protestant party was awakened by wrens pecking on the drums just in time to avert a surprise attack by the Catholics and to rout the enemy. Hence the Irish Catholics despised the birds, considering them agents of the devil, and killed all they could: "You'll see sometimes on holidays a whole parish running like madmen from hedge to hedge a wren-hunting."[13] A second attempt to account for the practice, equally dubious (Aubrey probably misinterpreted the holiday activity), is found in the annals of the Percy Society. The first Christian missionaries are said to have been shocked at the veneration accorded the wren by the Druids and to have ordered the birds killed.[14] A more acceptable story is told by G. F. Northall: In ancient times a siren used to lure men from the Isle of Man into the sea, and when at length she was almost trapped, she escaped by changing herself into a wren and eventually to be killed during the hunt.[15]

These three explanations pertain to local custom and account for little in the ebb and flow of folk belief and custom in Britain.

It seems evident that the annual St. Stephen's Day custom was misunderstood by students of folklore in the nineteenth century. It was not as Northall calls it "a cruel persecution"; the wren was killed, not despite the reverence accorded it, but because it was or had been a hallowed bird.[16] It is not unusual in primitive religions for scared animals to be ceremonially killed on specified days every year. But the full meaning had been lost before the serious study of folklore began; hence the false assumptions of the nineteenth-century scholars.

In the light of this body of folk beliefs, it seems probable that the song "Lets Go Hunting" has its source in the St. Stephen's Day merry-making of the servants, peasants, and, especially, the young people. No one knows its age. The earliest printed version that I have seen is in David Herd's *Scottish Songs*, published in Glasgow in 1869 and said to be a reprint of the edition of 1776. The wren song which appeared in it is pleasantly Scottish:

1.   Will ze go to the wood? Quo' Foizie Mozie;
     Will ze go to the wood? Quo' Johnie Rednozie;
     Will ze go to the wood? Quo' Foslin ene;
     Will ze go to the wood? Quo' brither and kin.
2.   What to do there? . . .
3.   To flay the wren . . .
4.   What way will ze get here hame?
     . . . .
8.   I'll hae a wing . . .[17]

Doubtless more important is Joseph Ritson's version in his *Grammer Gurton's Garland; or The Nursery Panassus*, published in London in 1810. The first edition (which was the second of the English "Mother Goose" collections) was published earlier by some twenty-six to thirty-six years (opinions differ as to its date). Since the rhymes in the first edition are incorporated as parts one and two of the 1810 printing, we may assume that the poem below is identical with the eighteenth-century original. It is titled "Robin, Bobbin, Richard, and John, or The Wren Shooting."

1. We'll go a shooting, says Robin to Bobbin;
   We'll go a shooting, says Richard to Robin;
   We'll go a shooting, says John all alone;
   We'll go a shooting, says everyone.
2. What shall we kill? Etc.
3. We'll shoot that wren . . .
4. She's down, she's down . . .
5. How shall we get her home? . . .
6. We'll hire a cart . . .
7. Then hoist, boys, hoist . . .

So they brought her away after each pluck'd a feather, and when they got home shar'd the booty together.[18]

Halliwell, who published the song in 1842, says in his preface that "these pieces have been current in our nurseries for nearly two centuries, in all parts of England."[19] If he is correct, the song goes back at least to the mid-seventeenth century. The fact that in its earliest printed version it is a bit of pleasant nursery nonsense suggests that it must be very old. In its original form it was a probably serious and possible ceremonial. It is not possible to estimate how many generations or centuries must be followed for its metamorphosis into nursery humor. One bold team of folklore editors, Edith Fowke and Joe Glazer, run its age back to the Peasants' Revolt of 1381; but their argument is more entertaining than plausible. According to them the wren is "a likely symbol of baronial property, and thus this song was probably sung at secret meetings when the peasants were planning to seize and redistribute the land among the poor."[20] We are not told on what authority or evidence from folk history the editors would make this old song a militant proletarian cry for aristocratic blood. Actually, the Scottish version they offer is lighthearted rather than antagonistic: its repetition of the phrase "That will not do" wittily exaggerates the nature of the quarry. The characters are Milder, Malder, Festle, Fose, and John the Red Nose.[21] When the proposal is made to hunt the wren with bow and arrow,

That will not do, said Milder and Malder . . .
Oh, what will do then? . . .
Big guns and cannons . . .
How will you bring her home? . . .
On four strong men's shoulders . . .
That will not do . . .

Oh, what will do then? . . .
Big carts and big wagons . . .

It is incredible that this sportive rhyme was ever a song of protest. As for its going back to (or past) the Peasants' Revolt, no one can say. The Opies are on much safer ground when they say that it is likely to be "exceptionally old."[22]

The British variants are many; some of them alter the names, others add details. From the Isle of Man, one of the principal sources of information about the hunt, comes—

We hunted the wren for Robin and Bobbin;
We hunted the wren for Jack of the Can . . .[23]

A frequently found version is given in *The Oxford Dictionary of Nursery Rhymes:*

We will to the wood, says Robin to Bobbin;
We will to the wood, says Richard to Robin . . .

The Opies report that in other versions the King and Queen are invited to the wren-feast, and that the left-overs give "eyes to the blind, legs to the lame, and pluck to the poor."[24]

The wren has survived in very few American texts, of which the fullest appears to have been sung by a Massachusetts woman, Elizabeth Wheeler Hubbard. It begins, "Let's go to the wood, says Robbin to Bobbin," and continues through the shooting, the retrieving "with a cart and six horses," and concludes with leaving "the bones for the crows."[25] It could easily pass for an English version. Mary F. Lindsay's Nebraska text, reported by Louise Pound, is very like the Massachussetts song, but little more than half as long.[26] In the fragment printed in *North Carolina Folklore,* a squirrel, not a wren, is the game hunted. Such a change was inevitable in this country. Perhaps the rarity of the song on this side of the waters is due to the small appeal which a wren-hunt had as a nursery song.

A somewhat cloudy and puzzling page in the American history of "Let's Go Hunting" is its alleged use as a minstrel song titled "Billy Barlow" in the late nineteenth century. There is no question about the existence of the song, which may be heard on Burl Ives's Decca record DL 8248. Yet if it enjoyed very considerable popularity in the minstrel shows, one would expect to encounter it frequently among American collection of late folk songs. I have found no specific accounts of its history or popularity as a minstrel song.

Henry M. Belden mentions only four states in which it has been reported, Texas, New York, Massachusetts, and Nebraska (the last two discussed above), and he remarks that it "persists only fragmentarily in American tradition."[27] Our Mixon-Cotter song, however, with its sixteen stanzas recounting a complete story, can hardly be called fragmentary. With the crow as the quarry instead of the wren, it misses some of the pleasant absurdity of the British version, but as a folk song for American children it seems to me to compare favorably with any of the printed British versions.

Notes

1. Sir James Frazer, *The Golden Bough* (London, 1919), Part V, Vol. II, p. 317.
2. Eloise Hubbard Linscott, *Folk Songs of Old New England* (London, 1962), 230–233.
3. *Folk Lore of the Northern Countries* (London, 1879), 124.
4. Ibid., 123.
5. Ibid., 125.
6. G. F. Northall, *English Folk Rhymes* (London, 1892), 275–276. Other rimes of the same type are found on the pages cited.
7. Frazer, *Golden Bough,* Part V, Vol. II, p. 318.
8. Ibid., 318–319.
9. Henderson, 125.
10. Frazer, *Golden Bough,* Part V, Vol. II, p. 318–319.
11. Iona Opie and Peter Opie, *Oxford Dictionary of Nursery Rhymes* (Oxford, 1952), 369.
12. Henderson, 125.
13. James Orchard Halliwell, *A Dictionary of Archaic and Provincial Words* (New York, 1924), 469.
14. *Early English Poetry, Ballads and Popular Literature of the Middle Ages* (London, 1841), IV, 11.
15. Northall, *English Folk Rhymes,* 115.
16. That the wren was a sacramental bird is evident from Frazer's account (*Golden Bough,* 321–322).
17. Page 210.
18. Page 6. Good fortune was thought to come to those who carried a feather from the ceremonial wren (Frazier, *Golden Bough,* 319).
19. *Nursery Rhymes of England* (London), Preface, vi. The song is on 144.
20. *Songs of Work and Freedom* (Garden City, N.Y., 1961), 117.
21. According to Iona Opie and Peter Opie, editors of the *Oxford Dictionary of Nursery Rhymes,* 370, these characters are Welsh, not Scotch.
22. Ibid., 369.
23. Henderson, 125.
24. Page 369.
25. Linscott, *Folk Songs of Old New England,* 230–233.
26. *American Ballads and Songs* (New York, 1922), 253.
27. *North Carolina Folklore* (Durham, N.C., 1952), Vol. II, p. 215.

Cockfighting in East Tennessee and Western North Carolina [1978]

Charles R. Gunter Jr.

Cockfighting, one of the oldest sports in the world, occurs under a wide variety of circumstances in the United States since it may be prohibited by state and federal laws. To the uninitiated, cockfighting may appear to be an uncomplicated "sport" that's cruel, barbarous, and unfair;[1] however, the sport is more complicated than it appears, and often those associated with the sport are people of integrity.

My initial interest in this sport was generated by my students who have interviewed cockfighters in this region. Rather than attempting a literary study of cockfighting, this paper seeks to present the viewpoints of principally three cockfighters. Pseudonyms, rather than real names, have been used, and objectionable language has occasionally been omitted.[2] At the time of the interview, "Mr. Sawyer" was engaged full time as a cockfighter, while "Mr. Hammer" considered the sport as an enjoyable yet time-consuming hobby. Mr. Sawyer was interviewed by Rosa Lee Cooper and Karen M. Smith, both East Tennessee State University undergraduate students, in spring 1978. Mr. Hammer was interviewed by Anthony A. Anderson, an ETSU undergraduate student, in spring 1976. Since both men frequently used in their vocabulary lingo which might not be easily understood by those unacquainted with cockfighting, an additional interview was arranged with "Mr. Toole" in order to clarify these terms. I myself interviewed Mr. Toole in fall 1978. So the information in this paper is the result of a joint effort by a number of people.

Cockfighting is much too complicated to consider every facet. Therefore, this paper is limited to examining briefly the conditioning of the game fowl, especially what often is referred to as "the keep"; the mechanics of the fights or derbies; the legal aspects of cockfighting; and the point of view of cockfighters concerning their continued involvement in a sport which may be prohibited by state and federal laws.

Concerning the conditioning of game fowl, let's assume that the cockfighter has crossbred his own birds and finally has come out with a pretty good strain. What could be said concerning the conditioning process employed in preparing the birds for a derby? On this question, one finds that cockfighters are not entirely in agreement. Hammer, who has been involved with cockfighting for over twelve years, thinks that the man who owns the chicken and who takes good care of him is a more important factor in the cock's success than his breeding. Let's listen to Hammer's response to other questions related to the conditioning of game fowl.

QUESTION: What do you think is the most important thing about taking good care of chickens?

MR. HAMMER: The most important thing is making sure he has plenty of food and water; if he has plenty of both he will be a healthy chicken. There is definitely certain kinds of food that you feed game fowl. A lot of people have spent thousands of dollars just paying veterinarians to find a particular method of feeding game fowl. When a man is winning, his competition naturally thinks he's got a secret formula.

Hammer's secret is hard work and tender loving care; he is willing to take better care of his chickens than of himself. He says, "Anything them chickens need, I get for them; I will do without things sometimes."

QUESTION: What do you do on your "keep"?

MR. HAMMER: The "keep" refers to the training or the conditioning of game fowl, especially the last few weeks before a fight.

Hammer mentioned that he feeds his game fowl anything that Purina makes for a chicken. Game fowl at six months of age are penned and are fed twice a day. A routine schedule of feeding before Hammer goes to work and every evening when he returns is begun and rarely changes. In a year's time he might miss only three or four feedings.

Each month about sixty dollars worth of chicken feed is mixed together (this assumes that thirty game fowl are involved). In addition to the various grain mixtures, several foods like lettuce and portions of apples help to supplement the diet since they have a high content of both water and vitamins.

Hammer begins intensive preparations some two months before a fight or derby. The weight of game fowl is a critical issue; if overweight, the fat must be taken off. One method of removing this excess weight is to construct "flight pens." These flight pens are approximately four feet wide, ten feet long, and ten feet high. Corn shucks are placed knee-deep in the pens, and feed is scattered among these shucks. In a week's time, game fowl will lose quite a bit of weight, but the "feeder" has the dilemma of maintaining the desired weight for several weeks prior to a fight. The flight pens also serve a purpose in building up a rooster's endurance. As they scratch around looking for their feed, they build up their muscles and their wind so that they can go the length of a rooster fight.

Some two weeks before a fight, what often is referred to as the "keep" begins. A considerable amount of time will be spent by the cockfighter in increasing his bird's endurance for these fights. A form of padding, shaped like boxing gloves (called muffs), is placed over the natural spurs, and two birds will be allowed to box or spar, much as professional boxers would do. The birds could easily maim one another if it were not for these "gloves."

Conditioning also includes "flying the birds"—a training procedure which builds up their endurance. A mattress is placed on a table, and the rooster is thrown up into the air; the wings obviously are used in reaching the mattress. Initially, some twenty-five flights are conducted per bird, but this number easily could increase to thirty-five to forty per day before the end of the keep. Assuming that one is conditioning ten birds for a given fight, it "gets to be pretty much work," noted Hammer, "when you consider throwing five pounds in the air 350 times for several consecutive days."

Assuming a two-week keep, on the twelfth day, Hammer, rather than working the roosters, will pet them and also change their diet somewhat. During the keep, the game fowl have been allowed to drink all the milk that they can consume; now, however, the amount is reduced.

Unlike the professional boxer, who can work himself up emotionally for a big fight, a rooster doesn't know what is about to happen. You can't say, "Hey, Old Red, you've got a fight tonight; you've got to get ready." But you can start getting him hungry and resting him. Taking some of the water and food away from him—called "drying him out"—makes game fowl get meaner. Game fowl fight naturally, but the more ornery he is and the more the bird wants to fight, the greater the odds for success.

The experiences of another cockfighter, Mr. Toole, suggest that maybe the gamecock is aware that he is going to fight. If a rooster has fought at two or three previous derbies, the bird may sense what is going on. For example, Toole has had high-strung and nervous birds that are completely changed; that is, they settled down once they were removed from their carrying case or while their handler was tying on the gaffs at a fight.

Furthermore, he insists, it's amazing the difference that the two weeks (of the keep) will make in a gamecock if he is handled properly. All of a sudden his head is even redder than it has ever been; he's almost on his tiptoes,

◻ Gamecock. Photo courtesy
of Charles R, Gunter Jr.

crowing every minute, flapping his wings, and flying up and down. He is a built-up bundle of muscle and "shiny blue steel," so to speak.

Hammer maintains that the secret of the keep is in knowing when to take away the food and water. If the feeder takes the food away too early, the bird is too weak; he can't fight. He's almost as pitiful if the feeder waits too long to take it away.

If ten game fowl are involved in the conditioning process, only half of them can be used in a "five-cock derby." In response to a question regarding how these five are selected, Hammer said, "Well, I get to know them; it's kind of like your dog. You can tell on days when he's feeling bad . . . and, I get to know my roosters the same way you know your dog. I can tell when they are ready to fight, and I can tell when they don't feel particularly good on a certain day."

Another cockfighter, Mr. Sawyer, on being asked questions about the conditioning of game fowl, stated that raising game fowl was not a "hit-or-miss" affair but that accurate records were kept of the age, weight, and diet of the birds. Being a good feeder or conditioner, he said, is not sufficient if one doesn't have a good strain of game fowl. Not only did he have the opportunity to acquire the knowledge of an old-time feeder of game fowl when he started in this business, but he also had the financial backing of others in order to purchase good brood stock.

Historically, cockfights have been conducted in America at many sites—near a village, at a courthouse, at a tavern, or near a country store. The cockfight frequently took place out of doors. Today, most cockfights are managed inside a building. Hammer stated that cockfights often take place in tin buildings which can accommodate spectators in bleachers built around the cockpit. The term pit may, depending upon the context, refer to the building or the designated area in the building where the fights take place.

Toole said that the pit could vary according to the facilities. It's quite common to find cockfighting conducted in either a livestock barn or a tobacco barn. Frequently, in this region, these converted or remodeled barns include concession stands and rest rooms. The more sophisticated type of facilities may include air-conditioning and heat in a metal or aluminum-type of building.

On the average, the pit itself will have a diameter of sixteen to twenty feet. The size of the pit may vary according to the desire of the pit owner to accommodate more people. The pit floor frequently will be raised five to eight feet so that those people sitting in the first row will not obstruct the view of others sitting behind on the bleacher-type seats. A wall surrounds the pit floor, which may be composed of a claylike substance. Occasionally, this wall is made of glass to permit spectators to see better, but most likely the wall is made of plank or concrete block.

Both Sawyer and Hammer, in a rather perfunctory manner, tended to slight the preliminary activities, such as matching and weighing game fowl, which must be accomplished before the cockfight begins. Nevertheless, their comments, plus those of Toole, do shed some light on these activities.

Hammer remarked that the chickens must weigh between four and six pounds. Let's say you are entering five gamecocks in a five-cock derby; you will put in five cocks, and they will be matched with cocks of equal weight. If one of your entries weighs four pounds and twelve ounces, it will face another weighing four pounds and twelve ounces, or one within two ounces of it. Sawyer commented that six pounds and over is a pretty heavy rooster and that one rarely ever matches him to another rooster that heavy.

Once your game fowl have been weighed and matched with other roosters, Hammer observed that officials at the pit will begin calling the weights and will tell you which rooster you are supposed to "heel by band number." The banding of cocks is a very important phase of conducting a cockfight and refers to placing a monogrammed band on each leg of the rooster. Since numbers rather than names are used on the bands, the matchmaker cannot be accused of deliberately matching certain entries.

A much more complete description of these preliminary activities before the actual fight was given by Toole. When the cockfighter reaches the pit after driving a few miles or 500 miles, he is interested in getting his birds out of the car and into "scratch pens" or "exercise pens" so that these birds can pull themselves together. After flapping their wings, scratching, and crowing for thirty minutes or so, the roosters are put back into their carrying cases, and an effort is made to quiet them.

Should the cockfighter arrive at the pit location the day of the event rather than the night before, which is a more common occurrence, the first step would be that of weighing the birds and having them banded by the management. Once the band number and the weight of the cock are recorded, this information is given to the matchmaker and entry fees are paid.

Since the matchmaker must have similar information from all entries before he can begin the process of "blind-matching" the cocks, there is usually a waiting period. Frequently, cockfighters will engage in "hack fights" during this lull before the derby begins. Hack fights may be described as simply a fight between two birds arranged by two handlers. Usually a cockfighter brings more birds to a derby than will be entered. After a decision is made regarding which birds will be entered in the derby, the extra birds may be fought during these "hack fights."

"Heeling," as described by Sawyer, refers to putting the steel spurs (the proper name is "gaffs") on each leg of the rooster. Since the gaffs replace the natural spurs of the rooster, moleskin is placed on the rooster's leg and on his spurs. The gaffs, in turn, are so constructed as to permit these natural spurs to protrude through a hole in them. Pieces of leather are lapped over the gaffs and moleskin, and wax string is used to secure the gaffs on each leg. There is a degree of skill, apparently, associated with heeling.

After both cockfighters have either "heeled" their roosters personally or allowed someone else to accomplish this task, Hammer indicates that the birds are taken into the pit. Once they are in the pit a lot of people think that something has to be done to make the birds fight. However, all that has to be done is to turn them loose. When they see another rooster they will fight. But the handlers always hold the roosters up in front of each other, allowing them to peck each other.

The referee, at the appropriate time, tells the two handlers to "get ready." When the referee says, "Pit," each handler sets his rooster down on scorelines which are drawn some eight feet apart. The handlers then step back approximately six feet from the birds, and the fight begins. These scorelines usually are drawn with corn meal and need to be redrawn repeatedly.

Sawyer describes the cockfight like this: "The roosters fight until they hang, which means that one of these metal gaffs, which is needle-sharp on the point, has stuck in an opponent's rooster. It's up to the referee to order 'a handle,' and when he does so, if my gaff is in your rooster, you will take the gaff out of your own rooster. This rule would certainly prevent me from damaging my opponent's rooster."[3] Toole says that both handlers rush into the pit when the referee says, "Handle" and "Pin the birds" to the floor so that they won't be shaking around and hitting each other. Sawyer says that twenty seconds elapse between "pittings" before the referee again says to "get ready" and "pit." If both roosters reach the point of exhaustion after several "picks" or rounds, the referee may instruct the handlers to move to the "short line" or, as it is often called, the "center scorelines," which are drawn some sixteen to twenty-four inches apart.

Suppose you and I are contestants. We set our roosters down with one hand on the scoreline after the order to "pit," and if my rooster pecks at your rooster last, I say, "Count me." The referee counts to ten; then he says, "Handle," which commences another twenty-second rest period. If my rooster never pecks or tries to fight, the count continues. One must have three ten-counts and one twenty-count to win a fight. The count can be broken if the cock being counted out fights.

According to Toole, if my rooster has the count, when I set him on the short score, I may tip him backward just a little bit. Frequently, he is tired and he sinks to the floor. If I tip him the other way toward the other rooster, mine is likely to peck him, and I don't want him to since he already has the count. But, says Sawyer, a lot of times one doesn't go to the count. During the first "pitting," my rooster hits yours and it flops over just like it's dead—"He's just graveyard dead," pronounces Sawyer. You might not have to continue the count, but if there is still some life in the rooster, it is permissible to try to revive him.

The handler, according to Hammer, must know what to do for that rooster; he has to be a good first-aid man. There is some conjecture concerning putting the rooster's head into one's mouth and blowing on him, or covering portions of the rooster's body with cold water. Sometimes by knowing what to do, the handler may win a victory rather than suffer defeat.

Winning or losing obviously would be of tremendous importance to someone like Sawyer, who makes his living from this sport. He does not consider himself a big fighter, but others have judged him to be pretty fair. Financially, he has the backing of a medical doctor.

The financial arrangements at various cockfights vary according to the entry fees paid by the contestants. For example, at Newport, Tennessee, earlier this year (spring 1978), Sawyer tied for the lead, but the entry fee was just $50. Three or four people split the pot, and he came home with only $800. If the entry fee had been $150, as it was a few weeks later, he would have made more money.

Additionally, side bets can be placed with the spectators or with the opposing handler. Sawyer's method is to holler out, "I've got a hundred dollars over here!" Usually somebody in the stands calls him. If a handler is confident, he sometimes gives odds.

Toole indicates that he doesn't know of another sport involving gambling where there is the same situation as in cockfighting. Frequently, in a crowd of several hundred spectators, there will be betting across the pit. Toole isn't sure whether it is a matter of tradition or what, but he says there is a tremendous amount of pride, integrity, and honor among cockfighters in that they will not welch on a bet.

Considered by many to be one of the oldest sports in the world, cockfighting today occurs under a wide variety of circumstances in the United States. Participation in this sport often is illegal; yet thousands are involved in cockfighting.

Today, according to Sawyer, cockfighting is illegal in Tennessee. He notes, "It's always been illegal; I've never known cockfighting to be legal, and I've been fighting eleven years, and I've been around it for fifteen years. I've been to a lot of fights and I would say that over a span of fifteen years about twenty-five to thirty fights were raided by the police. I've never been put in jail, but three times, mainly because I can run fast. Four years ago (1974), I got caught in Cocke County, and it cost me $142 plus the court costs to get out of that one. I was trying to get charged as a spectator, but because I had rooster fighting equipment in my pocket, the police rationally assumed that I had been fighting them."

Sawyer observes that most pit owners know when they are going to be raided. He assumes that sheriffs or other law enforcement personnel are paid so much per month, week, or fight. "Generally, one officer will call and tip us off that we are going to be raided." About one humorous incident, Sawyer said, "The law tipped us and we thought we would fool them, so we just set up two horseshoe pegs in the pit. It was down below Lynchburg, Tennessee. Anyway, we were all pitching horseshoes when the law broke through the wall!"

In response to a series of questions involving the law; Hammer mentioned that it looks pretty bad right now. He commented that it is all right to go out and kill a cow, butcher it, make hamburger out of it and eat it, but it is not all right to go out and fight a game chicken—that's cruel! "I don't know what the future is going to be; it's going to be determined by some big wheels up there in Washington, and they don't fight cocks."

"I guess," asserts Sawyer, "the largest problem in rooster fighting is the humane society; they just don't like us. They just don't like the idea that two chickens can fight each other to the death or until one of them can't move. There is no difference, in my opinion, in the processing of fryers where they run them through conveyer belts and big blades are utilized to chop their heads off. A rooster, in contrast, can make up his own mind whether he wants to live or not; it's his own fate."

Toole responded to a number of questions which considered the legal aspects of this activity. Since he has a legal background and is also a participant in cockfighting, he was able to explore another facet of this sport.

In 1976, a federal law titled "Animal Welfare Act Amendments" was passed, and Toole believes that this legislation became effective on July 1, 1977. The part of this act which most concerns cockfighters is in Section 26 and is referred to as "Animal Fighting Ventures." A curious feature of this act is that where a given state does not prohibit cockfighting, there can be no federal offense. This legislation becomes ambiguous in many places. Moreover, regardless of its uncertain interpretation, the law has not been enforced since no money was appropriated to implement it.

There are many variables concerning the prohibition of cockfighting among the states, but the most common situation is for a state to have a law prohibiting cruelty to animals. In some five states the highest courts have ruled that cockfighting per se does not come within a cruelty-to-animal statute. Other states prohibit cockfighting on Sunday. Obviously, that law has nothing to do with cruelty, because if it is cruel, it is cruel any day of the week. Does cockfighting come within the cruelty-to-animal statutes in Tennessee and North Carolina? Toole observed that the average cockfighter likely is not willing to carry his case to the Supreme Court on a constitutional question but had rather pay a twenty-five-dollar fine and go on down the road. Somewhere along the line, these laws will be tested, but Toole hopes not to be involved as an indictee.

The cockfighter has his reasons for his involvement in this sport and has a definite philosophy. In a five-part study titled "Profiles of the American Cocker" published in *Grit and Steel* in 1974–75, the authors suggested that cockfighters are involved in this sport because they enjoy raising and fighting their own birds.[4] The great majority of cockfighters are more interested in the competition than in raising game fowl as a business. It is evident that the general public often has an incomplete and sometimes distorted picture of the cocker himself.

Toole declares that neither he nor his family is embarrassed when it is known that he is a cockfighter. He has learned to be positive rather than negative about it. On occasions when others have found out indirectly of his involvement, rather than "going low and copping out" by saying, "I don't know what you are talking about," he would say, "I am a cockfighter, and if you have a couple of days I will tell you why." Toole's philosophy is that so long as I am not hurting you or bothering you, why should you dictate to me what my pursuit of happiness should be?

Sawyer considers cockfighting not as a money-making hobby but as a means of making a living. He strongly intimates that one can't fight chickens as a hobby and make money; one has to do it for a living and have money behind him. Without the aim of making a living at it and without financial backing, one will win a few fights but will lose a lot more.

Hammer, in contrast, fights game fowl as a hobby, but apparently he has been extremely successful. In response to the question why he has excelled at cockfighting, he mentioned that the first time he attended a cockfight he saw one fellow carrying home four thousand dollars, and he told himself, "I'm going to get good at this chicken fighting." He traces his involvement with this sport to family ties. Although his father was involved, his brothers apparently were the first members of his family to encourage him to attend cockfights.

He welcomes the opportunity to talk with others about this sport. "That is the one thing I love to do better than anything else," he declared. He seems willing to share his techniques with others even though he may be facing them in competition at some future date. "I intend," he said, "to keep on raising good game roosters and try to keep on shipping 'em." His response to the question of what his greatest ambition is in cockfighting makes an appropriate conclusion to this paper and certainly would represent the viewpoint of most cockfighters: "I guess it would be my ambition to have as good a rooster as anybody and have everybody recognize that I have."

Notes

1. Edward L. McKenna and Louis F. McCabe, "Sports," *Colliers* 89 (January 23, 1932): 17.
2. Since cockfighting is illegal in the states where the respondents reside, fictitious names were supplied. Two of the respondents gave their permission verbally to be interviewed and to have these tapes transcribed for future use, whereas the third respondent signed a written release form.
3. Some minor rules of cockfighting vary from one region to another in the United States. Also, in a given region, house rules or pit rules may differ. However, rule books for cockfighting do exist. *Wortham's Rule* published by the Gamecock, in Hartford, Arkansas, probably is the best-known publication containing modern tournament and derby rules.
4. Clifton D. Bryant and William C. Capel, "Profiles of the American Cocker," *Grit and Steel* 76 (October 1974): 27–28; (November 1974): 32–33; (January 1975): 27–28; (February 1975): 33-D, E, F; and (April 1975): 27–30.

    TFSB Editor's Note: Several years ago a person told me of an experience at a cockfight. A cock was dying. The owner of the dying cock was challenged by the owner of an uninjured cock, who offered odds of twenty to one that his cock would defeat the dying cock. The owner of the injured cock bet one hundred dollars. The cocks were placed in fighting position. The miracle happened: The dying cock killed the other, then expired. The owner pocketed two thousand dollars.

    I asked, "Did the other person hesitate to fork over the two thousand dollars?"

    The answer was, "At a cockfight, you don't hesitate."

Further Reading in Play and Recreation Lore

Bronner, Simon J. *American Children's Folklore.* 2007.

Jones, Bessie, and Bess Lomax Hawes. *Step It Down: Games, Plays, Songs and Stories from the Afro-American Heritage.* 1987.

Opie, Iona, and Peter Opie. *The Singing Game.* 1988.

Page, Linda Garland, and Hilton Smith. *The Foxfire Book of Appalachian Toys and Games.* 1993.

Snow, Russell J. *Blood, Sweat and Feathers: The History and Sport of Cockfighting.* 2004.

Spalding, Susan Eike, and Jane Harris Woodside. *Communities in Motion: Dance, Community, and Tradition in America's Southeast and Beyond.* 1995.

Speck, Frank Gouldsmith, and Leonard Broom. *Cherokee Dance and Drama.* 1993.

Spurgeon, Alan L. *Waltz the Hall: The American Play Party.* 2005.

Sutton-Smith, Brian, Jay Mechling, Thomas W. Johnson, and Feicia R. McMahon. *Children's Folklore: A Source Book.* 1995.

PART SIX

Folk Speech

The founders of the Tennessee Folklore Society encouraged its members to collect the "natural antiquities" of the state, and these included elements of folk speech. What the founders undoubtedly had in mind were aspects of quaint or archaic speech (vocabulary, pronunciation, and grammatical forms) evident among the older, less educated, and primarily rural peoples whose language had been least influenced by formal education, travel, and modernization. The *Bulletin* ran an occasional feature called "Picturesque Speech" in the early 1940s in which members shared colorful terms and expressions. Later, from 1954 to 1961, Gordon Wood, a dialectologist located at the University of Tennessee at Chattanooga, edited a similar feature called "Heard in the South."

"Riddles from West Tennessee" by Herbert Halpert examines a form of verbal play that was a type of popular entertainment at various social gatherings in the past. One of Halpert's informants observed, "These riddles I remember hearing in Henry County, Tennessee, about 1936 to 1940, when I used to go to those little high school parties. We didn't have all that 'new-fangle-dangle paraphernalia' to provide entertainment. . . . Everybody would be seated. Someone would say a riddle. The one who guessed the answer got to tell one. If you were wise and 'up' on your riddles, you could be the star of the show." The riddles reflect an agrarian life in that many of the referent objects (e.g., a churn, three-legged pot, and wagon.) are things or situations unfamiliar in today's world.

Kelsie B. Harder's "Pert Nigh Almost: Folk Measurement" (1957), illustrates well the kind of material the founders wanted to capture. Of interest is how most of the folk units of measure reflect farming life and an intimate relationship with the environment. A native of Perry County, Harder was a professor of English at the University of New York at Potsdam for many years and a regular contributor of articles on onomastics to the *Bulletin*. This article and two others on folk speech he contributed the *Bulletin* are based on materials he collected in Perry County.

According to many Tennesseans, the distinctions between the three grand divisions of the state are more than geographical and political; they are also marked by deeply rooted cultural differences. One cultural difference that Tennesseans have debated for years is whether each of the grand divisions is distinguished from the others by dialect. As noted in Michael Montgomery's article, "Does Tennessee Have Three 'Grand' Dialects?: Evidence from the *Linguistic Atlas of the Gulf States*" (1995), when Tennesseans are asked what features distinguish one sectional dialect from another, most are hard pressed to provide examples. The responses are usually vague and nonspecific, such as "They speak with a twang" or "They have a nasal kind of speech." Some residents of Middle and West Tennessee conceive of East Tennessee as exotic as the Far East, and they harbor the unfounded belief shared by many Americans that there are some isolated mountain communities where people speak Elizabethan English. In contrast, some East Tennesseans maintain that the speech of whites and blacks in Middle and West Tennessee is much the same. Montgomery, a native East Tennessean and linguist who recently retired from the University of South Carolina, locates only faint phonological and lexical differences between the sections of the state in the linguistic atlas reports, but his analysis of the enduring belief in sectional dialects is both entertaining and insightful.

Riddles from West Tennessee
[1952]

Herbert Halpert

As far as I know, no extensive group of "true riddles" has hitherto been published from either East or West Tennessee. Middle Tennessee riddles have been reported in two excellent general collections. The first, by T. J. Farr, "Riddles of Middle Tennessee," appeared in this *Bulletin*, Vol. I, No. 3 (October 1935), 28–40, and was reprinted in Professor Farr's article, "Riddles and Superstitions of Middle Tennessee," *Journal of American Folklore*, XLVIII (1935), 318–326. The second was by W. A. Redfield, "A Collection of Middle Tennessee Riddles," in *Southern Folklore Quarterly*, I, No. 3 (September 1937), 35–50.

The West Tennessee riddles given here are fewer in number than those in either of the Middle Tennessee collections. There are two reasons for this. The riddles were reported by students in my folklore classes as part of their term collections contributed to the Folklore Archive at Murray State College. Since I had made no special effort to stress the riddle in my classes, only an occasional student has been interested. Of the seventy-three items given here, the majority were contributed by two students from Henry County, Mr. Ewing Jackson and Mr. Horace Derrington. Mr. Jackson recalled twenty-nine riddles from his childhood and collected fourteen more from a Negro informant. The significance of his contribution to this collection is understood when it is seen that I have given independent numbers to only sixty of the seventy-three items. Four other variants are also given in full; the remainder are merely noted with an indication of their variations, source, and contributors.

The second reason for the comparatively small number of items in this collection is that it has been limited to what Professor Archer Taylor calls "true riddles." There are a number of other kinds of riddling questions in the Tennessee collections of the Folklore Archive at Murray. At some later date, after they have been annotated, I hope to present them in this *Bulletin*.

Professor Taylor's exhaustive collection, *English Riddles from Oral Tradition* (Berkeley and Los Angeles, 1951), lists under eleven large categories 1,749 distinct items as the corpus of "true riddles" in English. Some of these numbers have single illustrations; others are reported from a dozen or more English and American collections. These West Tennessee riddles have been grouped under the Taylor headings for ready reference. I have listed all eleven of the Taylor categories, though we have no examples of three of them.

If one of these riddles is also found in the same form in the Taylor volume, my reference reads, "Taylor No." followed by the number assigned to the riddle in that book. If the Tennessee version has some variation, the reference is "Compare Taylor No. (etc.)." I have usually noted what the variation is. Where the riddle apparently belongs in a certain category but differs from the texts in Taylor, my note reads, "Compare Taylor Nos." followed by two numbers, usually joined by a hyphen. For six items (my numbers 6, 13, 41, 46, 53, and 55) on which I queried Professor Taylor by mail, he was kind enough to comment on, or approve, my classification.

Both as a folklore collector and as a teacher interested in stimulating others to collect, I am impressed by one surprising fact. Even a collection as small as this has produced several texts which Professor Taylor says are new to him. In addition, as my notes show, there are interesting variations from the Taylor texts both in the riddle questions and the answers given. See, for example, numbers 11, 29, 36c, 39, 40, 54, and 57. The answer to No. 54 seems to be the first English version of a particular European riddling theme.

I stress these items in order to urge folklorists interested in collecting riddles not to become discouraged by the exhaustive nature of Professor Taylor's book. Taylor's figure, 1,749, should not be allowed to become canonical for the English riddle as Child's figure, 305, too nearly has for the English ballad. Professor Taylor's own notes, with their stress on themes not reported hitherto in English riddling, should be a challenge to the collector.

The Tennessee collector has, I believe, two particular opportunities for important work. It is startling that no Tennessee folklorist, as far as I know, has harvested the rich field of Negro riddling. Among rural Negroes in most of the United States, riddling was, and probably still is, extremely popular. Tennessee should prove no exception. The other project would be to secure information from riddlers on the function of riddles. Who tells riddles? How are they learned? When are they asked? Are they used as a complete entertainment or along with other activities? Does the riddler like certain kinds of riddles and not others? Under what circumstances are riddles such as No. 60 asked? Has the riddler lost interest in some riddles but become fonder of others which he originally did not find interesting? Though we can guess some of the answers from our own experience, I think the question of why riddling is or has been popular is in itself a riddle that needs to be proposed and solved.

Here is a tabulation of contributors.

Abbreviation	Contributor	County	No. of Items
DC	Doris Castellaw	Crockett	5
HD	Horace Derrington	Henry	12
EJ	Ewing Jackson	Henry	43
TRJ	T. R. Jones	Stewart	2
CK	Clarence Kennedy	Henry	1
SL	Sara Leonard	Weakley	1
MCL	Mary C. Long	Marshall	3
MR	Marie Rowlette	Stewart	1
CSS	Charles S. Speed	Maury	1
NJT	Nancy Jane Terry	Shelby (Memphis)	4
(HLS)	(Harris Lee Stubblefield, EJ's Negro informant)		

Only a few of my student collectors gave any notes with their riddles, apart from data on source. (See Nos. 3 and 23.) Mr. Ewing Jackson wrote: "These riddles I remember hearing in Henry County, Tennessee, about 1936 to 1940, when I used to go to those little high school parties. We didn't have all that 'new-fangle-dangle paraphernalia' to provide entertainment that they have in a lot of sections. Riddles were a part of the entertainment at a party. Everybody would be seated. Someone would say a riddle. The one who guessed the answer got to tell one. If you were wise and 'up' on your riddles, you could be the star of the show.

"As for Negro riddles, I went to the homes of Negroes and asked them to tell me riddles and they did. They told me they tell them to the kids, and they use them when a large number of people gather at one place for entertainment."

I. Comparisons to a Living Creature, Nos. 1–335

1. It goes east and west;
   It goes north and south;
   Has ten thousand teeth
   And no mouth

   —"Cards you card 'bats' with" (i.e., cotton cards).

   > (EJ from memory)
   > Taylor No. 20

2. What stands on one foot, has its heart in its head, and grows in mother's garden?

   —A cabbage.

   > (EJ from memory)
   > Compare Taylor No. 32

3. Blacky under blacky,
   Blacky over blacky;
   Three legs up,
   Two legs down.
   What is it?

   —A Negro carrying a wash pot on his head.
   ("This riddle is not very good; I always thought they were supposed to rhyme. I've known it for a long time.")

   > (HD from A. B. Jeffrey)
   > Compare Taylor No. 64. For
   > the answer compare No. 67.

4. Three legs up,
   Six legs down;
   White in the middle,
   And black all around.

   —Man riding horse with a wash pot on his head.

   > (EJ from memory)
   > Compare Taylor Nos. 64–66

5. Four legs up,
   Four legs down;
   Soft in the middle,
   Hard all around.

   —A bed.

   > (EJ from memory)
   > Variant inserts "and" after lines 1 and 3
   > (HD from Hattie Davis, aged 72).
   > Taylor No. 69

6. Goes to the spring once a week, and leaves the bed at home.
   —Bed clothes.

   (Collector's note: "Everybody usually washes
   by a spring in Delno Community.")

   (EJ from HLS, Negro)
   Compare Taylor Nos. 112–122. Professor
   Taylor writes that the text is new to him.

7. Up hill
   And down hill,
   It goes to mill,
   And stands still.
   —Road.

   (EJ from memory)
   Compare Taylor No. 124. Here the reversal of lines 3 and 4 makes the comparison to an animal more precise and less
   paradoxical.

8. What goes up the chimney, but won't go down the chimney?
   —Smoke.

   (Marshall Co., MCL from Mrs. R. L. Long)
   Compare Taylor No. 141, except for "the
   chimney." Possibly some confusion has
   entered from the "umbrella" riddle, Taylor No. 1604.

9. Over the water,
   Under the water;
   Ten against two.

   —Woman walking across bridge with a jug of water on her head.
   (Collector said informant didn't know what "two" was.)

   (EJ from MLS, Negro)
   Compare Taylor No. 165. The "ten" must
   mean the fingers, but the "two" baffles
   me. Her ears, the ears of the jug, or
   simply the two sides of the jug, are all
   possibilities.

10. What goes up stairs on its head?
    —Tack in a shoe.

    (EJ from memory)
    Taylor No. 188

11. Give it hay, it'll live;
    Give it water, it'll die.
    —Fire.

    (EJ from memory)
    Compare Taylor No. 235. "Food," not
    "hay," is given for line 1 in Taylor.

12. What has eyes and cannot see?

—Potato.

> (Marshall Co., MCL from Mrs. R. L. Long)
> Taylor No. 277

13. Long tongue,
Hollow head,
Lot of fuss
And nothing said.

—Dinner bell.

> (EJ from memory)
> Compare Taylor Nos. 292–296,
> "tongue." Professor Taylor writes that
> the text is new to him.

14. What has four legs, a long tongue, goes to water but never drinks?

—Wagon.

> (HD from Dan Smith)
> Taylor No. 293

15. What has eyes and can't see,
A tongue and can't talk,
Has no legs but it can walk?

—A shoe.

> (EJ from HLS, Negro)
> Compare Taylor Nos. 296 and 311

16. What is it that has a tongue and can't talk,
Can run but can't walk?

—A wagon.

> (Stewart Co., TRJ from J. L. Hicks)
> Taylor No. 316

17. Eyes and can't see;
Legs and can't walk;
Pipe in its mouth;
It can't talk.

—Stove.

> (EJ from HLS, Negro)
> Compare Taylor Nos. 319 and 320

18. What has four eyes (i's) and can't see?

—Mississippi.

> (EJ from memory)
> Taylor No. 328

II. Comparisons to an Animal, Nos. 336–458

19. Tippy up stairs;
    Tippy down stairs;
    If you don't mind,
    Tippy will bite you.

    —"Wasper" (wasp).

    (EJ from HLS, Negro)
    Taylor No. 338

20. Hippy Tippy up stairs,
    Hippy Tippy down stairs;
    If you don't watch out,
    Hippy Tippy will bite you.

    —A wasp.

    (Maury Co., CSS from his grandmother)
    Taylor No. 338

21. What goes over the hills in the daytime and sets in the pail at night?
    —Milk

    (It's in the cow's bag in the daytime; the cow goes over pasture. You milk it out, and it's in the pail at night.)

    (EJ from memory)
    Compare Taylor Nos. 449–452

22. What is it that travels all over the hills and valleys in the daytime and stands on its head at night?

    —Tack in a shoe heel.

    (Stewart Co., TRJ from J. L. Hicks)
    Taylor No. 457

III. Comparisons to Several Animals, Nos. 459–512

No Tennessee variants in the Folklore Archive at Murray State College.

IV. Comparisons to a Person, Nos. 513–826

23. Little white nettie coat,
   In a white petticoat,
   She has a little red nose;
   The longer she stands, the shorter she grows.
   —Candle.

> (HD from Hattie Davis, aged 72)
> ("I don't think that is the way it goes
> but it has been so long since I heard
> it that I'm not sure. We used to tell it
> when I was a little girl about sixty years
> ago.")
> Compare Taylor Nos. 607–610

24. Little Nancy Edicoat
   In a white petticoat;
   The longer she stands
   The shorter she grows.
   —Candle.

> (EJ from memory)
> Taylor No. 611

25. I go all over the house in the day and sit in the corner at night.
   What am I?
   —Broom.

> (HD from Hattie Davis, aged 72)
> Taylor No. 695

26. Up she jumps,
   Out she runs;
   Now she squats
   And out it comes.

   —A woman milking a cow.

> (EJ from memory)
> Taylor No. 734

27. Long, tall, slim fellow;
   Pull his tongue and make him bellow.
   What is it?
   —A shotgun.

> (Crockett Co., DC from a 60-year-old
> neighbor)
> Taylor No. 755

28. As I went over London Bridge,
    I met my brother Bill.
    I cut off his head,
    And sucked his blood,
    And left his body standing still.

    —Jug of whiskey.

>   (Memphis, NJT from her mother, who
>   learned it in Missouri)
>   Compare Taylor No. 805

29. As I went over London Bridge,
    I met dear old Nancy;
    I pulled her neck and sucked her blood,
    And left her body dancing.

    —Jug of whiskey.
    ("Drank contents of jug; threw it in river. When it hit the waves,
    it danced.")

>   (EJ from memory)
>   Compare Taylor No. 805, but the body
>   "dancing" rather than standing is con-
>   nected with No. 806.

V. Comparisons to Several Persons, Nos. 827–1035

30. Whitey went in Whitey;
    Whitey run Whitey out of Whitey.

    —White dog running a white dog out of a cotton patch.

>   (EJ from memory)
>   Compare Taylor Nos. 842–844

31. Whitey went in Whitey;
    Whitey came out of Whitey,
    And left Whitey in Whitey.

    —White hen went into cotton patch, laid a white egg, and came out.

>   (EJ from memory)
>   Compare Taylor Nos. 860–861, but this
>   text is closer to the cotton field series.

32. As I went over London Bridge,
 I met a heap of people;
 Some were nicky,
 Some were nacky,
 Some the color of brown tobaccy.

 —Bees.

> (Memphis, NJT from her mother, who learned it in Missouri)
> Compare Taylor No. 898. For the answer compare Nos. 899–902.

33. As I went over London Bridge,
 I met a heap of people;
 Some were nick,
 An' some were nack,
 Some were color of brown tobacco.

 —"Waspers" (wasps).

> (EJ from HLS, Negro)
> Compare Taylor No. 898a (quail); for answer, compare No. 901 (wasps).

34. Down in the meadow there is a green house;
 In the green house there is a white house;
 In the white house there is a red house;
 In the red house there lived a bunch of little Negroes.

 —Watermelon.

> (EJ from memory)
> Taylor No. 916

VI. Comparisons to Plants, Nos. 1036–1099

No Tennessee variants in the Folklore Archive at Murray State College.

VII. Comparisons to Things, Nos. 1100–1259

No Tennessee variants in the Folklore Archive at Murray State College.

VIII. Enumeration of Comparisons, Nos. 1260–1408

35.   As high as a house,
        Then as low as a mouse;
        As bitter as gall,
        But sweet after all.

        —A walnut.

        (The walnut was first high on a tree, then low when it falls to
        the ground. The shell is bitter, but the nut is sweet.)

                              (Crockett Co., DC from a 60-year-old
                              neighbor)

        Variant omits "Then as" in line 2, and the first "As" in line 3.

                              (Henry Co., CK from a lady about 45
                              years old)
                              Compare Taylor Nos. 1270–1272.

36A. Crooked as a rainbow,
        Teeth like a cat.
        Guess all your lifetime,
        And you can't guess that.

        —A briar bush.

                              (Crockett Co., DC from a 60-year-old
                              neighbor)

36B. Crooked as a rainbow, teeth like a cat,
        Guess all your life and you can't guess that.

        —Briar

                              (HD from Hattie Davis, aged 72)
                              Taylor No. 1295

36C. Cracked (crooked) as a rainbow,
        And claws like a cat;
        Guess all your lifetime,
        You can't guess that.

        —Briar.

                              (EJ from HLS, Negro)
                              Compare Taylor No. 1295. No variant
                              with "claws" is listed.

37. Round as a biscuit,
    Busy as a bee;
    Prettiest little thing,
    You ever did see.
    —A watch.

> (EJ from memory)
> Variants: Line 3: "The prettiest."
>
> (Memphis, NJT from her mother)
> Line 4: "I" for "you."
>
> (Henry Co., HD, who says it is very common)
> Taylor No. 1310.

38. Round as a biscuit, deep as a cup,
    All of the king's horses can't pull it up.
    —Well.

> (HD from Minnie Smith, aged 76)
> Taylor No. 1318

39. Round as a biscuit, deep as a cup,
    The whole Mississippi River can't fill it up.
    —Well.

> (Memphis, NJT from her mother, who
> learned it in Missouri)
> Compare Taylor No. 1319 where the answer
> is a "sieve."

40. Round as a biscuit,
    Steep as a cup;
    Mississippi River
    Can't fill it up.
    —A strainer.

> (EJ from memory)
> Compare Taylor No. 1319, but for answer
> compare No. 1321.

41. Round as a biscuit,
    Bitter as a gall;
    In the middle
    The best of all.
    —A walnut.

> (EJ from memory)

I do not find this in Taylor, but to compare other walnut riddles, e.g., No. 1346, "round and rough," and No. 1270, "bitter and sweet." Professor Taylor, in a letter, says he is "inclined to believe (this riddle) is *compositum mixtum* of themes belonging to other riddles." He suggests "round as a biscuit" is borrowed from the watch riddle, and that "in the middle the best of all" also belongs to an eye riddle.

42. Round as a biscuit,
    Slick as a mole,
    Great big tail
    With a thumbin' hole*?

    —Frying pan.
    (* "That's what we call the hole where you hang the pan up on a nail.")

> (EJ from memory)
> Compare Taylor No. 1349

43. Soft as silk,
    White as milk;
    Green coat and thick wall
    Covers me all.

    —Walnut.

> (EJ from HLS, Negro)
> Compare Taylor No. 1359. This riddle
> lacks the usual phrase, "bitter as gall."

44. White as snow and not snow;
    Green as grass and not grass;
    Red as blood and not blood;
    Black as tar and not tar.

    —Blackberry in process of growth.
    ("Bloom; green berry; then after it turns red; then it turns ripe.")

> (EJ from HLS, Negro)
> Taylor No. 1391

45. Opens like a barn door,
    Shuts up like a bat.
    Guess all your lifetime,
    You can't guess that.

    —Umbrella.

> (EJ from HLS, Negro)
> Taylor No. 1401

IX. Enumerations in Terms of Form or of Form and Function, Nos. 1409–1495

46. Under your apron
    Black as a crow,
    Hair all around
    Thick as will grow;

If you will touch it,
It will do no harm;
Stick something in
Long as your arm.

—"Muffler" (i.e., woman's muff).

(EJ from memory)
Compare Taylor No. 1428, though the
action suggests it belongs with Nos.
1739–1749.

47. What is:
Big at both ends,
Little in the middle,
Digs up dirt,
And sings like a fiddle?

—"A dirt-dauber" (an insect).

(EJ from HLS, Negro)
Taylor No. 1421

48. Dead in the middle
And live at each end.

—Man plowing with horses.

(EJ from memory)

49. Big at the bottom,
Little at the top.
Right in the middle,
A thing goes flippity flop.

—Churn

(Crockett Co., DC from a 60-year-old
neighbor)

Variants of lines 3 and 4:
Something in the middle Goes flippity flop.

(EJ from memory)

Thing in the middle Goes flippity flop.

(Weakley Co., SL from his mother)

A thing in the middle Goes flippity flop.

(HD from his mother)
Taylor No. 1445

50. Two lookers,
    Two crookers,
    One switcher,
    Four hangdowns.

    —Cow.

                              (HD from A. B. Jeffrey)
                              Taylor No. 1476

51. Two lookers,
    Two hookers,
    Four downhangers,
    One switchabout.

    —A cow.

                              (EJ from HLS, Negro)
                              Taylor No. 1476

X. Enumeration in Terms of Color, Nos. 1496–1572

52. What is black and white and read all over?

    —Newspaper.

                              (EJ from memory; also HD from memory)
                              Taylor No. 1498

53. Black without and white within,
    Raise your leg and poke it in.

    —A boot.

                              (EJ from memory)

Compare Taylor No. 1538, though the color is usually "red within."
Later boots (as I recall from childhood) had a white lining. Professor
Taylor writes the original form of the riddle properly belongs in Nos.
1739–1749, and that the variant "white" shows the speaker is now aware
of what is intended.

54. What is first white; then green; then brown?

    —Chestnut.

                              (HD from Minnie Smith, aged 76)

Compare Taylor No. 1561. Although the arrangement of colors in
chronological sequence "ordinarily refers to the blackberry," Professor
Taylor points out (p. 635) "the Rumanians and modern Greeks use it for
a nut."

55. It's red, it's blue,
     It's tassel, it's green;
     The king can't touch it,
     No more than the queen.

     —(No answer recalled.)

(EJ from memory)

Compare Taylor No. 1570. I have tentatively classified this with the "rainbow" riddle. The informant did not suggest a meaning for "tassel." Professor Taylor writes: "I have no idea of what 'tassel' might be and I hope that you may recover more versions and establish its meaning. I should expect it to be a color."

XI. Enumerations in Terms of Acts, Nos. 1573–1749

56A. House full and yard full,
      Can't catch a spoonful.

      —Smoke.

(Setwart Co., MR from her mother)

Variant omits "and" in line 1.

(Marshall Co., MCL from Mrs. R. L. Long)
Taylor No. 1643

56B. House full, yard full,
      You can't catch a tablespoonful.

      —Smoke.

(EJ from memory)
Compare Taylor No. 1643 and No. 1649a

56C. Yard full, house full,
      Can't catch a thimbleful.

      —Smoke.

(Crockett Co., DC from 60-year-old neighbor)
Compare Taylor No. 1643

57. What is it that can be broken by a whisper?

     —A secret.

(EJ from memory)

Compare Taylor Nos. 1668–1669. These versions give "silence" as the answer.

58. What do you cut at both ends to make it longer?
    —Ditch.

> (EJ from HLS, Negro)
> Taylor No. 1693

59. Riddle me, riddle me, rocket.
    What a poor man throws away
    A rich man totes in his pocket.

    —Snot.

> (EJ from HLS, Negro)
> Taylor No. 1724

60. Old man went to bed and forgot it,
    Old lady went to bed and forgot it,
    The old man turned over and stuck it in.

    —Door key. ("They think everything but that.")

> (EJ from memory)
> Taylor No. 1744

Pert Nigh Almost
Folk Measurement
[1957]

Kelsie B. Harder

When Chaucer says of the Squire that "he was of evene lengthe, I guesse," he was voicing the measuring inexactitude of human folk. Man seems to have been a slave to measurement for thousands of years, and there is little doubt that exactitude of the yardstick has had about as much to contribute to human "progress" as thinking. Nevertheless, measurements in feet, inches, centimeters, millimeters, pounds, ounces, etc., can never take the place of such unscientific, but subtle, even cruel in their ironic way, statements as Mercutio makes about the size of his mortal wound, which will do, or as that of the young boy, barefoot, obviously in itching anguish, who cried out, "I jist know I got forty-lebm chiggers all over me." One is dying and the other is in itching misery. Both are serious, if not "scientifically" correct.

In this paper I wish to list and discuss "somewhat" a number of "pert nigh almost" or "I guess" measurements, ones which find no sanction among the dead metaphors and similes used by the white-robed priests of the laboratory, whose feet, inches, and ounces are in reality metaphors when we come to think about it, a trifle dull perhaps, though useful for laboratory purposes no doubt. This list that follows has some expressions that are standard, some substandard, and many which must be considered dialectal. All are part and parcel of my own speech background on Cedar Creek, Perry County, Tennessee, and all were heard, unless otherwise noted, during the latter part of the summer of 1956. The list is not exhaustive, for combinations and similes continuously arise; the material can certainly be supplemented or corroborated.

The grouping is arbitrary. I shall begin with the English suffix *-ful,* a conventional method for forming new words. The qualifier *almost* frequently precedes the use of the *-ful* formations. Among the *-ful* words are the following (remember that *-ful* is free-compounding): *bagful:* Relatively recent and rare in the singular but known widely in a nursery rime line, "Yes, sir, yes, sir, three bagsfull." A *baitful* is a quantity of something edible: "Them 'possum grapes was almost a baitful." As for *bedful,* I recently heard in reference to a newly married couple: "Them two'll make pert near a bedful." A *crawful* cannot be measured, but it can be felt, especially when *craw* is jocularly substituted for the human stomach. *Cribful,* a standard term, occurred in this bit of comment: "John ain't goin' make much corn offen that hillside, but I betchy he could gather a cribful o' snakes."

Other related terms that can be heard are *diaperful* (and the inevitable *hippinful*), *dipperful* (rarely now), *doorful* (joc., "He sure makes a doorful"), *fruitjarful, goardful* (archaic), *handful* ("a handful of smoke," "too big a handful"), *lapful* (can be taboo in some locations), *loadful* ("How much hay ye got on?" "I got a loadful on"), *mouthful* (occ. heard instead of *drink:* "Pour me out a mouthful"), *pokeful* ("I jis' bought 'em a pokeful"), *shirtful* (rarely, but once widely used by boys who fished by swimming under the water, grabbing fish, and depositing them in their shirts until they came out of the water with their shirts filled with fish), *shoeboxful* ("He saved them old marbles till he got a shoeboxful"). *slop-bucketful, smokehouseful, squirtful* (joc.), *stomachful* (but *bellyful* is often substituted), and a few taboo *-fuls* that most of us can fill in as we chose. A few expressions complete the distension: "so full he's about to bust," "so full he can't bend," "She's so full she's runnin' out both ends," and the especially slick, full-blooded image, "full as a tick." That is *plumb full.*

Unfortunately, we do not have a suffix for *empty.* But expressions denoting emptiness are many. A water jar may be empty; it may also be *out* or *plumb out.* "They ain't nary slap-dab drop o' water in that branch run" is perfectly good usage in its place. To outsiders, some of the expressions seem to be wisecracks or lamp-smellers. Within the community, however, one can hear quite naturally, without any apparent self-consciousness on the speaker's part, such statements as "That bucket's bone dry," "I'm so empty my stomach's growed to by backbone," "The well's done dried up," "The bottom fell out of the spring last week," "I'm so empty I got the weak tremmels," and "The pond's so empty the frogs dried up and blowed away." "That jar's empty as a sucked egg" moves into the category of wisecracks, and so does "empty as Hell's half-acre," along with "empty as a church on takin'–up-plate Sunday."

Nearly empty is not expressive enough either. These specimens, some rather trite, I have heard recently: *near 'bout(s) dry, pert nigh almost dry, ain't hardly none, pert nigh is out, jist enough to wetchy gizzard, might nigh ain't none, jist a little dab, a drop or two left, orter be a squirtful (thimbleful) left,* and *maybe a dram's there. Dram* is used almost universally in the area for "a drink of any liquid," but I believe that the speaker is always aware of a relationship with alcoholic drinks.

Expressions of depth often draw upon the human body for measurement similarity and scale from "jist deep enough to wetch shoe soles" to "forty foot over ye head, I guess." To fill the range, I mention first my own favorite, *shoe-mouth deep*: "That hoglot's shoe-mouth deep" indicates that the mud and muck are rather deep, but not as deep as it would be if the depth was "over the shoe-tops." *Half shoe-mouth deep* is also heard, but not *half over the shoe-tops*.

Next in order up the human body measuring stick are *ankle deep, half knee deep, knee deep, hip deep* (around this depth can be found at least two taboo depth expressions), *waist deep, belly deep, middle deep, middlin' deep, chest deep* (to humans, but *breast deep* to mules and horses), and *shoulder deep*. I do not remember hearing or using *neck deep*. The expression used was always *up to the neck*.

Up to indicates that the depth is such that it barely touches the object, as distinguished from *over*, which means that the object is completely covered. *Over* can also be qualified by "just lapping." *Up to* can be used with *shoe-mouth, ankle, knee, hip, waist, middle, belly*, and *shoulder*.

Beginning with another extremity, the arm, we have *fingernail deep, finger deep, elbow deep*, and *shoulder deep*. *Up to* can be used with *wrist, elbow*, and *shoulder*. Qualifiers, such as *jist about, pert nigh, just past, near 'bouts, around*, etc., attach themselves naturally.

Besides the human body, farm implements and animals are often pressed into duty for measuring depth. A stream can be *rim deep* (i.e., barely over the wagon tire and fellers—st. "fellies"), *spoke deep, over the spokes, hub deep, over the hub cap, over the tongue, over the coupling pole, over the hounds, over the rocking bolster, over the running gears, flat deep* (in reference to the wagon frame or *flat*), *wagon-bed deep*, and *up to the standards*. Then the depth becomes *over*.

Shallowness depends on the emphasis of depth. If *just* is used, the stress is on the shallowness. For instance, "Buffalo River's purty shaller there, just shoulder deep" implies that Buffalo River is normally deeper along this section. But *shallow* cannot be substituted in sentence positions where *deep* appears. Usually shallowness is expressed by the use of the negative with *deep*: "It's not deep," "It ain't ebm ankle deep," "It's not deep enough to wetchy finger in," etc., although *shallow* appears in such expressions as "It's too shaller to wade," "It's too shaller for minners to swin in," and, facetiously, "It's shaller enough to paddle a steamboat in" or "That sankhole's shaller enough to swaller a team o' mules." Shallowness and depth overlap in a number of wisecracks: "'Tain't deep enough to hide a gnat's posterior" expresses extreme shallowness, even though several taboo terms can be substituted for *posterior*. The word *posterior* is never heard. Another vivid, but logically meaningless, expression is "It's just about knee deep to a grasshopper." But one of the more vivid depth metaphors that I have happened upon comes from a letter written to me in 1945. The writer had been angered by an imagined wrong. She wrote, "I would have kicked her so hard it would take a shoe shop to pull the shoe out."

Tall and *high* are for all practical purposes synonymous and can often be interchanged. Growing boys usually "shoot up tall (high) as a house." I have heard that a mule was both 15-hand high and 15-hand tall. The fact that a hand's span is supposed to be four inches or 10.17 centimeters cannot be taken seriously. A hand is a hand, and a muletrader's hand is quite narrow, narrow as a slat, figuratively, of course. On the other hand, a buyer's hand is "sort of" broad, broad as a board, so to speak.

High can be found in combination with *ankle, knee, hip, shoulder, neck, chin,* and *head.* Height can also be measured in fingers, as *one-finger high, two-fingers high,* and *three-fingers high,* but not *four-fingers high,* for that would constitute a *hand.* Except for one well-known obscene jesture, the thumb does not contribute to dimensions. "As high as you can reach" is standard, as is "as high as Haman," but "tall as the loft (ceiling)" and "tall as a bird-house pole" speak more for the normal expressions in the area. Also, "He's tall as he can be," logically true, means that "he is quite tall." Rail fences are also pressed into service to donate degrees of height. To the farmer, richland weeds grow incredibly fast and tall; consequently, "tall as a richland weed" is common. "Tall as a sprout," however, relegates us to a different stature.

Shortness and lowness may or may not assume the same proportions. In matters of clothes, *short* of course can mean high, viewed from certain angles. "My overalls is too short" or "My overalls are so short I could wade the creek and never git wet" means that they crawl up too high on my legs and need to be let out to "lengthen the legs." But if I say that my overalls are too low (too long), I imply that they need to be let up (taken up) to shorten them. The same situation occurs with dresses, but the expressions are more colorful—some would say salacious.

Short and low, to indicate human height, can often be interchanged, as, for example, in "He's too low (short) to reach the table." But in "He's awful low down," the context is needed to clarify the ambiguity of whether the reference is to character or to position of the body.

Witticisms pertaining to short and low can always be heard. Among those I have collected are "His watergap's low enough for a cow to crawl through," "He's swaggin' so low his runnin' gear's draggin'," and "That plowline's so short I'll have to use the mules' tails for plowhandles."

Length, or "length," can be as long as, or about as long as the fingernail, arm, leg, or "you are." But I suspect that the length of snakes has called for more tall talk than truth telling in the area of measurement, that is, if we eliminate some taboo boasts. Some of the more or less exact expressions of snake length are "long as a fence rail," "about as long as ye arm (leg)," "long as a hoehandle," "long as a peephole," "as long as its mammy's mouth," or just "the longest I ever did see or hear tell of." Other comparisons, applicable to different objects, are "as long as, or longer'n a cat's hair," "long as a mare's tail," "long as a crane's neck," "long as my coattail (apron strings, stocking)," and "long as from here to Utah." One of the more ambiguous comparisons occurs in "about as long as a stick, or maybe a bit longer." "About as long as a broomstraw" is another just as indefinite. All these expressions when used with the negative denote shortness.

Width is sometimes expressed in breadth. In addition, *thick* is occasionally synonymous with *wide* and *broad*. In the statement, which I have bowdlerized a mite, "She's as thick as a washtub," both *wide* and *broad* could be substituted for *thick*. Comparisons of width are "wide as a straddle," "the barn," "the river," "the creek," "ye hand," "the door," "too wide to paddle across" (which may or may not have any connection with water), and "about as wide as the pan o' ye hand." With *broad* are "broad as a barn," "as a beam," "a plank," "a board," "a half-bushel," "a washtub," "a washkettle," "a barn door," and "a turn o' corn." Narrowness is expressed in the negative *no broader'n*.

Thick also denotes intimacy of friends or member families: "Them folks is thick as hair (or fleas) on a dog's back," "so thick ye can't pry 'em apart," "thick as thieves," "thick as sorghum 'lassies in winter-time," and the smart-alec elegancy of "thick as maggots on a dead groundhog." One family was described as "thicker'n a old sow 'n' pigs." Besides objects being as "thick as Johnson (or crab) grass," "as mush," or "burrs," they are also "just as thick as can be."

Next in the order of my listing, I come to the size of holes. Holes in or under fences come in two sizes, pigholes and hogholes, the former "little bitty holes" and the latter "pretty big holes." There are rabbitholes, chickenholes, ratholes, and mouseholes, all pertaining to the size and not necessarily to the animal that makes use of them. *Big* enough usually appears in the comparisons, as in "It's a hole big enough for a cow to go down," "to get your head in," "to swaller a wagon and team," "for a hog (cow, mule) to crawl through," "to put a house (barn, crib) in," "to bury ye in," and "for Noah's ark." *Deep* can be substituted for *big* in all of these, depending on whether the speaker wishes to emphasize depth or size. A hold can also be "as big as the side of the house." Holes in doors or walls are "big enough to get your finger, fist, or arm through." In the floor, they are big enough for a dog, baby, or any other mobile object to fall through. I heard one preacher describe Hell as a "hole big as creation." That, of course, is big enough.In an assortment of odds and ends, I have collected the following sizes:

"That snake's big 'round as ye leg."

"That old black cow has a tiny calf about the size of a little lamb."

"She ain't no biggern'n a scantlin', just skin 'n' bone."

"The Peaches are as big as Birds eggs and some are as big as Partridge eggs." (Letter, Apr. 27, 1945.)

"That watermelon is about half size a half-bushel."

"His old belly's as big as a keg."

"Them girls is just fryin' size."

"He's got more hair'n you could shake a stick at."

"That old nose is swelled almost as big as a small hen egg."

"Them little boys ain't no bigger'n sprouts."

"That risin' swole up as big as a pone." (In this instance, *pone* means "a hard ridge or swelling around a wound.")

"I got chickens 'bout the size of pa't'idges."

"I aim to raise a knot on ye head as big as a goose egg."

"We had hail the size of large marbles."

"That air's a dost big enough to kill a mule."

"Ye got a hunk o' bread in ye mouth now big as a hen egg."

"That old box is as big as a bale of hay."

"He's a-goin' to bite off more'n he can chew."

"That gal ain't big enough for a washing o' soap."

"It ain't room enough to cuss a cat without gettin' hair in ye mouth."

"John's wife's as big as a cow carryin' a calf."

"That little old girl wasn't much more'n big as a pound o' soap."

"My little chickens is big enough to swaller corn, but 'ey ain't a-growin' none."

"Them ice sticks was hangin' off the house, long as ye arm."

"Them young'uns'll be puffed up big's a hog bladder."

"His foot ain't big. She's just his leg turned up."

"We got watermelons 'bout size ye head."

"We got watermelons 'bout size small pumpkins."

Temperature: "Man, she's hot as a blisterbug today."

"That little old kid ain't light as a feather."

"He's heavy's a fatt'nin' hog."

These comparisons are almost inexhaustible. I have omitted several scatological ones in my attempt to list only those that seem to occur naturally. I shall stop with this one: "He's big enough to sleep by hisself."

Everyone in unfamiliar territory has been chagrined by the odd answers given to questions about direction or distance. Among the expressions I have heard and used are the following: "God, they live way over yonder. They's a million dirt roads 'tween here and there. And they all look alike." "It's just a little piece," "a little ways," "a step or two," "just over the ridge," "just up the hill," "down the holler," "up the road," "a hop, skip, and a jump," "a right smart piece," "way over (down, up, outch) yonder," "just down (up) the creek," and "a little ways around the bend." However, "Ain't far the way the crow flies, but she's a purty good hike around the cowpath" draws laughter from groups gathered in the local stores.

In the art of cooking, amounts are measured off in pinches, dabs, dribbles, drops, and handfuls. An area of land is stepped off, three steps to the yard for a short-legged person and one pretty long step for a long-legged person. Also, a yard measures "from the tip of the nose to the tip of the thumb and forefinger on the right hand pinched together." A foot is equal to the hands placed so that the thumbs overlap at the first joint. Center is "square center" or "slap dab in the middle." It is no wonder, I suppose, that many buildings are erected "by guess and by God," as one hears it said frequently when a building is started.

For extremely small sizes or amounts, *a thimbleful, a mite, just a tinsy dab, just enough for a bird, a little dribble, about the size of a chigger (flea, nit, chicken mite)*, and *big as a pinch of snuff* can be heard. Women, who would be embarrassed if they became conscious of what they had said, often call little chickens "little bitchy, tintchy chickens." This is also heard of small babies, although "little bitsy, tinsy" is also heard. In a barber shop, I heard one barber, who was quite busy and was irritated with an elderly man who would not await his turn, comment heatedly, "I don't see why that old man was in such an all-fired hurry. He ain't got but a frazzlin' dab o' hair noway." On the other hand, *just scads* and *forty-lebm* represent many.

This listing of folk expression of measurement is, as I have pointed out above, not complete. It does, however, open an area of folk-speech collecting that has not been thoroughly treated. I have tried throughout to emphasize that the majority of the terms and comparisons are spoken naturally without any overt attempt on the part of the speaker to be ornate, vivid, or pretentious.

Does Tennessee Have Three "Grand" Dialects?
Evidence from the
Linguistic Atlas of Gulf States
[1995]

Michael Montgomery

This paper is dedicated to Kelsie Harder, a native Tennessean who has written more on the language of the Volunteer State than any other person, especially on his native Perry County.[1] Professor Harder, who has spent his academic career largely at the State University of New York at Potsdam, is most widely known for his work on onomastics and is familiar to readers of this journal as the longtime, faithful reviewer of hundreds of books on names. It is thus fitting that the present essay, which combines name study with dialectology with reference to Tennessee, should pay tribute to his work by examining the linguistic dimensions of a long-held, popular truism—that the state has three distinct "grand divisions" of East, Middle, and West. Is this a linguistic as well as a political differentiation? Beyond considering some of the types of linguistic evidence available and determining what they tell in this regard, we will see that deeper issues of continuing interest to folklorists, sociologists, and historians are raised, such as "What are the elements of linguistic behavior that people use to classify one another as belonging to a certain regional or social group?" "In what objective way are sectional divisions manifested in the behavior of Tennesseans?" and, more elusive, "What is the psychological reality of dialects and on what exactly are they based?"

Early in his 1986 Pulitzer Prize–winning novel *A Summons to Memphis,* the late Peter Taylor has the teenage protagonist move with his parents and sister from their native Nashville to the river city of Memphis; the latter, according to the young man, was marked by "the peculiar institutions of the place—the institutions, that is to say, which one associates with the cotton and river culture of the Deep South" (p. 2). Taylor frames this relocation from one city to another in terms of a deep cultural contrast between the two regions in which the cities were located: "On the whole the move was made quietly and without fanfare, in the best Upper South manner. There was nothing Deep South about our family—an important distinction in our minds" (p. 3). A more recent story in the *Tennessean* newspaper (December 25, 1994) dealt with the longtime contrast, even rivalry, between the two cities:

> They have spent two centuries growing up together, have traded sons and daughters for countless generations, have battled for similar spoils and opportunities, developed distinct cultural heritages, nurtured waves of entrepreneurs, and done it all under the roof of the same state government.
>
> And they are stranger unto each other. Or is it rivals? The nature of their relationship—or lack thereof—is one of the great puzzles of the age.
>
> "I don't really know the dark secrets between these two cities, why it is that they are brothers and yet strangers," says Nashville author John Egerton. "It just seems it's always been that way."
>
> To hear lifelong residents of both cities tell it, there is an eerie gulf between Memphis and Nashville. Each city tends to take a dim view of the other, latching on to a few simple stereotypes and supposing that somehow the other is worse. Nashville is country music, hifalutin snobs, churches, Opryland, and state government. Memphis is rhythm and blues, decadent partygoers, barbecue, cotton and Elvis. (Parsons 1994:1F)

In many ways the distinction between the two cities is a real and important one. Most Tennesseans would feel that Taylor's description is neither artificial nor exaggerated and would have an intuitive sense of the difference between both the cities and the regions of which they are a part. But they would likely add something to this—the consciousness of a third division of the state, with its own culture and people and identity—East Tennessee.

It is all a bit strange. One can hardly begin a volume on Tennessee history without the author referring to the state's three grand divisions, sometimes called the "Three States of Tennessee," which are enshrined on the state flag by three white stars in a circle of blue. Nor can one read about significant facts and events in the history of the state without the interplay of these divisions coming to the fore. Though just about everyone native to the state, regardless of social class, knows that these divisions are there in very human terms, it is usually right nigh impossible for them to pin down what they consist of. It is one thing to say that Memphis is the home of rhythm and blues while Nashville is the capital of country music, but this implies little, if anything, about differences between the people of the regions. There's no obvious test that can objectively detect East, Middle, and West Tennesseans today by their political inclinations, cultural affiliations, athletic allegiances, or social manners, but there seems to be agreement that the differences are as real as they can be. Might their speech have something to do with this? This possibility has motivated the author over the past decade to conduct of his fellow Tennesseans an unscientific, intermittent oral survey consisting of three questions: "Are people in the three parts of the state different?" (to which the response has almost invariably been "Yes"), "Do you think they talk differently?" (also usually answered "Yes"), and "In what way is their speech different?" (to which respondents have rarely been able to be specific, except occasionally to suggest that East Tennesseans pronounce the name of the state with the accent on the first syllable, while other Tennesseans pronounce it on the third).

The political angle to this intrastate division can in part be documented and understood. The June 14, 1987, issue of the *Atlanta Journal and Constitution* ran a piece that must have seemed a little off the wall to many of the newspaper's readers. The story was headlined "Cumberlanders Want a 51st State" and reported how residents in a nine-county area of southeast Kentucky, northeast Tennessee, and southwest Virginia had met to declare themselves a separate entity. This would doubtless have been viewed by most readers as a publicity gambit or stunt, and this it surely was (after all, the nickname of the State of Cumberland was "Mountains Are Fun"), but this proposal for separation strikes a familiar note to many Tennesseans and has nothing to do with refighting the Civil War—in fact, the idea long predates that conflict. Since the late eighteenth century, the very earliest days of settlement, the territory later to become the Volunteer State has been marked by sectionalism. East Tennessee hill folks haven't been at all sure they've wanted to be part of the same state as Middle Tennesseans, and vice versa. For instance, in the 1780s, East Tennesseans in the Watauga settlements were involved in the abortive attempt to create the State of Franklin for themselves, and in Middle Tennessee a group of 256 pioneers in 1780 formed an independent government in the Nashville basin by drafting and signing the Cumberland Compact. Tennesseans in different parts of the state have long had their own ideas about their sectional independence.

Political as well as economic forces conspired to crystallize the three-way division of Tennessee in the early days of statehood. (Their economies have long been based on distinctive patterns of agriculture and land use, with, for instance, cotton dominating West Tennessee and tobacco in East and parts of Middle Tennessee.) The division was manifest in the rivalry over locating the state capital in the early 1800s and also in the 1834 state constitution, a document that institutionalized the three sections by decreeing equal representation on the state Supreme Court. It was cemented by differences in their participation in the Secession Convention of 1860 and in the Civil War. The latter, as we read in the state's history, split a tragically large number of Tennessee families, and the high enlistment rate of East Tennesseans in the Union cause solidified the political isolation of the eastern third of the state during and following the war. The elevation of the East Tennessee tailor Andrew Johnson, considered a turncoat by many of his fellow Volunteers, to the presidency in 1865 widened and embittered the rift. That the sectional feeling may consequently be strongest in East Tennessee is echoed by historian Charles Crawford of (then) Memphis State University: "It has been traditional in the mountain counties to view those of different experience and culture as real or potential enemies. And the local residents [of East Tennessee] make little distinction between Middle and West Tennessee. All are outsiders" (Crawford 1986:68).

In politics East Tennessee has seen itself as a separate entity down to the modern day. It's not just that Jimmy Quillen, the First District congressman representing Upper East Tennessee, proposed as one of his first actions in Congress in 1963 that East Tennessee be split off and declared the fifty-first state in the Union. The reporting of statewide election returns is normally broken down three ways, reflecting the divergent political climates and party loyalties in East, Middle, and West Tennessee and the expectation that the different political histories of the three will be revealed in the vote counts, which it usually is. The state guidebook to Tennessee produced by the Federal Writers' Project of the Work Projects Administration (1939) characterized the situation in this way: "In politics, as in most things, the East Tennessean shows his independence, for here in an otherwise Democratic State is a strong Republican district that regularly chooses Republican representatives in both State and Federal elections. To the East Tennessean, West Tennessee is almost as far away and unknown as Missouri. He looks upon this western section as a swamp and resents the weight of the powerful Shelby County political machine in state-wide elections. What West Tennessee is for, he is 'agin'" (4). As evidenced particularly in the November 1994 elections, the political allegiances of Middle and West Tennessee have shifted markedly toward the Republican Party since this statement was written, but it is not at all clear that residents of the state's three divisions feel any closer to one another.

When Tennesseans identify with one division of the state or another today, in the late twentieth century, does this reflect anything more than regional pride? Or to put it more bluntly—do Tennesseans claim identity with their section of the state as a way of expressing some kind of local clannishness and sectional prejudices against other Tennesseans, while using the history of the state as justification?

This last question is probably easy enough to discount, but the persistent belief by the residents of the state in sectional differences is difficult to explore in any concrete way. The three grand divisions are not markedly distinguished by geographical cleavages, as is Michigan's Upper Peninsula, for instance, from the lower part of the state, or by settlement history, as Up Country South Carolina is from the Low Country. Stanley Folmsbee et al. in *Tennessee: A Short History* surely overstate the case in saying that "had the natural contours been followed, Tennessee would be three states or parts of three states, instead of one" (1969:3). The boundary between West and Middle Tennessee is the short hop across the Tennessee River. Hardly anyone but the state legislature and professional geographers have known where Middle Tennessee stops and East Tennessee begins, and the legislature has changed its mind several times about this.

The three sections of Tennessee were settled largely by the same groups of people, at least among whites, who migrated from east to west across the territory and state from the 1780s to the 1820s. David Crockett represents an archetypical Tennessean in this regard. Born in Washington County in Upper East Tennessee, with his family he moved seventy miles southwest to Jefferson County at an early age, as a young husband to south-central Tennessee (Hickman County), which he represented in the state legislature, and later to "the last frontier" of the state, what was to become Gibson County in the extreme northwest corner of Tennessee, which he represented in the U.S. Congress. While Middle and West Tennessee were not settled entirely by East Tennesseans looking for more open spaces, they were populated by the same European-derived stocks of people (this is not to discount the numbers and influence of black settlers, particularly in West Tennessee).

Yet many Tennesseans perceive that the three divisions of the state have had distinct histories, and today the Volunteer State is, so far as this writer knows, the only one with three regional historical societies, each with its own library and journal.[2] Despite mobility between the sections and many recent common political and economic developments, Tennesseans remain as conscious of the divisions of the state. Natives of Knoxville or Johnson City or elsewhere in the eastern third of the state, when asked where they are from, tend to say "East Tennessee" rather than "Tennessee," when meeting outsiders.[3] This does not reflect any lack of state pride. We come back to a question posed at the beginning: In what objective way are sectional divisions manifested in the behavior of Tennesseans? Why are the divisions so clear cut in the minds of the state's citizens?

Though problematic to distinguish on physical geography and settlement history, the three grand divisions of Tennessee have sometimes been recognized by geographers and correlated with cultural artifacts. For example, in his *Cultural Regions of the United States* (1975:174), Raymond Gastil outlines a three-way division of the state based on analysis of material features such as barn and fence construction, between the Mountain, Upland, and Lowland cultural areas. This is a more refined division than that of most other geographers, who consider both East and Middle Tennessee as part of the Upper South and West Tennessee a northward extension of the Lower South Plantation Belt (see Zelinsky 1973; Jordan 1976). However, the regional distinctions made by cultural geographers hardly bring us closer to understanding the perceived differences between the sections of the state, because it is quite doubtful that material culture has much to do with the consciousness of regional divisions in our urban age.

As far as research and discussion on Tennessee speech is concerned, more than two hundred articles and notes have dealt in whole or in part with the state, beginning with a five-page article, "Dialectal Survivals in Tennessee," that Calvin S. Brown, a Vanderbilt University professor, published in 1889.[4] As voluminous as this literature may appear to be, most of it, including all nine dissertations that have been written, focuses on single communities or other small areas and thus provides no basis for a statewide view or a comparison between regions within the state. Because of this basic limitation, no material has been collected, with the exception of two projects, to permit the exami-nation of regional linguistic distinctions within the state. Actually, nearly all the scholarship on Tennessee speech has been concerned with East Tennessee. This is explained by the longer and greater interest in mountain speech, but it means that the western two-thirds of the state have been almost entirely neglected by researchers—other than Kelsie Harder.

One researcher to collect evidence statewide is Gordon Wood, who began his Vocabulary Change project while on the faculty at the University of Chatta-nooga in the 1950s. A number of preliminary reports of his research were pub-lished in the present journal and a summary volume appeared in 1973. Because Wood assumed a two-way division of the state and accordingly sought the rela-tive frequency of items in these regions, his findings do not bear directly on the question at hand about a possible three-way distinction. In more recent years, however, research in linguistic geography, in the form of data from the *Linguis-tic Atlas of the Gulf States* (LAGS), has become available to analyze, and this offers the first realistic opportunity for a three-way contrast of language pat-terns within Tennessee.[5] LAGS data provide two unique features for exploring intra-state differences and similarities. First, LAGS interviewed 141 natives of the state (60 in the East, 47 in Middle, and 34 in West Tennessee) at roughly the same time—in the early and mid-1970s.[6] Second, the data are largely com-parable in that informants generally answered the same questions (the survey encompassed approximately 800 questions which sought responses that were known to vary in pronunciation, vocabulary, grammar, or otherwise). In short, LAGS data offer the prospect of identifying linguistic contrasts within the state, perhaps even quite subtle ones, that play a role in the perceptions Tennesseans have of intra-state differences among its citizens. Such data will help us answer, or come much closer to answering, whether it is possible to identify three dif-ferent dialects in the state and whether there may be shibboleths that mark the speech of East Tennesseans vs. Middle vs. West Tennesseans.[7] We will examine some of the LAGS lexical and phonological evidence to answer these questions.

For those unfamiliar with the LAGS project, a brief summary is in order. Directed by Lee Pederson of Emory University throughout its history (1968–92),

LAGS is a broad-based study of regional and social dialects in eight southern states: Tennessee, Arkansas, Louisiana, Mississippi, Florida, Alabama, Arkansas, and Texas (as far west as the Balcones Escarpment). It is the largest and most inclusive research project ever undertaken on southern speech, providing basic texts for the study of speech in the region and a description of the sociohistorical and sociolinguistic contexts necessary for their interpretation.[8] Ultimately, the project has sought to achieve four additional, interrelated goals: an inventory of the dominant and recessive patterns of usage in the Gulf States; a global description of regional and social varieties of southern speech; an abstract of regional phonology, grammar, and lexicon; and an identification of areas of linguistic complexity which require further study (Bailey 1989; Pederson 1977:28).

Linguistic geography is the discipline that attempts to map, through various devices, individual linguistic features and then to generalize the results of these maps into distinct language or dialect areas. LAGS is an extension of the direct method of linguistic geography, which was initiated by Jules Gillieron in France at the turn of the century and refined by Hans Kurath in the United States in the 1920s. These methods involve the following: selection of a network of communities, including focal, relic, and transitional communities, on the basis of the history of the region; conversational interviews with natives of these communities conducted with a questionnaire of selected items; and recording of the responses in finely graded phonetics. In LAGS, informants were of three types: Type I, folk informants with a grade-school education or less (40%); common informants with some high school education (35%); and cultivated informants with some college education (25%). Blacks comprised 22% of the sample, which also included several informants whose language was Spanish, French, or German. Although faithful to the methods and the questionnaire of other regional linguistic atlas projects, LAGS was innovative in a number of important ways: for example, every interview was taped, producing a total of nearly 5,500 hours of recording for the project as a whole, most interviews elicited at least one hour of free conversation, and approximately 160 informants in urban areas were asked a supplementary set of questions about city life.

From the very earliest days of research in linguistic geography in Germany over a century ago, it has been the case that rarely, if ever, do dialects (or even the distribution of individual words) pattern geographically in an absolutely clear-cut fashion. Words and other linguistic features are rarely confined to a given territory; nor is there a one-to-one correspondence between linguistic form and land area. (For instance, they frequently have a social dimension and are shared by social groups across regions). It is therefore most likely that any differences found between East, Middle, and West Tennessee will be relative ones, and, of course, it is possible that no significant contrasts will show up—after all, the perception of regional differences may be a figment more than reality. The perception may also be based on stereotypes that once corresponded to reality but do so no longer, or on more subtle and elusive features of speech like intonation that are difficult to identify and almost impossible to quantify.

LAGS Lexical Evidence

From LAGS evidence on vocabulary, the differences between the three divisions appear to be rather few and not so revealing. Table 1 lists some of the terms, out of hundreds that were elicited, that show a distinct distribution across the state.

Table 1: Vocabulary Showing Regional Patterns in Tennessee

	West Tenn (n = 34)		Middle Tenn (n = 47)		East Tenn (n = 60)	
airish (cool weather)	3	8.8%	0	0.0%	17	28.3%
baker (a type of frying pan)	0	0.0%	3	6.4%	17	28.3%
barefooted (black coffee)	2	5.9%	1	2.1%	12	20.0%
barn lot	1	2.9%	9	19.1%	22	36.7%
blinky (thick sour milk)	0	0.0%	1	2.1%	18	30.0%
branch (small stream)	11	32.4%	32	68.1%	46	76.7%
family pie (deep-dish dessert)	2	5.9%	0	0.0%	13	21.7%
fireboard (mantel)	0	0.0%	5	10.6%	19	31.7%
grub (to clear land)	0	0.0%	0	0.0%	16	26.7%
mountain boomer (mt. resident)	0	0.0%	0	0.0%	7	11.7%
mountain hoosier (mt. resident)	0	0.0%	4	8.5%	18	30.0%
paper poke (paper sack)	0	0.0%	5	10.6%	15	25.0%
poke (paper sack)	3	8.8%	9	19.1%	34	56.7%
rock fence	3	8.8%	21	44.7%	22	36.7%
rock wall	2	5.9%	11	23.4%	20	33.3%
snake doctor (dragonfly)	21	61.8%	26	55.3%	8	13.3%
snake feeder (dragonfly)	1	2.9%	7	14.9%	43	71.7%
spicket (outside outlet)	4	11.8%	0	0.0%	19	31.7%
spicket (inside outlet)	1	2.9%	3	6.4%	27	45.0%
tommyto (miniature tomato)	11	32.4%	16	31.0%	38	63.3%

From this table, which gives a good idea of the relative frequency of twenty selective vocabulary items in Tennessee, several points emerge:

1) The vocabulary of East Tennessee appears to be the most distinctive of the three divisions, the speech of West Tennessee the least distinctive. Many terms occur frequently in East Tennessee but much more rarely elsewhere: *airish, fireboard, baker, poke* and *paper poke, barefooted, grub* (to get rid of trees and stumps on a plot of land), *blinky, snake feeder, mountain hoosier, mountain boomer,* and so on. The only term that appears most often in West Tennessee is snake doctor, but it occurs nearly as often in Middle Tennessee and is hardly unknown in the East (eight occurrences).

2) However, lexical differences within the state turn out to be quite relative. With two exceptions (*grub, mountain boomer*), no term is found in only one section of the state. The table actually underrepresents this uniformity to a significant degree, in that the vast majority of vocabulary items collected by LAGS reveal a far more even spread and are thus not cited here.

Social differences, especially between generations, are actually greater than sectional ones, though this is not represented in the table. For instance, nearly all the terms mentioned in the table were used by middle-aged and older speakers, rather than speakers under age 30, in East Tennessee. This writer, a Knoxville native (born 1950), was acquainted with only two terms in Table 1 (*spicket* and *tommyto*) from growing up there.

Further, the distinctive vocabulary in sections of Tennessee is largely recessive, constituting almost entirely what are known as "secondary" responses to terms (i.e., synonyms for more common terms known and used throughout the state). While most Tennesseans knew the term *dragonfly,* fifty-one also knew *snake feeder,* forty-three of them in East Tennessee, and fifty-five knew *snake doctor,* only eight of them in East Tennessee. Terms like *fireboard, barefooted,* and *tommyto* have competition from national alternatives (*mantel/mantelpiece, straight/black,* and *cherry tomato*). There is another obvious reason for the recessiveness of this vocabulary—most of the terms in Table 1 have to do with rural and agricultural life, which younger and increasingly urbanized speakers usually have little contact with. While urbanization can explain the fact that fewer and fewer speakers know many terms, and while the importance of documenting how language changes is not to be denied (the LAGS data directly call into question the assumption that some type of "media influence" is behind such changes), this matter is not germane to the question of this paper. For vocabulary, perhaps the most crucial point is not just that more and more speakers don't know the terms in Table 1, but that the opportunity for the terms to be used is occurring more and more rarely; people don't talk about barns and clearing land and fences and dragonflies much anymore. At the very least, these topics would hardly seem to arise often enough in conversation for vocabulary pertaining to them to become widespread markers of East, Middle, and West Tennessee speech.

Thus, relying on patterns of vocabulary to distinguish the sections of Tennessee runs into the same problem that cultural geographers have tended to face—the differences revealed pertain primarily to the older, rural population and have little reality for modern urbanites—who still do express intra-state sectionalism.

Pronunciation Data in LAGS

This brings us to pronunciation. There are many reasons why we might expect to find significant variation in this aspect of language and why this area might be more productive in our search for intra-state differences. Vowels, consonants, and combinations of sounds occur with far greater frequency than specific words. They occur in the speech of everyone and are not dependent on a topic of conversation. As revealed by many different languages and dialects, sounds are highly prone to vary in any number of ways—socially, regionally, articulatorily, etc. It is thus intuitively far more reasonable that there may be phonological shibboleths to being an East, Middle, or West Tennessean—nuances of pronunciation that enable Tennesseans to categorize one another. To explore whether it is one's pronunciation that may reveal what section of Tennessee a person is from, five place names (four cities—Knoxville, Chattanooga, Nashville, and Memphis—and the state of Tennessee) were examined in the speech of the 141 Tennessee informants for LAGS to determine the common variations in their pronunciation and then to see if these variant pronunciations correlate with the three divisions of the state. Among the linguistic forms sought by LAGS for studying pronunciation, place names have two important advantages over vocabulary: they were elicited by investigators for most informants and they are items that occur with far greater frequency in everyday life, for speakers of all ages and groups, and thus differing pronunciations would be more likely to develop associations with different groups. (This view receives some support from the few concrete responses to the "unscientific" survey of the author cited above.)

Tables 2a–2f show the results of the analysis of the five names. The first two tables examine the pronunciation of unstressed vowels (the variation between [ə], the central vowel or "schwa" or "uh" sound, and [ɪ], what is traditionally called "short i"). This variation affects the vowel in the second syllable of *Chattanooga* and *Tennessee* (producing "Chat-*uh*-noo-ga" vs. "Chat-*ih*-noo-ga" and "Ten-*uh*-see" vs. "Ten-*ih*-see") and the final vowel of *Memphis* ("Mem-fus" vs. "Mem-fis") and *Chattanooga* ("-noo-*guh*" vs. "-noo-*gih*" or "noo-*gee*"). The unstressed syllable in all cases is only very weakly pronounced. In Table 2a we see that no distinct correlation with region emerges for the middle vowel in *Chattanooga* or *Tennessee*. For the former word, the unstressed [ə] occurs at a highest rate in West Tennessee (61.1%); however, in this region *Memphis* was never pronounced with [ə]—West Tennesseans tend to say "Chat-*uh*-noo-ga" but "Mem-fis." At the same time, a third of West Tennesseans (9/27, 33.3%) use this vowel in pronouncing "Ten-*uh*-see." What is most striking is that the percentages of [ə] vary greatly from name to name for each section of the state. This means that if any one of these names does represent a shibboleth in the minds of Tennesseans and used to classify their fellow Volunteers, it is only the individual name rather than the pattern of pronouncing a sound in a certain way in a certain context that is involved. For the final vowel in *Chattanooga* (Table 2b), a clearer pattern is seen, with a high front vowels [i]/[ɪ] occurring only in East and Middle Tennessee, although at a rather low rate.

Table 2a: Medial Unstressed Vowels in *Chattanooga* and *Tennessee*

Section	Chat-uh-noo-ga		Ten-uh-see	
East Tenn	25/53	47.2%	12/56	21.4%
Middle Tenn	17/43	39.5%	14/41	34.1%
West Tenn	11/18	61.1%	9/27	33.3%

Table 2b: Final Vowels in *Memphis* and *Chattanooga*

Section	Mem-fus		Chattanoo-gih/gee	
East Tenn	9/56	16.1%	8/53	15.1%
Middle Tenn	2/43	4.7%	6/43	14.0%
West Tenn	0/30	0.0%	0/18	0.0%

Table 2c shows whether speakers in the three sections pronounce the vowel in the final syllable of *Knoxville* and *Nashville* as either -*vil* [vɪl] or -*vul* [və] (strictly speaking, the latter has a "syllabic l" rather than a vowel). The percentages of speakers who say "Knox-*vil*" is relatively even across the state, those who say "Nash-*vil*" slightly less so. While West Tennesseans pronounce the names of the cities consistently, East and Middle Tennesseans show a somewhat higher rate of -*vil* in pronouncing the principal city in their own section of the state than other Tennesseans do. The samples are too small and the differences too limited to make too much of this, but it does represent an intriguing pattern of reversal. What is probably most important here is that Tennesseans everywhere overwhelmingly say -*vul*, which would tend to make this pronunciation (and that of many other towns in the state—*Rogersville, Smithville, Brownsville,* etc.) a marker of being a local rather than a new arrival. A number of years ago this writer made a presentation at East Tennessee State University, in the course of which he stated that he was from Knoxville; after the talk a member of the audience told him that she could recognize this by his pronunciation of "Knox-*vul.*"

Table 2c: Pronunciation of *-ville* in *Knoxville* and *Nashville*

Section	Knox-*vil*		Nash-*vil*	
East Tenn	16/56	28.6%	6/54	11.1%
Middle Tenn	7/41	17.1%	13/46	28.3%
West Tenn	4/18	22.2%	4/18	22.2%

Two of the five names (*Memphis* and *Tennessee*) show variation between the vowels [ɪ] and [ə] ("short I" and "short e," respectively). A frequently noted feature of southern American speech in the twentieth century is the merger or identical pronunciation of these two vowels before certain consonants—specifically before /n/ and /m/. As a result, pairs of words like *ten/tin* and *hem/him* are pronounced identically by many Tennesseans. This, however, is not borne out by the pronunciation of the two names by LAGS speakers, many of whom, especially in East Tennessee, say "*Mem*-phis" and "*Tenn*-essee" rather than "*Mim*-phis" and "*Tinn*-essee"; Tennesseans may in fact pronounce *pen* and *pin* exactly alike, but this doesn't imply that the same tendency extends to proper nouns. If anything, "*Mem*-phis" and "*Tenn*-essee" may distinguish East Tennesseans from others in the state.

Table 2d: Front Vowel in Initial Syllable before Nasal in *Memphis* and *Tennessee*

Section	[mɪm-]		[tɪn-]	
East Tenn	5/56	8.9%	8/56	14.3%
Middle Tenn	15/43	34.9%	17/41	41.5%
West Tenn	7/30	23.3%	10/27	37.0%

Two further, unrelated patterns of variation with the name *Memphis* are worthy of attention. One of these is the variable addition of a "p" sound at the end of the first syllable; the other involves the stretching of the vowel in the first syllable and the attention of another vowel sound (the "schwa" vowel), so that the name sounds like "Me-*um*-phis." The latter tendency, which is frequently called the southern drawl, is pronounced most often in East Tennessee, occurring at a level of nearly 50%, although the rate in West Tennessee (30%) is not too far behind.

Table 2e: Pronunciation of First Syllable of *Memphis*

Section	Mem*p*-phis		Addition of schwa	
East Tenn	23/56	41.1%	26/56	46.4%
Middle Tenn	23/43	53.5%	6/43	14.0%
West Tenn	10/30	33.3%	9/30	30.0%

A final aspect of pronunciation involves stress. While *Memphis, Nashville,* and *Knoxville* are invariably accented on the first syllable, this is not true for *Tennessee* and *Chattanooga,* which may have the primary accent on the first or third syllable. Table 2f shows the rate of pronunciation of the latter two names with initial accent. The evidence provides some support for the anecdotal reports given to the investigator's "unscientific" survey cited earlier, in that the name of the state more often than not receives stress on the first syllable in East Tennessee; the contrast with Middle Tennessee is strong, but less so with West Tennessee. The same type of pronunciation of *Chattanooga* is most prevalent in the East but does not occur for the speakers interviewed in West Tennessee.

Table 2f: Accent on First Syllable of Chattanooga and Tennessee

Section	*Tenn*-essee		*Chat*-tanooga	
East Tenn	34/56	60.7%	14/53	26.4%
Middle Tenn	11/41	26.8%	5/43	11.6%
West Tenn	13/27	48.1%	0/18	0.0%

Conclusions

The results of this rather brief study, this sectional comparison of Tennessee speech using *Linguistic Atlas of the Gulf States* data, are mixed and seemingly ambiguous in that there are no dramatic differences in vocabulary or pronunciation between the three divisions. Looking at these results in a larger perspective, however, does tell us a number of things about the language of the state in general. Tennessee vocabulary is marked by sectional differences not so much as it is by widespread change. Many differences once existing for older speakers no longer hold for their younger counterparts, who may know several synonyms for an item or none at all. This does not necessarily mean that national or larger regional patterns are erasing the distinctiveness of the three grand divisions of the state or that all Tennesseans will be talking alike in another couple of generations. Sociolinguists have long pointed out that one speech community will often differ from another community not because of the historical derivation of its speech but because it (often unconsciously) wants to be set off and recognized as different from another speech community and have its own identity. In theory at least, East Tennesseans will be distinctive in their speech as long as they have a strong identification as East Tennesseans and they don't want to be mistaken as "them flat landers," "those Democrats," or whatever. The psychological reality of the three grand divisions of the state, then, is at least as important as the geographical reality. Linguistically speaking, the divisions within the state are still most likely to be based on variation, not in lexical items, but in the pronunciation of vowels, although this did not turn out very clearly to be the case for the five names examined in the present study. Even if they may no longer be geographically or linguistically valid or if they linger in the subtle, hard-to-discuss, impossible-to-quantify areas of manners and disposition, the divisions may be real nonetheless because they have become part of mental maps of the state. They are part of what makes some of us Tennesseans.

While only weak intra-state divisions of speech in Tennessee are suggested in this study, this does not mean that the citizens in one section of Tennessee do not maintain notions and stereotypes about how those elsewhere in the state talk. Nor does it mean that the identification of Tennesseans as being from the East, Middle, or West is not based on something else: this question needs to be investigated through other approaches, including direct surveys which ask a variety of Tennesseans about whether and how they classify one another. It is the impression of this writer that sectional identification (for categorizing both oneself and others) is still potent in the state, but this is surely a question that is fascinating enough to be explored by sociologists, anthropologists, folklorists, and others. Perhaps Kelsie Harder will take up the challenge and bring us closer to an understanding himself.

Notes

1. His publications relating to Tennessee are listed and annotated in *Annotated Bibliography of Southern American English*, edited by James B. McMillan and Michael Montgomery (1989).
2. The oldest of these is the East Tennessee Historical Society in Knoxville, which published a journal since 1929 (*East Tennessee Historical Society Publications* until 1989, when it became the *Journal of East Tennessee History*). The Tennessee Historical Society in Nashville has published the *Tennessee Historical Quarterly* since 1941, whereas the West Tennessee Historical

Society in Memphis has published *West Tennessee Historical Society Papers* since 1947.

3. I am indebted to Bethany Dumas of the University of Tennessee–Knoxville English Department for this observation, who pointed out to this writer, a Knoxvillian, that he exemplified it.

4. A survey presented by the author at a gathering of the Tennessee Conference on Linguistics (Montgomery 1986) identified 195 items. A number of others have been published in succeeding years, bringing the total well over 200.

5. For research purposes not important here, Tennessee was classified as a "Gulf" state by the LAGS project, which was edited at Emory University.

6. This is better characterized as a judgment sample (LAGS sought primarily older, rural speakers) than as a random sample. It is inappropriate to use the results of the survey for statistical comparison for this reason and others as well (for instance, it is not discernible from transcription records whether a given question was in fact asked in a given interview).

7. The term *shibboleth* originated from the pronunciation of the stream by the name by the Gileadites (Judges 6).

8. The publications generated by the LAGS project are many and diverse, ranging from microfilm to oversized volumes to computer files. A survey and critique of these can be found in Montgomery 1993.

References

Bailey, Guy H. "Linguistic Atlas of the Gulf States Project." *Encyclopedia of Southern Culture,* ed. by Charles R. Wilson and William Ferris, 788. Chapel Hill: University of North Carolina Press, 1989.

Brown, Calvin S. "Dialectal Survivals in Tennessee." *Modern Language Notes,* v. 4 (1889): 205–9.

Crawford, Charles W. "The Nature of the Volunteer State: What Makes Tennessee Different?" *The Egyptians 1985–1986 Yearbook,* 1986, 61–70.

Folmsbee, Stanley J., Robert E. Corlew, and Enoch L. Mitchell. *Tennessee: A Short History.* Knoxville: University of Tennessee Press, 1969.

Gastill, Raymond D. *Cultural Regions of the United States.* Seattle: University of Washington Press, 1975.

Jordan, Terry G. *The Human Mosaic: A Thematic Introduction to Cultural Geography.* San Francisco: Canfield Press, 1976.

McMillan, James B., and Michael Montgomery, eds. *Annotated Bibliography of Southern American English.* Tuscaloosa: University of Alabama Press, 1989.

Montgomery, Michael. "One Hundred Years of Tennessee English: A Bibliographical Survey." Paper read at the Tennessee Conference on Linguistics
meeting, 1986.

———. 1993. "Review Essay of Basic and Descriptive Materials of the Linguistic Atlas of the Gulf States." *American Speech,* v. 68 (1993): 263–318.

Parsons, Clark. "Nashville and Memphis: Why Can't Tennessee's Two Biggest
Cities Be Friends?" *Tennessean,* December 25, 1994, 1F, 4F.

Pederson, Lee A. "Toward a Description of Southern Speech." *Papers in Language Variation: SAMLA-ADS Collection,* ed. by David L. Shores and
Carole P. Hines, 25–31. University: University of Alabama Press, 1977.

———. "East Tennessee Folk Speech: A Synopsis." *Bamberger Beitrage zur Eng-
lischen Sprachwissenschaft 12.* Frankfurt/Main: Peter Lang, 1983.

Wood, Gordon. *Vocabulary Change: A Study of Variation in Regional Words
in Eight of the Southern States.* Carbondale: Southern Illinois University
Press, 1973.

Work Projects Administration. *Tennessee: A Guide to the State.* New York: Viking
Press, 1939.

Zelinsky, Wilbur. *The Cultural Geography of the United States.* Englewood
Cliffs, N.J.: Prentice-Hall, 1973.

Further Reading
in Folk Speech

Abrahams, Roger D. *Talkin' Black.* 1976.

Carver, Craig M. *American Regional Dialects: A Word Geography.* 1987.

Fink, Paul. *Bits of Mountain Speech.* 1974.

Hall, Joseph S. *The Phonetics of Smoky Mountain Speech.* 1942.

Holloway, Joseph. *The African Heritage of American English.* 1993.

Kurath, Hans. *A Word Geography of the Eastern United States.* 1949.

McMillan, James B., and Michael Montgomery. *Annotated Bibliography of Southern American English.* 1989.

Montgomery, Michael, and Guy Bailey, eds. *Language Variety in the South: Perspectives in Black and White.* 1986.

Montgomery, Michael, and Joseph S. Hall. *Dictionary of Smoky Mountain English.* 2004.

Plotkin, David George, ed. *Dictionary of American Proverbs.* 1955.

Prahlad, Anand, Sw. *African American Proverbs in Context.* 1996.

Shuy, Roger. *Discovering American Dialects.* 1967.

Still, James. *Rusties and Riddles and Gee-Haw Whimmy Diddles.* 1989.

Taylor, Archer. *A Dictionary of American Proverbs.* 1958.

Williams, Cratis. *Southern Mountain Speech.* 1992.

Wolfram, Walt. *American Voices: How Dialects Differ from Coast to Coast.* 2006.

Wolfram, Walt, and Donna Christian. *Appalachian Speech.* 1976.

Wolfram, Walt, and Erik Thomas. *The Development of African American English.* 2002.

PART SEVEN

Legends

It is not coincidental that the International Storytelling Center and the National Storytelling Festival are located in Tennessee (both are situated in Jonesborough), as the people of Tennessee, like southerners in general, have a gift for storytelling. Many of these stories are legends, that is, narratives that commemorate and often celebrate the significant aspects of places, people, and animals. Legends emerge because the subjects of legends embody significant qualities valued by the communities that create them. Some legends never circulate widely from the place where they are created, and some highly localized legends do not survive beyond a generation or two. Other legends, however, proliferate widely over time and space because they hold relevance for larger populations.

A famous legend of the latter type concerns Tennessee native David Crockett, whose death at or shortly after the Battle of the Alamo led to him becoming the national folk hero known as Davy Crockett. In his essay "Davy Crockett, David Crockett, and Me: A Personal Journey through Legend into History," Michael A. Lofaro, a noted Crockett scholar, recounts his own experiences as a student of the Crockett legend and as a fan. Lofaro reports that after publishing a book in which he deconstructed the Crockett legend, he received numerous letters from people angry with his effort to reconcile the popular image of Crockett with historical fact. People thought that such an effort was unpatriotic, even an act of blasphemy, when in fact Lofaro was simply trying to celebrate the true Crockett as opposed to the image constructed by such agents of the popular media as Walt Disney.

Another Tennessee legend that has received considerable national exposure concerns the Bell Witch of Middle Tennessee. In "Twentieth-Century Aspects of the Bell Witch," Teresa Ann Bell Lockhart discusses the lasting influence of that local legend traceable to an alleged supernatural incident involving a phantasm that occurred during the 1820s in Robertson County,

Tennessee. What the author could not anticipate was that the Bell Witch legend would become even more widely known in the twenty-first century after its adaptation in 2006 for a nationally distributed feature film titled *An American Haunting*.

The Civil War was a national event that produced numerous local legends in the states the war affected, and Tennessee was no exception. One Tennessee legend created during this critical event in American history is that of Champ Ferguson, a leader of a band of Confederacy-sympathizing guerrillas in Pickett and Fentress counties who was eventually hanged for siding with the losing cause of the war. Linda C. White's essay, "Champ Ferguson: A Legacy of Blood," reconstructs who Ferguson was and why his exploits were spun into legend in East Tennessee. To provide a well-rounded portrayal of Ferguson, White draws on portions of stories about Ferguson she collected from residents living in the area. Legendary figures like Ferguson are often interpreted from multiple perspectives. To capture the declining legend of Ferguson, White offers a variety of recollections without declaring any specific version as definitive.

Like the legend of the Bell Witch, another Tennessee legend presented in Thomas G. Burton's essay "The Hanging of Mary, a Circus Elephant" has recently received wider attention outside the local community (Erwin, Tennessee) from which it emerged. A 2006 song based on the legend composed by singer-songwriter Chuck Brodsky has transmitted the story of Mary the elephant to new audiences. Burton's analysis of the bizarre sequence of events that led to the hanging of an elephant draws on a wide range of accounts of the event, including newspaper and oral history sources.

The Hanging of Mary, a Circus Elephant [1971]

Thomas G. Burton

Incredible as it seems, late Wednesday afternoon, September 13, 1916, Mary, a circus elephant, was hanged in Erwin, Tennessee.

The day before, in Kingsport, Tennessee, after the daylight performance, Mary had killed Walter "Red" Eldridge, who reportedly had joined the "Sparks World-Famous Shows" only two days earlier in his home town of St. Paul, Virginia, because he wanted to be an animal trainer.

According to some reports, Eldridge was not Mary's first victim. One Erwin resident (Bud Jones) who witnessed the hanging, stated: "She'd killed one man up in Virginie and killed a man in Kingsport." Another witness of the hanging (James Treadway) said: "She killed—one at Kingsport, one at Bristol, and one over there [Erwin]. But I didn't see that there at Erwin." Others (Mont Lilly and W. H. Coleman) thought she killed two before the one at Kingsport. The number expands in various oral accounts, such as the following (by Kary Gouge): "He took spells that he'd kill 'em, you know, and that's made about six or seven that he'd killed."

In one published account, carried ten days after the event in a Chicago newspaper and illustrated by a 7x10 sensational drawing, Mary was reported to have killed seven other men (*Saturday Blade*, Sept. 23, 1916, 1); and the *Johnson City Comet* stated the day following the hanging: "It is said that Mary had killed 18 men" (p. 1). The Ripley's "Believe It or Not" cartoon of August 29, 1938, numbers the victims as three. On the other hand, another article in the

Johnson City Comet (Sept. 14, 1916, 1) quoted Mr. Heron, the press agent for the Sparks World-Famous Shows, as saying: "'I have been with the shows for three years and have never known the elephant to lose her temper before.'" The *Nashville Banner* (Sept. 13, 1916, 9) reported similarly: "'Murderous Mary,' as she was termed by spectators, has been . . . performing . . . for fifteen years, and this is the first time anyone has come to harm."

Mary was billed as "THE LARGEST, LIVING, LAND ANIMAL ON EARTH. 3 INCHES TALLER THAN JUMBO AND WEIGHING OVER 5 TONS." The *Johnson City Staff* (Sept. 13, 1916, 3; Sept. 14, 1916, 6) reported her to be one of a trained quintette, 30 years old (interestingly, only half her life expectancy in captivity), and estimated her loss to the show at $20,000; another newspaper valued her at $8,000 (*Saturday Blade*, Sept. 23, 1916, 1).

Her attack on Walter Eldridge was flamboyantly reported by the *Johnson City Staff* as follows: "Suddenly [Mary] collided its trunk vice-like about his [Eldridge's] body, lifted him ten feet in the air, then dashed him with fury to the ground. Before Eldridge had a chance to reach his feet, the elephant had him pinioned to the ground, and with the full force of her biestly [*sic*] fury is said to have sunk her giant tusks entirely through his body. The animal then trampled the dying form of Eldridge as if seeking a murderous triumph, then with a sudden . . . swing of her massive foot hurled his body into the crowd" (Sept. 13, 1916, 3).

Twenty years later Mary's attack was reported quite differently: "The elephant's keeper, while in the act of feeding her, walked unsuspectingly between her and the tent wall. For no reason that could be ascertained, Mary became angry and, with a vicious swish of her trunk, landed a fatal blow on his head" (*Johnson City Press-Chronicle*, Aug. 16, 1936, 1). (Reasons for Mary's attack, however, are in circulation. David Hatcher told me that it was commonly said when he was growing up in Erwin that the person Mary killed had once given her a chew of tobacco to eat instead of peanuts and that Mary, keeping the incident in mind over a period of years, took her revenge when she recognized her offender during a parade. Eugene Harris says that another local explanation for Mary's violent behavior is that she had two abscessed teeth, and the pain incurred from Eldridge's striking her with a stick drove her into a fury.)

W. H. Coleman of Kingsport, who witnessed the event as a youth of 19, described to me Mary's attack on Red Eldridge as follows:

> There was a big ditch at that time, run up through Center Street, . . . [an]
> open ditch that had been put there for the purpose of draining all of King-
> sport. . . . And they'd sent these boys to ride the elephants. . . . There was, oh,
> I don't know now, seven or eight elephants . . . and they went down to water
> them and on the way back each boy had a little stick-like, that was a spear
> or hook in the end of it. . . . And this big old elephant reach over to get her

a watermelon rind, about a half of watermelon somebody eat and just laid it down there; 'n' he did, the boy give him a jerk. He pulled him away from 'em, and he just blowed real big; and when he did, he took him right around the waist . . . and throwed him against the side of the drink stand and he just knocked the whole side out of it. I guess it killed him, but when he hit the ground the elephant just walked over and set his foot on his head . . . and the blood and brains and stuff just squirted all over the street. [Later, Mr. Coleman specifically said Mary did not gore Eldridge.]

According to Mr. Coleman, Hench Cox, who was 65 or 70, came out of the blacksmith shop close by when he heard the elephant "blow" and shot it five times with a 32–20 pistol; the elephant "just doubled up and just groaned and carried on, you never heard the like; he just stooped down and shook all over." Then, as Mr. Coleman related: "The crowd kept hollerin' and sayin', 'Let's kill the elephant, let's kill him,' an' he [the management or owner] said, 'People, I'd be perfectly willin' to kill him, but there's no way to kill him. There ain't gun enough in this country that he could be killed; there's no way to kill him.'"

Nevertheless, Mary was quickly brought under control and even performed in the evening show—according to the newspaper "without having exhibited the slightest indication of 'bad temper'" (*Johnson City Staff*, Sept. 13, 1916, 3). Nothing was apparently done by the circus officials at that time to exterminate the elephant; furthermore, Mr. Coleman thought that they did not plan then to execute Mary and would not have executed her solely for the killing of Eldridge. He based his opinion on a conversation, held some six or seven years after the hanging, with one of the operators of the Sparks side shows. The showman told Mr. Coleman that Mary "wouldn't never been destroyed if he [Mary] hadn't of come in an ace of destroying the owner. . . . He . . . come so near of gettin' him that he said, 'That'll be the last of you,' and just took and had him killed." In reality, according to Mr. Coleman, Mary was executed because she was old, mean, and dangerous to handle, not because she had taken a human life. And not, one might add, because of the analysis, seemingly serious, offered by one newspaper: "It is stated that when an elephant kills one or more people that they are liable to do the same thing again and at a time that they [*sic*] keepers are least expecting it" (*Johnson City Staff*, Sept. 14, 1916, 6).

It is difficult to establish definitely, however, the authority responsible for sentencing Mary to death. The *Johnson City Staff*, the day after the execution, reported: "Not wishing to take any more risks as to the loss of life, the Sparks Circus management had Mary . . . hung and killed" (p. 6). The 1916 December issue of *Popular Mechanics* stated that Mary "was condemned to death by the state authorities and executed" ("Vicious Elephant Hanged for Killing Man," 803). Some of the residents of Erwin also placed the decision on the state of Tennessee; as one (Mont Lilly) said: "The state of Tennessee preferred charges against [Mary]. . . . They charged her with first degree murder"—or as implied by another (Bud Jones): "They couldn't take her out of Tennessee, you see, and they had to do somethin' with her." Erwinians certainly do not hold their city responsible, as it is made perfectly clear by one lady (Mrs. E. H. Griffith): "It was decreed that she [Mary] must be killed in the interest of public safety by whom I do not know, certainly not by anyone here" (from a typed manuscript of an answer to Bert Vincent, furnished by P. O. Likens, Clinchfield Railroad).

At any rate, on Wednesday, September 13, the day following Eldridge's death, the Sparks circus moved from Kingsport to Erwin, taking Mary with it.

In Erwin, it had rained; and Mary, along with the other elephants, helped push the wagons out of the mud. James Treadway described the scene to me as follows: "They come in there and there was a wet spell, rained awful for several days. . . . They shipped them [the animals] in there by train at that time—they wasn't any trucks then—and the railroad just set 'em on the sidin' there and rolled them wagons off. . . . They was mired down, and they couldn't pull 'em with horses. And this feller took this elephant down there, and she just pushed 'em out with her head."

Later that day, following the afternoon show, Mary was taken down to the shop yards of the C C and O Railways. Mont Lilly, at that time a 16-year-old relief man on the derrick car crew, gave me the following details of the hanging (he was present that day but not on duty):

> They brought those elephants down there, they had four or five of them together. And they had this here Mary . . . she was bringin' up the rear. It was just like they was havin' a parade, holdin' one another's tail. . . . These other ones come up . . . and they stopped. Well, she just cut loose right there . . . and the show men, they went and put a chain, a small chain, around her foot, and chained her to the rail. Then they backed the wrecker up to her and throwed the big ⅞" chain around her neck and hoisted her, and she got up about, oh, I'll say, five or six feet off the ground and the chain around her neck broke. See, they had to pull this chain loose; it broke the smaller chain, and that weakened the other chain. And so, when they got her up about five or six feet from the ground, why it broke.

Bud Jones, the fireman on the 100-ton derrick car that was used to hang Mary, gave me the following details:

> They had eight or ten other elephants. The brung 'em all down there and she seemed to know there was somethin' wrong someway, you know, and she'd walk off around to one side, you know, and wouldn't stay hardly with the others a-tall. And finally got her up close enough to throw a chain around her neck. And we picked her up about, well, I'd say about three foot off the ground, and then the chain broke. And it kind o' addled

□ The only known photograph
depicting the hanging of Mary,
a circus elephant, September
1916. Courtesy of the Archives
of Appalachia, East Tennessee
State University.

her when it fell, you know. And we quick 'n' got another chain and put it around her neck then and hooked it before she could get up.

James Treadway told me that Mary "kicked with both feet, one at a time, and that broke the chain." When the chain broke, he says, "she sat down just like a big rabbit . . . she haunkered down, and a fellow ran up her back and throwed the cable 'round her neck and hooked it." According to Mr. Lilly, it was not two minutes before the circus people had the second chain around Mary's neck, and Sam Harvey, the regular fireman acting as engineer that day, had her hoisted once again: "She kicked a little bit and that was about all; see, that thing choked her to death right quick."

Incidentally, the absence of the regular engineer of the derrick car, Jeff Stultz, is also a subject that evokes varying explanations. According to Bud Jones, he was replaced that day by Sam Harvey, "a one-eyed feller," because Stultz was in Roanoke. Another elderly citizen of Erwin (O. C. Hale) told me that Stultz would not hang the elephant because he had to go out at night to wrecks, and he was afraid that having the hanging on his mind would bother him. Columnist

Bert Vincent also reported that Stultz refused to hang the elephant (Willard Yarbrough, ed., *The Best Stories of Bert Vincent* [Brazos Press, 1968], 146).

Amid the drama of the hanging, however, occurred one incident of comic relief. When the chain broke, some of the spectators yelled out and began to scatter. Jim Coffey, a blind banjo picker over six feet tall, who had come to "see" the elephant hanged, ran into some people trying to get away. According to Mrs. E. H. Griffith (daughter of S. W. Bondurant, the derrick wreckmaster), one man yelled at Coffey, "'Can't you see?' Mr. Coffey replied, 'No, I haven't seen a lick in 20 years.'" The story is a popular one in Erwin; Kary Gouge, for example, said: "Bud [Jones] told me about it a hundred times and laughed about that blind man a-runnin' so fast. He run over everybody to get away from there." Not only Mr. Coffey, but also, according to a conversation I had with Mrs. B. O. Bailey, all the other people "got to runnin'"; and, in particular, her son "started to run and scratched his legs all to pieces in the briars."

As the story of Mary's hanging grows in oral tradition, the number executed also grows. A few area residents have held, as expressed by one (Lanny Phillips), "Not many people know it, but the elephant's two Negro keepers were also hanged with her." This belief may stem from a fusion of the hanging with another incident that occurred in Erwin, the burning on a pile of cross-ties of a Negro who allegedly abducted a white girl. (The fusion of these two incidents might also explain the belief of some that Mary killed a young girl.)

After Mary's execution and after the pronouncement of her death, supposedly by local physician R. E. Stack, her five-ton corpse had to be disposed of. P. H. Flanary related, "We . . . buried him with a steam shovel. I dug the grave after we hung the elephant . . . and also covered him with a steam shovel." According to Bud Jones, she was held swinging about ten minutes before the derrick dropped her in the hole, some four or five hundred feet away from where she was hanged. The site itself, however, is a disputable subject, but according to Mr. Treadway it was "south of the roundhouse, below the tracks where the river [Nolichucky] comes up so far there." The reported length of time Mary was held aloft (before her shame was decently covered) also varies considerably—from a short period of 5, 10, 20, or 30 minutes to a long period of several hours. After Mary was dropped into her grave, her tusks reportedly were sawed off—according to some (e.g., M. D. Clark) before she was buried, according to others (e.g., James Treadway), "They dug down that night and cut her tushes off." With one of the tusks, says Lilly, "one fellow . . . made a set of dice."

The details of Mary's burial are also sometimes apparently fused with the burning of the Negro, referred to earlier; in one reminiscence of the burial (by Mrs. B. O. Bailey), crossties were piled in on top of the elephant and burned, the fire from which could be seen long into the night.

Mrs. Griffith stated that "the Associated Press learned of the event and came here [to Erwin] ten days later, had the animal dug up." Mr. Lilly had no recollection of Mary's ever being dug up; however, Chief Engineer Jim Goforth said that a request, long after the hanging, was made by a geological school to exhume the remains, although the project was not attempted.

A photograph of the hanging was made, but the details concerning it are as cloudy as the day on which it was taken. One report says that when Johnny Childers submitted an article titled "Vicious Elephant Hanged for Killing Man," published in the December issue of *Popular Mechanics,* a picture was requested to accompany the article. Childers is quoted as stating: "I got hold of one in Erwin, but it was too dim for reproduction. The picture used with the magazine article was a sketch by the magazine artist" (from an unidentified newspaper article contributed by Betty Chandler, Erwin *Record*).

The drawing deserves a brief comment; the following is attributed to Childers himself: "It showed the huge elephant swinging from the derrick [the drawing, however, does not show Mary hanging; it presents her being driven by the other elephants to the track]. Standing nearby alongside a circus tent, was a group of young lady circus bareback riders, using lace handkerchiefs to wipe tears from their eyes as they watched the hanging of the elephant Mary. The artist's conception of what happened was not erroneous. Circus people told me that they all were saddened by the hanging." (Mrs. Monk commented on this attitude of the circus people, some of whom, she was told, "cried like a baby"; and Bert Vincent in his article on the hanging of Mary also referred to the sentiment displayed by the circus folk. He gave the following comment by W. B. Carr, pipe foreman at the C C & O shops who observed the hanging: "A circus woman must have loved Mary, this elephant, a whole lot. She had ridden her in the circus parades, and had never been afraid of her. . . . This woman . . . wouldn't come down and see the elephant die. She stayed in a hotel and cried" [p. 147].)

Focusing on the photograph again, however, Mrs. Griffith related: "The hanging occurred between four and five o'clock in the afternoon on a dark and cloudy day, a local photographer by the name of Mitchell, I believe, made a picture of the event, but when it was developed it was very dim and he faked the picture of the elephant, and my father standing under it can only be distinguished as a man." In this photograph, claimed as the only existing one of the incident, Mary, unnaturally hanging from the derrick with trunk extended, is suspiciously sharper than her background. (Incidentally, when submitted by Eugene Harris to the editors of *Argosy,* the photo was rejected as "phony.")

There are no available photographs to record the size and reaction of the crowd, but apparently the hanging to them was an extension of the circus spirit. As J. C. Monk, who watched the event from the tipple about 100 yards away, said: "It was excitement, you know . . . to see the elephant hung." Word was spread and the people gathered from miles around to witness the event. The crowd estimates, however, of the people to whom I talked vary widely. Mr. Lilly stated, "I'd say they was, well, Erwin wasn't very big then, but I'd say there was two or three hundred down there at least." Even the women came, Mr. Lilly said: "They had a lot of dead engines—no fire in 'em, you know, just stored down there, engines—and there was women . . . standin' all over the tops of 'em engines to watch that elephant hung." Mr. Monk's estimate of the crowd was approximately that of Mr. Lilly's: "I would say there was perhaps 200—just the whole show, nearly, went down." Bud Jones's estimate was much larger; the following is his description of the crowd: "Everbody was excited about it, you know—'n' come down there; I guess the coal tipple was three hundred—four hundred feet long from the ground up to the top of the tipple; and it was covered up with people just as thick as they could stand on that tipple, you know, besides what was on the ground. I'd say their was three thousand people there."

The published estimates of the crowd also vary considerably. The issue of *Popular Mechanics* previously mentioned stated, "The hanging was witnessed by a crowd of about 1,500 persons." One recent local journalistic treatment, that of the *East Tennessee Times* (Aug. 15, 1969, 3), reported: "It appeared as if Erwin's three thousand population and surrounding country were on the scene." But as early as 1936, the attendance according to one newspaper had grown to "more than 5,000 curiosity-seeking people from all parts of East Tennessee" (*Johnson City Press Chronicle,* Aug. 16, 1936, 1); and the most recent article that I have seen published about the hanging uses the same figure: "As was the custom in those days for all hangings, whoever the victim, a crowd of some 5,000 persons gathered to witness the vengeance reaped" (James Ewing, "Tennessee Tales," *Tennessee Conservationist,* June 1970, 10). Similarly, "The Ballad of Murdering Mary" by William E. Mahoney stated: "Five thousand gathered in the gloom / To see her hoisted on a boom." (As a point of comparison, it is interesting to note that the *Johnson City Staff* reported that 2,000 persons attended the evening performance of the Sparks show in Johnson City the day following the hanging [Sept. 15, 1916, 1].)

From another point of view the hanging of Mary was a serious matter. Mrs. B. O. Bailey said that the people were quiet: "They's just standing around, just like anybody else, you know, a-watchin'. . . . They just wanted to get rid of that elephant that was killing everybody. . . . Nobody was sorry for it, for it was a-killin' too many people." Bud Jones said that everyone was "very serious" about the hanging. "They was all mighty quiet," but, he said, "the people, most of them, thought she ought to be killed." Mr. Lilly stated: "Well, the general attitude was they just wanted to see the elephant hung. . . . They, of course, a lot of 'em, thought too that the elephant ought to be killed . . . they ought to destroy her, you know, for killin' so many people." Similarly, Mr. Monk recalled, "There wasn't much sympathy for old Mary. . . . [M]ost people thought that the elephant ought to be hung—at least I did." Mrs. Griffith went even further in saying, "We did not sit in judgment on her fate, and I don't believe any of those who witnessed the event felt it was inhumane under the circumstances. She paid for her crimes as anyone else would."

According to local belief, however, hanging was not the only means attempted or at least considered to punish Mary for her crimes. Mr. Treadway said: "They thought about just putting her between that two engines and just mash her to death, and they decided, better not do that, might get somebody hurt." Bud Jones told me: "They shot her eight or ten times with one of these high-powered rifles. . . . There wasn't a bullet that went through the hide, they claimed. Now that's what they said over there in Kingsport." Mr. Treadway related to me another incident: "The sheriff thought he could shoot her, but he couldn't with a .45. Sheriff Gallahan, I believe, was sheriff at that time. And it had knocked chips out of her hide a little. . . . He shot her six times. . . . He thought he could shoot her in the heart, but that gun wouldn't go through her." Mr. Lilly added another attempted method: "They tried to electrocute her in Kingsport—they put 44,000 volts to her, and she just danced a little bit. . . . And then they decided, well, they'd shoot her and they was afraid to try that—afraid they'd just shoot her and maybe make her mad, you know, and she would hurt somebody." Bud Jones also mentioned a proposed electrocution, but he said, "They didn't have power enough here to do it." One story that Don Whitlock, a native of Erwin, told me he always heard is that the railroad chained Mary to the rail and transferred the power from the turntable at the round-house to the rail in an unsuccessful attempt to electrocute her.

Regardless of the other means of execution attempted, however, or of what other course of action might have been taken, or of why what took place occurred, late Wednesday afternoon, September 13, 1916, Mary, a circus elephant, was hanged in Erwin, Tennessee—an incredible incident that has become part of the oral and written tradition of the surrounding area.

Champ Ferguson
A Legacy of Blood
[1978]

Linda C. White

While there were no major battles fought in the Pickett-Fentress County area of Tennessee during the Civil War, small wars were waged in this section of Appalachia, and the aftermath of these involvements is still remembered within many families. These recollections are still collectible from natives of this area who came from a culture in which these tales were passed from generation to generation.

According to historical accounts, the Civil War began in this section of western Appalachia with the murder of Colonel Stokley Huddelson in the summer of 1861.[1] The people of this area were divided in their loyalties during the war. Even though very few farms had slaves, men left behind their wives, children, and homes to fight on one side or the other. Some of these soldiers would never again see their homeland, while others would return from war only to continue violent feuding with neighbors, family, and former friends.

Remembering accounts of this time, Luther York, nephew of Sgt. Alvin C. York, asserted,

> In this area of the Wolf River Valley in Fentress County, Tennessee, there were a number of instances of killings . . . bushwhackings . . . some of them just plain murdered . . . at that time due to their being either sympathizers for the North or the South. And this particular area right through here was one of the worse areas of that kind because of the almost even division between those who sympathized with either the North or the South.[2]

A Pickett County native, Cordell Hull, who was secretary of state under Franklin Roosevelt, described this area during the war in this way:

> For several years during the Civil War bands of guerrillas and bushwhackers operated back and forth across the borderline, pillaging, robbing, and killing. They stripped the entire area bare of livestock and movable property. Only old persons incapable of military service, widows, and small children were left at their homes. To them life was a perfect hell.[3]

Mr. Hull, son of the notorious Civil War bushwhacker, Billy Hull, was accurate in his observations. Just how accurate was made vividly clear by the tales from this blood-filled time, which describe a "perfect hell."

"From Jamestown, Tennessee, westward to Nashville suffered from battles and skirmishes between the Union men and the Southern Confederate soldiers, or friends, whether they were taking any part in the war or not."[4] It was these "friends," who in most instances took no part in the war, that are now instilled in the memories of these people. The exploits of these men are told with admiration for the cunning arts of killing and escape that they are reputed to have possessed. Stories of guerrillas and bushwhackers have displaced accounts of brave and heroic deeds in this area during the war.

Names such as Champ Ferguson, "Tinker" Dave Beatty, and "Coon-Rod" Pyle were found readily on the tongues of informants, with the Ferguson tales being dominant. Ray B. Phillips of Byrdstown, Tennessee, gave one reason for the popularity of the Ferguson stories:

> There weren't many stories in this area about "Tinker" Dave Beatty, all I heard was about Champ Ferguson. I guess it was because Champ Ferguson lived and did his killin' in this part of the country. Most of these people who lived in this area where I come from [Pickett County] were Southern sympathizers, as Champ was, and naturally they talked about his exploits.[5]

Stories of Tinker Dave Beatty, a Union sympathizer, are collectible in small numbers, but predominantly in connection with Champ Ferguson. An example of this is the story of Beatty meeting Ferguson on the streets of Jamestown, as recounted by Luther York.

> Now, one thing in regard to Champ, which I've heard but I'm not sure I can repeat it like it was supposed to have happened. "Tinker" Dave Beatty was a native of Fentress County, and he was a Union sympathizer. Led a guerrilla band that sympathized with the Union, where Champ Ferguson's guerrilla band sympathized with the Confederacy. So the story goes that they met one day in Jamestown, got up in shooting distance before they recognized each other. Then Ferguson shot "Tinker" Dave Beatty.

"Tinker" Dave, in order to escape, swung over on his horse. Hanging on to the horse's neck, the horse shielding him from further shots from Champ Ferguson. He escaped over into the head of Rock Castle Creek, which is one of the canyons that head up near Jamestown, and spent quite a few months over there then recuperating from the wounds inflicted by Champ Ferguson on the streets of Jamestown.[6]

These two men, Ferguson and Beatty, kept this part of Appalachia in terror during their own time, and at the end of the Civil War, when men returned home, it seemed their troubles were multiplied. Former war guerrillas continued their raids and soldiers coming home found it difficult to settle down again next to people who had fought on the opposite side and in many cases had killed members of their own family. Feuds flared up, and soon full-scale wars raged in this once peaceful segment of Appalachia.

Ferguson's exploits were related with almost a sense of reverence. One reason for the admiration and awe of the atrocities he committed was because the older residents of this area had seen so many acts of bloodshed and retaliation during the early years of the Civil War that these older atrocities seemed mild in comparison with his. The remainder of this article will be composed of some of the Ferguson tales collected from Pickett and Fentress Counties, Tennessee.

There were several versions of stories collected which explained Ferguson's beginnings as an outlaw. Each story places Ferguson in a role of a peaceful, law-abiding farmer who was caught up in personal emotions of the time.

> Now to my understanding, . . . they was having a meeting at Chinook, and a bunch of fellers, you know, roughed him. Actually, was aiming to kill him, you know, they killed people there. And, well, he got away from them, and left, and they follered him, and he killed three or four of them that time. And from that time on every time he met one of them, he killed him.[7]

Another, perhaps more colorful, account of Ferguson's deadly career was told by Ray B. Phillips.

> You have probably heard enough to know that Champ was just a savage butcher, that he just killed for the thrill of killin'. You probably already heard of how he went into a military hospital in Virginia and shot down a Lieutenant Smith. Well, there's a story that is known through this area on that deal. You see, this section was the meeting ground of North and South, and feelings ran high. Champ lived just across the state line in Clinton County, Kentucky. He was a Confederate sympathizer, and most those people were Union sympathizers. Champ left home, came over to Tennessee, and joined the Confederate Army. To get even with him, a

group of Union sympathizers—about twelve of them, and one of them was supposed to be Champ's half brother, and Smith was that one—they went to Champ's home. Champ's first wife died without children, and by his second wife he had a twelve-year-old daughter. These twelve men went into Champ's home, made his wife and daughter completely disrobe, prepare lunch for them, and then paraded them up and down the country road completely disrobed. When Champ heard of the story, he vowed to kill every man that heaped this indignity on his wife and daughter. Lieutenant Smith was the last of the twelve. Champ found him wounded in the hospital and shot him.[8]

Bromfield Ridley revealed a story in his book on the Army of Tennessee in which Ferguson's three-year-old child was killed by Union troops who shot at Ferguson but hit the child. Ferguson supposedly vowed to kill one hundred "blue coats" in vengeance. Champ admitted to the murder of one hundred and twenty people.[9]

The next two stories revealed a method the Ferguson gang employed in keeping their whereabouts from the authorities. Since these men were fugitives, their safety depended on secrecy. Anyone who accidentally uncovered their hideout was given little chance for survival.

There was a woman lived on my daddy's place, name of Net Yates. Her son saw Ferguson coming down through the Little South Fork rise. He [Ferguson] got a hold of that and left his home near Albany [Kentucky], and he walked clear across—he might have had a horse—but he went across there, it must have been about twenty miles.

He went over there, and he went prepared to kill this boy, and that's all the business he had. There's nobody home but just her and her son. He told him to step out, he's going to kill him. That boy told his mother about seeing Ferguson, and it got out, you know.

He told the boy to come out there, and when he come he [the boy] grabbed a hold of his mother's dress and run around and around two or three times. Champ's trying to get a bead on him, you know. And he [Ferguson] told him to shove off from her or he'd kill her. Then he'd kill the boy too. He aimed to kill them both anyway. And she shoved him [the boy] off, and he killed them both.

The next thing I heard about him was ol' Cross-eyed Billy Pyle and Bill Delk came upon him [Ferguson] and he'd found out about it. The gang came over there and aimed to kill them. Ferguson generally got three or four men in his crew. They came by and told Cross-eyed Billy to come out, he'd come to hang him.

Cross-eyed Billy got up and come out. He knew he had to do something. Billy came right on across with him and walked across the Joe York foot-log right up by Sam Williams', came right over there to the top of that little hill. Old Champ told one of the men to hold ol' Cross-eyed Billy there, and he'd go across there and get Bill Delk.

And Cross-eyed Billy knew he had to do something 'nuther, so he bided the thing to do was wait till 'bout the time he [Ferguson] got there. And, he told them, he said, he cussed at them, "By God, if you fellers aim to kill me, hang me! If you don't, I got to go feed. I can't fool with you damn fellers!"

He jus' got up and walked off. He walked off in the bushes and hit the run. They run after him, but he knowed the way, you know. And he went over to his house and got his pistol. He got on into the hills, and in the woods, and they never follered him. They wouldn't foller him in the woods.

So, they got Bill Delk and brought him over, and hung him right in sight of Sam Williams's house. They hung him and Cross-eyed Billy got away![10]

There were two contrasting accounts of Ferguson's acts told back to back by informants Pyle and Patton. The first was a vicious story, while the latter was of a humorous nature. These informants made no distinction between the seriousness of the two incidents.

Well, now, this I heard about him. I heard my granny tell about him a-cuttin' a man's throat, and stuck a twist of 'baccer down his guzzle![11]

He went in on this ol' womern. She didn't have nothin' ta eat, just a little bowl of butter. She was down sick, and she didn't have nothin' ta eat. She said she couldn't get nothing to lay on her stummick except the butter. He told her he couldn't get nothin' ta put on his stummick.[12]

Ferguson's reputation as a cruel killer spread throughout the Pickett-Fentress area. Informant George Patton gave the following opinion of Ferguson:

He didn't have to have a thing in the world agin him [the victim]. He's jus' a blood-thirsty maniac! What I mean, a maniac's crazy ta kill somebody all the time. And, everybody of course that could, tried to shun 'selves away, but he'd run across a feller that wadn't ta suit him well enough. If that feller had a gun, alright. If he didn't, he'd just shoot him down.[13]

Champ Ferguson later moved his family to White County, Tennessee. He sought to settle into the peaceful farming existence which he'd known before the conflict. After the North won the Civil War, Champ's past caught up with him. Even though Union sympathizers, such as Tinker Dave Beatty, may have committed as many atrocities as Ferguson, Champ was on the losing side. He was brought to trial and hanged in Nashville on October 21, 1865.

Notes

1. Patsy Crouch, "Pickett County First Settled About 1786 by Soldiers of Revolution," 10th Anniversary Edition, *Pickett County Press,* June 15, 1972, Section II, 1.
2. Collected from Luther York, Pall Mall, Tennessee, July 1, 1972.
3. Crouch, 1.
4. "Pickett was 'No Man's Land' During Civil War Days," 10th Anniversary Edition, *Pickett County Press,* June 15, 1972, Section III, 1.
5. Collected from Ray B. Phillips, Byrdstown, Tennessee, July 13, 1972.
6. Luther York.
7. Collected from Willie Pyle, Jamestown, Tennessee, July 3, 1972.
8. Ray B. Phillips.
9. Bromfield Ridley, *Battles and Sketches of the Army of Tennessee* (Mexico, Miss.: Missouri Printing and Publishing Co., 1906), 522.
10. Collected from George Patton, Jamestown, Tennessee, July 3, 1972.
11. George Patton.
12. Willie Pyle.
13. George Patton.

Twentieth-Century Aspects of the Bell Witch

[1984]

Teresa Ann Bell Lockhart

Almost everyone in Tennessee is familiar with the legend of the Bell Witch. The traditional legend is about a witch, commonly referred to as Kate, who tormented John Bell and his family. Even President Andrew Jackson was supposed to have witnessed some of the witch's antics. Several authors have recorded this phenomenon, and the legend is an important part of any southern folklore collection. Most important, however, is the fact that the traditional Bell Witch legend is still generating new legends that continue to circulate today.

According to the original legend, the Bell Witch is, or was, supposed to return after a certain number of years. However, in typical legend fashion, the exact number of years after which the witch is to return varies. Some legends reported the witch's return to be 1935, or after 107 years. Other legends have estimated the return of the witch to be about every seven years. Newspaper accounts, on the other hand, gave the date of the supposed return as 1937.

In 1937 a series of articles appeared in the Nashville *Tennessean* during the first week of August. Each of the articles reported strange events that occurred near the original site of the witch's first visit. For example, Louis Garrison, who farmed the land adjacent to the original homeplace of John Bell, reported noises coming from the Bell Witch Cave. Garrison said, "It sounded like birds rising in a convoy." However, after a thorough search, he found no birds or bats in the cave. Garrison blamed the weird event on the Bell Witch, as one might expect.[1]

Queen of the Haunted Dell.

□ "Queen of the Haunted Dell":The Bell Witch
of Robertson County,Tennessee. From Ingram,
Authenticated History of the Famous Bell Witch,
ca. 1894. Courtesy of Sherrod Library, East
Tennessee State University.

In another 1937 incident, the Adams Epworth League was having a wiener roast about a quarter mile from the cave. After making joking remarks about whether or not there was a Bell Witch, the group noticed "high up on the cliff, a white figure sitting on a rock with its feet hanging down." Miss Mary Jean Mayes related the story. It was her great-great-great grandfather who was Jack Johnston, friend of the Bell family. Johnston was said to have actually held the witch's hand in 1817. He described it as being "soft and tiny" like a baby's hand.[2]

The Bell Witch legend seems to forever be of interest to people. For example, articles continue to appear in the newspapers. Hugh Walker, reporter of the *Nashville Tennessean,* has written several articles about the Bell Witch. In one account, Walker decided to investigate the story himself. He took his family to Adams and tried to summon the witch, but with no luck. On the return trip (and according to Walker), Kate struck. Walker witnessed a wreck with a fatality—the only one ever witnessed in years on a midstate highway. He wanted to call another photographer. Walker's story of the automobile accident appeared in a new section of the *Tennessean,* but since it was a new section, the Tennessee State Library and Archives did not include the article on microfilm. (Walker naturally blames this incident on Kate also.) Fortunately, Walker's article did give information on how to obtain additional copies of the article. Unfortunately, however, the information was no good. Walker included a photograph with his story, too. The picture was taken near the Bell cemetery. An old farmer, as well as Walker's family, was included in the photograph, but the old man's name was not included in the caption. Walker had intended to mention the farmer in the story, since he was kind enough to guide his family to the cemetery. Unfortunately, the farmer's identity was lost, and no doubt (as stated in the caption) the lost identity was blamed on the witch.[3]

In 1980, Walker also reported on the sale of the Bell Witch Cave. According to the article, the cave continues to be a popular spooking place—especially around Halloween. The owner of the cave, Wayne M. "Bims" Eden Jr., wanted to sell the cave to "someone with time and resources to cope with the throngs of visitors to the scene."[4] Mr. Eden apparently chose not to sell the cave, as he still owns it today.

Another article appeared in a Nashville newspaper in 1965. This article is about a woman who sat in a mysterious old rocking chair that belonged to the late Charles Willet, a descendent of the Bell family. The rocking chair was in an antique shop in Adams near the old Bell homestead. The woman mentioned seemed quite peculiar because she sat in the chair for twenty minutes after she was told it was not for sale. Two weeks later, the woman's daughter appeared at the shop. She told the owner about an unusual experience that her mother underwent after having sat in the chair. According to the daughter, her mother heard a strange voice. The voice told her mother to look in a field along the highway; there she would find something "of great value." The woman decided to disregard the voice and get in her car. However, her car would not start. Again, the voice told the woman to look for the object. Finally, the lady did search for "something," and she found a very old, valuable mother-of-pearl buckle.[5]

The Bell Witch legend and its modern versions appear not only in newspapers but in other forms of print as well. For example, "at various times the *Folklore Magazine* has discussed the Bell Witch legend, placing it in North Carolina and Mississippi, as well as Tennessee."[6] Charles F. Bryan has also helped spread the fame of the Bell Witch legend through his composition *The Bell Witch Cantata*. The cantata premiered at Carnegie Hall in 1948, with Robert Shaw conducting. Bryan, like several other writers, placed the setting of his version in North Carolina.[7] The Bell Witch legend even appeared in the November 1968 issue of *Playboy*. The writer suggested that the Bell Witch was a male ventriloquist who was in love with Betsy and wanted to run off her sweetheart, Josh Gardner.[8] Additionally, Kathryn Windham, well known for her ghost story collections, claims that the Bell Witch legend was mysteriously included in one of her books. She did not intend to include the legend, but "something happened in the printing of the book which the editor cannot explain. The book came out with ten blank pages at the end."[9] Windham believes that the Bell Witch was trying to give her a hint.

In addition to being circulated by newspaper articles and other forms of print, the Bell Witch legend is being circulated today by oral tradition. Many of the current legends are spread by children and are considerably less sophisticated and complicated than the legends communicated in print. The legends that children tell have very little in common with the original Bell Witch story.

For instance, in many southern towns there is a place that the Bell Witch is supposed to inhabit. In Tracy City, Tennessee, the Bell Witch was said to have lived in the tower of the old Shook School. The school was built in about 1891 and burned down in 1978. Before the school burned, as the local legend has it, a man (possibly the school janitor) went up to the tower and hanged himself. He was left hanging for a long period of time because everyone was afraid to go up there. The man might have hanged himself because he saw the Bell Witch. In Manchester, Tennessee, the Bell Witch is said to live in the old Hickerson house on Powers Bridge Road. The house is dilapidated and a family cemetery is located right across the road—the perfect setting for a haunted house. People who visit the house are told to listen carefully for the sound of a crying baby coming from one of the rooms. In Murfreesboro's tale, the "Bell Witch and her two sisters once inhabited" a huge white home on North Highland. The part about the Bell Witch's two sisters is very different from the original legend. It is also quite interesting to note the great differences between the modern legends as compared to the traditional tale.

Universities in Middle Tennessee have also attracted their share of Bell Witch legends. In 1974 a student at Middle Tennessee State University in Murfreesboro collected two such legends for an unpublished paper. A 21-year-old student described the incident that happened to a family friend who was then a professor at David Lipscomb College in Nashville. He had had a "passing interest" in the legend and studied it casually when, about 1955, he encountered her. "He had gotten off the bus one night and a woman dressed in black got off behind him. She walked beside him. She said nothing. He got to his destination, turned to her to say goodbye, and she had disappeared."[10] There was also a widely circulated student legend on the MTSU campus in Murfreesboro about a girl living in Lyon Hall who was tormented by the witch. Most versions of this story have the girl writing a term paper on the Bell Witch for a class in 1968. Shortly after she started her research, she began to return to her room in Lyon Hall to find her drawers ransacked and a fresh rose on her pillow. This happened repeatedly. The rose, she was told, signified death by the witch. The torment continued until the girl hanged herself, or was hanged, in a closet in her room. The room remained vacant for some years and has now been converted into a storage closet. The housing office on campus denies that a death ever took place.[11]

Then there are the Bell Witch stories that children tell among themselves. Some of these stories involve a type of ritual to be performed and are usually told at slumber parties and sleep-overs. For example, ghost stories are very popular among children, especially during a slumber party. Children seem to enjoy the spine-tingling process of being scared. Often kids will have a séance

◘ "Kate Batts' Troop," Robertson County, Tennessee. From Ingram, *Authenticated History of the Famous Bell Witch,* ca. 1894. Courtesy of Sherrod Library, East Tennessee State University.

◘ "John Bell's Death," Robertson County, Tennessee. From Ingram, *Authenticated History of the Famous Bell Witch,* ca. 1894. Courtesy of Sherrod Library, East Tennessee State University.

and try to conjure up a ghost—just for fun. Similar to conjuring up ghosts, children in the South make up a game of trying to conjure up the Bell Witch. This process usually includes a ritual like this:

> A person must go into a dark room and stand in front of a mirror. Then he says, "I don't believe in the Bell Witch." He must say this three to ten times. (Legends vary.) After he does this, the Bell Witch will appear in the mirror, and the person's face will be scratched. The scratch marks are described as being long, deep, and bleeding. They are supposed to look as if a human being with very long nails made them.

One variation of the process suggests the person simply repeat "Bell Witch" three times while standing in front of the mirror. Another so-called method of getting in touch with the Bell Witch is through the use of a telephone. Children in Manchester, Tennessee, claim that if four identical numbers are dialed, the Bell Witch will answer the phone. Another legend states the caller must dial all the numbers (1, 2, 3, 4 . . . 10) before the Bell Witch answers the call.

Even individual families have their own versions of the Bell Witch legend. I can remember hearing about the Bell Witch for most of my life. My grandmother, Mrs. William Houston (Beatrice) Bell Sr., tells her own version of the story, although the validity of the story remains unchecked:

> Sometime after Andrew Jackson was president, John Thomas Bell and his family moved to Beech Grove, Tennessee, from Robertson County. There he purchased 14,000 acres of land between Beech Grove and Bell Buckle. Among his descendants was John Thomas Bell, who later married and settled at Bell Springs located near Highway 41 between Murfreesboro and Manchester. He was the father of nine children, one of which was her [my grandmother's] grandfather's grandfather. He was sheriff at Coffee County in the later 1800s. Among John Thomas Bell's children was one daughter named Bessy Bell. Bessy first married Jim Black. After he died, she married a Reams man. Bessy claims that the power of the Bell Witch came through her, enabling her to communicate with the dead and to forecast the future. Many of her predictions actually came true. For example, Aunt Bessy (as we called her) claimed that a vision came to her from beyond and told her that her sister was going to die. Aunt Bessy told my grandmother the exact date she would die, and sure enough her prediction came true. She had another vision that told her that her other sister was going to be bedridden before she died. This also came true. Aunt Bessy had a brother who had been very ill for some time. Suddenly he became quite well, and everyone thought he would be fine. Bessy predicted he was not well and that he would die unexpectedly and soon. A few mornings later he died while combing his hair.

Aunt Bessy was indeed a very strange woman. She didn't trust anyone and believed that all the people who visited her were out to get her money. I remember visiting her while I was a youngster. She would lie on her couch and pretend to be asleep. Actually she kept one eye open and watched me. It was very scary; I used to think Aunt Bessy was the Bell Witch.

Besides the connection between Aunt Bessy and the Bell Witch, my grandmother also believes other versions of the legend. According to my grandmother:

> Our family says that the Bell Witch returns every seven years to bring disaster. During the seven-year period, one to seven Bells will die, usually two or three. There is also one year between the seven years that the "death angel" is supposed to visit three people. In 1981 Aunt Bessy and her nephew died. During the same year, Aunt Bessy's great-nephew died. During the same year, Aunt Bessy's great-nephew was killed in an airplane crash in Wyoming.[12]

Although no one is sure about the validity of this family legend, my grandmother says that Dr. T. Bell is presently doing research on the subject and has contacted her and my uncle, Charles Bell of Manchester.[13]

All of the current Bell Witch legends mentioned are quite interesting. Perhaps some of the most interesting current Bell Witch tales are being circulated today in the Robertson County area. H. C. Brehm has written a book *Echoes of the Bell Witch in the Twentieth Century*. It consists of unexplained events that have occurred near the site of the old Bell homestead. Most are the results of personal experiences and first-hand knowledge of Mr. W. M. Eden, who owns the Bell Witch Cave and surrounding property.

A large number of strange happenings have taken place at the cave. For example, it is almost impossible to take a good picture of the cave entrance. For some unknown reason, the finished picture comes out blurry when developed. In another case, a white form is often seen floating inside small passages of the cave. Sometimes the form is in the shape of a woman. On other occasions, visitors to the cave feel like some unseen being is touching or actually hugging them.

Brehm also mentions the legend of the missing grave marker. In this story, three young men had been to the old Bell graveyard and had stolen the headstone from John Bell's grave. They put the headstone in the trunk of their car. Then they headed back to their home which was in Nashville. During the return trip, the car became involved in an accident. The owner was killed, but the other two boys were not seriously injured. Within a few days of the accident, one of the two survivors was killed on his job and the other lost his hand. The accidents happened a few days apart. The automobile was returned to the home of the owner's mother. She checked the wrecked auto for any of her son's belongings and found the old tombstone in the trunk. The marker must have had John Bell's name on it because she returned it to Adams and placed it on the edge of a roadside ditch in front of what she thought was the old Bell farm. The marker remains undiscovered and is said to lie somewhere on the back-roads just off Highway 41 near Adams.

Except for the strange events that have been reported, Adams remains a small, quiet town. There are no department stores, movie theaters, or bowling alleys. In fact, Adams had nothing to do after the sun went down. Now, however, residents and visitors can enjoy bluegrass music every Saturday night in what is called the Bell Witch Opry. The opry is located in the Old Bell Elementary School, which also serves as an antique mall. Mr. and Mrs. Ken Seeley converted the school into the mall and named it Bell Witch Village Mall. The Seeleys, musicians since childhood, also traveled around the surrounding areas on weekends performing as a bluegrass and "ole-timey" country music band. In March 1981, they decided to move the weekend "jam session" to the abandoned auditorium located on the second floor of the old school building. The Bell Witch Opry features country, western, and bluegrass music. Frequently, Grand Ole Opry performers and their relatives entertain at the Bell Witch Opry. Dolly Parton's aunt and uncle, Bill and Kathy Owen, are regulars in the Adams musical show. In January 1983, a Springfield radio station, WDBL-FM, began broadcasting the Bell Witch Opry show live every Saturday night from 7:30 p.m. to 9:30 p.m.

There is another event that takes place every second weekend in August. It is the Bell Witch Bluegrass Festival, a two-day event. The festival, which allows no electric instruments, includes competitions in guitar, junior guitar, flatfoot dance, mandolin, harmonica, old-time banjo, fiddling, etc.[14]

In conclusion, the legend of the Bell Witch has existed for years. Furthermore, new versions of the legend are being circulated every day. The town of Adams even celebrates the popularity of the Bell Witch. Although no one has been able to explain the unusual mystery, the "spirit" of the Bell Witch is flourishing.

Notes

1. Jack Tucker, "Something Goes on at Adams; It May Be Kate, the Bell Witch," *Nashville Tennessean,* August 1, 1937, p. 1, col. 3.
2. Jack Tucker, "Form Lately Appears on Cliff Overlooking Bell Witch Cave," *Nashville Tennessean,* August 4, 1937, p. 1, cols. 3–4.
3. Hugh Walker, "The Bell Witch Strikes Again," *Nashville Tennessean,* February 23, 1980, p. 4, col. 1.
4. Hugh Weaker, "Robertson Bell Witch Cave for Sale," *Nashville Tennessean,* February 23, 1980, p. 4, col. 1.
5. Bill Preston Jr., "Has Bell Witch Returned Home?" *Nashville Tennessean,* February 23, 1980, p. 4, col. 1.

6. Gladys Barr, "Witchcraft in Tennessee," *Tennessee Valley Historical Review* II (Fall 1983): 29.

7. Carolyn Shoulders, "Is Bell Witch Giving Arts Center Premier?" *Nashville Tennessean,* April 24, 1980, p. 19, col. 4.

8. Barr, 29.

9. Kathryn Windham, *Thirteen Tennessee Ghosts and Jeffrey* (Huntsville, Ala.: Strode Publishers, 1977), 151.

10. Lisa Human, "Mystery Still Unsolved at Bell Cave," *Sideline,* October 30, 1979, p. 1, cols. 4–5.

11. Kay Horner, "A Collection: Ghost Stories in Middle Tennessee," unpublished manuscript #74–16-A, Tennessee Folklore Society Archives, Middle Tennessee State University. The manuscript contains names of original informants.

12. Horner manuscript.

13. Mrs. William Houston Bell lives on the Woodbury Highway in Manchester, Tennessee. Bessy Bell, born in 1887, was confined to Crestwood Nursing Home in Manchester. She died in 1981 at the age of 94.

14. The information listed was obtained from various pamphlets from The Bell Witch Village in Adams, Tennessee.

Davy Crockett, David Crockett, and Me
A Personal Journey through Legend into History
[1994]

Michael A. Lofaro

"Davy Crockett Not a Hero?" "Professor Shoots Holes in Crockett Myth." "'King of the Wild Frontier' Dies Hard by the Pen of Lofaro the Giant Legend Killer."

Who me?

My book, my tribute to my childhood hero, generated headlines in 1985 and 1986 that whipped the Crockett faithful into a minor frenzy. A woman wrote anonymously from Alamo, Tennessee, the seat of Crockett County, to let me have it with both barrels: "How dare you dishonor Davy Crockett. He was a REAL man, a patriot who fought and died for this country and our freedom. Not like you, you communist, intellectual, wimp. If the newspaper stories about what you wrote in your book are true, its [sic] a good thing you already got a job teaching at the University because your [sic] not fit to do anything else."

Didn't she know that I carried my Crockett lunch box to school longer than any other kid? Didn't she know that I was one of the few people who could still sing "The Ballad of Davy Crockett" without forgetting the line that came after "Born on a mountain top in Tennessee, / Greenest state in the Land of the Free"? Didn't she realize that my most cherished childhood possession was my never-crack plastic, simulated cowhide Davy Crockett wallet? And that every time I looked at the picture of Fess Parker on the front of it, I hoped that some day I'd have a coonskin cap too and grow up just like Davy?

With only a postmark to guide me, I had no way of telling her that I and the other scholars who contributed to the book had no intention of debunking Davy Crockett. We merely tried to separate the man from the many myths, both bad and good, that had grown up about him in over a century and a half of hero worship.

Pinning Davy down and explaining exactly who he is and what he did has been a problem for writers ever since he came into the public eye. Crockett himself made the situation worse. He loved a good joke and encouraged many of the outlandish tales told about him to gain further political mileage from his "ring-tailed roarer" backwoods image. But you can untangle the myths; you can peel back the accumulated layers of media-created hype to recover the real Davy Crockett. And in an age where true heroes are hard to come by, you quickly see that his life has a special relevance for Americans and particularly for Tennesseans. Remember that Davy is our only statewide hero. East, Middle, and West Tennessee rightfully claim him as their own because he lived in all three grand divisions of the state.

Interestingly enough, the process of stripping the myths from the man doesn't cut Davy down to size by revealing his "dirty linen"; instead it highlights the humanity and heroism of the actual, historical Crockett. You find that in life, he fought for the rights of the underprivileged and dispossessed, whether they were white squatters or Cherokee Indians, no matter how adversely it affected his political career, and in death, he became the supreme symbol of American grit and independence. You find that his values weren't new, but in him they found a new champion, a self-made man whose rough-hewn courage, honor, and determination gave an added dignity to our fledgling democracy.

So what really happens when you separate the man from the myths? If you take away, for example, the wildest of the fictional images given to Crockett, the tall-tale Davy created from 1835 to 1856 in the Crockett almanacs, you don't diminish the stature of the real man at all. These illustrated comic almanacs, the direct ancestor of today's superhero comic books and Saturday morning cartoons, offered their readers a make-believe Davy who, when he was at his best, twisted the tail off Halley's Comet, treed a ghost, drank up the Gulf of Mexico, rode his pet alligator up the face of Niagara Falls, and reenacted the role of Prometheus to bring fire back to save a nearly frozen Earth.

No one, then or now, believed the stories. This tall-tale Davy was a projection of our boundless optimism or perhaps egotism, the superhero who reinforced the belief that we Americans could do anything. We had defeated the military might of England not once but twice, were sure that our borders

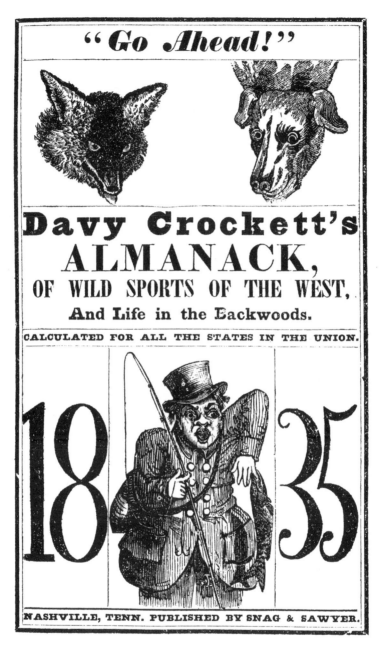

□ Cover of Davy Crockett's Almanack, 1835. From Lofaro, *Davy Crockett.*

□ Cover of Davy Crockett's Almanack, 1835. From Lofaro, *Davy Crockett*.

would soon stretch from sea to shining sea, and saw the eventual domination of this hemisphere as part of our manifest destiny as a nation.

But to the modern mind, empire building has a dark side that doesn't square with the American dream. What about the rights of the people and nations who might be in the way? The same fictional super-Crockett provides us with the answer we hoped not to hear. Our old enemies, the English, had no more right to the Oregon Territory than Mexico had to its land, and battle-scarred Davy was there to convince them of it by brute force. The other side of the comic hero was dark indeed. Once, when he was feeling ornery, he killed an Indian and boiled him down to make a spring tonic to cure the stomach ache of his pet bear, Death Hug, and he most always saw blacks, "red niggers," and Mexicans as less than human and fit only for "extarmination."

This half of the Davy of the Crockett almanacs mirrored the worst of the savage, racist, and extreme behavior associated with America at that time but did not mirror the opinions of the historical Crockett. He had already been dead for some years when the fictional stories about "his" actions and beliefs were published. Needless to say, any present confusion of the man and the myth usually incorporates this negative side of the almanac Crockett into the depiction of the man. That these attitudes existed is undeniable. But when they are mistakenly associated with Crockett, the fact that they are eagerly seized upon by editors and publishers who can't or won't discriminate between fiction and history is an unfortunate commentary on today's society. The decision to print or broadcast these stories is clearly economic, but it has more to do with us than the simple media truism that bad news sells better than good. It's that we get what we want; we seem to revel in discoveries that puncture or destroy a hero's character or reveal his feet of clay. Perhaps that's why when you ask a group of kids today who their heroes are, they nearly always name a fictional rather than a historical hero.

Fortunately some of the attempts at Crockett-bashing are too ridiculous to be taken seriously. Imagine my surprise at the dogged determination of one radio talk show's host to pursue the sensational. In an aborted interview with Capitol Radio, London, the host's opening statement was "Dr. Lofaro, I understand that you have proved in your book that Davy Crockett was fat, bald, and gay. [Ten-second pause.] I assume that your protracted laughter means that you have indeed proved that Crockett was fat, bald, and gay." At that point, I had to choke off my belly laughs long enough to explain that I had done no such thing. Very disappointed, he cut short our interview after I convinced him that I had neither printed nor proved a bizarre enough reversal of Crockett's physique (actually about five feet eight or nine and 160 pounds) or of his sexual preferences to warrant part of his program's air time.

Folks who cut their Crockett teeth on the likes of Fess Parker and John Wayne may be disappointed to find out that Davy literally didn't measure up

◘ Replica of David Crockett's birthplace home, Davy Crockett State Park, Tennessee. From the Appalachian Photographic Archive. Courtesy of the Archives of Appalachia, East Tennessee State University.

to the height and weight of the actors who portrayed him. They may also be surprised to learn that he was almost always called David and that he seldom if ever wore a coonskin cap. But do these minor details really lessen our admiration of the man? I think not. When you take the time to examine the real David Crockett, the pioneer, the Indian fighter, the politician, and the hero of the Alamo, you find that, while he was by no means perfect, he was an extraordinary individual and perhaps one of the best models of all that is right in the American spirit.

Born on August 17, 1786, fifty-two years after the birth of Daniel Boone and only ten years after the Declaration of Independence, Davy grew up with the new nation, and, more important, he helped it to grow. Living in Tennessee for all but the last few months of his life, he was one of the settlers who gradually pushed the frontier to the west through Tennessee toward Texas. In his search for a better life for himself and his family, he participated fully in the American dream. He wanted to own a home and to ensure his family's financial security. The means may have been different—hunting, farming, and a bit of land speculation—but the goal was the same.

Although Davy was known early on in his life as a first-rate hunter and backwoodsman, his public service began and ended with his volunteering as a soldier and had nearly twenty years of local, state, and national politics in between. His brief career as a soldier in the Indian Wars lasted a total of only nine months. It began in September 1813—when he enlisted for ninety days in the militia in Winchester, Tennessee, to avenge the attack on Fort Mims, Alabama, in which the Creek Indians killed some five hundred settlers and soldiers, a number that included about one hundred children—and ended on March 27, 1815, after a six-month mopping-up operation trying to ferret out the British-trained-and-supplied Indians from the Florida swamps.

Two incidents left a sour taste in his mouth for the regular army and undoubtedly later led Congressman Crockett to favor a force of volunteers and to oppose what he regarded as the aristocratic tendencies of West Point by attempting to limit the academy's appropriations. Chosen as scout on his first tour of duty by his commander, Major Gibson, Davy picked young George Russell (yes, that's where Disney came up with the name for Crockett's side-kick played by Buddy Ebsen) as his companion. Davy recorded in his autobiography that he was a "little nettled" when "Major Gibson said he thought he [George Russell] hadn't enough beard to please him,—he wanted men not boys" and reflected that "I didn't think that courage ought to be measured by the beard, for fear a goat would have the preference over a man." Davy's insistence eventually convinced the major, but the need for such an argument made him wonder about the wisdom of men who judged by age and appearance rather than by ability.

His fiery dislike of army brass was fueled further in a few weeks. Davy and his scouts had traveled night and day to bring back the news of a Creek war party advancing to attack Jackson's troops, but Colonel Coffee disregarded the intelligence until the next day when Major Gibson returned with the same news. Davy wrote:

> This convinced me, clearly, of one of the hateful ways of the world. When I made my report, it wasn't believed, because I was no officer; I was no great man, but just a poor soldier. But when the same thing was reported by Major Gibson!! why, then, it was all true as preaching, and the colonel believed every word.

Fortunately for the unprepared forces, the information proved a hoax. Jackson had time to consolidate his forces and revenge the murderous attack on Fort Mims by surrounding and massacring the Indian town of Tallussahatchee on November 3, 1813. Indian warfare was a savage business on both sides. Davy saw a group of braves retreat into a house and noted, "We now shot them like dogs; and then set the house on fire, and burned it up with the forty-six warriors in it."

Commentators have tried to make both too much and too little out of Davy's words and actions by contrasting them to his speech in 1830 against the

Indian Removal bill and to his efforts to help provide redress and compensation for three Cherokee Indians who had been dispossessed of their land by white men. While we can never fully know his motives in all these instances, they may not be contradictory. Davy may well have been guided throughout by the same straightforward notion of frontier justice that he said he used in making his decisions as a Lawrence County magistrate:

> I gave my decisions on the principals of common justice and honesty between man and man, and relied on natural born sense, and not on law, [and] learning to guide me; for I had never read a page in a law book in all my life.

Was it so far-fetched to believe that the massacre of the Indians at Tallussahatchee was simply the equivalent in rough frontier justice of an eye for an eye for the slaughter at Fort Mims? Or that Davy would later try to prevent the unjust treatment of peaceful Indians by land-hungry whites?

One of the few times that Davy's honesty was evidently overpowered by his political desires came out when he wrote in his autobiography about his role in the mutiny of volunteers against Andrew Jackson after the end of their sixty-day term of enlistment in the Creek campaign. The famous mutiny scene at the bridge made memorable by Walt Disney did occur, but Jackson backed down the rebellious troops; they were not released until Governor Blount convinced the general that it would be a wise political move. Davy, whose ninety-day enlistment had not expired at that time, did not lead or even participate in the rebellion. He was "improving" his war record along the lines of his anti-Jackson campaign for the presidency for the election of 1836. So it seems that Pat Robertson's famous "inaccuracy" concerning his war record in the 1988 presidential campaign may be a part of a longstanding tradition in American politics and a reflection of the same mentality that led Bill Clinton to state "But I didn't inhale" in regard to his trying marijuana.

Fortunately, Davy's autobiography of 1834 showed a great deal more political savvy than misrepresentation. He used his image and reputation well. His fame was already in part ensured because he came into his own just as the American ideal of the noble pioneer of the eighteenth century was giving way before the brash and cocky backwoodsman of the nineteenth century. He also had the good luck to enter his pubic career as the centers of political power were moving from the control of the upper class to within reach of the common man. Davy was, therefore, in the forefront of a major shift in American politics that helped to define the shape of many present-day campaigns.

If you don't think that his grassroots image and down-home style has had an effect, try to recall the last time someone was elected who emphasized wealth, status, and family privilege as assets for holding public office. What we see instead are staged "media opportunities" that feature George Bush driving any large truck or piece of heavy equipment that he can lay his hands on, Michael Dukakis setting records for the number of Greek folk dances done, and Bill Clinton playing his saxophone on national television. To be electable, you have to appear to be a man of the people.

True to the common-man image that Davy projected in his autobiography, he never tells you that he rose to the rank of fourth sergeant by the end of his military service. His summation of the time he spent as an Indian fighter was both prophetic and poignant:

> This closed my career as a warrior, and I am glad of it, for I like life now a heap better than I did then; and I am glad all over that I lived to see these times, which I should not have done if I had kept fooling along in war and got used up at it.

The next time that he would bear arms as a soldier would occur twenty-one years later at the Alamo and last only thirteen days.

His military experience served Davy well. After he returned home, he was elected a lieutenant in the 32nd Militia Regime of Franklin County in 1816 and, within a year, could tell us that his political fortunes "took a decided rise in the world." In quick succession Davy became a magistrate of Lawrence County, town commissioner of Lawrenceburg, colonel of the 57th Militia Regiment in the county, and then resigned all offices but his colonelcy in 1821 to run successfully for a seat in the state legislature as the representative of Lawrence and Hickman counties. From the very start of his state political career, he took an active interest in public land policy regarding the West, an interest that was to be his political undoing in the national arena.

Davy quickly made himself known when the legislature met in Murfreesborough. He introduced, amended, and helped to pass a number of bills, but perhaps more important for the legacy which he left to all Tennesseans, he set an example and a high standard of behavior by continuing to rely on the "natural born sense" that he used as a magistrate, by making honest judgments, and by keeping his relaxed, informal style, his natural grace, and his keen sense of humor.

Were he able to give a rapid evaluation of some of his political descendants in Tennessee, he might follow the lead of the almanac Davy, who raised his historical counterpart's comic boasting to a high art. Instead of statements such as "I can run faster, jump higher, squat lower, dive deeper, stay under longer, and come out drier than any man in the whole country," Davy might well tell us that he could out-fiddle either Bob or Alf Taylor, the brothers who ran against each other for governor in Tennessee's famous "War of the Roses," find better uses for raccoons than Estes Kefauver, out-joke Howard Baker, out-barbeque John Duncan, and at least give Ned Ray McWherter a run for his money in eating vanilla wafers.

So it is that this lighter side of Davy lives on as a firm part of Tennessee's informal political tradition. Storytelling, the use of slang and everyday language, an anti-Washington, anti-intellectual independence of thought and action, and a fondness for stumping all found a comfortable home in the state's political scene. Davy underscored the idea that politicians have to remember their roots and keep their sense of humor if they hope to gain reelection and to do their best for themselves and their constituents.

Crockett obviously knew better than to take himself too seriously, but at first, some of his fellow elected officials didn't take him seriously enough. Ironically termed the "gentleman from the cane," Davy was viewed as a country bumpkin by some of his fellow members of the Tennessee legislature. They thought that he had stepped directly from the wild recesses of a West Tennessee canebrake onto the floor of the House. Crockett turned their mockery to his advantage by pinning to his shirt a fancy cambric ruffle of the same cut as that of his main antagonist, a Mr. James C. Mitchell. When he rose to speak after one of Mitchell's particularly informative addresses, Davy's newly affected finery stood out on his rough backwoodsman's shirt in such a ridiculous fashion that the members of the House burst into an uproar of laughter that forced an embarrassed Mitchell from the chamber. Davy's "working man's" shirt was just as much one of his campaign trademarks as was Lamar Alexander's. And the pairing of Davy's shirt and the cambric ruffle presented just as vivid a contrast as Lamar's checkered shirt did to Jake Butcher's finely tailored suits on the nightly news.

Davy was no fool. He knew his image and continued to manipulate it to his political advantage, especially in his early campaigns. His run against Dr. William E. Butler in the state elections of 1823 provided some of the best examples of his humor and wit. Crockett played up his "gentleman from the cane" image and labeled Butler as an aristocrat. When visiting his opponent's fine house, he refused to walk upon a particularly expensive rug and subsequently incorporated a telling comparison as a high point in his speeches: "Fellow citizens, my aristocratic competitor has a fine carpet, and everyday he walks of truck finer than any gowns your wife or your daughters, in all their lives, ever wore!" He told Butler that he would have a buckskin hunting shirt made with two pockets large enough to hold a big twist of chewing tobacco and a bottle of liquor. After a prospective voter took a taste of "the creature," Davy said that he would immediately hand him a replacement for the "chaw" he had to discard to take the drink and thus "he would not be worse off than when I found him; and I would be sure to leave him in a first-rate good humour." Crockett once even memorized Butler's standard campaign speech and delivered it word for word just before it was Butler's turn to speak. The two men fortunately remained on good terms, and Butler often enjoyed Crockett's brand of entertainment as much as the rest of their audiences.

Davy's sense of humor was one of the reasons that he was likely a better symbol of the spirit of Jacksonian democracy than Andrew Jackson himself. Never reaching the heights of Jackson's achievements in military combat or in the political arena in his three terms in the House of Representatives (1827–29, 1829–31, and 1833–35), Davy's humor and, somewhat ironically, his lack of extraordinary success may well have kept him a more identifiable ideal and representative hero in the popular mind during his public career. Davy could have succeeded as a legislator, but for him the price would have been too great. Had he not opposed Jackson so vehemently by opposing the Indian Removal bill that eventually led to the Trail of Tears, had he not supported the national bank, and had he not argued for the cheap sale of land to squatters in West Tennessee, he would have been more effective in gaining support for his positions. Had he been willing to compromise on his stands, he might well have been able to gain passage for some of his key pieces of legislation.

Impractical? Yes. Foolish? Perhaps. But there was not an inch of give in Davy's backbone when his dander was up, and he continued to pursue policies that he knew would cause political problems for him at home. He seemed determined to live up to his motto of "Be always sure you're right— THEN GO AHEAD!"

Davy's actions created an irreconcilable rift between him and his party, a gap that became a canyon when he was taken up by the opposing Whig Party as their anti-Jackson presidential candidate. In so doing, he unwisely gave the Jackson forces plenty of ammunition to use against him in his try for a fourth term for a seat in the House. He had taken time from his congressional duties to tour the northern and eastern states to test the presidential waters and, egged on by his new-found cronies, intensified his overt antagonism to anything and anyone associated with the still popular president and his administration. The outcome of Crockett's political career was nonetheless in his own hands and his downfall ultimately hinged on his dwindling political clout. At the end of the legislative session, he could not even get his squatters' land bill, on which he pinned his congressional reelection hopes, to the floor of the House for a vote.

Davy's personal popularity kept the election of 1835 close, but when the ballots were counted, he lost the election to Adam Huntsman, a peg-legged lawyer supported by Jackson, and Governor Carroll of Tennessee, by a vote of 4,652 to 4,400. It was because of this defeat that he decided to explore Texas, or as Davy himself put it: "Since you have chosen to elect a man with a timber toe to succeed me, you may all go to hell and I will go to Texas." At this point, he had no intention of joining the fight for Texan independence.

His last surviving letters, however, show that Texas changed his plans. On January 9, 1836, Davy wrote:

I have taken the oath of government and have enrolled my name as a
volunteer and will set out for the Rio Grand [*sic*] in a few days with the
volunteers from the United States. But all volunteers is entitled to vote
for a member of the convention or to be voted for, and I have but little
doubt of being elected a member to form a constitution for this province.
I am rejoiced at my fate. I had rather be in my present situation than to
be elected to a seat in Congress for life. I am in hopes of making a fortune
yet for myself and family, bad as my prospect has been.

Davy was confident that Texas would allow him to rejuvenate his political
career and to acquire the wealth that had eluded him all his life by becoming
the land agent for the new territory. He clearly felt that he was in the right place
at the right time.

In early February, Crockett arrived at San Antonio De Bexar; Santa Anna
arrived on February 20. On the one hand, Crockett was still fighting Jackson. The
Americans in Texas were split into the two main political factions that divided
those who supported a conservative Whig philosophy and those who supported
the administration. Davy chose to join Col. William B. Travis, who had deliberately disregarded Sam Houston's orders to withdraw from the Alamo, rather
than support Houston, a Jacksonian sympathizer. And on the other hand, he saw
the future of an independent Texas as his future and he loved a good fight.

Davy's part in the battle of the Alamo, and particularly his death on
March 6, 1836, continued in uncertainty until the publication of the diary of
Lt. José Enrique de la Peña in 1955. When this eyewitness account was placed
together with other corroborating documents, Crockett's central role in the
defense became clear. Colonel Travis stationed Davy and his men at the most
vulnerable point, behind the rough log palisade between the Alamo church and
the south wall. In a letter written during the first bombardment, Travis said that
Davy was everywhere in the Alamo "animating the men to do their duty." Other
reports told of the deadly effect of his rifle that killed five Mexican gunners in
succession, as they each attempted to fire a cannon bearing on the fort, and that
he may have just missed Santa Anna, who thought himself out of range of all the
defenders' rifles.

Crockett fought so well and courageously that he survived the battle and
was offered his life by Gen. Manuel Fernandez Castrillón despite the fact that
Santa Anna had ordered that no prisoners be taken. Santa Anna was infuriated
when Davy and five or six other Americans were brought before him and commanded that they be executed immediately. De la Peña recorded that Castrillón
and the officers who accepted the surrender

> were outraged at this action and did not support the order, hoping that
> once the fury of the moment had blown over these men would be spared;
> but several officers who were around the president and who, perhaps, had

not been present during the moment of danger, became noteworthy by an infamous deed, surpassing the soldiers in cruelty. They thrust themselves forward, in order to flatter their commander, and with swords in hand, fell upon these unfortunate, defenseless men just as a tiger leaps upon its prey. Though tortured before they were killed, these unfortunates died without complaining and without humiliating themselves before their torturers.

Crockett's reputation and that of the other survivors was not sullied by the way in which they died. His bravery and dignity was underscored by de la Peña and noted in all the accounts of the battle. If Davy's end was less than satisfying by Hollywood standards, then so be it. That he didn't die on the battlements swinging his broken rifle as a club and surrounded by a mounting pile of Mexican soldiers made him no less a hero and no less a man. Was Robert E. Lee's reputation somehow clouded by his surrender to Grant? Honorable survival is no disgrace.

An interesting sidelight perfectly in keeping with Davy's character was also noted by de la Peña. It seemed that Davy bent the truth a bit and let it be known that he was merely a tourist who took refuge in the Alamo at the approach of Santa Anna's forces. Had he had a bit more time, he may well have talked his way out of his execution. Nothing would have been more fitting.

Nothing except the fact that Davy died pursuing his dream.

In the final tally, that's all that matters. His heroism and patriotism were proven long before he went to Texas. His actions at the Alamo merely confirmed the beliefs that guided his life.

While his martyrdom was the springboard from which a series of outlandish legends were launched, it was also a truly fitting end for the historical Crockett, the fighting congressman and "gentleman from the cane." It should be clear to everyone that Crockett the man was the source for all that was admirable in the myths. Davy's willingness to pay the ultimate price for his beliefs made him a role model for Tennesseans and for the entire country.

This is why Davy won't die. Invested in him are the hopes and beliefs, the virtues and the values, and the shortcomings and the triumphs of each generation that takes him up as a hero. Davy's own words of praise for Andrew Jackson, when they were on friendly terms early in 1828, capture our regard for Crockett himself equally well, for he too "is like the diamond in the hill . . . the harder they Rub him the brighter he Shines."

And to those of us raised on Walt Disney, Davy really didn't die. We looked at the final scene and saw Davy swinging Old Betsy as a club, knocking the enemy left and right, and then the picture faded to a shot of the Lone Star flag as the strains of "The Ballad of Davy Crockett" grew louder and louder. We never saw him die. For us, the simple faith that Davy lived on was also testified to by the last verse of the ballad:

[His] land is biggest an' his land is best,
From grassy plains to the mountain crest,
He's ahead of us all meetin' the test,
Followin' his legend into the West,
Davy—Davy Crockett,
King of the Wild Frontier!

If, as you're singing along, there are still some Crocketteers out there who haven't come up with the elusive third line to the first stanza of the ballad, the verse goes like this:

Born on a mountain top in Tennessee,
Greenest state in the Land of the Free,
Raised in the woods so's he knew every tree,
Kilt him a b'ar when he was only three.

I've learned my lesson. I didn't say anything about the mountain top. I'm not saying anything about the b'ar.

Further Reading in Tennessee Legends

Duncan, Barbara R. *Living Stories of the Cherokee,* 1998.

Ingram, M. V. *An authenticated history of the famous Bell witch : the wonder of the 19th century, and unexplained phenomenon of the Christian Era : the mysterious talking goblin that terrorized the West End of Robertson County, Tennessee, tormenting John Bell to his death : the story of Betsy Bell, her lover and the haunting sphinx.* 1894.

Lindahl, Carl. *American Folktales: From the Collections of the Library of Congress.* 2004.

Lofaro, Michael A. *Davy Crockett: The Man, the Legend, the Legacy, 1786–1986.* 1985.

McKnight, Brian D. *To Perish by the Sword: Champ Ferguson's Civil War.* 2008.

Mooney, James, and George Ellison, *James Mooney's History, Myths, and Sacred Formulas of the Cherokee,* 1992.

Price, Charles Edwin. *The Day They Hung the Elephant.* 1992.

———. *Infamous Bell Witch of Tennessee.* 1994.

Russell, Randy, and Janet Barnett. *The Granny Curse and Other Ghosts and Legends from East Tennessee.* 1999.

PART EIGHT

Folk Ballad and Song

While Tennessee is known worldwide for its country music industry and for having played a significant role in the rise of several other forms of popular music, including southern gospel, rhythm and blues, and rock and roll, the state has in fact been equally renowned for its ballad and song traditions. Most of these traditions have been covered in the *Tennessee Folklore Society Bulletin* over the years. The five essays in this part offer five particularly compelling scholarly explorations of ballads, songs, and traditional singers associated with the state.

Some of the ballad traditions in Tennessee evolved from Old World prototypes, such as traditional ballads of English and Scottish origin sung throughout the state but particularly in the eastern and middle sections. Thomas G. Burton's article "The Lion's Share: Scottish Ballads in Southern Appalachia" explores the tradition of British balladry in southern Appalachia and is based on his extensive fieldwork in the mountains on Tennessee's border with North Carolina. Much of this fieldwork was conducted with Ambrose Manning, who like Burton taught in East Tennessee State University's Department of English. Burton also incorporated into his article information from other seminal documentary collections of ballads, including those assembled by well-known investigators Cecil Sharp, Frank and Anne Warner, and W. K. McNeil. "The Lion's Share" makes a significant contribution to ballad scholarship by disproving the long-held notion that the primary ethnic influence on Appalachian balladry was English. His survey of popular ballads in Appalachia convincingly revealed that five of the ten most commonly sung ballads in the region were in fact of Scottish origin. This article achieved wide exposure when it was mentioned on a nationally syndicated radio program dedicated to promoting Celtic music, "Thistle and Shamrock."

The article by Debra Moore, "'Jim Bobo's Fatal Ride': A Study in Progress of a Tennessee Ballad" (1984), explores the ballad making process by examining the historical context for one topical ballad that originated in Tennessee. While identifying variants of this particular ballad collected across the southeastern United States, Moore definitively traced the ballad to an 1894 incident in Tullahoma, Tennessee, in which James S. Bobo was tragically killed from a fall off a bicycle, with Bobo's neck breaking in his effort to protect a little girl who was riding with him. According to Moore, this ballad is based on a text of a "ballit" published in a Middle Tennessee newspaper on August 16, 1894, the day after the accident. The "ballit" was attributed to a mysterious author listed in the newspaper as D. H. H. (likely a Mr. Honeycutt). Speculating that "Jim Bobo's Fatal Ride" was written during the wake the night before its first printing in the newspaper, Moore asserts that the ballad entered oral tradition immediately because people were moved by the event depicted in the ballad, filled as it was with both tragedy and pathos. This article demonstrates the origins of much folk culture in popular and high culture sources, and suggests that the line between these three levels of culture are not always that clearly defined.

Ethnomusicologist Kip Lornell's article "Successes of the 'Spirit'" (1991) chronicles the career of the Spirit of Memphis, a vocal harmony group active during the early years of commercial black gospel. Presently based at George Washington University in Washington, D.C., Lornell points out that the group, a male vocal quartet, during its long existence (dating back to 1928) was archetypal in that it embodied the history of black music during that era. For one thing, the group was semiprofessional, necessitating its members to work other jobs and leading to frequent line-up changes. Also, like other black gospel groups across the country, the Spirit of Memphis served as a training ground for popular secular singers in two commercial music genres: rhythm and blues and soul. One well-known soul singer who emerged from the group was O. V. Wright. Lornell's article on the Spirit of Memphis represents one of the few articles in the *Bulletin* to examine either the traditional or the popular music of West Tennessee, yet this relatively short article provides an authoritative historical context for commercial gospel music, an important manifestation of urban black music.

W. H. Bass's article, "McDonald Craig's Blues: Black and White Traditions in Context" (1982), discusses a different type of music produced by another black musician from West Tennessee. A professor long associated with Carson-Newman College, Bass presents a well-rounded portrait of Craig, a native of rural Perry County, Tennessee and an award-winning interpreter of the music of "the father of country music," Jimmie Rodgers. In Bass's eloquent phrase, Craig's music "represents an unusual cultural mixture: a black man preserving a type of blues popularized by a white singer who in turn partially derived his material from an earlier black blues tradition." One of the strengths of Bass's study is its combining of oral history—that is, direct transcribed statements from Craig—with Bass's perceptive analysis of the interplay of race and tradition in contemporary music making in Tennessee.

McDonald Craig's Blues
Black and White Traditions
in Context
[1982]

W. H. Bass

McDonald Craig is a black man dedicated to preserving the memory and songs of the "father of country music," Jimmie Rodgers. The fifty-one-year-old guitarist and singer lives with his wife Rosetta and son Irving in the rolling Tennessee River hill country near Linden, Tennessee. Four generations of the Craigs have been deeply rooted in this remote scenic area near the line between Middle and West Tennessee. McDonald Craig lives on the same property where his great-grandfather, a former slave who was the first black to own property in Perry County, built a log house. His mother still occupies one of his grandfather's properties. After years of working in a saw mill and service in the Korean conflict, Craig is now employed by the state highway department and raises a few cattle.

Just as Jimmie Rodgers's music exists in both folk and popular idioms, McDonald Craig's performances combine these elements. On one level, he is a traditional musician who has committed Rodgers's songs to memory and performs for pleasure within family or social circles. But as an artist and entertainer, he dreams of reaching more people with his music and being recognized for his talent and achievement. He has performed at the Neshoba County (Mississippi) Fair, the Illinois Traditional Country Music Festival in Griggsville, and for radio on the *Ernest Tubb Midnight Jamboree* (WSM, Nashville). Winning trophies for yodeling and singing, he in 1981 played before 30,000 people at the Old Time Country Music Pioneer Exposition in Council Bluffs, Iowa. In 1978 he took top honors at the Jimmie Rodgers Memorial Festival Talent Contest in his hero's hometown, Meridian, Mississippi. He represents an unusual cultural mixture: a black man preserving a type of blues popularized by a white singer who in turn partially derived his material from an earlier black blues tradition. A starting point in exploring this anomaly is Craig's own history and cultural tradition.

Craig is both knowledgeable and articulate about his family history.

My great-grandfather was the one that owned this place here. Tapp Craig was my great-grandfather's name . . . and his wife Amy. He came out of Linden . . . off of Craig property on Buffalo River, in what is known as the Chestnut Grove Community area. He was a slave, he was held by this Craig family. . . . He came here immediately after slavery and bought this place. My great-grandfather's . . . was the first black-owned home of the county (Perry).

The home that my great-grandfather and his family lived in was an old log house up the holler a little bit further about 500 yards. It was . . . a homeplace. They did grow a little crops.

This is the only place my great-grandfather had. . . . . He was up in years before he had a chance to own a place. For the chance that my great-grandfather had, I think of him as being one of the most outstanding people. . . . He was a very strong man. He was about five-ten, weighed about 225 pounds. He was good at blacksmith work, he was good at farmwork, and he was also very good at doctoring, though he never had a chance to go to school for it. Both the Africans and the Indians are well known for their herb practice of medicine . . . and they say that he was very, very good.

Now my grandfather, he married Lizzie Wilburn, who was born and raised over in the Beardstown community area that is east of here about five miles. To them were born twelve children.

My grandfather has two places on up the road, or had two places, that are still in our family. My mother and one of my brothers lives on the first place that you come to and the next one is on up the creek, on up the valley a mile and a half up. He bought an 88-acre plot right on the Tennessee River just below the Alvin C. York Bridge about a mile and a half below . . . on what is known as the Spring Creek–Mousetail Road.

My father was the seventh child in his family. Newt Craig was my father's name, and my mother, Conna, she was a McDonald, and that's where I got my first name. She was born and raised in Decatur County, the little town of Perryville. And to my mother and father were born seven children.

I went to work at the sawmills at a very, very early age for that type work. I was only twelve years old. At the time I was working at the sawmill, I wasn't sure I'd ever get to go to high school. There's always been a pretty good problem in this particular location for lower classes of people to make a substantial living. And just as soon as my oldest brother and I got old enough . . . to hold down a job, we started working. I started working at the steam-powered saw mill.

Lived around here all my life except for two years in the service. I served in the Korean Conflict. I was with the 175 recoiless rifle. I was gunner on a 175 recoiless rifle with the 5th regimental combat team on the front lines.

McDonald Craig's pride in family and place are obvious. He rightfully respects his great-grandfather as a hard worker, folk doctor, and landowner. What must be a fascinating story, how Tapp Craig acquired land after slavery, is lost from the family's recollection. Neither does McDonald Craig know any details about his great-grandfather's herb medicine except to assume its origin in retained African folkways. What is clear is his deep affection for family members of past generations and his attachment to home and place. It's not an attachment bred in the conceit of superiority, but in the confidence and contentment of fulfilled satisfaction.

I have been exposed to different people right here in my community that played when I was a child but directly it [appreciation of music] came from my mother and father and these old recordings I listened to on the old spring-operated Victor machine. . . .

When my dad was about seven years old, my grandfather bought the two older boys . . . two fiddles. . . .

Well, they never did play, that was Ashley and Black. He passed them on down to the ones who did have ability. The oldest of my uncles that played was Excel, but the best two of the family was my father and his brother . . . Clint. Clint and Newt were the two that really did the fiddle playing.

No one in my father's family before that time, before his time, played. . . . My dad always said that his father had to be gifted to music. . . . He was able to help him a lot with the fiddle. . . . He'd hum or sing different tunes . . . like "Buffalo Girls" . . . "Red Wing." . . .

My mother, she had a little more advantage in music, because she was raised out to where they had different kinds of music, and more music over here at Perryville, right on the river. There used to be a lot of showboats to come and stop off there and she would attend those. . . . She made about every show that came by. . . . She was exposed to various kinds of music.

We used to all just gather around the piano with my mother when we were children, and we would sing along with her at first. Have you ever heard the old Titanic song? . . . "The Sinking of the Titanic," "When My Blue Moon Turns the Ocean Blue to Gold," "Steamboat Bill," "Casey Jones." . . .

All of us played some. My baby brother was a fiddle player, the only one of seven children. He was very good instrumentally. He was a good singer also.

Asked whether his mother played from memory or sheet music, he replied, "Both. . . . She could read some music."

McDonald Craig credits heredity and environment for his musical talent. Both his mother and father performed, and he grew up in a house filled with song. He traces his musicality to his grandfather who bought his sons fiddles and encouraged them to play.

The picture of Craig's father and uncles learning to play is a scene of traditional music being transmitted in a traditional manner. They had no sheet music nor could read any, but by listening and copying songs like "Red Wing," they learned to play. Encouraged in their appreciation and performance, the most talented brothers, Clint and Newt, became accomplished folk musicians.

McDonald Craig's mother was exposed to music via a once popular and familiar entertainment vehicle, the showboat. Carrying commercial amusement to otherwise isolated communities like Perryville, the showboat introduced Tin Pan Alley's latest hits to rural audiences. It became a means to transmit popular culture into folk tradition. Mrs. Craig heard the music, recreated her favorites at home on the piano, and transformed these songs into part of the family's traditional folk culture.

Growing up in an environment filled with song, McDonald Craig naturally and rightly credits this atmosphere for his musical appreciation. In the manner of a past but not remote generation, his family entertained themselves with singing and playing. Interestingly, the songs he remembers his mother playing, "Buffalo Gals" and "The Sinking of the Titanic" are commonly field collected in folk versions. They are songs that still exist in both popular and traditional modes.

It's many different kinds of exposure that I've really been exposed to right here in my community. I can remember back when I was small, groups of people walked—anywhere from three to maybe a dozen—coming to my mother and father's home on the weekends. . . . All of them would get together and play. . . .

They were all white except one, a fellow by the name of Fred Dixon. He and my father grew up together. He was a banjo player.

> We were raised right here in this community where it was just all whites, all white settlement. . . . Of course, you know they played . . . their kind of music. Because of the fact that we were exposed to the type of music that they played as individuals and the recordings . . . and the type of music that my father played, I never had touch chance to do anything else. I've never even wanted to do anything else. I respect all music to a degree.
>
> [My father's music had] guitars, fiddles, banjos, mandolins.
>
> It was all the old pioneer type break-down tunes about the same as Bill Monroe. The only difference is he had his own idea of how he had rather for it to be done.
>
> Well, the old fiddle tunes, he played what is called "Sally Goodin," "The 8th of January," "Buffalo Gals," "Red Wing," "Possum Up a Gum Stump," "Black Mountain Rag," and such as that.

A black man growing up surrounded by white culture, McDonald Craig's musical background bears witness to some degree of environmental acculturation. It was natural that he internalize the predominant cultural norms, and one of those norms was country music. But the fact that his father and Fred Dixon played country fiddle tunes suggests that perhaps there is more to the story than a black man assuming white culture. It suggests, as some folklorists contend, that there was an earlier tradition of black country-style music using the standard string instruments—guitars, fiddles, banjos, and mandolins. Theorists propose that this once vital musical tradition disappeared from folk culture when it was overwhelmed by the twentieth-century popularity of Afro-American blues.[1]

McDonald Craig's passion for Rodgers's music generated his lifelong respect and curiosity about the man. Today in conversation he speaks of Rodgers as if he knew him, and, indeed, Craig does know the spirit of the man through his songs. Talking with Rodgers's friends, relatives, and sidemen have lent personality to the legend and drawn Craig even deeper into a lifelong devotion to his music. Asked when he heard his first Jimmie Rodgers's song, Craig replied:

> I was very, very young. I was just really walking age, very, very young. At my closest white neighbors' homes that had this spring-powered player machine that I heard my first recordings. . . . They had always been good friends to my father and his people before my mother came to this county. . . . Who had the Victrola? Bill Young's family, he and his wife and daughter that remained at home with them, Sally Mae. From a small child up, I loved his [Rodgers] songs better than anyone else.
>
> The very first would be "Soldier Sweetheart," "Old Pal of My Heart," and "Mississippi River Blues." I guess those are the very first that I can really say I remember.

After the radio's finest started coming in up in the 30s . . . they just kind of put the old spring Victor playing machines aside and kind of forgot about it.

The Warren family came in . . . they had a radio. . . . About '42 Ernest Tubb was getting to be well known and Ernest . . . has always used a lot of Jimmie Rodgers songs. That just kind of renewed all of this . . . the midnight jamboree show . . . because of the fact that he was going to do some Jimmie Rodgers songs. . . . I'd sit up all Saturday night until the show would come on. . . . I learned mainly from listening to his recordings, at home on the radio, and also through other artists who did his songs like Hank Snow, Ernest Tubb.
 . . . Maybe you'd hear them on the radio, or you'd hear a phonograph record or once in a while you'd learn them from a song book. . . . Sometimes maybe it might be related to you by a friend. About every way that it could be to give you the knowledge of a song, I have received it. . . .
 What little I know about playing the guitar actually came about, it was a white family. . . . The children were about the same age as we were . . . and . . . two of the girls which their father had taught them to play the guitar a little bit, Jessie and Odell Warren, and Odell taught me the first three chords, G, C, and D . . . and it was on a guitar my father had borrowed from another Warren. . . .
 I was eleven. I was actually about fourteen until I got further enough along to where I felt I was really doing some good . . . as far as being able to play.
I bought my first guitar when I was eighteen. Now, my baby brother was given a guitar by my oldest sister when he was seven. So we used that little guitar up until I bought my guitar. I still have my old guitar up in the loft somewhere or another. Well, he still has his, too.
 They [Rodgers songs] are more complicated to play on the guitar than just about anyone else's songs that I have ever attempted to play. . . . I actually started in there about seventeen or eighteen doing some of his songs. But some . . . of his most complicated songs I really had to [play] them for awhile before I could accompany myself with the guitar.
 . . . And he [Ernest Tubb] would tell a lot of stuff about Jimmie Rodgers. . . . Mrs. Jimmie Rodgers had a book out on the market. . . . Ernest was selling a lot of these books at the record shop, so I ordered me one . . . [and] talked with older people who knew something about Jimmie, just any source that I could get, and that's how I got what knowledge I have about Jimmie. If they let it get away [the memory of Jimmie Rodgers], they will have let the greatest one of all that will ever be get away.
 I have talked with his relatives in Mississippi, his grandson in Texas, and very strong fans of his in different places across the country.

I did the very first song that I ever did in public . . . out of my mother and father's house. That was in '49 on Cypress Creek at an Indian family's home, the only Indian family that I reckon we've ever had in my lifetime to live in Perry County. And she was forever inviting my family to come down and make music. Most of the time it was always my dad and the two younger brothers to go and play because my oldest brother and I worked out every day at the sawmill. The very first song that I did out in public was a little song that Ernest Tubb had going pretty good . . . called "My Tennessee Lady." I was then about seventeen years old. It would have to been around '48.

I have done performing work in the various schools around . . . and social gatherings.

Well, one of my best, I won't say it was the very first time I have a clear view of this right now . . . was at the Pineview School . . . northwest of here about six, seven miles. . . .

I didn't get to go to high school until I was up in years pretty good. I used to sing . . . for the school and . . . all of them marveled at it because they had never heard no one black do the kind of songs that I was doing and they would all whisper to one another and say why does he sound that way.

I played for several people when I was in the service overseas . . . barracks of about twenty-eight or thirty people. And then later on was at the Ernest Tubb record shop. I sang there twice before a record shop full of people. That was about '69 or '70.

The first large group of people I had a chance to sing for . . . was in Meridian, Mississippi, in '78. . . . before something like three thousand people.

They are about all white. It's very seldom that you'll have blacks in the audience.

From his earliest years, McDonald Craig's favorite was Jimmie Rodgers. In Craig's own words, he has acquired Rodgers's music in every way possible—phonograph, radio, song books, and personal contact. Within a strict folkloric definition, these are non-traditional means of transmission. But many of Rodgers's songs exist in both popular and traditional texts, in folk and commercial modes. McDonald Craig actively searched and learned Rodgers's music from any available source, then committed it to memory, preserving and performing it traditionally. The immediate origin of the music is non-traditional, but the spirit and manner in which it is maintained are solidly within the mainstream of folklore.

Craig's passion for country music was nurtured in a supportive atmosphere. His family—mother, father, brothers, and sisters—all loved music and reinforced his determination to play. Especially interesting given the times and place was the support and interest of his white neighbors. The picture he describes is a mutually affectionate and respectful relationship. He spent time at the Youngs' enjoying the Victrola and later at the Warrens listening to their radio. The Warren daughters taught him his first guitar chords. Evidently the Craigs and their white neighbors had developed a trust and cooperation that avoided the negative extremes of southern racial relations in the 1930s and 1940s.

McDonald Craig's performances have broadened from intimate family and social circles to include public appearances at music festivals. The history of his musical growth is the gradual union of formal and traditional performing contexts. His first appearances were for small groups of friends in traditional settings. But as he grew musically, his aspirations as a performer and entertainer grew. Currently performing outside the folklore context for larger audiences, he reaches more people with the music he has such a passion to preserve.

> You asked me earlier in our discussion if I changed Jimmie's songs in any way, and I told you that I did not and I try to not. However, this song that I just finished, "Way Out on the Mountain," I use a word or two differently . . . it gives a stronger meaning. Now to Jimmie, he's going to this great land away out on the mountain. He's going to be provided with all the things of nature that he needs. . . . Jimmie says, "I'm going says I to the land of the sky away out on the mountain." But I get this feeling . . . when I use the term "going to survive to the land of the sky," I really believe that I am going to survive and hold out in faith . . . to the land in the sky. It doesn't only tell about the great life that he is going to live there being provided for the things of nature. . . . It also goes into the heavenly land that will survive to the land of the sky. Jimmie does it really in a boastful way of being provided with the natural things on earth. I do it in appreciation of the natural things that we [are] provided with for the survival of life on earth, but it . . . carries me beyond this point. It carries me even to a great point . . . spiritually. . . . So you can get both the appreciation of . . . nature and also the great benefit of . . . beyond this point after life.
>
> You do have your own individual feeling. You will never be able to eliminate your own individuality. . . .

Variation is both part of folklore's definition and part of the problem in identifying it. Variation, or variant texts, occur naturally and unintentionally as folklore is passed traditionally from one person to another. Paradoxically, folklorists' problems are created by the most imaginative artists who change traditional music to express their own creativity. Disrupting the natural transmission of folklore, they are at once satisfying their artistic impulses and distorting traditional folklore texts.

McDonald Craig is a creative artist who occasionally changes Rodgers's lyrics for the best of reasons, to try to improve them. He's obviously given this particular variation deep consideration, and it expresses his conviction of faith. It's hardly a change taken lightly. Craig's testimony is graphic witness to the kinds of feelings, impulses, and motives that move an artist to create or change a song. He is fulfilling his role and function as an artist by interpreting the music in a newly creative way. That makes good art but bad folklore.

> It is not a typical thing for a black man to play country music.
>
> However, Jimmie Rodgers, who is the father of country music, he got a lot of his experience from the old black blues singers that worked on the railroad. . . . He did a lot of recording with Louis Armstrong, and he was exposed in many different ways . . . [to] black culture and music and you can tell in some of his work that he did have, just how closely related . . . his work was . . . with some of the blacks. I guess that is one thing that helped me to, maybe be so much in love with Jimmie's work, just because of the fact he did have an awful lot of respect for black people and their singing.

Actually, in 1928 Jimmie Rodgers recorded once with Louis Armstrong on "Blue Yodel No. 9." He performed with other black musicians, including Clifford Hayes's Dixieland Jug Blowers on "My Good Gal's Gone Blues."[2] McDonald Craig is accurate in his assessment of Rodgers's respect for Afro-American music. His widow, Carrie Rodgers, claimed that as a boy Rodgers would carry water to the railroad section hands, and they taught him to plunk melody from a guitar and sing "darkey songs, moaning chants, and crooning lullabies."[3]

Many Rodgers songs were sentimental ballads, but his most innovative and popular records were his blue yodels. From black blues singers Rodgers learned to vary the length of words to fit the music's meter. Instead of guitar riffs at the end of stanzas, he yodeled. By combining the structure and imagery of Afro-American blues with the white tradition of yodeling, he forged a national popularity and success unsurpassed by any country music artist since. Like another young Mississippian years later, Elvis Presley, he captured the public's imagination by making black music acceptable to white audiences.[4]

Besides his style and technique, Rodgers incorporated whole stanzas of folk blues in some of his songs. Early blues musicians had a stock of traditional lyrics which they combined in an infinite variety to create fresh and original compositions. In "Blue Yodel No. 1" or "T for Texas," Rodgers borrowed some of these stanzas to tell a story of betrayed love. His hit "In the Jailhouse Now" had been previously recorded by Blind Blake, and some of the lyrics of "Brakeman Blues" were from Ma Rainey's "Southern Blues." Because they were such fluid musical devices and existed in the folk tradition, many of these stanzas went undocumented and perhaps forgotten except on Jimmie Rodgers's records.[5]

In an intricate symbiosis of cultures, Rodgers was an active catalyst in transforming folk music into commercial culture, and then reversing the process by transmitting commercial music into folk tradition. The first step is easy to recognize. He borrowed traditional black blues lyrics and made them white commercial successes. But in the 1940s many of these same commercial successes were being collected "on the ground," performed traditionally as legitimate Tennessee folk songs. Included were "Blue Yodel" ("T for Texas"), "Brakeman Blues," and "In the Jailhouse Now."⁶ The traditional music had traveled full circle, from folk to popular to folk, but in the process it had also crossed racial lines. Traditional black blues had become part of white popular culture and then passed into white folk culture, with little or no recognition of its racial origins. Completing this complex interface, black blues musicians later borrowed Rodgers's music, which he had borrowed from earlier black composers. Some copied his blues-style lyrics, some his guitar work, and the Mississippi Sheiks even featured a yodel.⁷

In performances, McDonald Craig precedes each song with a narrative introduction. To him, Rogers's music evokes the story of American settlement and civilization. His own words are the best evidence.

> Even though it was many years after, a lot of the songs Jimmie Rodgers wrote and recorded . . . coincide right along with the lives that the people lived . . . when they first came here. . . . The terrain features of this locality always reminds me of one particular song that Jimmie did . . . "Way Out on the Mountain," because of the fact that Tennessee is known and loved for its hills.
>
> Back when I was a child, I just loved to have some older person to tell me the story of what it was like when the settlers came over here, or to read from a book . . . what it was like [He then sings "Way Out on the Windswept Desert"].
>
> As the settlers of this country moved west, the cattle business became one of our giant businesses, which it still is today, and the western life is a life that people all across the United States and across the entire world fell in love with; and I think this song that Jimmie Rodgers wrote and recorded, titled "When the Cactus Is in Bloom" paints a beautiful picture of that life. . . .
>
> While the country was growing and business expanding, transportation was very essential. Though there was very little transportation back in those days, I guess the major way of getting freight about was by boat, and I believe it was the Egyptians that referred to the Nile River as a god, because it was such a great provider. Our rivers and streams have provided for us in the same way, including giving us a great source of transportation; and I'm sure Jimmie Rodgers had something in mind along that line when he wrote what I think is the most beautiful river route song I've ever heard, "The Mississippi River Blues."

When asked when and why he began introducing the songs with comments, he replied:

I started about the same time that I started performing the songs because . . . I was impressed with the songs . . . to where I could tell the story . . . about what it was like.

I do it quite often. You see, Jimmie's songs actually told the life of different people at different stages . . . of time, because everything moves along. . . . He just kind of kept pace with history and told these things. Just the songs themselves, the way that they describe a certain life or certain scenery encouraged me to do this. I was encouraged by the songs themselves to do it. I'm very fond of all Jimmie's songs. "Way Out on the Mountain," I'm very, very fond of that song because of the fact that I was raised in this type of area where it was kind of rugged; and it tells of the rugged life and . . . it insinuates the faith that he . . . will be able to hold out for a better time.

That ["Mississippi River Blues"] is one of my favorite songs, special favorites of Jimmie's, because . . . I know how much Jimmie loved his home state, Mississippi; and another reason is because of the many different types of work that went on, on the river. I get great pictures from doing this song. . . .

That ["When It's Peach Picking Time in Georgia"] is one of mine [favorites]. One reason it is, is because it tells a little bit of something about several different states of my beloved South. . . . It tells a great story. There's no doubt about him loving [the South], and I love it just as much as Jimmie.

Asked what the South means to him, Craig replied:

Not only just the joy of home itself, but many joys, many joys that reach out beyond the home. It was that way with both Jimmie and myself; that is because he's covering all this different territory. You get a different type of enjoyment from every different area that he mentions. I can get enjoyment of scenery in Mississippi that I can't get in Tennessee. I can get enjoyment in Tennessee from different observations that I can't get in Texas.

They have lost some of it [the pioneer spirit]. However, there is nothing that will ever be . . . greater than the different skills that were used during those particular times. I think it would be very beneficial for every child today to have knowledge of what it was like because that's the only . . . way he will ever be able to appreciate the things . . . that keep him from having to go through some of the things that earlier generations had to go through.

For McDonald Craig the history of the American experience is reflected in the songs of Jimmie Rodgers. Creating a musical sequence illustrating the pioneer story of Tennessee's mountains, the Old West, and Mississippi River life, he interprets the songs through his own experience and imagination. In his mind these are the images Jimmie Rodgers intended. According to Dr. Charles Wolfe, Kelly Harrell's "Way Out on the Mountain" was probably written about the Blue Ridge, but in Craig's mind Rodgers was singing about Tennessee. Craig's boyhood fantasies of pioneer life and the Old West are reflected in "Way Out on the Windswept Desert" and "When the Cactus Is in Bloom." The romance and tradition of river life are painted in "Mississippi River Blues." The songs and their introductions create a framework in which McDonald Craig visualizes and expresses his hopes and ideals about his historical and cultural heritage.

Craig's empathy for the music is expressed in his explicit, visual imagery and emotional interpretation. He becomes more than an entertainer performing to please a crowd (though that's important to him); he is a communicator of pride, emotion, and love. Jimmie Rodgers's songs are real, personal elements in his life; they reflect his ideas, beliefs, and experience. In performing the music he loves so much, McDonald Craig combines the passion and creativity of artistic expression with the preservation of his cultural tradition.

When asked what it was about Rodgers's music that appealed to so many people in different walks of life, he replied:

> He brought out a lot of it, hardship, hardship. He was able to understand the hardship of people like he himself. It made him have the feeling . . . that enabled him to come up with these songs.
>
> He saw every man as a very important individual. He made a quotation that he was no better than a good dog, but he was just as good as the greatest king. Now, you can see the feeling he had for everything.
>
> Sincere love that he's able to get to the people with. . . . Normally, a lot of people may have never felt, if it hadn't been for songs of his. . . .
>
> From a small child up, I have always been able to appreciate the work of all people. . . . A lot of people will look at a doctor . . . and will be highly impressed, and will look at a man working with a plow and a hoe in a field and be depressed. But . . . just as much respect is due to one man as it is to the other, as long as they're both doing a good job.
>
> And there is no better way to express your appreciation of different kinds of work than through music. And my love for people, I had to have love for people in order for me to respect the different work . . . that people have done; and I just think that its the greatest way of all for a person to truly express his appreciation through music, through country-style music.
>
> Because it [music] would bring out the strongest feeling that can be had, and of course every song is somewhat different from the song before or the song after, so you get a lot of different pictures.

According to Craig, Jimmie Rodgers's popular appeal was his empathy and respect for working men and women, and their identification with his life's hardship and success. Evidently, Rodgers had the common touch that didn't alienate those poorer or richer than he. To Craig, his songs transcended entertainment and conveyed a sincerity that touched deep emotional chords in his audience.

In McDonald Craig's interpretation of Rodgers's social philosophy, all people are due respect for a job well done, and music is the media to communicate that respect. Again, it is clear that to Craig music transcends amusement; it is a means to touch people, convey emotion, and stimulate feelings appropriate to the moment. For Craig music is a communicator, a means to reach people on a profound instinctual level, a means to convey his respect, appreciation, and love.

> There's many a day that I've gone out to work, and I could work very satisfactorily just thinking in my mind over the different songs of Jimmie's that I know. Normally, I would not have been able to have gone out and had such an enjoyable [time] that I had, had it not been for Jimmie Rodgers's songs. They encouraged me in a lot of different ways. There was a whole lot that I didn't have when I came up. I was barred racially, I was barred off in the remote area I was raised in, and there are different reasons that caused me to have holdups beyond some of the people that I have known. But the songs of Jimmie Rodgers have helped to inspire me through the days, the weeks, months, and years of most of my life.
>
> . . . And as far as I'm concerned [Rodgers is] the greatest singer the world has ever had. . . . I hope you can accept my comparison. Jesus Christ is Jesus Christ of the world. Jimmie Rodgers is the Jesus Christ of country music. It's just that simple to me.

Eloquently summarizing Jimmie Rodgers's meaning in his life, McDonald Craig is devoted in his belief that Rodgers was the greatest singer of all time. His music has been a living force throughout Craig's life. Struggling to make a living, Rodgers's songs lightened his heart and eased his day. As a black man in the racially segregated South, they inspired him to work hard and persevere. Craig appreciates the potential power of music because of its impact in his life. He recognizes that art is not an external irrelevancy unrelated to human life; he understands it as a psychological reality and an integral instinct in an individual's drive for emotional satisfaction and fulfillment.

A man of faith, McDonald Craig intends no disrespect in comparing Rodgers's musical significance to Jesus' religious significance. He is merely making the point emphatically that to him no singer can ever approach the stature of Jimmie Rodgers. He is stating directly what is obvious throughout his conversation, his devotion to Rodgers and his music.

In talking with Craig, Jimmie Rodgers becomes real. The quaint figure in a railroad hat on a dusty record jacket assumes life as a dynamic musical and personal force. Craig's enthusiasm and dedication is contagious and his devotion unrelenting. Within a folklore context, McDonald Craig has helped complete a cultural transition of Rodgers's music. From bits and pieces of traditional music, Rodgers fashioned hugely popular commercial successes. Many years later performers like Craig have reintroduced these commercial successes into traditional folk culture. McDonald Craig is proud of his role as a preserver of Jimmie Rodgers's music, and he should also be proud of his role in the larger sphere, as a communicator and preserver of a vital element in his country's cultural legacy.

Notes

1. Edwin C. Kirkland, "A Checklist of the Titles of Tennessee Folksongs," *Journal of American Folklore* 59 (1946): 423–76.
2. Nolan Porterfield, *Jimmie Rodgers: The Life and Times of America's Blue Yodeler* (Urbana: University of Illinois Press, 1979), 211, 259, 297.
3. Patrick Carr, *The Illustrated History of Country Music* (Garden City, N.Y.: Doubleday, 1979), 55.
4. Ibid., 54–55; Porterfield, *Jimmie Rodgers,* 364; Bill C. Malone, *Country Music U.S.A.: A Fifty-Year History* (Austin: University of Texas Press, 1968), 95; Bill C. Malone and Judith McCulloh, eds., *Stars of Country Music: Uncle Dave Macon to Johnny Rodriguez* (Urbana: University of Illinois Press, 1975), 122–24.
5. Jan Harold Brunvand, *The Study of American Folklore: An Introduction,* 2nd ed. (New York: W. W. Norton & Co., 1978), 425; Porterfield, *Jimmie Rodgers,* 123; Malone and McCulloh, *Stars,* 37.
6. Kirkland, "Checklist," 423–76.
7. Malone, *Country Music,* 94–95; Malone and McCulloh, *Stars,* 137

Appendix 1
Jimmie Rodgers's Songs
Performed by McDonald Craig

1. Away Out on the Mountain
2. The Wind-Swept Desert
3. When the Cactus Is in Bloom
4. Cowhand's Last Ride
5. Yodeling Cowboy
6. Mule Skinner Blues (Blue Yodel No. 8)
7. Frankie and Johnnie

8. The Mississippi River Blues
9. The Gambling Bar-Room Blues
10. Never No Mo' Blues
11. T for Texas (Blue Yodel No. 1)
12. Waiting for a Train
13. The Soldier's Sweetheart
14. Sleep, Baby, Sleep
15. California Blues (Blue Yodel No. 4)
16. Every Body Does It in Hawaii
17. Moon Light and Skies
18. Ninety Nine Year Blues
19. Nobody Knows But Me
20. My Little Lady
21. Mother the Queen of My Heart
22. Daddy and Home
23. Dear Old Sunny South by the Sea
24. Hobo's Meditation
25. In the Jail House Now
26. Why Did You Give Me Your Love?
27. Any Old Time
28. Brakeman's Blues
29. Blue Yodel No. 6
30. She Was Happy Till She Met You
31. T.B. Blues
32. Jimmie's Mean Mama Blues
33. Peach-Picking Time Down in Georgia
34. Roll Along Kentucky Moon
35. I'm Lonesome, Too
36. My Blue-Eyed Jane
37. Sweet Mama Hurry Home or I'll Be Gone
38. You and My Old Guitar
39. Standing on the Corner (Blue Yodel No. 9)
40. Ground Hog Rooting in My Back Yard (Blue Yodel No. 10)
41. Blue Yodel No. 11
42. Pistol Packing Papa
43. Miss the Mississippi and You
44. Old Pal of My Heart
45. No Hard Times
46. My Carolina Sunshine Girl
47. For the Sake of Days Gone By
48. Take Me Back Again
49. Why Should I Be Lonely?

50. Traveling Blues
51. I'm Free from the Chain Gang Now

Appendix 2

This is a list of Tennessee folk songs that were being perpetuated traditionally and were collected in the field. They were published in different M.A. theses and then organized into one listing by Edwin C. Kirkland in "A Checklist of the Titles of Tennessee Folksongs," *Journal of American Folklore,* 1946, 59:423–76. After the title is the name of the collector, the thesis page number, the form of the song (text, tune, or recording), the county it was collected in, and the JAF page number.

Buffalo Gals, Perry, 283 (Title), Carter, 429.

Casey Jones.

Red Wing, Mason, 92 (Text), 461.

Sinking of the Titanic, Jackson, 210 (Text), White, 464.

Sinking of the Titanic, Library Congress (Recording), Crossville.

Sinking of the Titanic, Library Congress (Recording), Gatlinburg.

Sinking of the Titanic, Anderson, 216 (Text).

Steamboat Bill, 465.

Jimmie Rodgers Songs in Tennessee Folk Culture

Away Out on the Mountain, Crabtree, 168 (Text), Overton, 426.

Brakeman Blues, Crabtree, 193 (Text), Overton, 429.

For the Sake of Days Gone By, Crabtree, 233 (Text), Overton, 437.

I'm Lonesome, Too—I'm Lonely Tonight Sweetheart, Crabtree, 263 (Text), 441.

In the Jailhouse Now, Crabtree, 80 (Text), Overton, 443.

Jimmie's Mean Mama Blues, Crabtree, 195 (Text), Overton, 445.

Jimmie's Texas Blues, Crabtree, 196 (Text), Overton, 445.

Memphis Yodel, Crabtree, 194 (Text), Overton, 452.

Moonlight and Skies, Crabtree, 78 (Text), Overton, 453.

Mother, Queen of My Heart, Crabtree, 33 (Text), Overton, 453.

My Little Lady, Crabtree, 221 (Text), Overton, 454.

Never No Mo' Blues, Crabtree, 194 (Text), Overton, 454.

Peach Picking Time in Georgia, Crabtree, 278 (Text), Overton, 459.

The Soldier's Sweetheart, Crabtree, 40 (Text), Overton, 465.

T for Texas, T for Tennessee, Henry, 100 (Text), 467.

Those Gamblers Blues, Crabtree, 200 (Text), Overton, 465.

Waiting for a Train, Crabtree, 201 (Text), Overton, 469.

You and My Old Guitar, Crabtree, 305 (Text), Overton, 469.

"Jim Bobo's Fatal Ride"
A Study in Progress of
a Tennessee Ballad
[1984]

Debra Moore

On August 17, 1894, the *Nashville Daily American* ran the following article:

FATAL BICYCLE RIDE
J. S. BOBO, OF TULLAHOMA, HAS HIS NECK BROKEN BY A FALL

TULLAHOMA, Aug. 16.—(Special.)—Mr. J. S. Bobo, an old and well-known citizen of Tullahoma, was almost instantly killed late yesterday afternoon while riding his bicycle. He had Mr. Pelham's little daughter on the wheel with him, and was riding on Jackson Street, when from some cause he lost control of the wheel and ran into the fence, throwing him and the little girl off. In falling he succeeded in saving the girl from injury, but his head struck the hard brick pavement, breaking his neck.

It is supposed that the handle-bars were loose in the steering-head, therefore in trying to turn the wheel he lost control of it. Mr. Bobo was about 60 years old and leaves a wife and one son.

I first became acquainted with the Jim Bobo story late one Sunday night over brownie cakes and sherry in Miss Sarah Thomas's kitchen in Shelbyville, Tennessee. Richard Hulan, folklore consultant from the Smithsonian Institution and the instructor for the American Folklife Institute at Vanderbilt Uni-

278

versity, introduced me to Miss Thomas, who showed me an 1896 version of a ballad based on this incident, a song called "Jim Bobo's Fatal Ride." During an earlier visit with Miss Thomas, Hulan had encountered this ballad in one of the manuscript song collections preserved by Miss Thomas's deceased mother and aunt. He had subsequently learned from Mrs. Elizabeth Coble, the county historian of Moore County, that the song originated in nearby Tullahoma, and that other song collectors such as George Boswell, Ralph Hyde, and Charles Wolfe had also found information about the song. It soon became obvious that "Jim Bobo's Fatal Ride" was one of the state's most unusual topical ballads— probably the only one dealing with the specific subject of a bicycle wreck—and that it was surprisingly widespread. The study of the song that I began in 1973 was to move from Middle Tennessee to Rome, Georgia, to Bessemer, Alabama, to Houston, Texas. What resulted was an outline of the song's dissemination and of the events that inspired it.

Although the historical material I have collected about Jim Bobo is not vast, it is sufficient to set his place in a typically gay, fun-loving, sentimental, late-19th-century Tullahoma community. After sketching this setting, I will discuss the mysterious ballad commemorating Jim's tragedy.

An ancestral history compiled by Catherine Bobo Debois, Jim Bobo's third cousin, states that Jim's forebears were French Huguenots who settled in Virginia in the 1730s. They changed the spelling of their name from French "Beaubais" to the American "Bobo" after the Revolutionary War. Great Uncle Lecil Bobo, an early-19th-century settler in the Bedford/Coffee County area, was a commissioner of Coffee County and later a state legislator. Where Washington Bobo witnessed the birth of his son James Simpson, the figure in the ballad, on March 13, 1842, is uncertain. Mae Bobo Timberlake, Jim's granddaughter, 78 years old in 1974 and living in Houston, Texas, was told that they came from Mississippi. Mae, who emerged as one of the key informants in this study, drew on her grandmother's scrapbook and her own memory to provide most of the following information about Jim Bobo.[1]

"During most of his service in the Civil War, Jim was a prisoner," Mae commented when she found a picture of her grandfather and his gun taken prior to his entry. On January 17, 1864, Jim married Mary Josephine Philpott in either Franklin or Bedford County, near Shelbyville. Before settling permanently in Tullahoma, they lived in Countyline between Shelbyville and Lynchburg and possibly in New Herman.

Coffee County records support Mae's claim that Jim dabbled a bit in real estate. She related this "family joke" about Jim's early investment ventures.

Mary Bobo was a very religious person when they married, a staunch member of the Christian church. Jim had a fortune invested in the Jack Daniel distillery, which at that time was just a country still. His wife objected. So he sold his stock and bought a sawmill near Lynchburg. Since he was too busy getting organized in his Tullahoma residence to purchase insurance in the county seat at Manchester, he lost his $3,000 when the sawmill burned down.

Mae said that carpentry, especially cabinet making, was a hobby of Jim's. He had fine tools in a workshop behind his spacious residence on the corner of Jackson and Lauderdale in Tullahoma and was famous for his work. Mae wrote: "I have what I believe to be the only remaining piece of his work. It is a table of oak about 20 inches wide and maybe 40 inches tall. It has three drawers with locks set in each drawer."

Two other anecdotes reflect Jim and Mary Bobo's fondness for animals. One post-mortem story in the October 12, 1902, issue of the *Nashville Banner*, reports the discovery of a terrapin with "James S. Bobo, 1886" and "Mary Bobo, 1897" engraved on its belly.

TALE OF A TERRAPIN
Turns up a third time within sixteen years
Tullahoma, Tenn. Oct. 12

Yesterday morning a dry land terrapin walked in the back door of R. A. Conger s warehouse. One of the attaches of the house immediately captured his terrapin-ship and preceded to look over his hull. The investigating incident opened up a most interesting incident. On the belly of the terrapin the names of James S. Bobo, 1886, and Mary Bobo, 1897, were engraved in clear cut letters. Upon inquiry the following facts in regard to the matter were obtained from Mrs. James S. Bobo, the widow of James S. Bobo of Tullahoma.

In the spring of 1886 James Bobo while driving through the barrens five miles from Tullahoma captured the terrapin, engraved his name and date as set forth and turned it loose in the blackjacks.

In 1897 the terrapin was caught by Mr. Winde, in the eastern suburbs of Tullahoma and seeing the name sent it to Mrs. Bobo, her husband having been killed by a fall from a bicycle a short time before. Mrs. Bobo kept the crustacean around the house for some time but it finally became annoying, so she had her name engraved beneath that of her husband and set it at liberty in the barrens again. The terrapin had not been seen again until yesterday.

Mrs. Bobo said that the terrapin was an inmate of her home for several months, that he came to be fed regularly, his menu consisting of raw chicken, beef, sweet milk and mush. The terrapin will again be turned over to Mrs. Bobo who will decide what shall be done with it in the future. She will doubtless have more engraving done, with the date and give the terrapin a new start in the world from the blackjacks where he was first found by James Bobo sixteen years ago.

Jim's granddaughter related another pet story accompanying a picture she sent me:

> The parrot shown here with my grandmother was called Polly. Jim Bobo bought Polly for my grandmother in the 1880s, as I see she was 48 when this picture was made. Polly lived and was a well-loved pet in the family until I was about 5 or 6 years old. When the bird died my father had a small wooden coffin made and Polly was buried under a snowball bush in the side yard of the Bobo home on Jackson Street. I remember my grandmother crying as the family gathered around for the bird's burial.

By the early 1890s, Jim Bobo was well known as a carpenter, and was a member of a train crew that worked on the branch line from Tullahoma to Sparta.

Family tragedies found their way into the Bobo house to mar three consecutive decades. In 1884, under a wave of yellow fever that struck the region, Lillie Mae Bobo, Jim's 18-year-old daughter, died. In 1909, Mary Bobo, her daughter-in-law and granddaughter, Eva and Mae Bobo, and Tullahoma mourned the deaths of Walter Bobo, Jim Bobo' s son, and two other men, "all of whom were killed in the wreck of a coal train near Doyle, Tennessee on the Sparta branch of the N.C. & St. L."[2] Jim Bobo's death in 1894 clouded the decade between the deaths of his daughter and son. The epitaph on the back of his gravestone in the old Tullahoma cemetery on North Jackson conveys his family's sense of loss:

> We miss thee from our home, Father
> We miss thee from thy place:
> A shadow o'er our life is cast,
> We miss the sunshine of thy face.
> We miss thy kind and willing hand,
> Thy fond and earnest care;
> Our home is dark without thee,
> We miss thee everywhere.

The fact that a ballad appeared commemorating Jim's death is not surprising, considering the late-19th-century vogue for ballads, and especially ballads describing unusual death tragedies. In the discussion that follows, first I will trace the paths to the two contacts who supplied the 1894 version of the ballad—Mrs. Shirley Majors of Sewanee, Tennessee, and Mrs. Mae Bobo Timberlake. I will then return to one informant, who was a participant in the accident, to compare her account with the 1894 text and the newspaper article printed above. I will conclude with a comparative examination of the six ballad variants I have found.

The path to Mrs. Majors began in Murfreesboro, Tennessee, in the office of Dr. Ralph Hyde. During my visit on July 17, 1973, Dr. Hyde played for me a

taped version of the ballad, arranged by Mrs. Nancy Majors, a former student of
his who had used the tape with an oral report. On Friday of the following week,
Nancy Majors responded by telephone to my letter, stating that her mother-
in-law, Mrs. Shirley Majors, had provided her with a copy of the ballad text.
Mrs. Majors had found the newspaper clipping with the ballad tucked between
pages of an old family Bible. One week later, when I visited Mrs. Majors at her
home on the University of the South campus, she allowed me to photograph the
"Family Record" page of the old Bible where James Simpson Bobo's birthdate
was entered, gave me a copy of the Bobo family history referred to above, and
presented me with a Xeroxed copy of the ballad. As with most newspaper "ballets," no tune was assigned to the words, and the text was followed by the initials
"D. H. H." and the subscript, "Tullahoma, Tenn., Aug. 16, 1894"—the day
following Jim Bobo's death. Since this represents the earliest text of the song, it is
important to consider the text in full.

JIM BOBO'S FATAL RIDE

I.   Jim Bobo rode a "safety wheel"
      He rode with all his might,
      T'was very safe he seemed to feel—
      To ride was his delight.

II.   Where 'ere he went he rode his wheel—
      A happy man was he,
      Until at last he rode that wheel
      Into eternity.

III. The wheel was built for only one—
      Much smaller man than he,
      But he had often made the run
      With two and sometimes three.

IV.   While riding out one evening late
      A little girl he 'spied.
      The little tot ran through the gate
      And asked him for a ride.

V.   With little Willie on the seat
      In front of Uncle Jim,
      They soon were gliding down the street
      As day was growing dim.

VI.   Then little Willie looked so neat—
      O, happy little child.
      Into her face so fair and sweet
      Jim Bobo looked and smiled.

VII.   Then angel Death put forth a hand
And turned the fatal screw
That soon would end his life, poor man,
(But nought of this he knew.)

VIII.   "Dear Uncle Jim, just look at this!
My seat is slipping down"—
He gave the little girl a kiss
And gave the wheel a bound.

IX.   Just then he saw—alas, too late—
The wheel he could not guide,
Before he slacked his fearful gate
The wheel had turned aside.

X.   It ran against the fence so wild
And bounded back so quick,
He barely saved the little child
But broke his own brave neck.

XI.   "What might have been"—no one can tell,
Instanter there he died,
But long will be remembered well,
Jim Bobo's fatal ride.

D. H. H.
(Tullahoma, Tenn., Aug. 16, 1894)

In addition to Mrs. Majors, Mrs. Frank Timberlake, Jim Bobo's grand-daughter, later sent me a copy of this same clipping, one found in her grand-mother's scrapbook. Unfortunately, neither clipping contains enough peripheral material to allow the newspaper source to be determined. One can assume it came from a Middle Tennessee county newspaper. Nor do we have a clear indication as to who the initials "D. H. H." stand for. The term "safety wheel" also requires some explanation; invented by Englishman H. J. Lawson in 1874, the safety wheel made possible the reduction in size of the front wheel of the bicycle by use of a chain drive which permitted the pedals to drive the rear wheel.

Although the ballad seems to have had its origin in a printed newspaper account, it quickly entered oral tradition, where it apparently flourished for some years in Middle Tennessee. Indeed, it was soon obvious that the song still existed in the repertoires of singers alive today. On July 17, 1973, I met with Mrs. Elizabeth Coble at her home in Lynchburg. She expressed delight at seeing the words of the ballad, and when she heard a taped version of the song I had gotten from Dr. Hyde, she was even able to sing a few verses herself. Mrs. Coble said that as a child she had learned the ballad from Emma Noblitt (now living in Rome, Georgia, as Mrs. Thurman Tolley), who had learned the ballad from her grandmother, Sara Bobo Noblitt. My brief correspondence with Mrs. Tolley revealed only the following:

> I was very small during Uncle Jim's life and can't remember one thing about him, other than his tragic death. Hearing my Grandmother tell us all the details. However, I remember visiting Aunt Mary.[3]

Mrs. Coble's second lead proved to be more fruitful. After phoning some Bobo kin in Lynchburg, she confirmed her supposition that Willie Pelham Waggoner, the "little Willie" in the ballad, was still living. Mrs. J. D. Templeton of Shelbyville, Mrs. Waggoner's stepdaughter, should know her address. After talking with Mrs. Templeton the following day, I contacted Mrs. Waggoner by phone on Thursday to schedule an interview. On Sunday, July 22, at her daughter's residence in Bessemer, Alabama, 84-year-old "little Willie" and I talked about Jim Bobo, his fatal ride, and the ballad's account of the incident.

In response to my inquiry about living relatives of Jim Bobo or informants, Willie provided three leads: (1) From the last she had heard, Mrs. Frank (Mae Bobo) Timberlake, Jim's granddaughter, was living in Scottsboro, Alabama. (2) Mrs. Charles (Willie Parker) Sehorn, a "lady friend" of Willie's, was living in Tullahoma. (3) Several years ago, a lady named "Macon" had sent Willie an article written in the Shelbyville area concerning the ballad.

Traveling east to Scottsboro, Alabama, I checked the telephone book only to find there was no listing for Mrs. Frank Timberlake. In fact, no Timberlakes at all were listed. But two drugstore patrons told me how to get to Stevenson, where a "whole bunch" of Timberlakes lived. At Stevenson, I became a bit skeptical when the telephone directory showed no listing for a Mrs. Timberlake, but the gas station attendant drew me a map with curves for corners, directing me to the house of a Mrs. H. Kenan Timberlake. After familiarizing myself with the east side of Stevenson, I finally rang Mrs. H. Kenan Timberlake's doorbell. During two hours of visiting, she gave me cousin Mae Bobo Timberlake's address in Houston, Texas, with an added note that I should "receive a clever letter from Mae." And so I did, along with pictures, anecdotes, and the second copy of the 1894 ballad version that she found in her grandmother's scrapbook.

Concerning her former residence in Alabama, Mae wrote:

> I lived in Stevenson while my children were growing up and moved to Montgomery in 1943. Worked for the State of Alabama 15 years then followed my children to Houston. Good to learn that an old friend, long lost to me, is living and remembers me. It will be good to get in touch with Willie Pelham again.

Meanwhile, "Little Willie" had shed some important light on several references in the ballad. She had been born Willie Pelham—"I was named for my father"—in 1890 in Tullahoma, Tennessee. She was one of four children, but never knew her oldest sister, Belle, who was killed in a pistol accident during Christmas time in 1889. Willie later married Mr. Waggoner in Tullahoma, lived in Lynchburg for several years, and moved to Alabama in 1940 to be near her brother.

Willie had a colorful childhood, in which the safety wheel accident was only one incident. Quite dramatically, Willie told me what she remembered about her accident with Jim Bobo.

> I think I was around four years of age. And we lived on Jackson Street in Tullahoma, Tennessee, and Mr. Bobo lived next door to us. They were our neighbors. We had had a . . . this is a quote . . . I'd often heard my mother speak of the fact that we had had a terrible storm that afternoon. And after having finished my evening meal, as I always did, I went out and sat on the gatepost. Mr. Bobo came by on his bicycle and said, "Come on Willie, I want to ride you down the street." So I clambered on the bicycle, and away we went. And he had on a huge harvest hat. And the wind was blowing and we had gone as far as the public school, when he decided he'd better turn around and go back. So, the wind tilted his hat, and he reached up to catch the hat, and when he did, he lost control of the bicycle, and it ran into the fence, and threw him off. He fell on me. I was pinned under him. And a neighbor saw the accident and he came rushing to us when he saw that Mr. Bobo didn't make a move to get up. When he came to us, well, he as well as myself heard him breathe his last breath. I was pinned under him, you know. Aside from that, child, that's about all I know. And a whole lot of that is quote. I've heard my mother tell it. Well, of course I knew that something horrible had happened, so I went rushing home to my mother, and told her, "Come quickly. Something has happened to Mr. Bobo." So they all rushed down and he was lying there dead. And that's about all I remember about it. . . . I remember what my mother had said about it. I didn't remember too much from my own mind, because I was too . . . well, I don't know that I was too small, but I was just a little kid . . . just a little barefoot kid.

The incident had a traumatic effect on Willie, one that lingered for some time.

> Robbed me of my memory and most everything for the time-being, you see. And I remember how it aroused my fear, even. . . . I was afraid, just so afraid. I wouldn't go from one room to the other. And, extremely nervous for my age.

And so we have our first mystery presented: What caused the accident? A gust of wind and a huge harvest hat are keys in Willie's explanation. Indeed, printed below the account of Jim Bobo's accident in the *Nashville Daily American* was an article describing how "Wind and Rain (played) havoc with things in Tullahoma" on the afternoon of August 15.

> One of the severest wind and rain storms that has visited this section of the country for many years, struck here about 3 o'clock Wednesday afternoon. Everywhere the corn is greatly damaged, in some places being flat on the ground. Several houses were slightly damaged. The bridge connecting Park Hotel ball room and the Hurricane Hall was wrecked. The smoke stacks of Raht Bro.'s flour mills are down. A box was blown more than 100 feet through the plate glass window of the Trader's National Bank. Hundreds of the beautiful shade trees that abound in Tullahoma are ruined.

This verifies Willie's reference to the storm and confirms the presence of a strong wind. In recounting the accident a second time, Willie further explained that Jim lost control of the bicycle when the wind tipped his harvest hat and he grabbed at it with one hand, while holding her steady with the other hand.

In the ballad, the "fatal screw" in Stanza VII, line 2 and the "slipping seat" in Stanza VIII, line 2 are the key causal elements of the accident. Similarly, the newspaper account attributes Jim's loss of control to loose handle-bars. Upon closer examination I found the following similarity of terms and phrases between the ballad and the newspaper notice:

Newspaper	Ballad
–Fatal Ride	–Fatal Bicycle Ride
–had little daughter on the wheel	–little Willie on the seat
–late yesterday afternoon	–as day was growing dim
–ran into the fence	–ran against the fence
–succeeded in saving the child	–barely saved the little child
–breaking his neck	–broke his own brave neck
–almost instantly killed	–Instantly there he died
–handle-bars were loose in the steering-head	–My seat is slipping down
–in trying to turn the wheel he lost control of it	–the wheel he could not guide –the wheel had turned aside

We could attribute these similarities to the ballad writer's dependency on the newspaper account, but more likely the ballad writer and reporter shared the same informant or informants. Willie, in fact, offered an identity for the original "D. H. H." who composed the ballad.

> A man by the name of Honeycutt wrote it. I remember hearing my mother say that. He wrote it the night he led corpse. He was one of the few who sat up with him. You know, they used to sit up with the corpses back in my younger days. He was one of the men who sat up with him, and he composed this song while he was sitting there.

According to this explanation, Mr. Honeycutt wrote the ballad on August 15, the night before the newspaper article, dated August 16, appeared in the *Nashville Daily American* on August 17.

Still we have not completely solved the cause mystery. Dick Hulan suggests that Mr. Honeycutt talked to police/newspaper types, and Mrs. Pelham talked to Willie. But who talked with the newspaper reporters? Who talked to Mrs. Pelham? Willie? Would not a neighbor who saw the accident have reported the same story? If a neighbor actually did not see the accident occur, and no one else witnessed it, then Willie was the only witness.[4] It is possible that she told her mother what happened and subsequently Mrs. Pelham refused to talk with reporters and others about it. "My mother never discussed this with me, nor would she allow anyone else to discuss it with me too much, because it always made me nervous," Willie explained. She claims never to have heard the explanation the ballad offers. Given the absence of witnesses, if Willie did not know what happened, then the cause was left to conjecture. In their examination of the bicycle, the investigators could have found the handle-bars loose and concluded what the newspaper account "supposed." Just as plausible is the strong wind and harvest-tipped hat explanation.

What do we know about Mr. Honeycutt, or D. H. H., as he initialed the newspaper printing of the 1894 ballad? Willie does not remember him as an habitual ballad writer. Mrs. Charles Sehorn, Willie's "lady friend," who also grew up in Tullahoma, vaguely remembers a Mr. Honeycutt who worked for the railroad in Tullahoma. Mr. Dick Poplin in Shelbyville, the Bedford County historian and author of the weekly column "Scraps of Poplin" in the *Times Gazette,* wrote the following in the article about Jim Bobo that Willie had mentioned:

> The Mr. Honeycutt who wrote the song was a detective who had been sent to Tullahoma to investigate the case of the death of a night watchman, who, it is said, was killed by two men to keep him from testifying against them in court. Mr. Honeycutt was in Tullahoma at the time of Jim Bobo's death and wrote the song.[5]

During a conversation with Mr. Poplin on August 4, 1973, he revealed his source of information as Mrs. O. M. (Macon Brown) Prince. She "was one of the best historians in Bedford County," reflected Mr. Poplin. "She was also a good friend to Willie Pelham. They were neighbors, and I believe cousins. But Mrs. Prince passed away about a year ago." Mr. Poplin was uncertain about his suspicion that Mr. Honeycutt came from New York. He agreed that it seemed strange for an out-of-town detective to sit up with a corpse and write a ballad. "It seems that what I learned . . . from what Mrs. Prince told me . . . seemed that he was sort of a mysterious character."

Whoever Mr. Honeycutt was, he did accurately portray the close relationship between Jim and little Willie by having her address her friend as Uncle Jim, "not because they were kin," explains Jim's granddaughter, "but because she loved him so much." D. H. H. also correctly described Jim as "a happy man" and knew that he "often made the run / With two and sometimes three" (Stanza III). Willie remembered that "in the afternoons he'd take the children in the neighborhood for little rides, you know, and entertain them that way. I guess we were all so bad, he had to resort to something."

I have received varying opinions on the status and reception of the ballad in the Middle Tennessee area. In response to "Do you recall the song? Is it familiar to you?" Willie answers, "No . . . honey, that song's a nightmare to me." She said it was printed in the town paper but the people did not receive it enthusiastically.[6] Jim's granddaughter recalls that at one time the song was set to music and professionally printed. Later, she says, it lost popularity and was considered passé after such tragic, emotional pieces began to go out of style.

Still, there is evidence that the song was for a time fairly well known in Middle Tennessee. It appears to have been transmitted vertically, from one generation to the next, more than horizontally. A look at these transmission lines indicate that the ballad fared better in areas outside of Tullahoma and with families not immediate to Willie Pelham's or the Bobos.

Figure A is a map showing the ballad's dispersion in Middle Tennessee. For this study, we collected seven different versions of the song:

1) The first was the 1894 newspaper clipping of the printed and initialed ballad found by Mrs. Shirley Majors of Sewanee; Mrs. Majors was a distant niece of Jim Bobo's.

2) This was the 1896 version found in Shelbyville; it was an entry in the songbook of Zadie and Lula McGill, written when they were 17 and 21, respectively, and living near Shelbyville.

3) This was a version sent by Mrs. B. A. Evans of Nashville to a column, "The Query Box," in the *Nashville Banner* in 1927. It was discovered in the newspaper files by Dr. Charles Wolfe. According to Mrs. Evans's note to the paper, "I was living near Tullahoma at the time of Jim's death. The story is

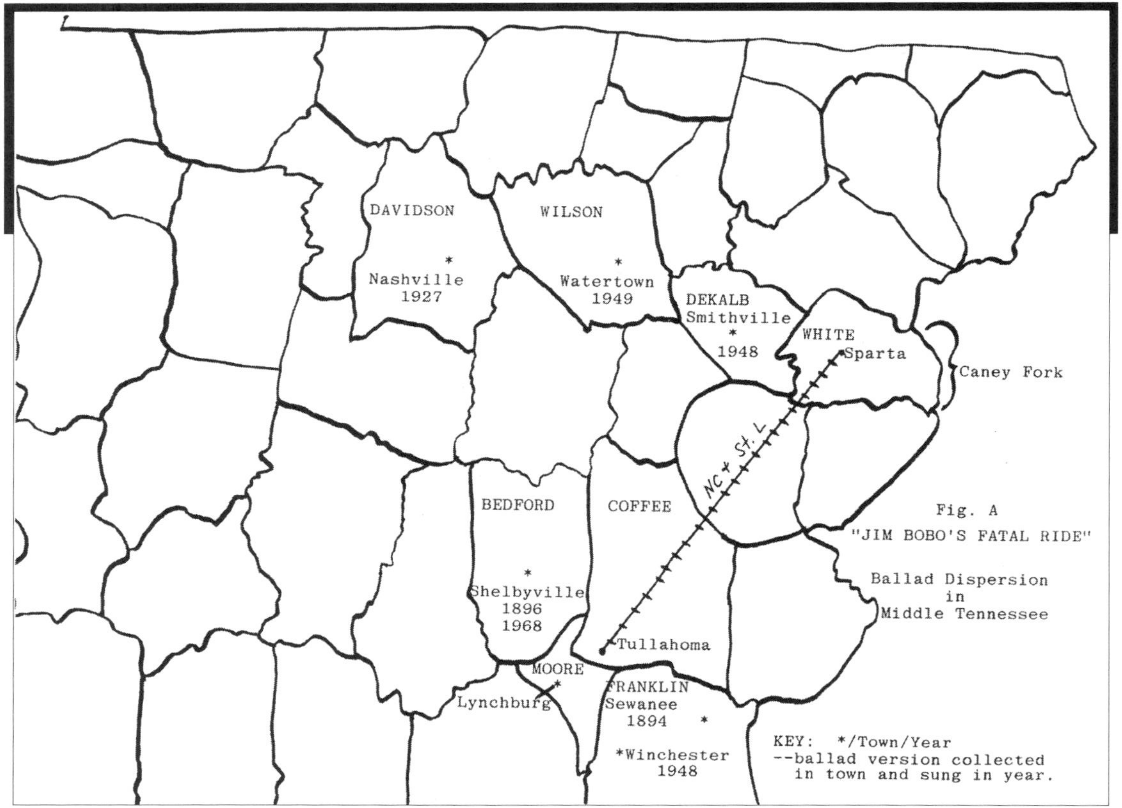
DAVIDSON
Nashville
1927
WILSON
Watertown
1949
DEKALB
Smithville
1948
WHITE
Sparta
Caney Fork
NC + St. L
BEDFORD
Shelbyville
1896
1968
COFFEE
Tullahoma
MOORE
Lynchburg
FRANKLIN
Sewanee
1894
*Winchester
1948
Fig. A
"JIM BOBO'S FATAL RIDE"
Ballad Dispersion
in
Middle Tennessee
KEY: */Town/Year
--ballad version collected
in town and sung in year.

Dispersion of ballad "Jim Bobo's Fatal Ride" in Middle Tennessee. Courtesy of the *Tennessee Folklore Society Bulletin*.

true. The song is sung to the tune of 'Home, Sweet, Home.' If it was ever set to music, or printed, I never heard of it. But everyone was singing it about 30 years ago."

4) This version was printed in 1947 by Mr. and Mrs. L. L. McDowell, Smithville residents, pioneer Tennessee folk song collectors, and early officers of the Tennessee Folklore Society. It appears in their last of four collections, *Memory Melodies,* published in 1947. Mrs. McDowell supplied the text from memory and supplied as a melody an adaptation of "Home Sweet Home." They too believed the ballad was well known throughout Middle Tennessee, especially in the western foothills of the Cumberland within the Caney Fork region. If this is so, the N.C. & St. L. railroad (the "Dixie Line") might have provided a prime source for horizontal transmission of the ballad from Tullahoma up through Middle Tennessee to Sparta and Caney Fork.

5) and 6) were both collected by George Boswell, then teaching at Austin Peay. The first was a 1948 version gathered from a J. Mathis in Winchester, a version which used the melody of "The Blind Child." The second was from J. B. Lasater of Watertown, who used the more common "Home Sweet Home" melody. Because the words in both of these are generally consistent with the 1894 ballad, Mr. Lasater and Mr. Mathis probably set to a tune the words they found in a printed or other horizontal transmission source.

7) This is a 1968 version assigned to Shelbyville and published by Dick Poplin in his article. Although Poplin gathered his text from traditional sources, more than one person contributed to the text. He noted that some people would substitute "the little elf," possibly in reference to Willie, in place of "angel Death" in stanza VII.

All six versions appearing subsequent to the 1894 printing of "Jim Bobo's Fatal Ride" deviate in words, lines, and the number and order of stanzas. The 1947 McDowell version is the prime variant. All stanzas except I, X, and XI are out of order. She misplaces lines within stanzas and exchanges lines between stanzas. She substitutes for line two of Stanza VIII "My feet are slipping down," and for Stanza X, line 1, "the wheel ran wild and struck the curb."

As a group, four out of six ballad versions misorder at least two stanzas, and all four switch stanzas III and IV. Five versions change "Then angel Death put forth a hand" to "Then angel Death put forth his hand," or "put out his wing," or "The angels of death put forth their wings." The word that changes five times is "Instanter" in the last stanza. The *Oxford English Dictionary* says that the word was originally, and still is technically, a law term but now is chiefly an emphatic substitute for "instantly." People changed it to "in an instant," "an instant," or "and instant."

All six versions omit the quotation marks around "safety wheel" in the first stanza. The term appeared around the 1880s to differentiate the new bicycles from the old ordinaries, used to describe the more dangerously built bikes. The quotation marks in the original version emphasize the irony of the term, at least in regard to "Jim Bobo's Fatal Ride."

Notes

1. This information was shared with the author through a series of telephone conversations and letters from June to October 1973.
2. *Nashville Banner,* May 3, 1909.
3. Correspondence with author, July 22, 1973.
4. Elmer Pelham, Willie's older brother, was a classmate of Mr. Walter W. Richardson, who was 90 when interviewed in 1973. Mr. Richardson was 12 at the time of the accident, and recalled, "I didn't see him riding his bicycle, but I remember the day. . . . We lived on the corner facing . . . and they [the Bobos] lived diagonally across . . . facing Jackson Street."
5. The article appeared in the October 10, 1968, issue of the *Shopper's Weekly Journal,* Shelbyville, Tennessee.
6. A search of newspaper files in Tennessee State Archives has not yet revealed this original printing.

Successes of the "Spirit"
[1991]

Kip Lornell

T he history of the Spirit of Memphis in many ways encapsulates the development of postmodern commercial gospel quartets not only at the Mid-South's cross-roads, but across the entire country. From their beginnings in 1928 as the TM&S Quartet, the "Spirit" (as they are often called in Memphis) slowly, masterfully, and in retrospect, inevitably, emerged as the city's best-known and most financially successful religious vocal harmony ensemble. The Spirit of Memphis continues as a regional semi-professional outfit, but its glory days with Little Axe, Jet Bledsoe, James Darling, O. V. Wright, Silas Steele, Earl Malone, and other great singers are behind them.

Not only was the Spirit of Memphis one of this era's most potent commercial groups, they also helped to pioneer several new approaches to quartet singing. The most important of these, "spiritual sermons" or "sermonettes," was an innovation of Silas Steele, who jumped from the Famous Blue Jay Singers late in 1947. Such "cante-fables" (a combination of singing and speech) exploded with a spontaneous, incendiary impact on the black gospel scene. Spiritual sermons caused near pandemonium when audiences heard Steele, and later Bledsoe, testifying and vocalizing. The Holy Spirit became intense with men and women "falling out" under the spell of this unique style, which combined preaching with singing. Both "Jesus, Jesus" and "Lord Jesus, parts 1 & 2" (recorded live at Masons Temple in Memphis) are sterling examples of sermonettes with Silas Steele and Jet Bledsoe exploring the lead vocals.

The Spirit of Memphis also assisted in introducing the concept of "lead-switching" between at least two singers. Until the late 1930s most quartets were egalitarian with no designated lead singer fronting all of the selections. This style of quartet singing is best illustrated by the modal harmonies of the moving "Blessed Are the Dead," quietly led but not dominated by Jet Bledsoe, and "There's No Sorrow." During the 1940s the concept of a distinctive lead singer with three- or four-part background harmony began to emerge. This album demonstrates that the concept of switching among two or more lead singers within a single group quickly became acceptable, even desirable. Between 1949 and 1952 the Spirit of Memphis simultaneously featured three superior ones: Bledsoe, Little Axe, and Steele. This versatility permitted the Spirit to perform both jubilee numbers like "Surely, Surely, Amen" and harder gospel such as "There's No Sorrow."

These new musical approaches were developed during a period of popular support for groups like the Spirit of Memphis. In fact, the decade between 1945 and 1955 is usually presented as the "Golden Age" of black gospel quartet singing. This is certainly true purely in terms of its popularity across the entire country. Pushed by the exposure provided through the independent record companies and local and regional radio station, quartets such as the Golden Gate Quartet, the Dixie Hummingbirds, the Harmonizing Four of Richmond (Virginia), the Swan Silvertones, the Soul Stirrers, and the Fairfield Four reached a large audience of eager fans. The fans themselves were spread across the entire country, from the poorest, flattest Alabama fields to Oakland's sometimes foggy "black bottom."

The fans not only purchased their favorite quartet records on Score, King, Gothan, and other labels, they also clamored for personal appearances. Touring became the norm for these groups, many of whom spent at least part of this decade on the road as full-time professional groups. The Spirit of Memphis proved to be no exception, traveling America's highways between 1950 and 1956 in a fashionable, well-used limo. They went through a series of vehicles, driving an estimated 200,000 miles yearly during their halcyon days. Between April and September 1952 the Spirit counted San Antonio, El Paso, Phoenix, San Francisco, Topeka, Detroit, Buffalo, and Washington, D.C., among their stops.

The Spirit of Memphis put on wonderful performances. Dressed in uniform, tailored suits, they were lively and energetic on stage. Its triumvirate of lead singers soon mastered the art of "working" crowds with both vocal and physical gymnastics. These performance arts combined with the religious frenzy of the crowd to create a highly charged atmosphere, lifting everyone closer to the spirit of God. By the end of a lengthy show, most attendees had their fill of musical and religious ecstasy. Although they often headlined shows at churches, schools, auditoriums, and other venues, the Spirit of Memphis frequently appeared as part of packaged shows featuring several nationally recognized groups. Such programs were most often held on weekends and allowed local and regional groups to share the stage with "stars." Five- and six-hour shows were not uncommon as quartet after group appeared on stage, saving the Spirit of Memphis, the Golden Gate Quartet, or the Sensational Nightingales for last.

And the Spirit of Memphis were stars—they toured with the best quartets and commanded top money for singing. On the road they often served as the guest artists on local radio programs. In between the big city shows the Spirit drove to smaller towns and hamlets, filling in the Tuesday-through-Thursday evening slots with shorter one-night stands. When they returned to their base of operation or were not on extended engagements, the singers often performed in the communities within an easy drive of Memphis: Marked Tree, Arkansas; Dyersburg, Tennessee; Robinsonville, Mississippi. They could make easy money, stay with their families, and spread God's word.

The importance of the electronic media in their career is difficult to underestimate. Their relationship with WDIA as well as the King and Peacock Record Companies proved critical to their commercial success. Not surprisingly their first recordings were for a small local label, the Hallelujah Record Company, whose precise origins and ownership is not entirely clear. The year was 1948 and the Spirit was on the verge of commercial success. The group was approached by a Birmingham, Alabama, promoter named Polk who proposed to record them. A June 1949 newspaper advertisement lists the group as Hallelujah Record Company artists, though "Happy in the Service of the Lord" and "How Many Times" was their sole release on the Hallelujah label (no number).

Their first real success came with King Records. This Cincinnati-based company operated by Syd Nathan developed into one of the premier entrepreneurial labels of the late 1940s with the Delmore Brothers, Swan Silvertones, and Grandpa Jones among its roster of artists. Between 1949 and 1952, when the Spirit of Memphis severed their relationship with Nathan over disputes related to fiscal agreements, they recorded some of the best black religious harmony singing. Their King repertoire ranged from a Martin and Roberts penned spiritual, "Every Day and Every Hour," to the lyrically inventive, topical "Atomic Telephone"—a clever contemporary reworking of the "royal telephone" theme.

Almost immediately they signed with the volatile, imaginative Don Robey, owner of Duke/Peacock Records and one of the 1950s most artistically successful black record executives. Robey was notorious for trying to convert religious singers from the sacred to the profane, but this was not one of the moves he pulled on the Spirit of Memphis. By the late 1950s, however, two members of the Spirit—O. V. Wright and Joe Hinton—had left the fold. Both ultimately recorded popular selections after leaving religious music. The association between Peacock and Robey proved to be long and fruitful, lasting from 1953 until their final 1967 session. The first two years proved to be their brightest period as the group recorded such strong selections as "Surely, Surely, Amen," "Come and Go with Me," "Doctor Jesus," and "Storm of Life." The Spirit of Memphis continued to revise older hymns and spirituals such as the rubato "When Mother's Gone," which echoes "Motherless Children Have a Hard Time." This is also one of the handful of their early selections that is supported by instruments (drums and trombone). Later sessions included some artistically suspect material—"Pay Day," "Voo-doo-ism," and "Christian Chain Gang"—that sometimes borders on the edge of novelty status.

The late 1940s and early 1950s proved to be the group's most fecund period; a half decade of great artistic and commercial success not only for touring and recording, but for radio exposure. Most of their broadcasting occurred over Memphis' legendary WDIA, home to Joe Hill Louis, Rev. Herbert W. Brewster's "Camp Meeting of the Air," Riley B. King, the Songbirds of the South, Rufus Thomas, and the Southern Wonders. Shortly after WDIA signed on the air in 1948, the Spirit of Memphis joined the broadcast team. In its early years, WDIA served the black community of Memphis with its mixture of news, church services, public service announcements, and music. Most of the programs ran in fifteen- or thirty-minute blocks sponsored by local or regional merchants.

The fifteen-minute broadcast reproduced on Gospel Jubilee 107 (Sweden 1991) is typical of these daily in-studio "live" programs. It also reflects the values of contemporary radio: carefully scripted and timed segments that allowed for a small degree of improvisation and spontaneity. The Carnation Milk name is prominent throughout the broadcast—the advertisement sung by the group itself adds a nice touch. But the Spirit of Memphis shines through on their a capella numbers. This program includes three older spiritual numbers, "Joshua Fit the Battle of Jericho," "Freedom," and "Ezekiel Saw the Wheel A'Rollin'," not commercially recorded by them. Another vintage song, "Mother Gone On," is a fine example of how spirituals were traditionally elongated through the process of incremental additions to the lyrics. The Spirit carefully included one of their more popular jubilee numbers "Swing Down Chariot," which was to become one of their favorite concert numbers. The group itself was one of the strongest assembled and is almost certainly the same line-up as appears on the first King session. One song from this session, "Blessed Are the Dead," immediately follows the WDIA broadcast and is one of the few pieces in their recorded repertoire cast in a minor key.

The impact of WDIA itself increased dramatically in July 1954, when the station boosted its output to the maximum allowable power of 50,000 watts and began around-the-clock operations. This change brought the station and groups such as the Spirit of Memphis into homes across the entire Mid-South and nightly into many parts of the nation. WDIA stepped up its local promotions, expanding its "Goodwill Revue" (a fund raiser for local children) by bringing in national acts such as Ray Charles, Little Walter, and the Moonglows. Within a year WDIA had expanded its audience and sponsorship from a local market to a strong regional presence.

Ironically, this happened just at the time that the Spirit of Memphis and the quartet movement in general was beginning to lose its thunder. The mass popularity of gospel quartet harmony singing had begun nearly a decade before and popular tastes were slowly shifting. Soloists such as Professor Alex Bradford, Mahalia Jackson, and Queen C. Anderson, as well as slightly larger, gender-mixed ensembles such as the Ward Singers, began to erode the dominance of quartets. Some church-goers also thought that the quartet singers were becoming "worldly" by driving expensive cars, wearing flashy clothes and jewelry, and grandstanding like pop singers.

The Spirit of Memphis remained full-time professional singers until about 1960, but their popularity had greatly diminished. So had their artistic talents. By 1955 Silas Steele, Wilbur Broadnax, and James Darling had departed. Though their replacements were fine singers, the Spirit was clearly not the powerhouse it had been in 1950. Nor was the gospel quartet movement itself, which by 1960 had lost much of its commercial punch.

The Lion's Share
Scottish Ballads in Southern Appalachia
[1997]

Thomas G. Burton

T he spirit of Scots ballads in southern Appalachia may be described in
terms of an extended whiskey metaphor.

I understand that, even in reused Tennessee charred Jack Daniel
barrels, up to 5 percent of Scotland's "water of life" evaporates and is rarified
into the mists. Similarly, in the importation of ballads, according to a study
by Herschel Gower, there is great evaporation—only a third of the cask of 305
Child ballads made it to the United States. And of that third, some 40 percent
may be labeled "Scotch" (154).

But what about Scottish balladry in southern Appalachia, where in the
minds of some, the Celtic blood runs thickest and makes us the lawless, shift-
less folk we are?

First, we need to delineate what is meant in this study by Child ballads that
are "Scots." Here I am accepting Herschel Gower's designation which he based
on certain primary and secondary criteria, including the following: ballads
with a basis in Scottish history; those collected only in Scotland; those which
have always had wide currency in Scotland but limited currency in England
and Ireland; and those with a long period of currency in Scotland and "natu-
ralized" before emigrating to America (84–85).

Second, after identifying which ballads are Scottish, we need to identify the area "southern Appalachia." Not many agree definitively on the boundaries; but in general southern Appalachia is accepted as the region defined by that portion of the Appalachian chain that extends from West Virginia south to the northern parts of Georgia and Alabama, including the western portions of Virginia and North Carolina, and the eastern portions of Kentucky and Tennessee.

But before we can attest to the spirit or vitality of Scottish ballads in southern Appalachia, we must examine the bill of importation—that is, which Child ballads made it to the region. This is not an easy task for a number of reasons, but principally because there is no readily available checklist of southern Appalachian Child ballads and because collections of ballads are not commonly published according to their Appalachian identification.

To work up such a list of southern Appalachian Child ballads, Ambrose Manning and I examined the major ballad collections as well as numerous other sources which potentially identified ballads from southern Appalachia. The list we compiled is drawn from forty-six of the sources consulted, and it tallies the variants of Child ballads collected from the early part of this century by the well-known Cecil Sharp down to those gathered in our own collection housed in the Archives of Appalachia at East Tennessee State University. The list is by no means complete, and it is not devoid of many inherent problems involved in such a compilation. But it does provide a reasonably sound, representative canon of southern Appalachian Child ballads and a tally of their variants. The checklist can be viewed online at this World Wide Web address: www.utpress.org/downloads

Our checklist enumerates one hundred individual Child ballads, a number that comes with little surprise. The Appalachian region has always been viewed as fertile ground for the ballad, and it has continued to be so for longer than have most other parts of our country.

The focus of this paper, however, is upon the Scots ballads in southern Appalachia. The compilation reveals that only two of the Child numbers collected in the United States that are Scottish have not been found in this area ("Archie o Cawfield" 188 and "The False Lover Won Back" 218). And of the total Child numbers collected in Appalachia, the Scots ballads represent 41 percent.

This percentage represents a strong tradition of Scots ballads. But the number alone of individual ballads does not indicate adequately the pervasiveness of Scots ballads in the Appalachians. To gain a better perspective of their vitality, one needs to look also at the number of variants of these forty-one Scottish Appalachian ballads.

Our tally of variants indicates 1,023 for the Scottish ballads, a number which represents 40 percent of the total. I had expected the percentage of variants to be higher than that for the number of individual Scottish Child ballads. In fact, it falls a little short but is within the same range. Perhaps we should expect approximately 40 percent since this percentage correlates with what is a reasonable estimate of the proportion of Scots (Lowland, Highland, and Ulster) to all the other ethnic groups who settled in southern Appalachia during the great migration of the 18th century (see Fischer 608–9; Blethen and Wood 34).

As an aside, it may be mentioned that the percentage of the variants as well as of the individual Scots ballads substantiates the misjudgment or prejudice of Cecil Sharp in designating his collection of folk songs from the southern Appalachians as solely English rather than as English and Scottish (cf. Gower 83).

I don't think, however, that even these rather high percentages of Scots ballads and their variants give a clear picture of their vitality in southern Appalachia. For example, a collector might uncover a number of obscure Child ballads sung in an isolated holler by some elderly woman with a sweet gum snuff brush perched in the corner of her mouth. But the discovery of those rare songs sung by that singer wouldn't necessarily indicate what ballads were generally sung in her part of the mountains, whereas a count of the number of variants collected in her locality would. Such a singer might know a fragment of "Thomas Rhymer," whereas a dozen of her neighbors might sing lengthy texts of "Lord Randal." Both ballads would be evidenced in the community, but "Lord Randal" would apparently have greater vitality.

In order to obtain a perspective of just how vital Scottish ballads have been in Appalachia, I ranked the composite list of ballads according to the number of their variants. I discounted the variants of "Bonny Barbara Allen" (Child 84), although hesitantly, because its total of 295 (influenced disproportionately by non-traditional publications and commercial recordings) skews statistical analysis. (If indeed this ballad is English, it is interesting that the earliest reference to it by Pepys in 1666 is as a "little Scotch song" [Child 2:276]; and when Percy in the eighteenth century "ransacked Scotland for traditional materials which he failed to find in England," it was from his Scottish correspondents that he received "Sir John Grehme and Barbara Allen" [Gower 120].)

The ranking of the variants by frequency of collection reveals that the top three ballads in Appalachia are Scottish. I like to think of this frequency as the lion's share of Appalachian balladry.

Not only are the top three ballads Scots, but also, of the top ten Child ballads, five are Scots. In order of rank by frequency of variants, these five are as follows:

1. "James Harris (The Daemon Lover)" (Child 243)
2. "Lord Thomas and Fair Annet" (Child 73)
3. "The Gypsy Laddie" (Child 200)
4. "Young Hunting" (Child 68)
5. "Lord Randal" (Child 12)

In the Burton-Manning Collection at East Tennessee State University, which contains approximately two hundred variants (189) of Child ballads gathered in the middle of southern Appalachia, the ranking of Scots ballads is even greater. Excluding "Barbara Allen," the top five ballads are Scots. These top five ballads are the same as those cited above, with the exception of the substitution of "Our Goodman" (Child 274) for "Lord Randal." Since the Burton-Manning Collection represents what was current in the 1960s and 1970s (rather than over the last seventy years, as represented in the composite list), this increased ranking of Scots ballads may indicate a superior survival quality—at least it is a proposition worth pursuing.

If you were to go into a number of pubs in Scotland and scan the shelves behind the bar for American whiskeys, you would probably see one, two, or three different labels. But chances are if there were only one bottle, it would be a Tennessee sour mash, Jack Daniels. Similarly, if you were to go into southern Appalachia looking for traditional ballads, you would probably come across several British ballads. But chances are if you heard only one—and it wasn't "Barbry Allen"—it would be Scots.

Another interesting matter to explore relative to Scottish ballads in Appalachia is the place of origin. They are Scottish, but what was their portage—to continue the whiskey metaphor. That is, where did they come from, what part of Scotland, Ireland, or England?

As a means of arriving at some understanding relative to this question, I chose to look carefully at "The Gypsy Laddie" (Child 200). The choice was based not only on its being one of the most popular Scottish ballads in Appalachia but also on its being one that I had collected in Appalachia, as well as in Scotland from the Travelling community. The ballad's popularity, no doubt, has been both a cause and an effect of its interesting commercial recording history. Records of this ballad were issued in the 1930s, 1940s, and 1950s by such varied artists as folk singer Woody Guthrie and Memphis rock-and-roll singer Warren Smith (Wolfe 29).

I compared approximately fifty motifs, key words, and stanzas in some seventy-five Scottish, English, Irish, and Appalachian variants of "The Gypsy Laddie." Non-Appalachian texts analyzed were from personal audio tapes and commercial recordings, from the archives of the School of Scottish Studies and the Ulster Folk and Transport Museum, as well as from the Child, Greig/Keith, and Bronson collections.

It is immediately clear from these texts that the principal narrative of this ballad migrates well: A lady is influenced to follow the Gypsies, generally by their singing, and to leave family, home, and belongings. The lady's husband on returning home rides out to reclaim his wife, but in most instances he is seemingly unsuccessful.

Although the general plot is constant, there are a number of interesting elements in the ballad that do not make the voyage to the New World—for example, the identification of the Gypsy leader as Johnny Faa, the exchange of gifts between the wife and Gypsies, and the poignant descriptions of the wife's wading across a stream or of the Gypsy brothers' lament.

Among those elements that do transport, two are of particular interest relative to certain key features of the Appalachian variants. One is the pervasive identification of the Gypsy leader as some form of the name "Black Jack Davy." The second is the characteristic description involving the wife's clothing of high/low-heeled footwear made of Spanish leather.

The first element, a form of the name of Black Jack Davy, appears in only one of the non-American texts examined, and there as "a Gipsey Davy." The text is a Scottish one that Child includes from the Motherwell MS, a recitation of Agnes Lyle of Kilbarchan in 1825. (Child does include an American text [J] which indicates that "Gipsey Davy" was also current in Maine and Massachusetts in the 1840s.)

The second element, the lady's high/low-heeled shoes or boots made of Spanish leather, appears in three Child numbers: (1) Child G from a 1720 Roxburghe broadside, cited "doubtfully, as of Newcastle upon Tyne," and a later stall copy; (2) Child I from an 1860 Irish text; and (3) Child K from New York texts, one of which was derived from a woman in "1820, or a little later . . . and perhaps [italics mine] learned from English soldiers there stationed during the Revolutionary War." An 1888 text from Devonshire also mentions shoes of Spanish leather (Bronson 87). Another late English text (1904) speaks of "Spanish livery" (Bronson 73), and one of Cecil Sharp's English texts has the lady pull off her "highland shoes / And put on her Spanish leather" (Bronson 86).

One would anticipate these dominant Appalachian features—the name Davy and the high/low-heeled footwear of Spanish leather—appearing in one of the five Ulster variants examined, since the Ulster Scots were the single largest ethnic group to settle Appalachia (Fischer 609; Leyburn 184–223). But that isn't the case, though the sampling is admittedly small. Nor do they show up in a text from Donegal or in an Irish text from John Reilly, a Traveller who lived for a time in Belfast.

What appears likely is that the typical Appalachian version, the lady in the high-heeled Spanish leather footwear following her charming Gypsy Black Jack Davy, emanates from western Scotland and the border areas before migrating orally and in print to England, Ireland, and the United States.

Even if this assumption is correct, we still do not have a firm grasp on the answer to who transported "The Gypsy Laddie," as well as to who brought the other Scots ballads. Since most of these ballads, according to Gower's study, were found only in Scotland, Ireland, and America (113), the assumption is that they came to Appalachia for the most part directly or indirectly by Scots or by their descendants—many perhaps by way of Ulster, But no doubt the English, particularly from the North, had a voice in the matter.

Incidentally, we also do not have a clear view of who brought the barrels of English ballads to Appalachia, including "Barbara Allen." But very likely the transporters were in considerable numbers the same Scots and descendants of Scots who brought the Scottish ballads.

Neither is there much information as to how much balladry is left after evaporation—that is, how many ballads in general and Scots ballads in particular are still being sung throughout southern Appalachia. That is a difficult question to answer.

One reason is that field work in general is not presently considered a premier pursuit of American folklorists. Theory claims the day. As a result there is little encouragement to collect ballads. There is even a pejorative attitude toward focusing solely on Child ballads, which is viewed as reflecting a sort of "Cecil Sharp" elitism. Lack of funding and the deluge of non-academic demands on academicians are certainly other detrimental factors to ballad field work. At any rate, there is very little collecting being done in southern Appalachia.

The field is also simply not as fertile as it once was. The omnipresence of mass media continues to take its toll on the traditional arts, except those that are engulfed by pop culture, as for example story telling.

There is also an absence of external stimuli to the oral tradition of balladry. The folk song revival of the 1950s and 1960s promoted the recall and performance of ballads in the Appalachians, as did the early treks and commercial recordings of collectors in the mountains during the preceding two or three decades. Even without these stimuli there is still a lot of traditional music in the mountains, but there is more instrumental than vocal, more newer than older, more bluegrass than old-time, more country ballads than the "muckle sangs."

As a project for one of my classes a number of years back, I conducted a field study to investigate the vitality of the British ballad tradition in a restricted area of Beech Mountain, North Carolina (see Johnson and Burton). Benjamin Franklin Jones, an eighty-seven-year-old native, was one of our chief informants. What we learned about him may be seen as representative of not only what we found in Beech Mountain, but what is also pretty typical in the Appalachians in general.

Frank Jones had continued to sing the ballads, or as he called them "the old love songs." Three of his four Child ballads besides "Barbara Allen" were Scots: "House Carpenter," "Jimmy Randall," and "Heneree"—his versions of "James Harris (The Daemon Lover)" (Child 243), "Lord Randal" (Child 12), and "Young Hunting" (Child 68). We learned that although his parents had sung ballads, only Frank among the siblings had significantly sustained the tradition. This degeneration of the tradition continued through two genera-

◘ Buna Hicks, traditional ballad singer and old-time fiddler, Beech Mountain, North Carolina, near the North Carolina–Tennessee border. From the Burton-Manning Collection. Courtesy of the Archives of Appalachia, East Tennessee State University.

tions. Only three of his eight children sang the old love songs, and none of his grandchildren sang them. Taste for the old songs had turned toward the newly recorded Nashville country, bluegrass, and gospel music.

One element that reinforced the ballad tradition in the life of Frank Jones and the lives of others in Beech Mountain was a common pattern of marriage. Ballad families married into ballad families—sometimes too closely because, as Mrs. Rena Hicks, who married her first cousin, said to me, "There just weren't many around you could marry."

This reinforcement of balladry through marriage, as well as through the family and social structure in general, was very important. For example, Frank Jones's first wife was part of a family with a rich singing tradition. Her sister was a fine ballad singer and her step-mother's brother was Abe Trivett, one of the early mountain musicians recorded by Folk-Legacy Records. Frank's second wife was also influential in his repertory and performance. She was a ballad singer and sang for us the Scottish "Bolamkin" (Child 93). Her kin were also ballad singers. However, the family and general cultural context of Beech Mountain, which is now known for its ski slopes and resort centers, has almost completely changed, as has the traditional context of much of Appalachia. And that change has had a profound effect upon the ballad matrix.

As we have observed, the spirit of Scottish balladry has been strong in southern Appalachia. All but two of the Scottish U.S. Child ballads have been collected in this area. From the composite list we also see that 41 percent of the Child ballads collected are Scots, and 40 percent of all their variants. But a better perspective of the vitality of the Scottish Child ballads is provided by their rank according to the number of variants: The Lion's share is the top three ballads (excluding "Barbara Allen").

Evaporation of the ballads has been heavy, but perhaps less for the principal Scottish ones than for the English. Certainly, even without strong external stimuli the Scottish ballad spirit in the southern Appalachians has not completely dissipated, but authentic traditional singing of these old love songs is becoming about as hard to find as good homemade corn whiskey.

Works Cited

Blethen, Tyler, and Curtis Wood Jr. *From Ulster to Carolina: The Migration of the Scotch-Irish to Southwestern North Carolina.* 2nd ed. Cullowhee, N.C.: Western Carolina University Mountain Heritage Center, 1986.

Bronson, Bertrand Harris. *The Traditional Tunes of the Child Ballads.* Vol. 3, *Ballads 114 to 243.* Princeton: Princeton University Press, 1966.

Child, Francis James. *The English and Scottish Popular Ballads.* 5 vols. New York: Dover, 1965.

Fischer, David Hackett. *Albion's Seed: Four British Folkways in America.* New York: Oxford, 1989.

Gower, Herschel. *Traditional Scottish Ballads in the United States.* Ann Arbor, Mich.: University Microfilms, 1957.

Johnson, Martha, and Thomas Burton. "The Vitality of the Ballad Tradition in Beech Mountain." *Tennessee Folklore Society Bulletin* 39 (1973): 33–34.

Leyburn, James G. *The Scotch-Irish: A Social History.* Chapel Hill: University of North Carolina, 1962.

Wolfe, Charles K. *Folk Songs of Middle Tennessee: The George Boswell Collection.* Knoxville: University of Tennessee Press, 1997.

Further Reading in Folk Ballad and Song

Bufwack, Mary, with Robert K. Oermann. *Finding Her Voice: Women in Country Music, 1800–2000.* 2003.

Burton, Thomas. *Some Ballad Folks.* 1978.

———. *Tom Ashley, Sam McGee, Bukka White: Tennessee Traditional Singers.* 1981.

Escott, Colin. *Good Rockin' Tonight: Sun Records and the Birth of Rock 'n' Roll.* 1991.

Evans, David. *Big Road Blues: Tradition and Creativity in the Folk Blues.* 1988.

Goff, James R., Jr. *Close Harmony: A History of Southern Gospel.* 2002.

Guralnick, Peter. *Sweet Soul Music: Rhythm and Blues and the Southern Dream of Freedom.* 1986.

Jackson, George Pullen. *White Spirituals in the Southern Uplands: The Story of the Fasola Folk, Their Songs, Singing, and "Buckwheat Notes."* 1933.

Lornell, Kip. *"Happy in the Service of the Lord": Afro-American Gospel Quartets in Memphis.* 1988.

Malone, Bill C. *Country Music, U.S.A.* 2002.

Sharp, Cecil. *English Folk Songs from the Southern Appalachians.* 1917. Rev. ed., 1932.

Wolfe, Charles K. *Folk Songs of Middle Tennessee: The George Boswell Collection.* 1997.

———. *A Good-Natured Riot: The Birth of the Grand Ole Opry.* 1999.

Wolfe, Charles K., and Ted Olson. *The Bristol Sessions: Writings About the Big Bang of Country Music.* 2005.

Zimmerman, Peter. *Tennessee Music: Its People and Places.* 1998.

PART NINE

Folk Music
Instrumental Traditions and Folk Music Collecting

This part explores the legacy of Tennessee's instrumental (i.e., nonverbal) music traditions, including the sometimes controversial process of collecting folk music. Two essays focus on the African American contributions to Tennessee music. In his essay "John Wesley Work III: Field Recordings of Southern Black Folk Music, 1935–1942," Bruce Nemerov recounts the role of Work, a professor of music at Fisk University during the Depression era, in collecting and interpreting traditional African American music. Work's effort to preserve and promote black music in the South has been ignored due to the considerable attention devoted to folklorist Alan Lomax's work. As Nemerov notes in his insightful essay, Work, beyond his own scholarly accomplishments, played a significant role in facilitating Lomax's important 1941 collecting trip in the Mississippi Delta when bluesman Muddy Waters was "discovered." While Lomax has generally been given credit for first recording Waters, Work, as Nemerov observes, was a full participant in that "discovery," helping Lomax with the recording of Waters and interviewing the bluesman.

The other essays in this part of the book examine the folk heritage of three different musical instruments associated with Tennessee's musical heritage. Charles Faulkner Bryan's essay, "The Appalachian Mountain Dulcimer Enigma," was a pioneering study of the fretted dulcimer, an instrument with Old World ancestry that was historically played in scattered sections of Appalachia (including in East Tennessee). In the early 1950s, before this type of dulcimer (as opposed to the hammered dulcimer, which is a different instrument with a markedly different musical history) achieved national popularity in the urban folk music revival, Bryan traveled to various museums in the United

States and Europe to investigate the folk history of the fretted dulcimer. While Bryan's essay was historically inconclusive, it is nonetheless credited by several scholars as having narrowed the focus of subsequent dulcimer research, thus enabling a better understanding of the elusive origins of this instrument.

An instrument specifically native to Tennessee is the subject of the essay by Sandy Conatser and David Schnaufer, "Tennessee Music Box: History, Mystery, and Revival." Found primarily in southern Middle Tennessee, the Tennessee music box is in fact a local variation of the fretted dulcimer, and like the fretted dulcimer, the Tennessee music box fell into disuse before being revived in recent years. In the case of the latter instrument, the person most active in the revival was this essay's coauthor, David Schnaufer, a leading contemporary dulcimer player. This essay provides a wealth of descriptive information on how this regional folk instrument was built and who once built it.

While such folk instruments as the fiddle and the banjo were the most commonly heard musical instruments in Tennessee during the nineteenth century, the guitar became the most popular instrument across Tennessee and the South by the mid-twentieth century. While many people who played the guitar purchased factory-made instruments at retail stores or from commercial merchandise catalogs, a small number of luthiers (instrument builders) in Tennessee produced hand-crafted guitars. Since the 1960s, one of the nation's most acclaimed line of hand-crafted guitars was the Gallagher, produced by J. W. and Don Gallagher of Wartrace, Tennessee. David J. Brown's essay, "J. W. and Don Gallagher, Master Guitar Craftsmen," discusses the important role the Gallaghers play in the commercial music industry through providing superior-crafted instruments to numerous acclaimed recording acts. Presented primarily through an interview format, Brown's piece conveys a sense of the Gallaghers' knowledge of and attitude toward their craft.

The Appalachian Mountain Dulcimer Enigma
[1954]

Charles Faulkner Bryan

Those of us who engage in some sort of research project hold different ideas as to the presentation of our findings. In general, we are of two somewhat opposing kinds: (1) those who conduct a project to its finality and report only when all the findings are in and when definite, conclusive statements can be made and authenticated; (2) those who ask, "Do I have to wait until every fact is in before I speak out? Can I not give some findings with the hope others may be stimulated to assist?"

The first type of research procedure is, indeed, the more scholarly and conclusive. It offers to the public at one time the complete, well-wrapped, and securely tied package which one may receive as a whole before attempting to untie and challenge. Its greatest virtue is completeness and unity. Its greatest weaknesses are the span of time needed and the hazards of illness, death or other interruptions of work before others find out what progress has been made.

The second type of researcher formulates his thesis for search. He then engages in his work and from time to time speaks out on various phases of his activity, realizing his word may be challenged but also bearing in mind that his statements may draw from others new information and thinkings relative to the work at hand—information which might have been over-looked had the person waited until the completion of his work before speaking. The greatest virtue of this type of research is in its sharing and its wide channels of intake of information and thinkings unknown to the researcher.

Its greatest weaknesses lie in its temptation to speak out with little factual background and its tendency to propagandize for a result rather than speak after scientific evaluation.

In the elusive realm of folklore research there should sometimes be a combination of these two types of investigation. We like to read, "Thus and thus is so." But it is also good to read, "This is what I sense thus far in my research; can any come forward with their facts and ideas?"

Following the open-bore shotgun technique mentioned as the second type given above, I wrote three articles on "American Folk Instruments" for our *Tennessee Folklore Society Bulletin* (March, June, and September 1952). In the first article I stated:

> At the risk of erring on many points, I am taking on myself to put down my findings about the dulcimer, with the hope that this quaint and beautiful sound and this subtle shape will come to be known by all of those interested in the folk arts, as well as those engaged in the study of formal music.

I proceeded to stick my neck out in naming and classifying the different types of dulcimers and describing their shapes and parts. I did this because over the years the scholars writing on musical instruments had ignored this distinctive instrument. Since that time I have waited for someone to come forward and say: "Didn't you know of this reference or that fact?" The response to my informal articles of folk instruments brought only references (all most welcome) from "hin and yon" as to the existence of certain instruments, but no challenges.

During the past two years I have developed some challenges of my own. In the form of questions, they are:

> Why are these instruments found only in a comparatively small region of the United States—a circle of the southern Appalachians, taking in western North Carolina, southwestern Virginia, eastern Kentucky, East Tennessee, northwestern South Carolina, and the tip of northern Georgia?
>
> Did the dulcimer[1] come to this secluded section from the Colonial States? Are there any records of the instrument having been used in New England or other parts of the United States prior to the settlement of this mountainous region?
>
> Since this region was the richest in the use of the English and Scottish ballads, in early English lore and in so-called Shakespearian speech, is there any connection of this instrument with the British Isles?
>
> What are the ancestors of this instrument?
>
> Are there missing links which, if found, would connect this instrument with earlier foreign stringed instruments?
>
> Could the dulcimer be original and native to the Appalachian region?

With these questions in mind I set out last year to find some of the answers. This had to be done in a casual way and only as a side issue to the other work.

While in New York on business in March 1953, I spent most of my spare time at the Metropolitan Museum. Dr. Emannuel Winternitz, Keeper of Musical Instruments, was most helpful in permitting me a backstage look there. In this museum, said to have the second largest collection in the world, I found only three instruments which seemed remotely related to the dulcimer but they were so far removed historically and functionally as to make relationship seem a happenstance. These oblong instruments were the scheitholt of eighteenth-century Germany, having five strings, one fretted and four drones; the scheitholt of France (nineteenth century) with two fretted strings and three drones; and the hommel of Norway (1799), of five strings, four of which are drones. The last instrument had a short string fastened to an outside peg like the five-string banjo. "What an odious comparison!" the purist would say.

On the same trip I stopped off in Washington, hoping that the museums in our nation's capitol would contain an instrument so much a part of the cultural life of a segment of our country. By good fortune I was permitted to explore, in addition to the other sections, one of the floors in the National Museum which had been closed to the public. I admired as I had before the Hugo Worch instruments arranged in sequence to show the historical development of the piano; but, search as I would, I could not find our elusive dulcimer.

Last summer I spent two months "across the pond." Although my major purpose was not one of searching out the European roots of the dulcimer, I gravitated to every museum and musical collection which time and location permitted me to investigate.

The British Isles were first on my itinerary. Surely, I reasoned, in this very cradle of our region's ancestors I would find the dulcimer. To me the instrument has an Elizabethan air and certainly its fretting and delicate manner of speaking suggest that period when simple accompaniments were being used with the ballads by the folk. The drone bass of the instrument fairly burrs out "Scotland." Surely there, one could find an instrument like or near our Appalachian descendant.

The British Museum was, for this novice, a spell-binding experience. It was difficult to think of dulcimers with the Rosetta Stone, the Magna Charta documents, and the Elgin Marbles all about. The most helpful attendants soon advised me that the British Museum was not the place to look for musical instruments. Following this I made the rounds of a number of small museums only to run up against a stone wall. The officials in each place I visited seemed eager to help and would suggest some other place where I might find this "what-do-you-say—dulcimoor?"

At the Victoria and Albert Museum I encountered the first and only antagonism to my project. A member of the musical instrument section, who shall remain nameless, after one sentence of introduction started to lecture me on the word *dulcimer* in its philological aspects. Upon seeing the picture of my collection and the words *Southern Folk Instruments,* he stated that they did not have "savage" instruments in their collection. This brought on a slight verbal "set-to" during which the gentleman confessed he was referring to folk instruments and meant no offense. He truly felt, it seemed to me, that any instrument found in folk hands in the southern Appalachians should not call for serious inquiry. I thought of these highly creative and beautiful instruments and of my forebears who were the "savages" referred to and, after finding out for sure that the museum contained no such "trivia," took my leave.

A trip to Edinburgh for two and a half days made possible a look in all the museums there. As it was cold and rainy during the entire time, the slightly warmer insides of the Scottish museums held an edge over the streets. In the Royal Scottish Museum three very capable assistants showed me about the large building and afforded me every opportunity to examine the music holdings. I was extremely disappointed not to find a dulcimer here. I traced down another collection in the city with no greater success and then went to the University of Edinburgh. Here I had the good fortune of meeting Professor S. T. M. Newman of the musical faculty. He told me of the final drive to collect all of the possible folk music and lore remaining in Scotland. It seems northern Scotland is being electrified and with the coming in of electricity, especially in the rural areas, the remaining lore will probably be lost. Mr. Newman studied my photographs and stated he had never seen such instruments in Scotland. He expressed exceeding interest in my project and said he would be on the lookout for such instruments, although we both expressed a fear that we might never turn one up here, as Scottish historical collections are well promoted and, by this time, something should have been placed in a museum.

I left the British Isles with an enigma clouding the clear sky of my previous hopes, for, from this part of the world came most of the ancestors of the people of our mountain dulcimer circle.

In The Hague, Holland, I visited with great interest the Municipal Museum. The Keeper of Music, Dr. J. H. van der Meer, a young man of great charm and organizational ability, showed me the rare instrumental holdings both on display and in the vaults beneath the new building. He was most interested in my quest. Here I found my first general clue to a finding which later was to become significant and which was to form an even greater enigma than that remaining from the British Isles. Dr. van der Meer stated that he believed such instruments as mine were to be found in the Scandinavian countries. I remembered that my former pupil at Peabody College, Bertyl Boer, who was born and reared in Sweden, had mentioned having similar instruments in Stockholm.

A search of the Hague's museum revealed three instruments which resemble our Appalachian dulcimer. These were the langspil of Iceland, the noordse balk of the Netherlands (1800), and, to substantiate our growing Scandinavian theory, the langeleik of Norway. Each of these instruments had frets arranged much like our instruments. They had, also, drone basses. There was a marked similarity between the sound holes. The greatest difference between the two types was in the fact that these foreign instruments did not have the raised, lengthwise wooden section under the strings. The shapes of these instruments were more angular than ours and slightly larger.

In Brussels I found, rather by accident, the largest instrument museum in the world. The Royal Conservatoire of Musical Instruments contained 4,300 items. Three museum assistants made the rounds with me, climbing the many steps of the old building. We conversed through an interpreter, who had kindly directed me to the building. Our search did not reveal an instrument of further interest than those found in the Hague, but the delayed repartee between the four of us I will remember with a good deal of interest. The keepers seemed to be puzzled by my pictures. If I caught correctly what they intended to say through the interpreter, it went something like this:

"These instruments are not usual. They are, perhaps, phantasms."
"But they do exist. Here are the photographs!"
"They are some sort of bastard instrument."
"Of what parentage?"
"It would be hard to say from which ancestors these instruments came."

After many remarks and much puzzlement, one of the gentlemen made the comment which was to make the third time I had gotten such hints from widely different sources. He said that he had heard of such a strange type of instrument from Norway.

Before leaving this interesting place, I made the rounds again and was greatly amused to find on a wall covered with many rare oriental and occidental instruments this inscription over a very familiar sight:

"Americain Banjo"

Hanging there in dignity never dreamed of in our country was this humble instrument—but nary a dulcimer.

How I wished I could have gone right up to Sweden and Norway, but my schedule did not permit. Nor does space permit me to tell of a continued quest in fabulous Italy, Germany, Austria, Switzerland, and France, where I looked at hundreds of paintings hoping to find our dulcimer in the arms of some long forgotten subject. Of course, there were many large museums in cities which were out of my itinerary. I had, however, a pretty good taste of the difficulty of dulcimer hunting in Europe.

On the way home I had time to ponder the whole matter. Here was quite an enigma I had cooked up for myself! Scandinavia! What connection could this section have with our little, secluded Appalachian region? If there is some connection, what are the missing links? Our puzzled curator in Brussels came forward with a comment—facetious but tinged with credulity: "Perhaps Lief Erikson and the Norsemen brought them over."

Not being able, at this time, to take this theory, I shall continue my search and enlarge, no doubt, my area of puzzlement.

Notes

1. I am here speaking always of the plucked dulcimer. The hammered dulcimer is quite well known and amply described in many writings.

John Wesley Work III
Field Recordings of Southern Black Folk Music, 1935–1942
[1987]

Bruce Nemerov

"Shut up! Don't you mention nothing about 'John Henry' to me. Only low people sang that! Men used to work on public works and they used to holler for blocks singing those kinds of songs. No! I don't want to tell you nothing about them—those people had good voices and throwed them away. Christian folks didn't sing those kind of songs"!

Elderly Black woman to Professor John Work III, 1939

" . . . the Black man came from Africa, not Howard University."

Amiri Baraka (LeRoi Jones), 1963

When John Work stopped that matron on a North Nashville street some fifty years ago, he was looking for alternate verses to the old Negro ballad. He wasn't surprised by her response. He'd been exposed to a variety of Black middle-class opinion about assimilation and "proper" behavior. Three generations of the Work family had been members of Nashville's community of Black professionals. Though hard to imagine today, prior to World War II consensus among that community concerning the race's best interests—artistic, social, economic—was not to be found. Members were debating the merits of the back-to-Africa movement, total integration/assimilation, or an ill-defined separate—and somehow equal—Black American society.

Whatever the social directive, musical remnants of the slave culture—excepting for the music of the spiritual—were in the 1930s still largely ignored or actively suppressed. Despite her vehement denial, Work's 1939 informant obviously knew the song and what it signified; those segments of Black society which were least concerned with the Negro's social agenda in the abstract—the rural and urban poor—were in fact the curators of the history of Blacks in America: an unwritten history told in song, story, and dance. It was this culture that began to fascinate Black scholar John Work in the mid-1930s, and which led to his pioneering but largely unheralded research in the late 1930s.

For years before, the Work family had been closely identified with the spiritual. John Work II resurrected the Fisk Jubilee Singers in the mid-1890s, and by the turn of the century the official Jubilees were back in the public eye.[1] He recruited the best voices from Fisk's Mozart Society—the official name for the Glee Club and indicative of the musical emphasis desired by the University administration. Though early on they performed as a choral group, the Fisk Jubilees traveling group was usually a quartet. It was this group, with John Work II as first tenor and leader, that recorded for the Victor Company in 1909.[2]

When his son, John Work III, returned to Nashville in 1927, it was natural for him to accept a position at Fisk as Instructor of Music. He had been a student at Columbia University and the Institute of Musical Art during the Harlem Renaissance, and his student notebooks reflect a more than casual interest in New York's commercial music scene. Friends made in New York—Hall Johnson and W. C. Handy among them—remained life-long correspondents.

Upon moving to Nashville at the death of his father, John Work III assumed responsibility for the support of an extended family. Needing more income as well as more musical stimulus than that provided by teaching Fisk students theory and harmony, Professor Work ventured into two quite different musical fields. He began composing serious music, an endeavor which, he discovered, produced a nice cumulative income as the catalog grew. He also began collecting Black vernacular music, an avocation which was musically rewarding but more often than not was self-financed.[3]

By November 1935, Work had been back in Nashville for two years in his new position as assistant professor at Fisk. He had spent 1932 and 1933 at Yale on a Rosenwald scholarship, and his newly earned bachelor of music degree secured him his promotion in Fisk's music department. The time spent at Yale also seems to have stimulated his interest in the roots of Afro-American music.

In a letter dated 19 November 1935, Work's friend George Herzog wrote him:

> Glad to know more about your researches . . . especially interested in your saying that you plan, in your present work, to take up the statements of collectors who have questioned the purity of Negro folk-song. That is a question which has interested me all along. Whatever the ultimate origin, African or not, of American Negro folk-song—I personally believe little has survived from Africa, and that most of it grew on American soil—it is a distinct contribution of its own, and not a "copy" of European-American folk songs. It is here, I believe, that men of great scholarship like Guy B. Johnson and George Pullen Jackson may not see the problem in full perspective. . . . Happy to know that *you who have so much more access to the material and a more intimate acquaintance with the background are interested in a similar approach* [emphasis added]. . . . Thank you for your kind suggestions for my survey. My survey aims at listing collections of melodies. . . . Could you tell me, approximately, the number of melodies in your collection, whether collected by you personally or through other sources? Since you state that the size of the collection is such that publication of the whole is at present difficult, it is evidently a collection that ought to be made known, even though only through a reference by number of melodies. My survey will be published sometime this winter. . . . Hope it will be possible for you to make a guess at the number of your melodies so that I can refer to your collection with some accuracy.

Unfortunately, John Work didn't make carbons of his correspondence, so it is impossible to determine the size of his collection at this early date, or where it came from. It's possible he inherited some of the collection—apart from the songs published in 1915—from his father.

It's also possible that he personally collected a significant number of "melodies" in the years since his return to the South. By all accounts, Professor Work had a fine ear and could scribble a lead sheet for most folk tunes on first hearing. Four- and eight-measure music manuscript fragments in the margins of worn notebooks give evidence of this practice.

Professor Work also took advantage of the fact that Fisk in the 1930s functioned as a training ground for teachers from rural Black school districts throughout Tennessee, Alabama, and Georgia. During the summer educator's

◘ John Wesley Work III teaching students at Fisk University. Courtesy of the Fisk University Franklin Library, Special Collections.

sessions at Fisk, Work taught not only music education technique but the value of vernacular music in schools. As a result, teachers from rural schools in the South became good sources and local contacts.

In 1938, just such a source called his attention to a most unusual form of music and social custom. As Work described it in the *Musical Quarterly,* January 1941:

> My interest in this music was aroused in the summer of 1938 by Miss Ruby Ballard, supervisor of Negro Schools in Dale County, Alabama, who was in attendance at Fisk University. She described a musical activity, entirely new to me, which was deeply embedded in the culture of the section.
>
> She told how neighbors gathered in the evenings to sing; how birthdays, anniversaries, and holidays were celebrated principally in singing. Frequently music makers from the entire county gathered for a singing festival which might last from one to two days. Once a year singers from all the counties in the section would meet for two days.
>
> Early in September she wrote that the Alabama State Sacred Harp Singing Convention would meet in Ozark on the 24th and 25th of the month. Immediately I made plans to attend.

Work goes on to describe the performance practices of the shape-note singers in musically precise detail.[4] Two other visits to Sacred Harp singings are cited: the Coffee County Convention at Shiloh, Alabama, on October 2, 1938, and the Seven Shape-Note Singers' Convention at Samson, Alabama, October 22 and 23. Work neglected to mention in the *Musical Quarterly* one significant detail: He recorded the singing at a meeting at Dothan, Alabama, on November 28, 1938. It was his first effort at field recording.

Apparently Fisk owned a disc recorder—aural evidence indicates a machine in poor condition–but could not, or would not, supply Work with sufficient recording blanks. In a letter to W. D. Wetherford of Fisk's Humanities Department (November 1, 1938), Work asks for use of a car, movie equipment, and sound equipment for a Sacred Harp project. "I have already made three trips at my own expense." The self-financed field worker was beginning to search for institutional support, and was partially successful.

At least seven double-sided discs were cut at Dothan. Three are at Fisk. One was subsequently broken. The remaining six songs—"Newman," "Jubilee," "My Home Above," "Glory Shone Around," "I Love Thy Kingdom," and "Great God Attend"—are in the Library of Congress collection (AFS# 5151–5153), though they are misidentified as having been recorded during the Ozark trip.

1938 marked John Work III's first efforts at writing up the results of his private researches in "Negro Folk Music." He presented a talk under that title as a part of Fisk's annual Robinson Music Lecture Series.[5] Work addressed topics—including spirituals, blues, and instrumental music—from a solid musical, historical, and sociological foundation. In discussing the influence of tradition on audience "attitude" (a sociological term, he noted), Work revealed not only the wide range of his musical experience but a well-honed sense of irony:

> If I were to select the one singing occasion I have witnessed which received the most applause I would mention a program I attended in a large metropolitan center some nine years ago. Because of the deductions I am leading you to make, the occasion and place must remain nameless as must the performers. The occasion was highly cultural. An outstanding Negro soprano and pianist were on the program as well as our own Dr. James Weldon Johnson and an eminent professor from one of the country's largest universities. Also on this program was a Negro quartet. Nine years of constant search for an adjective to describe the singing of that quartet have provided no more fitting one than "terrible." The voices of the group were unusually poor. The harmony was of a particularly inferior grade. As an instance of this, the bass ignored a fundamental musical law observed rigidly by every musical unit—whether the bass instruments of a symphony orchestra, the bull-bass in a hill-billy band, or the bass in a barbershop quartet—that the bass must end on the tonic note. No matter how much wandering he might do in the body of the piece, he obeys the fundamental urge to end on the tonic. The bass of this quartet did not end on "do." He only wandered. He was typical of the

other members. The quartet was supposed to sing two spirituals—"Good News the Chariot's Coming" and "Steal Away to Jesus." But this quartet with all its bad harmony and voices were [sic] forced by the most tumultuous applause to sing six songs before they were allowed to leave the stage. From the standpoint of applause they easily overshadowed all other personalities on the program. The reason for all this? The tradition that America likes to see four Negroes together—singing. The audience, if you would like to know, comprised over a thousand university people!

Work's view of the distinction between authenticity and tradition was more pointed.

The Hall-Johnson Choir has established a tradition of performing the spirituals to which many influential important New Yorkers subscribe. When the Fisk Choir with its own established tradition of performing the spirituals went to New York in 1933, one of the prominent newspaper critics roundly scored it for not singing the spirituals as well and in the manner (what he meant was "tradition") of the Hall-Johnson Choir. I am perfectly sure that if the Hall-Johnson Choir were to perform in Nashville, many Nashvillians would condemn it for not singing in the Fisk tradition. And yet, if it were possible to transport a chorus from some rural church in the Deep South which could sing the spirituals in an authentic manner with the slow tempi, the ejaculatory style, and the absence of any graduations in dynamics to New York or Nashville, both places would find it uninteresting and disappointing. Authentic as it might be, it would not be traditional. This diversion into the realm of the aesthetics of the appreciation of Negro folk song merely intends to emphasize that the preponderance [sic] of interest in favor of the spiritual over the secular folk song can only be due to tradition rather than to the relative musical merits of the two types of songs.

This was a bold statement from the man whose father led the Fisk Jubilee Singers and used the phrase "paucity and utter worthlessness" in describing Negro secular song.[6]

In the same lecture, Work discussed the blues in terms that were surprisingly sophisticated for that day and time.

We have in the form of blues an unexpected phrase balance. As distinguished from orthodox forms which balance phrase by phrase, designated by the term's antecedent phrase and consequent phrase, the blues has two antecedent phrases balanced by one consequent phrase. The verse can illustrate this phrase balance easily. Let's quote from a well-known blues.

When I was home the door was never closed
When I was home the door was never closed
Where my home is now the good Lord only knows.[7]

You noticed that the second line was merely repetition. This is a feature. This repeated phrase has an important esthetic function in the form. It is definitely a tension factor making the third line, the release line, more welcome.

A few more verses will further illustrate this form as well as substantiate further my earlier description of the blues as music from sad, cynical, disillusioned souls.

> Sometimes I feel like nothing, something throwed away
> Sometimes I feel like nothing, something throwed away
> Then I get my guitar and play the blues all day.
>
> Money's all gone and I'm so far from home
> Money's all gone and I'm so far from home
> I just sit here and cry and moan.
>
> Standing here wondering will a matchbox hold my clothes
> Standing here wondering will a matchbox hold my clothes
> Got no money, got so far to go.[8]

This word structure is simple enough but the music is infinitely more complex. There are still three lines but they are each different and have a preconceived harmonic basis. Practically every blues conforms to a rigid harmonic mold. This is supplied by an accompaniment which is usually very highly embellished and highly rhythmical. In no manner must this accompaniment be considered subordinate to the singer. It is just as important. Together they form an integral whole. Actually to many the accompaniment is the more interesting. In authentic performances no written music is ever used and the accompaniment resolves itself into improvisation which, in the hands of the better instrumentalists, becomes a demonstration of genuine skill and imagination.

Professor Work's technical appreciation of the skill of blues instrumentalists was not indiscriminate. In this, as in all forms of music, he was quick to distinguish the superior performers. In a letter to Dr. W. D. Hand at the *Journal of American Folklore* (September 16, 1948), Work writes, "I have made several transcriptions of secular guitar playing as a part of a longtime study I have been making of folk rhythmic patterns." Two guitarists whose playing he undoubtedly transcribed are Muddy Waters—Work was present at Waters's first recording session in 1941—and Joe Holmes, an itinerant bluesman comparable to the best of the commercially recorded artists of the late 1930s, whom Work recorded in the field.

For most of 1939 and 1940 Work located and collected from musicians. Of the forty-one folk musicians listed in his notebooks, we have audio samples of twenty-four. Some of the musicians who didn't record yielded intriguing notes:

Thomas S. King—born Nolensville, Tennessee, in 1885. Lived in Nashville 38 years. 2nd Ave.—2nd house back of H. G. Hills. Learned banjo from Ida Redd. Self taught on fiddle—41 years. Saw Eph Grissom lynched in 1898.

John Carter—born near Murfreesboro [Tennessee]—1864. Farmer. Learned to play from his brother.

John Work was trying to find the authentic secular music of the first post-Emancipation generation—a generation whose music should be indistinguishable from that of the slave. It was not an easy hunt. Again from the 1938 Robinson lecture:

> This [instrumental] music was produced by small groups—from one player with a guitar, mandolin, piano and other less orthodox instruments. You will notice I did not mention banjos. In many of Dunbar's poems he mentions the banjo player. Stephen Foster mentions the banjo in his songs. Traditionally the banjo is considered a Negro instrument. But outside of the recognized jazz band, I personally have never seen a Negro banjo player. They undoubtedly do exist and these old songs and poems seem to indicate they were quite popular many years ago. But at least not in this vicinity, and in the other communities I have visited the banjo player is rare.

Some time between the autumn of 1938 and winter of 1940–41 John Work found Nathan "Ned" Frazier, "banjoist deluxe." Frazier was a remarkable player. Apparently a popular Nashville street musician in the 1930s, Frazier played a repertoire of minstrel songs ("Old Dan Tucker"), breakdowns ("Boil Them Cabbage Down"), and blues ("Corrina, Corrina")—all with the sweetest tone and liveliest rhythm. Similarity of style between Ned Frazier and White banjoist Uncle Dave Macon tends to support stories of a widespread Black banjo style in Middle Tennessee, which Macon had tapped in the early part of the century. A meeting of those two on a Nashville street corner has a certain speculative fascination.

By the end of 1940 John Work, using the borrowed disc recorder and Montgomery Ward recording blanks, was on his way to building a private collection of recorded Negro folk music. Call-and-response singing at a folk church in Pulaski, Tennessee; a South Carolina convict singing a work song; the Alabama Sacred Harp; Jesse James "Preacher" Jefferson playing blues on the harmonica—these were the start of the collection Work envisioned.

Realizing that a large folk music study could not be financed by an assistant professor of music—just borrowing a car to attend some local gathering was often difficult—John Work again sought to enlist the Fisk administration in his cause. In a letter to Fisk president Thomas E. Jones (June 21, 1940), Work suggested a complete folk music study at Natchez, Mississippi. The selection of Natchez was based on an unfortunate event in April 1939, when over two hundred Negroes were killed in a fire at a recreation hall in that town. As John Work stated in his proposal to Dr. Jones:

> To the abundance of folklore natural to the community, a new body of lore is due to be added. It is the ballads and music arising out of the holocaust of last April. . . . The impact of this terrible fire with its religious implications on the minds and imagination of the unlettered Negroes of that region must of necessity be of such weight as to stimulate the creation of a tremendous amount of folk expression.

President Jones discussed this idea with Harold Schmidt, chairman of the Music Department, and Charles S. Johnson, famed head of Fisk's Social Sciences Department. Schmidt had often spoken of a research branch for the music department. Dr. Johnson was also in favor of an intensive study within a limited territory; he encouraged Work to include folk tales, religious practices, foodways, and occupational lore with the music study.

So it was that on June 29, 1940, President Jones wrote to Jackson Davis of the General Education Board, New York:

> I am submitting herewith an appeal for a special grant to enable Mr. John W. Work, of Fisk University, to pursue studies on the Negro folk ballads in Natchez, Mississippi, and selected areas in the South.
>
> Mr. Work is the son of the famous John W. Work who published one of the first volumes of Negro spirituals and directed the Fisk Jubilee Singers for many years. John Work, Jr., was composing such as "The Tennessee Lullaby" and arranging Negro spirituals while he was yet in his teens. . . . He has published many choral numbers and arrangements of spirituals. He has just had accepted for publication by Simon, Howell, & Co., a volume entitled "Negro Folk Music" which will be off the press in October.

The book that came off the press in 1940 as *American Negro Songs and Spirituals* is a collection of 230 folk songs, religious and secular. The songs, which are printed from hand-lettered music manuscript, are mostly spirituals. Of these, most are in current use in Black churches and among professional quartets. Of some special interest are a few that have become standards in the bluegrass/country music repertoire. "I Want to be Ready" in the Work collection is identical to Bill Monroe's "Walking in Jerusalem Just Like John." Monroe says:

> Where I got this song was down in Norwood, North Carolina. I was visiting some friends of mine and they knew these colored folks, you know, and they had been fans of mine. They had this number "Walking

in Jerusalem Just Like John" and wanted me to learn it and record it. I went by these people's house and I talked to this man; I believe that maybe he was a preacher . . . it's been so long ago, but anyway he wanted me to record it and sing it on the Grand Old Opry. They sang it for me there kind of like the way I sing it.[9]

Problematic as is Monroe's account of his source's motivation for teaching him the song, Monroe has readily acknowledged the influence of Blacks on his music. However,

I believe I heard the Carter Family sing that song ["I'm Working on a Building"], and we got requests for it on our show dates and I thought that I should learn it. It's a holiness number I would say. You know there's holiness singing in my music, bluegrass music.[10]

Monroe's ear is not wrong. "Working on the Building," as the song is titled in Work's collection, is often sung in Holiness (Pentecostal) churches, Black and White; yet the composer's credit on Monroe's recording of the song lists A. P. Carter. One can assume that Carter copyrighted the song as his own just as Monroe did with "Walking in Jerusalem," which had been in print more than ten years before Monroe recorded it. Several other of the spirituals in the Work collection are easily recognized as songs in the hillbilly and bluegrass repertoire. It remains for a diligent researcher to trace the entry points for these.

Among the secular songs are three versions of "John Henry." Two are variants similar to John Hurt's "Spike Driver Blues," and the third is the version commonly identified as "John Henry" today. Another secular song of interest is "Goin' Keep My Skillet Greasy." Its appearance in Work's book seems to be the first publication for this song which is also known as "Keep My Skillet Good and Greasy" and was one of the more popular songs in Uncle Dave Macon's repertoire.

In addition to the song collection, *American Negro Songs and Spirituals* also contains a lengthy foreword covering the origins of the spiritual, the blues, the work song, and social songs. Except for the discussion of the origins, most of this foreword is a rewrite of material presented at the 1938 Robinson lecture. The section on origins centers on the spiritual and is a polite refutation of the position taken by Pullen Jackson and Newman White. Work's argument is telling as he cites Jackson's reliance on text similarities in hymns and spirituals.

These similarities have confused most collectors of American Negro folksong, but before they can be accepted as conclusive evidence that the Negro spiritual is an imitation of the White gospel song, several important factors must be considered. Among them are the Afro-American creative folkgenius, and the distinction between "imitation" and "reassembling."

In Africa native scales were purely melodic in their concept and were composed of tones which lacked the distinct character of rest or restlessness. There is no dispute over the fact that the Africans discarded these scales when they were introduced to the new country. But the substitution of scales and tonality can hardly be construed as imitation, especially when we attach to the term "imitation" its usual connotation. It is, rather, an *incorporation of free material for a distinctive use* [emphasis added].

In his letter of June 29, 1940, to the General Education Board requesting the Natchez Grant for Work, Fisk president Thomas Jones noted:

It has already become evident that such a study would be of much interest to the Library of Congress, to John and Allen [sic] Lomax, and to others who have been working in this field. Exchanges of material, comparison of recordings and general collaboration between Fisk University and the Library of Congress have already been agreed upon in case the project can be carried out. In celebrating the 75th Anniversary of the founding of Fisk University, from May 1st through 8th, 1941, it is hoped to present, together with other American music, Negro ballads as they are being created today.

In spite of this appeal, the General Education Board declined to fund the Natchez study. John Work continued teaching Fisk undergraduates theory and harmony and collecting Black vernacular music when and how he could.

An opportunity of a different sort presented itself in March 1941. That month Fort Valley State College at Fort Valley, Georgia, had its second annual folk festival. Twenty-five miles southwest of Macon and just one hundred miles east of the Alabama line at Tuskeegee, Fort Valley sits in the Black belt of counties which runs from Alabama, up through Georgia, and into South Carolina. An outgrowth of the traditional Spring Sing, which tended toward light classical chorale, the Fort Valley Folk Festival was equal parts folk and folklorists.

Festival director Linton Berrien offered cash prizes to the best string band ($10/1st place, $5/2nd), banjo, guitar, harmonica, and fiddle ($7.50/1st, $5/2nd, $2.50/3rd), and a special $5.00 prize for the best novelty instrument. The turnout of musicians must have been quite good; the guitar contest on Friday evening boasted ten entrants who had survived the even larger elimination round. Similarly, Sunday's program was made up of a "Singing Rally of Spiritual Songs"—church quartets and choral groups vying for cash donations to rural and city churches in Peach, Crawford, Bibb, Houston, and Macon counties. With such a gathering of singers and musicians—folks—it was fitting that the contest judges were for the most part folklorists. Willis James from Spelman, Sterling Brown of Howard University, and William Faulkner from Fisk, among others, were given a rare opportunity to study a broad range of Black folk styles from eastern Alabama and western Georgia.

John Work was at the 1941 festival, disc recorder in tow. While there he recorded forty-one selections by thirteen artists. The evidence indicates that Work financed this field trip himself. He traveled to and from in Dean Faulkner's car and the relatively few discs expended (thirteen) on the forty-one selections suggest an extremely economical approach. In addition, recordings made with blanks purchased with his own money he considered part of his personal collection; the Fort Valley recordings were donated to the Library of Congress at the same time as some Nashville recordings known to be from his personal collection.[11]

While John Work was at Fort Valley in early March 1941, Fisk administrators in Nashville were setting the schedule of events for Fisk's seventy-fifth anniversary celebration in May. From the first, President Jones, Dr. Johnson, Dean Faulkner, Professor Schmidt, et al. planned folk music programs as an integral display of Afro-American culture as nurtured by Fisk. The same phenomenon of nationalism and ethnic pride which gave birth to the Fort Valley festival—as well as Gertrude Knott's National Folk Festival, and the Library of Congress' folk-song collecting projects—made it acceptable for a normally stodgy Fisk to present on campus for the first time the music and stories of the Black underclass. To be sure, an academic veneer was carefully applied.

Minutes of the Anniversary Committee meeting of March 4 record a resolution to acquire the services of the Golden Gate Quartet. The report also notes that "Paul Robeson has prior commitments and can't attend but Alan Lomax is available and requires a fee to be negotiated with his manager." Ten days later in a letter to Dean Taylor, Charles S. Johnson reports that CBS will allow the Golden Gate Quartet to sing at Fisk. "CBS will pay the group's weekly salary of $2500.00, but Fisk must pay transportation from New York." So on Tuesday, April 29, 1941, Josh White and the Golden Gates performed at Fisk's Memorial Chapel. Emceeing the event were Alan Lomax and poet Sterling Brown.

In addition to the Tuesday evening program with the nationally known artists mentioned, a Friday afternoon program was authorized using local folk artists. Professor Work was given the responsibility for this. The program as originally projected was to feature the Sacred Harp from Alabama—the group Work had recorded in 1938—and William Faulkner telling the folk tales for which he had some reputation. A note to John Work a month before the celebration asks him to ask Mr. [Thomas] Talley to participate with Mr. Faulkner in the folklore portion of the program.

By the middle of April, the Friday program was set. The shape-note singers had been dropped—travel expenses were too high, most likely—and seven Nashville-area singers and musicians had been added, all in their own way as remarkable as the Sacred Harpers from Alabama.

In his introductory lecture at the program, Work said:

The despair of the folklorist arises over the necessity of his exhibiting and studying contemporary folk songs only. First because his interest in the lore began late in his career and thus the older lore had largely vanished by the time he had begun his investigations, and second because recording instruments are recent inventions and have become available far too late to catch the lore of 30 or 40 years ago. The best the folklorist can hope for today is to find occasional melodies of the old vintage written down and to have the playing of them described by the older folk. He realizes that he probably will have only the faintest idea of the real style of the older music.

We are very happy here at Fisk University to present to you an instrumental ensemble which plays the music of 40 or more years ago. The tunes you will hear played by these men are those Mr. Frank Patterson has been playing for 40 or more years and were handed down by the player who taught him. This ensemble is the answer to a folklorist's dream. I feel apologetic for having so little time to say the things needed to be said about this combine. They easily offer the opportunity and material for an entire lecture alone.

It does seem important to take a few more minutes to describe the individual functions of these instruments in the ensemble. The fiddle is the principal carrier of the melody with its many possible variants which are always idiomatic. The banjo has several subordinate functions. It may reinforce the melody, it may embellish the harmony, it may accentuate the rhythm, or it may perform all three functions simultaneously as you will observe in the playing of Mr. Nathan Frazier, Banjoist de Luxe.

Aside from supplying rhythmic support of minor importance, the sole function of the guitar is to provide the harmony. This is done with several harmonic formulas in the possession of the player to which the melodies must conform. Folk song is largely a matter of melody growing out of harmonic molds. And so every melody which Mr. Frank Patterson will play will belong to a harmonic mold known by Mr. Ford Britton, the guitar player. Many songs may fit one harmonic mold or formula.

Mr. Patterson's repertory is so large, he plays so many songs in such rapid succession with such speed that he usually wears down two, three or more guitar players a sitting.

Last night Nathan Frazier was complaining that guitar players were so soft that he could not find guitar players who could keep up with him. He usually wears them all down and so ends up playing by himself.

Imagine poor Ford Britton's unlucky plight being asked to play between such guitar exhausters as Frank Patterson and Nathan Frazier. At this time the group will play four songs of their own choice, each of which is of 19th Century vintage and might be antebellum songs. I am hoping Mr. Frazier will sing.

Ned Frazier was a superlative banjoist and singer. That Professor Work, an accomplished musician himself, should recognize Frazier's technical expertise is not surprising. Whether Frazier and fiddler Frank Patterson had worked as a duet before Work recorded them as such in 1941 is not known. Nashville resident octogenarian Wesley Copeland knew both men: Mr. Copeland grew up on the sharecrop farm in Antioch, Tennessee, next to Frank Patterson's. "Mr. Frank," Wesley, and Wesley's father played for dances in the area during the second decade of this century. In the 1920s Wesley moved to Nashville and began playing blues as a solo. In Nashville he came to know Ned Frazier, whom he describes as "a pretty good feller, a pretty straight feller. Ned acted like a monkey all the time. [He'd play the banjo] anywhere . . . on the street, anywhere you stopped him. I know every time I seen him he had that banjo. Wherever he was at he had that banjo." Wesley Copeland has no recollection of Frazier working with Patterson as a fiddle-banjo team.

Critical listening to the thirteen selections by Frazier and Patterson in the Library of Congress collection (AFS# 6679, 6680, 6682) tends to contradict Mr. Copeland's recollection. Ten of the thirteen tunes are fiddle and banjo duets; the shared stylistic values indicate a musical association of more than a few days. Of the ten shared tunes, six are common fiddler's repertoire—White and Black.[12]

"I Would if I Could" (titled "I Would but I Couldn't" in Work's notes), "The Old Cow Died," and "My Journey Home" are not common; at least, there appear to be no other recorded examples of these. "Texas Traveler" has the same melody as "Old Dubuque," a well-known tune—yet Frazier's idiosyncratic delivery of the lyric makes this version unique. The remaining three songs of the Frazier/Patterson recordings donated by Work to the Library of Congress in the summer of 1942 are songs with banjo accompaniment by Ned Frazier. "Bile Them Cabbage Down," "Old Dan Tucker," and "Corrina, Corrina" are in the minstrel style, with Ned Frazier "acting like a monkey."

Of special interest is a fourteenth tune, "Giles County," recorded by Frazier and Patterson but apparently not given to the Library of Congress. The title appears on a list in Professor Work's notebook but does not show in the LC's Archive of American Folk Song. Nor is the disc among Work's personal recordings. The tune "Giles County" is on a field recording made by Tennessee folklorist Robert Cogswell at the VA hospital in Nashville in 1974. Black Fiddler Walter Grier played the tune but did not indicate where he learned it. Grier was from Walter Hill, Tennessee, birthplace of fiddler Frank Patterson.

In addition to Nathan Frazier, Frank Patterson, and Ford Britton (who recorded four sides with Fiddler Dave Merritt for the Work collection—unremarkable performances of "Old Joe," "Billy in the Lowground," "Old Joe" reprised, and a blues),[13] Professor Work also brought a local group, the Heavenly Gate Quartet, to sing at the Fisk celebration. William Leftwich, Leroy Smith,

Woodrow Campbell, and Charles Wilson were in their late teens and early twenties in 1941. Singing in Nashville churches as the United Gospel Singers and the Zion Spiritual Singers, they became the Heavenly Gate Quartet shortly before meeting John Work. In the words of William Leftwich:

> We was singing one Sunday evening at a church and a fella named William Gilcrease heard the group sing. He was a barber. John Work went to his barber shop and he was telling John Work about our group. John Work said he would like to hear the group sing. We made an appointment and went to see John Work one Sunday afternoon . . . and he listened to us sing. And he liked the way we sang and our arrangements and everything. Then we made an agreement that he would supervise us and would train us.
>
> We met Mr. Lomax and the Golden Gate Quartet that [Tuesday] night at Professor Work's house . . . after the concert. They had us to sing a couple of numbers at the house. They were surprised. They liked it. We sang "Traveling Shoes" and, I think, "John the Revelator." Those two Professor Work liked. Now those were their [Golden Gate Quartet's] own arrangement . . . but John Work told us that we sang those better than the Golden Gate did. That's what John Work said.

At the Friday afternoon program the Heavenly Gates sang those same two songs. From Work's introductory remarks:

> The quartet does not have the long tradition in folk music as the instrumental combinations. But while much more recent it is just as genuine in its folk-ness. It is interesting to observe the evolution of the styles of performance by folk quartets. Their first emphasis was on harmony. They loved chromatic chords. You all remember the barbershop chords and "snakes" of the earlier part of the century. Next came the exploitation of the narrative type of spiritual with its parlando style. This style featured a long rehearsal of the events in a Biblical hero's life. You all remember the song "My Soul is a Witness." The present day quartet has absorbed the present day emphasis on rhythm and has fused it with the narrative style of spiritual. The performance of the Golden Gate Quartet was the epitome of such style. Folk instrumental combinations are made up of players who were attracted to each other by their mutual respect for their playing skill. The singers in a quartet are generally assembled by friendship and leisure. We will listen now to a group of friends in a quartet who sing pure Negro folk music.

In the spring of 1941 John Work recorded the Heavenly Gate Quartet at his house—two takes of "If I Had My Way" and one each of "Got on My Traveling Shoes" and "John the Revelator." These spirituals are in the LC collection

(AFS# 5163–64) as by an unidentified quartet and are mixed with the Work recordings from the Fort Valley Festival.

Audition of the performances of the Heavenly Gates reveals an excellent quartet in the "hot rhythm style" popularized by the Golden Gate Quartet. The similarity of names is probably no accident. John Work's knowledge of the Golden Gates' earning power—commercial recordings, network radio, personal appearances—must be granted. It's probable that Professor Work had a business arrangement in mind when he agreed to train the Heavenly Gates. "He was trying to get us to get arrangements of our own. You can make professional on that. You can not get professional on somebody else's arrangements."[14]

Given John Work's large financial obligations—he supported an extended family as well as his own research and composition expenses—it's likely that the opportunity to be an arranger/musical director for a commercial quartet would have appeal to him.

Unfortunately two members of the group were drafted later that year. "We didn't do much good after that . . . it broke up the quartet," remembered Leftwich.

The spring celebration of Fisk's seventy-fifth anniversary brought more than folk music to the campus for the first time. Alan Lomax had been an admirer of Charles S. Johnson, who had done some important studies of Negro housing patterns in the 1930s. Lomax proposed a joint study of a large Negro commercial center. After some discussion, Coahoma County, Mississippi, and its county seat, Clarksdale, were chosen.

Dr. Johnson selected Lewis Jones, an assistant professor in the Social Sciences Department, as Fisk's representative for the Coahoma Study Project. Lomax represented the Library of Congress and provided technical services— the LC's sound truck, plenty of record blanks, and needles. By July 1941, a year after John Work applied for a grant for the Natchez study, plans for the Coahoma study were set. Various Fisk faculty members were to spend portions of the summer in Clarksdale with Lomax doing the fieldwork. John Work was given the task of transcribing music from the field recordings—in his spare time at Fisk.

Lomax, however, had spoken to his superiors at the Library of Congress about Work. With their approval he proposed that Work collect folk songs in the Nashville area with Library of Congress support. Record blanks of any quality were getting hard to find due to war-related interruptions of raw material supplies; when available, quality varied greatly from disc to disc. Compounding such problems was Fisk's recorder. Lomax, from the start, expressed concern that the recorder was not in good working condition. Whether Work had played some of his private recordings for Lomax in April or merely stated some misgivings of his own, Lomax offered the repair services of the Library of Congress' Recording Laboratory. Lomax urged Work to send some of his personal recordings to the LC so the technicians could determine by listening if the recorder was working properly. A rather roundabout way of checking potentially faulty hardware, or so it seemed to Professor Work. He balked. Lomax assured him that the LC would give Work complete credit for any donations to the LC collection and would return duplicate recordings of such donations.

By the end of August 1941, a compromise of sorts had been worked out. Work sent twenty discs from his private collection for deposit—the Fort Valley recordings, Heavenly Gate and Holloway High School Quartet discs, and Alabama Sacred Harp sides among them. Apparently no duplicates were returned to John Work. Presumably the Fisk recorder was given a tune up, for subsequent recordings were of better quality. Alan Lomax did ship two boxes (twenty-five each) of blank discs to Work in the last week of the month. The 12" Presto glass-based discs used by the LC were a great improvement over the 10" Record-O-Disc and Audio-Disc blanks Work had been buying.

On August 28, 1941, Work again wrote Fisk President, Thomas E. Jones:

> I am very happy over your recent letter stating your favor toward the folk-lore projects in which I have long wanted to engage. I am eager to begin work upon some of these immediately which I believe will have much cultural value to the University.
>
> These projects fall into two categories. The first would be concerned with visiting nearby communities to record and study unique or interesting folk activities; i.e. camp meetings, revivals, barn dances, fiddler's meets, etc. Some of the more important of these are annual and have a lengthy history.
>
> The second category of projects would be concerned with interviewing creative individuals in the various communities and recording their songs. In our own city there is a Negro banjo player who is most unusual. I doubt if his style of playing and skill could be easily duplicated. His vast repertoire of secular folk songs should be placed in our archives, both on phonographic record and on paper. There is a famous Negro character in Pulaski, Tennessee, who is a sort of newspaper, chronicling the news events of the day in verse and song which he sings to the populace on the public square at frequent intervals.
>
> These are only two of a considerable number of such individuals that I would like to interview and record and, on occasion, bring to the campus. Most of these men eke out a living from their music and either demand money for their performances, or, if not demanding money, perform better when paid.

This is a pretty good definition of professionals—they perform better when paid. Work's interest in folk music, as should be clear by now, was not exclusively in repertoire. Most of the fieldworkers at that time were self-styled "song hunters." Work was a musician and his primary interest was performance and style.

Folk *songs* could be collected from anyone, but Work searched for the best exemplars of the various folk *styles*. Professionals—not to the same degree that jazz violinist Stuff Smith was a professional—but professionals nonetheless.

Work's earlier self-financed recording efforts wasted very little acetate on inferior performers. His practice of recording alternate takes of the same tune also indicates a stronger interest in performance than repertoire. His notebooks contain comments about the musicians which support this view: "Fairly good," "style of playing old fashioned and not very interesting," "entertaining type of player," "exceptionally good." Rarely does he comment on the material performed.

That he was aware of his unique qualifications for this work is indicated by this excerpt from the Fisk Anniversary program.

> Folklore belongs entirely to no special branch of science. Surely it is accurate and dependable sociology, but it is just as important in the field of anthropology. Strangely some of the most scholarly and comprehensive studies on American folk song have been written by students of English. More strange than this, however, is the fact that musicians themselves have rather avoided the field.

Even his definition of a folk song is stated in musical rather than sociological terms: "A folk song is any song which embrasing [*sic*] a consistent folk form, making use of common and traditional rhythmic and melodic idioms can be immediately identified with a race or a community, section or country."

By August 1941, the Coahoma Project had begun. On August 28, Work left Nashville to join Lomax, Lewis Jones, and a Mr. Ross (of Fisk's Drama Department) in Clarksdale, Mississippi. Lomax had been in the Delta scouting for talent and had found a local bluesman called Muddy Water—a *nom-de-guitar* which was pluralized later. John Work's only field trip with the project would have him in Mississippi for the first recording session made by this most important musician. In addition to the songs recorded at Water's cabin near Clarksdale are two interviews with the singer—one conducted by Lomax, one by Work. The contrast in interview style and areas of interest between the interviewers is more significant than the information extracted from the subject.

Work returned to his teaching duties at Fisk in the middle of September. To facilitate his work as a member of the Coahoma support team, he secured space in the Social Sciences building, recruited a student assistant (Mr. Harry Wheeler), and began the labor of transcribing the sixteen recorded discs that the summer expedition had produced. On those recordings are twenty spirituals, two blues, and a prayer and sermon by the Rev. C. H. Savage of Mt. Ararat Church. He later wrote Thomas Jones:

> In transcribing the spirituals I made an earnest effort to transcribe the songs just as they were sung—not as I thought they ought to be sung. Even

where there were obvious errors in the singing I transcribed them, in my effort to record these songs accurately. This has resulted in rather long transcriptions, necessary to record the many variations of the song.

A tremendously important folk expression is the old Negro folk-sermon. Very regrettably it is fast disappearing—never to return. Many folklorists have recognized the charm of these but while a few may have been recorded I doubt if one has been transcribed. Because of this, persons unfamiliar with these sermons have remained almost entirely ignorant of their nature. James Weldon Johnson caught some of their charm when he wrote "God's Trombone." The most significant thing about these is the fact that he recognized that these sermons were poems.

It is more important, however, to recognize that these sermon-poems are intoned. And the audience's response to these is due more to the preacher's tone and the pitch than to the words. Therefore I point with a great deal of pride to our transcription in musical notes of the folk sermon recorded at the Mt. Ararat church. To do this accurately and comprehensively required practically all of three weeks.

In February 1942, John Work was to be a judge at the annual Fort Valley Folk Festival. At Alan Lomax's request he agreed to record the event for the Library of Congress.

> This trip was taken upon the insistence of Mr. Lomax who in a long distance telephone call and a letter promised me all expenses. Having no car I was forced to carry the heavy recording machine and microphone by train and express the box of discs [leftover from the previous year]. Unfortunately the discs did not arrive in time for the programs with the regrettable result that I had no recordings to report to Mr. Lomax. But I did incur expenses to the extent of about $20.00. Although I sent receipts for all expenditures, the Library of Congress has not yet honored the expense account. (Letter to Thos. Jones, 21 November 1942)

Lomax, Lewis Jones, and other Fiskites spent the summer of 1942 in Mississippi recording 196 selections of folk material. By the time the duplicates were made for transcription, Work's assistant, Harry Wheeler, had enlisted in the Navy. World War II was bringing to a standstill a most ambitious undertaking. Professor Work could not find another student assistant as trustworthy as Wheeler and the transcription process slowed to a crawl. Lewis Jones was drafted later that year, removing the sociologist from the team; Lomax himself left the Library of Congress shortly thereafter, effectively ending the project without a summary of the two years' work.

On August 20, 1942, John Work turned over to Alan Lomax the Nashville-area recordings made with the LC-supplied blank discs. AFS# 6678–6690 contain the Frazier and Patterson and Britton and Merritt sides as well as hymns by Bessemer Bradley, the "Dry Bones in the Valley" sermon given every October by the Reverend Stratton of Nashville, and the first recording of Sam McCrary and the Fairfield Four singing "Don't Let Nobody Turn You Round."

Of the approximately 230 recordings made in Mississippi and duplicated for Fisk, less than a dozen remain at the Fisk library. The fate of the missing discs is a mystery. One of Professor Work's students mentions a "housecleaning" of the music department in the 1950s when "old records" were thrown out. John Work's personal recordings were well taken care of at his home, and after his death his widow Edith took great care to preserve his effects. To her we owe gratitude.

This is the end of the story—not John Work's story, for he went on to study Haitian music after the war, compose many fine choral and piano works, and lead the Fisk Jubilee Singers throughout the 1950s—but the end of the story of a nation committed to gathering the history of its most reluctant citizens, the African Americans. Never again would the combination of Depression-inspired federal programs and nationalistic fervor permit the collection of Black folklore on such a scale. Should such a confluence of circumstance occur again, the work could not be resumed, for the stream is dry.

Shortly after beginning the research for this project in March 1988 I realized I was going to be finding more than some "lost" field recordings. As a musician I was well aware that there were qualitative differences between Louis Armstrong's playing and Harry James's—even musicians of the same race, Bill Monroe and Ralph Stanley in the bluegrass genre, didn't inform their music with the same emphasis. That Monroe was exposed to the music of Blacks in western Kentucky while Stanley learned to play in the Anglo-American stronghold of Virginia's Clinch Mountains was the sort of pat answer which answers nothing. Why does Monroe's singing touch deeper emotions? Why does a single sustained note from Armstrong's horn convey more about what it is to be human than an entire eighth-note chorus by James? What made John Work's efforts particularly important was his acute bias in favor of musical values—style and performance—and his de-emphasis of the sociological veneer so popular during his time.

Ten months of examining John Work's thoughts, attitudes, and opinions produced a musical epiphany for me. Unfortunately, as with most expression of personal revelation, language is inadequate: One might as well try to send a kiss by messenger.

Notes

1. Though there had been groups performing under the name since the successful Fisk-sponsored tours of the 1870s, these later groups were not composed of students, nor were they sanctioned by Fisk.
2. For an excellent account of the Work family in Nashville, I refer the reader to Doug Seroff's booklet *Gospel Arts Day—Nashville—A Special Commemoration*, June 19, 1988.
3. It's hard to miss his father's influence here. John Work II had published (*New Jubilee Songs as Sung by the Fisk Jubilee Singers* 1901) and *Folk Songs of the American Negro* (1915). In addition, John Work II co-owned with Frederick Work a profitable music publishing company.
4. James Bryan and I visited the Sacred Harp meeting at Dozier, Alabama, on September 24 and 25, 1988—fifty years to the day after John Work. Remarkable as is the longevity of this musical gathering—Work put on the first annual Henry County Convention in 1880—I was struck by the utterly apt emphasis given its communal and recreational aspects by Professor Work. Since the youngest participants at the 1988 convention appeared to be in their sixties, one can guess that the post–World War II generations have found other social outlets.
5. Work also spoke at the 1939 series. His topic was French popular song.
6. *Folk Songs of the American Negro*, Chapter 3 (Fisk University Press, 1915).
7. "I'm Going Back Home," Memphis Minnie, Victor 23352.
8. This particular verse also appears on the commercial record "Matchbox Blues," Blind Lemon Jefferson, Paramount 12474.
9. Interview with Bill Monroe by Alice Foster and Hazel Dickens, September 1968.
10. Ibid.
11. AFS# 5147–5167 were donated in September 1941, not March 1942 as indicated by the Library of Congress. Some of Work's recordings have been reissued on LP, especially on the Flyright-Matchbox Library of Congress series (SDM 250, *Ft. Valley Blues*, 1973, o.p.). See also Pete Lowry and Bruce Bastin, "Ft. Valley Blues," *Blues Unlimited*, No. 111 (December 1974), 11–13, and Bruce Bastin, "Ft. Valley Blues Part 2," *Blues Unlimited*, No. 112 (March 1975), 13–16.
12. A selection of the Patterson-Frazier discs will be issued commercially by Rounder Records in spring 1989 under the tentative title *Altamont*.
13. AFS# 6678 and 6681.
14. Interview with William Leftwich, Nashville, Tenn., May 16, 1988.

J.W. and Don Gallagher, Master Guitar Craftsmen
[1978]

David J. Brown

Tennessee has a tradition of fine craftsmen that stretches back to the earliest days of the state. Residents of Greene and Sumner counties have produced fine furniture for many years, while the magnificent homes of Williamson, Maury, Rutherford, and Davidson counties speak of the skill of their builders. Tennesseans have also had a love for music that spans two centuries and that encompasses both Appalachian hill music and the Mississippi blues of Memphis. It is appropriate, therefore, that these two traditions meet as they have in the guitar shop of J. W. and Don Gallagher of Wartrace, Tennessee. Here one can find a pride in craftsmanship and a love for music seldom seen in today's mass-production world.

In the state's earliest days, many musicians developed their talent on home-made instruments such as the old cigar-box fiddle. As the fields of bluegrass and folk music grew, however, cults developed around certain instruments. If one played the banjo or mandolin, he was expected to own a Gibson, while Martins were the accepted brand of guitar. Only with the recent increase in the number of quality luthiers has this domination of the instrument field by these companies been broken.

It was back in 1965 that the guitar-making bug bit J. W. Gallagher. He had been working at a plant in Shelbyville turning out what he described as "the worse made guitars in the world." The company stopped production after a year and a half, but Mr. Gallagher had decided he could do better. Back in

Wartrace, he converted his cabinet-making business into a guitar shop and began work on the prototype for his G-50 model, so named "because my initial was G and I was 50 years old." After four years of changes and experimentation, Mr. Gallagher finally arrived at the form that he continues to use today.

The Gallagher guitar line has expanded from the original G-50 type to a total of fourteen models that range in price from $510 to $1,500. They currently make seven dreadnaught (very large) guitars, from the G-45 to the G-72S model, that come with rosewood or mahogany backs. These guitars, which are the type used by bluegrass and country musicians, have fourteen-fret necks, a twenty-inch body length, and require steel strings. Their line also includes three twelve-string models; two folk models with wider, twelve-fret necks and longer bodies; and two auditorium- or concert-size guitars with twelve-fret necks and smaller body depth and width, which makes them excellent finger-picking style guitars. The Gallaghers still maintain strict quality control, however, producing approximately one hundred guitars each year.

The fame of the Gallagher guitar has spread around the world in the thirteen short years J. W. has been in business. Such respected musicians as Randy and Steve Scruggs, Ramblin' Jack Elliot, Johnny Cash, Grandpa Jones, and Peter Yarrow own Gallaghers.

Perhaps the best-known figures that play Gallaghers, and the people J. W. feels have done the most to help spread the word about his guitars, are the blind singer/guitarist from North Carolina, Doc Watson, and his son Merle. Doc and Merle have purchased eight guitars from the Gallaghers through the years, and Mr. Gallagher delights in telling stories about his dealings with the Watsons. They first met in 1967 at the Union Grove Fiddler's Contest. Mr. Gallagher recognized Doc's picking (he had heard the *Southbound* album) and introduced himself. Doc invited him out to dinner the next day, and at that time decided he wanted a G-50. Merle later ordered a G-45, and Doc purchased a rosewood-backed G-70.

The friendship between the musicians and craftsmen is one that has grown through the years, typified by Doc's famous endorsement to Merle Travis on the *Will the Circle Be Unbroken* album. (On this 1972 landmark album, with many of the giants of country and bluegrass music, along with the Nitty Gritty Dirt Band, Merle comments that Doc's guitar "rings like a bell." Doc replies, "It's a pretty good little box. A Mr. Gallagher made this thing—lives down near Wartrace, Tennessee.")

After taking up an interest in slide guitar, Merle asked for the first of three modified guitars that the Watsons have ordered. Mr. Gallagher built his first cutaway guitar and his first classical guitar for Merle. The cutaway body, where a section of the body below the neck is taken out to allow easier access to the higher frets, is now available on any model guitar.

About two years ago, Doc asked for a custom-built guitar with special modifications. It has now been added to the Gallagher line as the "Doc Watson" model. When I interviewed the Gallaghers at their shop in Wartrace on January 14, 1978, Don Gallagher explained the modifications:

> The guitar we started making and call the "Doc Watson" model did have specific things that he asked for, which in a way was kind of like variations off a G-50. Instead of a rosewood fingerboard, it had an ebony fingerboard. Instead of it being the same shaped neck, it was a slightly different shaped neck which he requested. We also grade the wood a little differently for the tops, in that it has a cross-hatch in the grain as well as a good, tight grain which is something he asked for—the cross-hatch.

J.W. continued by explaining that the frets on the "Doc Watson" are also different.

BROWN—What's the difference in the frets on the "Doc Watson" model and your other guitars?

J.W.—It has a larger fret.

BROWN—"Larger" meaning higher or wider?

J.W.—Both. It's a wider fret and it's also higher when it's put in, but we take an oilstone and grind it down quite a bit to reduce some of that height. It's designed for fast action, and that's the one thing that Doc specified, particularly the neck and the size of the frets. He wanted a large fret.

BROWN—Does he seem happy with it as far as his finger-picking goes?

J.W.—He's very happy with it. This neck, you'll notice, is a little flatter on the back than a regular model.

BROWN —And that was something he specified?

J.W.—Yes, he thought it would give him a faster action. I told him I hadn't noticed him having any problem that way! (Laughter). Anything that I've seen him play, he seems to get around on pretty good.

The first time J. W. Gallagher saw the Watsons after making Doc the guitar was at the National Flat-Picking Championships in Winfield, Kansas. He relates that Merle told him he'd "outdone himself this time. Doc plays that guitar all the time, and I think he even takes it to bed with him."

Though J. W. still spends a lot of time at the shop, most of the work is now directed by Don. These guitar craftsmen, spanning two generations, took me through their shop, where we talked about design, the guitar-making process, and a great deal more.

During the interview the Gallaghers frequently returned to expand on earlier points or statements. I took the liberty, therefore, of editing the interview so that the guitar-making process is fully explained in the proper sequence. In the following transcript, J. W. Gallagher is identified as "J.W.," Don Gallagher as "Don," and the interviewer as "Brown."

BROWN—How long have you been working down here at the shop?

DON—The first time I worked in the shop was back when I was just a kid. I really grew up working in the shop. Back in '65, when we started making guitars on a full-time basis, I was working summers. I went to MTSU in the fall of '67, and was there in the year of '67–68. And then I joined the reserves and that summer I was gone four months for active duty, and then I worked the rest of that year here at the shop. In '69 I returned to MTSU, and I worked summers until I graduated in 1971. I then went to Akron to graduate school, and returned back here the summer of '75, and I've worked full-time since that time.

BROWN—What contributions have you made to the design of the guitar?

DON—I make a good sounding board. The pick-guard is something I designed, and in terms of anything independently designed, that's about the only thing.

BROWN—But you've worked with your father throughout the years on design?

DON—That's right.

BROWN—You're heading up the shop now, aren't you?

DON—Yes. There are two other people besides myself who work full-time in the making of guitars, and then two part-time people.

BROWN—What specifically do you do? Do you have a hand in each part of it, or do your workers have individual duties?

DON—Each person, pretty much, has his job that they do. I fit the necks to the bodies, carve the neck, and glue the necks into the bodies. I take care of that phase, but I also have a hand in all the phases. I check out the guitars and do a little help in the finishing room as the head arises, and help the girl with the bodies as the need arises.

J.W.—I'll say, essentially, that Don supervises all the work—keeps check on everything, quality control and so forth. If I see that there's any problem, I discuss it with Don, and he tends to do something about it if it develops that something needs to be done about it.

DON—*Tends* to do something about it? (Laughter) Let's be a little more positive there!

J.W.—I'm being truthful, Son. (More laughter)

BROWN—Don't you have another son who worked here at the shop?

J.W.—Yes, my older son Bill. He was here about two years, I guess. He came here in the summer of '74 and stayed until the summer of '76. He wasn't too happy with it, so he left. He went to Texas and got an engineering job, which is what he had been doing before he came down here.

BROWN—Can you explain the first step in making your guitars?

J.W.—The tops and backs are glued together, the inlay stripe put in them, and then sanded down to thickness. This is all book-matched wood—both sides are identical in grain structure. We have better than a two years supply of wood here at the shop, to give it ample time to cure.

DON—One thing a person does pay for when he pays for a more expensive model guitar is a better selection of wood. For instance, on the 72 Special, it wasn't just that I was putting abalone pearl on it. When we get woods in from the mill, we order the best grade wood the mill has. Of course there are variations within that. In essence, we designate the best that we have for the 71 Special on down the line. For the 72 Special, to give you an idea of the ratio, out of 200 tops, ten are selected for the 72 Special. I'd like to keep that ratio. Of course, it's kind of a relative term. I'm saying I'm using the best I've got and that could be the best of the junk you've got, but it does give it a little more meaning in terms like that.

BROWN—Yes. It's not like you're ashamed of what you put on your 45s or 50s.

DON—It's all the best grade wood, and some we don't use at all. We do have a bottom limit.

J.W.—It's all select grade wood. We order select grade to start with, because we don't feel there's any point in paying shipping charges on wood we can't use. Okay, we sand the sides down to thickness, which is about 90/1,000's [of an inch] and then we put them in a tank of boiling water and let them boil for about ten minutes. Then we put them in the press and press the shape. That has a heating element in it so they're dried out pretty dry in about twenty to thirty minutes.

BROWN—Can you describe what the tape is used for on the inside?

J.W.—It's simply used for reinforcement, to help keep them from cracking. Now this tape is stuck in place, and then we stick the whole frame . . . we just stick one end of it kind of loosely and hold it in place. We put it in a little oven back there and it's heated for about fifteen minutes and the tape will stretch. Then we take it out of the oven and we press it down tightly into place and the tape tends to shrink as it cools. If you glue wood strips, as some manufacturers have done, the strips will be across the frame—and wood is going to breathe. It's going to swell and shrink with changes in humidity and so forth, and after that had been done for a few years, some manufacturers found out that creates cracks. So this tape is elastic enough so that if the wood expands, the tape will stretch with it. But it just keeps a little tension on there, and if you did get a crack in the side it would keep it from spreading.

Then they're put in the rack to hold the shape until we're pretty sure—they stay in the rack at least two days. Then we take the sides out and the ends are trimmed to the exact length. Then the two halves are glued together with a block in each end, which you refer to as the neck block and the end block. The liner strip is glued in around the top and the back edge and this is faced off to give a gluing surface to glue our tops and backs on. This is known as a frame. Then the bracing is glued on the inside of the tops and backs and it's shaped down by hand and sanded smooth.

BROWN—Does the twelve-string have the bracing like the G-50?

J.W.—Right. It has the wider bridge plate for obvious reasons— you've got a larger bridge and two rows of holes.

BROWN—This bracing [flat across the top] is used only for the G-45s, the G-50s, and the twelve-strings?

J.W.—As you can see, the G-70s are identical, except we do put the scalloping in the bracing. [This refers to the practice of cutting a curve or scallop in the brace. It's called "voiced" bracing and is done to achieve a different tone.]

BROWN—What about the bracing in the Grand Concert models?

J.W.—We use the same bracing pattern.

BROWN—Are they scalloped, or does that also depend on the model number?

J.W.—Well, we don't make anything under a G-70 in the Grand Concert. Because the body of the guitar is smaller, we use a little thinner wood—we sand it down a little more. We also make the bracing a little thinner (in width) because it's smaller. It balances out. You don't need as much weight to get the same structural effect. Really, we think as much about structural strength as we do about tone. You have to have both, obviously. The greatest sounding guitar in the world is no good if it falls apart in your hands. So we try to make it as durable as possible.

BROWN—Is it difficult to get this balance of structure and tone, and are you satisfied with the balance you have now?

J.W.—Yes. I can't see any changes, really. I developed the guitar for about four years, just making minor changes until I got to the point of no return. I just can't see anything else that I can do that would improve the situation. We still occasionally do some experimentation, but I don't see anything we can do that would materially affect the guitar.

BROWN—Is this bracing pattern similar to that used by other companies?

J.W.—Yes. It's, I would say, a traditional pattern. Martin, Gibson, and most everyone who makes a dreadnaught, jumbo guitar uses essentially the same bracing. Mine is different in this respect: the two diagonal braces are tapered like an aircraft wing. Because I used to be a model maker [at Arnold Engineering], and I came up with that idea, and it seems to work very nicely. The point of the greatest strain is where you have the greatest strength, and it tapers out toward the end, where you don't have any stress on it.

BROWN—What are most other manufacturers doing?

J.W.—Most manufacturers make this bracing the same thickness out to within about two inches of the end, and then taper it off to go underneath.

BROWN—What's next?

J.W.—The frame is put in a form to hold it in its exact size, clamped in place in the form, and the top and the back of the frame are faced off to the exact contour to fit the top and back, and then the top and back are glued on.

BROWN—Did you come across any problems in building the cutaway body? Did you change your bracing?

J.W.—No, we didn't change anything. 'Course, when we cut that section out of the frame—the frame is put in an assembly jig to glue the top and back on, and the frame is shaped in such a way that by putting a spreader right through the waist, it holds it tight against the inside of the form all the way around even to the ends. That's simply due to the shape of the body, which we did a lot of developing on. Then we cut that big hunk out for the cutaway and the whole thing collapses. So we had some fun then figuring out ways to get it clamped into the form, until the cutaway section is glued in and it works normally. We had a little trouble figuring out how to get the thing shaped and glued up and so forth. That cutaway section is something that is formed separately; it's not formed in the press. I made up a little wooden form and we steam the cutaway section, clamp one end of the press, take a hot electric iron, and work it on over until we clamp the other end down. It's dried out pretty well with the iron. And then we leave it clamped up until it's thoroughly dried.

Then the next step. The body is sanded. We cut a groove around the top of the back edge to receive the binding [plastic strips around the edge of the guitar]. It is sanded down again, and we make another cut with a router around the edges to get to the exact depth to fit the binding, then the binding is glued in place. The whole body is sanded once again. The pick guard is glued on, and then the next step is the neck.

BROWN—Do you consider getting the neck correctly positioned one of the hardest jobs?

J.W.—Well, it is, yes. Everybody has trouble with their neck warping, to some degree. That's something that we have to work with all the time—and just simply getting the neck shaped right and set right, the correct shape that will give you the right action, and so forth. It's a pretty tedious job. Don pre-fits all the necks and hand-shapes all the necks now. We roughly shape the necks out, we put in adjustable reinforcing rods, the fingerboards we cut to exact dimensions and they're inlayed and bound in most cases. The headplate, which is a ⅛" thickness of rosewood and is inlayed in Wisconsin, is cut to shape. The binding is put on it and it's glued onto the headstock surface of the neck. Then the entire neck is clamped up in a vice and worked down by hand—all the finished contours are hand-shaped. There's a dove-tailed recessed cut in the body to receive the neck, and there's a dove-tail on the neck. That is hand-fitted to get the neck sitting at exactly the correct angle. And after it's fitted—actually the fingerboard and headplate are glued on and then the nut, then the neck is assembled with the body—the neck is shaped out. In every case where we cut, we'll cut outside the mark and then we sand it down to the mark, to get the accurate dimension on it.

BROWN—What type of wood are you using in your neck?

J.W.—The neck is all mahogany. All guitars have the mahogany neck. It's a light wood that's very stable. It doesn't tend to warp as much as other woods. The fingerboards are ebony, or rosewood on our lower-class guitars. Again, ebony is prettier. It has more aesthetic appeal, I guess. More contrast, and a little bit harder than rosewood. It would take an awful long time and a lot of picking to wear out a rosewood fingerboard, but ebony is somewhat closer grained and more durable. And they're an awful lot more expensive, I might add.

BROWN—How did you arrive at the shape of the back of the neck when you were developing your guitar?

J.W.—I can't give you a very good answer on that—well, not a technical answer. I should say I worked by the feel of it till I got what I considered a good feeling neck.

BROWN—What about your neck widths?

J.W.—Well, the neck width is pretty much a standard thing. $1^1/_{16}$" is the neck width on most dreadnaught guitars. That's the width Martin has used all these years. We do make a wider neck, a $1^7/_8$" neck for folk guitars. We do sell a few of them—not very many. Doc Watson wanted a neck like a Les Paul Gibson [a popular electric guitar developed by jazz guitarist Les Paul] which turned out to be a $1^3/_4$" neck. He brought one down here and left it with me to use as a guide in making the neck—duplicate it, in other words. But the $1^{11}/_{16}$" seems to be the most satisfactory width for 90% of the people, anyway. 'Course there's always this guy with the real long fingers that wants a wider neck. Sometimes a person will want an extremely slim neck, and when I first started making guitars I made two or three of them. But I found out the customer never was happy with it, because you can't get your fingers in there to note the individual strings too well. So I learned to refuse to make something really oddball unless people have very valid reasons for needing it that way. Then the guitar, after the whole thing is sanded once again, goes to the finishing room. We use a lacquer finish. First, it gets a wash-coat of very thin lacquer to stiffen the wood fibers so that they'll cut off easily with a sharp, fine-grade sandpaper. Then it's given two coats of paste wood filler, which is wiped off—then a sanding sealer. Then the backs and sides get about eight coats of clear-gloss lacquer, which, I believe, gets about three sandings between coats to get it down perfectly level. The top gets about five coats of lacquer. And after a final coat of lacquer is applied, we'll let it cure for a minimum of two weeks. Then they're sanded down with extremely fine 500–600 grade sandpaper, and bossed with electric polishers to gloss out the scratches and to get a nice gloss built up. Then we go again and hand-polish them to get any streaks or what-have-you out of it. Then we locate the bridge. We have a jig set up to give us an exact location on the bridge. The bridge is located, scribed around it, and we scrape all the finish off where the bridge glues on so we have a wood-to-wood bond. Then the bridge is glued in place with a clamping jig. For the final operation, we put on the keys and string the guitar up and adjust the action to insure the best playability, of course.

BROWN—How much guitar repair work are you doing?

J.W.—We always keep three or four guitars. Most of the cases are due to damage. We have one here someplace that this guy simply wants refinished. We don't work on anybody's instruments but ours, by the way. Occasionally we'll have a finish crack on one. We had this happen on about three guitars recently, because of the cold weather—shipping them out of state, one went to Oregon, I believe, and the finish was cracked on it. It was cold for several days, zero temperature, you know. We'll have a few of that during the winter. Of course we'll take it back, strip it, and refinish it. Sometimes we'll have a bridge crack and we'll replace that.

BROWN—But you don't have too many problems with guitars coming back?

J.W.—Of course, you're really going out on a limb when you put a life-time guarantee on a guitar. You're going to have some of it—but I think, on the whole, we don't have any more problems than other guitar makers, and probably less than most of them. It's annoying to have to spend time correcting a problem on a guitar, but we don't have to do much of that, fortunately.

BROWN—What is your biggest cost in guitar making? Is it wood, or is it labor . . . ?

J.W.—Labor is the big cost. Labor, by far.

DON—Labor is the big corker, so to speak, all the way around. In terms of trying to find somebody who has the ability to do the work, and then training that person and finding people that will stay with us long enough that they can really get efficient in what they're doing, and have a pretty good degree of competence in it. Dad said that an apprentice program is usually some five years for this type of work, which is about right. It takes a pretty good period of time, particularly if you're working with woods, to come up with 90% of the variations that are going to happen. Not every guitar is just alike, even in terms of finishing, let's say, because with the humidity and the changes you have to bend to accommodate the environment, so to speak. It might take a little more thinner this week than it did last week because the humidity's up a little bit this week. There's a lot to developing the skill to be able to see what's going on and compensating for it.

BROWN—Do you plan to keep it pretty much a family business—family owned?

DON—Oh yeah. The same basic way that we're making guitars now is how we plan in the future to continue making guitars. We don't have any plans to set up a production line.

BROWN—Do you have any plans in the future for new guitar models?

DON—This year we've introduced two new models, the 72 Special and the Auditorium, which is the small-bodied guitar. We might go up and make a 73 Special. The 72 Special has abalone pearl around the purfling and sound hole, and we might go with abalone around the sides and get a little extra trim on the headstock.

J.W.—Now I will say this: we're talking about the possibility of changing models. As the years go by and tastes change and so forth, there's no question but that we will make some variations on the existing models.

DON—And drop some models that we have now. There are a few models that we hardly ever make right now, and whenever we come out with the new catalog—those won't be in the new catalog.

J.W.—For some strange reason, the highest priced guitars are the ones that sell the best. Maybe it's kind of based on the theory that if you're going to get the best, you might as well get the best of the best. It may sound a little bit egotistical, but I think we do make the best guitar.

In this day of production-line guitars, more and more people are agreeing with J. W. Gallagher's statement, a statement that comes from pride, not egotism. True craftsmen are becoming more difficult to find, and meeting men like J. W. and Don Gallagher is as refreshing as hearing Doc Watson pick a fiddle tune on one of their guitars.

Tennessee Music Box
History, Mystery, and Revival
[1998]

Sandy Conatser and David Schnaufer

When one thinks of an Appalachian dulcimer, the vision is usually of a light, delicate, and graceful instrument featuring hourglass or teardrop curves and made of thin hardwoods such as walnut or cherry. These may have been the common styles in the mountainous regions of West Virginia, Virginia, and Kentucky, but the farming communities of southern Middle Tennessee produced an instrument that found its grace in the sound it made rather than its outward appearance. While the reasons for this development are still in part a mystery, the instruments themselves speak of the ingenuity of the builders and the importance of music in everyday life of Tennessee's pioneers.

Most often called "music boxes" by the people who created and played them over one hundred years ago, these dulcimers have striking commonalities, although they appear to have been made by various builders. They are folk instruments, made from materials at hand. Forty-eight music boxes, in addition to the eleven catalogued in L. Allen Smith's *Catalogue of Pre-Revival Appalachian Dulcimers* in 1983, have been located, with the majority of them found in southern Middle Tennessee. Giles, Lawrence, Wayne, and Perry Counties have supplied a large number. Family histories indicate that the music boxes were most likely built between 1870 and 1940, with the majority of them coming from early in that period.

Structure

Of the forty-plus instruments which we have observed, most were constructed of yellow poplar, and a small number were made of pine, chestnut, maple, and oak. The lumber used was ⅜" to ½" thick to construct a soundbox 10"–14" wide, 27"–28" long, and with a depth of 3" to 4". The raised fingerboard is generally 1½" tall and 1½" thick and is solid, not hollowed out like most mountain dulcimers.

Most boxes have a vibrating string length of 26½", which shows that they probably all had a common ancestor. The soundboxes are generally nailed and glued and feature either butt joints or carefully mitered corners, depending on the skills and the tools of the individual builders. Most of the music boxes have been painted, which has helped preserve them from the elements. We have observed little cracking or warping, and most of the instruments can be strung up and played without any repairs even after one hundred years.

One of the most unique characteristics of the music box is the tinwork that forms the nut and bridge (supports the strings at each end) and covers the end grain of the fingerboard from the weather to prevent "checking" or cracking. The metal also extends over the top of the fingerboard to protect the wood in the area used for strumming. The metal covering the ends also provides a solid screwplate for the four 2"-long eye screws used as tuners as well as the nails at the other end used to anchor the strings. Oral history tells us that at least one builder used old snuff cans for the tinwork because "everybody dipped snuff back then." It is interesting to note that the tuners are located at the bottom end of the instrument to be manipulated with the right hand as opposed to most other dulcimers which feature tuners at the other end of the fingerboard. On some instruments, even though the holes have been wallowed out with use, the eye screws hold

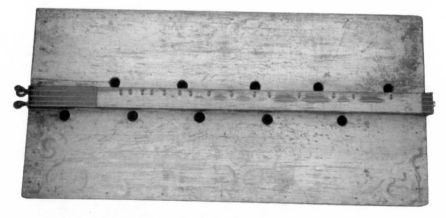

❏ From Lawrence County, this music box, like many others, is painted and decorated with milk paint. Courtesy of Sandy Conatser.

tune extremely well. A nail could be inserted through the eye screws to add leverage for tuning. One music box had two of the eye screws replaced by an old door latch, but the hook was not removed. This unique feature adds a special character to the box as well as a handle for tuning!

The fifteen frets, pieces of metal used to shorten the string length to make the various notes of the scale, are made of fence staples approximately ¼" wide. Only the first string is fretted, and the other three provide a continuous drone. Occasionally the frets were made of bent bailing wire, and one box has a nail added to provide an extra note. At least three of the builders fretted the instrument by ear. One man remembers watching his father touch a nail to the string and pluck it, moving the nail until the sound was correct. Another builder enlisted his wife's help. She was the player, and he would wait until she told him the sound was right. Then the spot was marked with a pencil, and the fret was installed.

Many of the instruments have three small feet attached to the back. With three balance points, the box would sit level if placed on a table for playing. Also, the feet raise the back from the surface and allow it to vibrate more freely, thus increasing the resonance.

Soundholes in the tops of instruments vary, but the most common pattern is ten ¾" holes, five on each side of the fingerboard. We have found two instruments that share a lyre pattern with curved cutouts radiating from a central soundhole. Many of the solid fingerboards feature indentations or scallops along each side, not only for design but to lighten up the top for more resonance. The scallops are usually aligned with the soundholes.

Playing and Tuning

To many observers the music box is a crude and primitive version of the dulcimer. The wood is too thick, the frets are staples, and the tuners are eye screws. What kind of music could so simple an instrument make? One only has to hear it played to dispel all preconceptions. It has a wonderfully full, rich tone and a mellowness not usually found in other dulcimers. It can delicately accompany a ballad or provide a driving, powerful rhythm and melody for a dance tune. Played with a bow, it can sound almost like a pump organ or a bagpipe to play hymns or a lonesome Scotch-Irish lament.

The fifteen frets of the box provide a diatonic musical scale (like the white keys of the piano) on the first string. The other three strings provide a continuous drone. There are many ways to tune the instrument to provide various scales and keys for particular songs. One of the simplest and most useful would have been to tune all strings to the same note (probably the pitch of A). This would provide two different scales and keys. From open A to the seventh

◘ A simple piece of hardware available to everyone, eye screws served as tuners on the music boxes. Courtesy of Sandy Conatser.

fret would give the Mixolydian scale, do, re, mi, fa, sol, la, ti-flat, do. This flattened seventh note is integral in much Appalachian music—"Old Joe Clark," "June Apple." Or the player could start on the third fret and play the regular major scale from there to the tenth fret. This would give the key of D major, and the drones in A would provide a harmony. A common variation on this would be to tune the outside drone string up to D to provide a more complete harmony in the key of D.

Many different string gauges have been observed on these old instruments, and personal histories have provided the knowledge that they were strung with piano wire or much thinner wire thread available at dry goods stores in the 19th century. The gauges of the strings used would greatly affect what keys would be possible. A wound or wrapped guitar string for the outside drone would provide a lower or bass harmony.

Oral histories and old photographs tell us that the music boxes were played with a noter in the left hand and were either plucked with the fingers of the right hand or strummed with a plastic plectrum or a turkey feather. The first music box which Schnaufer acquired in Lawrenceburg, Tennessee, had rosin residue under the strings, indicating that it had been played with a fiddle bow. All of these techniques are traditional Appalachian dulcimer playing styles.

Mrs. Ocie Pulley Burns of Wayne County and Lawrence Gamble of Lawrence County are traditional players. Ocie learned from her grandmother and

◘ Mattie Crownover is pictured with the George Washington Anderson family of the Poplar Springs, Tennessee, community in this 1894 photograph. Photo provided by Charles Fiddler and Brenda Kirk Fiddler and courtesy of Sandy Conatser.

Lawrence from his mother. Their playing styles are identical. Each used a noter in the left hand and anchored the right hand on the side of the fretboard with the ring finger and little finger. The strings were plucked and strummed with the thumb and index finger. Additional evidence of this playing style exists in an 1894 family photograph of the George Washington Anderson family of the Poplar Springs community (see fig. 9.7). Mattie Crownover, a neighbor, is pictured with the family. She is holding a music box in her lap in this same style—noter stick in the left hand and right hand anchored and poised to play.

Also, Miss Ida Sharp of Savannah, Tennessee, was photographed by researcher Donna Roe Daniell in 1973, and she is playing the music box in the same way as Mattie Crownover.

Lawrence uses a noter, which he calls a "chording stick," carved from hickory. A noter carved from mountain laurel was retrieved from one box which originated in Hickman County. The deep playing groove worn in the end and the owner's assurance that the box hadn't been touched in sixty years are evidence of the early noter style of playing. This particular noter was carved in the traditional style of noters common in the Galax area of western Virginia. Picks were also used for strumming and increasing volume. The boxes were also strummed with turkey quills, another traditional Galax style of playing.

The strings on some of the instruments were placed so high above the frets that it would be difficult to press the strings down to fret them in tune. Also, there was little wear on the fretboards. Atlas Qualls of Perry County is a third-generation builder who provided an answer to this mystery.

> My dad and granddad would just lay them across their lap and play, and they used a steel bar like a Hawaiian guitar that they would slide up and down. . . . They didn't necessarily push it down on the frets, just slide it back kind of like a violin. . . . You could push it down on the frets, but you didn't necessarily have to. I can remember how they could do it that a-way and make it quiver, you know.

Another example of this playing style came from Lynette Williams of Giles County, who remembers her mother, Sarah Ellen Skeets Kieff (born January 6, 1890), using a pearl-handled knife in her left hand to play the music box. She used a plastic pick in her right hand. Sarah Kieff built the music box which she played and was the only woman builder whom we have identified. Almus Crowe of Milan, Tennessee, built a music box in the 1950s patterned after a one-hundred-year-old box which was in his uncle's family. A newspaper article about Mr. Crowe described the box as a forerunner of the Hawaiian guitar. This is likely a reference to the fact that the sound produced by playing the music box with the metal slide was similar to the sound of that instrument.

Decoration

Many of the music boxes have some special decoration. A particularly striking box from Wayne County was painted red and decorated with primitive carvings, including a bird, a shamrock, and a figure eight. This music box originated in the family of Mrs. Ocie Pulley Burns of Waynesboro. It was built by her great-grandfather for her grandmother, Sarah Josephine Ford Pulley (born

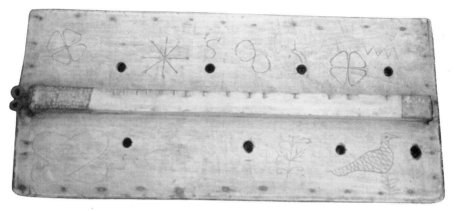

□ This box from Wayne County appears more primitive than many of the boxes and is decorated with unusual carvings. Courtesy of Sandy Conatser.

January 9, 1870), while they lived in Hardin County. Mrs. Burns believes the box to have been built in the 1880s.

Three of the music boxes in the Lawrence County/Giles County area appear to have been built by the same craftsman. The workmanship is consistent, and the playability is the same. Two of these boxes are decorated with yellow and red free-form designs in each of the four corners and along the sides. The box from Lawrence County appears to have been signed on the back. Barely perceptible is "by Joe S." The third box has a red floral design also, but is more geometric and covers the entire top of the box. It was owned and played by Emma Petty Richardson, who lived in Giles County in the 1880s, and it is now in the possession of her granddaughter who remembers hearing her play.

A clever and unique decoration added to several of the boxes is a checkerboard painted on the back. When the music was finished, the box could be turned over and placed on the knees for a rousing game of checkers. In addition to a checkerboard, one McNairy County box has "July 8, 1828" written on the back, but there is no additional evidence to determine the authenticity of that date. The current owner of the box found it in the garage of a house he purchased. Although the instruments were most often called music boxes, two of them have the word "harmonica" written directly on the soundbox. Decorative elements on other boxes include notches on the side of the fretboard, notches in the tinwork, and Victorian stenciling. The sides of three of the boxes appear to have been made from beaded ceiling boards or from door or window casings. Clever craftsmen used what was at hand. Several boxes have numbers stenciled above the frets, and one box has shape notes drawn above the frets. Sacred music was often played on the music boxes, but none of the memories collected place the boxes within church services.

The Memories

Several of the owners have active memories of the early players of these instruments. Joe Youngblood of Corinth, Mississippi, has his mother's music box and remembers very vividly hearing her play on the front porch late in the evening as they came in from working in the fields. Among the songs he remembers are "Red River Valley," "Down in the Valley," "Pass Me Not Oh Gentle Savior," "Redwing," and "Amazing Grace." She often sang as she played. The box was given to his mother in 1920 by Edna Garner of Wayne County. Gerald Young remembers his grandmother playing "Little Orphan Girl," "Old John Morgan," "Froggy Went A'Courtin'," and "Going Down to Lynchburg Town to Lay My Banjo Down." The traditional reference in the Lynchburg song is "tobacco," but she often was accompanied by her brother, John Garrett, on banjo, so perhaps she changed this reference to begin her own tradition. "Black Jack Davie" was a favorite song which Atlas Qualls's grandmother played on her music box.

Lawrence Gamble has clear memories of the music boxes which he got from his mother and his two uncles. Lawrence tells this story about buying the box from his aunt after his Uncle Charlie's death.

> My mamma told me, "Now she's got Charlie's music box, and you might buy it. Go up there and see if you can get it." It was 10 mile up there, and I drove a wagon up there and bought Uncle Charlie's music box. She said, "Yeah, I've got it," and I said, "What'll you take for it?" "By the leave of God I ought to have a dollar for it." I said, "Well, I'll give you a dollar for it if you've got it." She went upstairs, and I thought she was gonna tear that whole roof down before she ever come down with it. She had to go up steps, you know. I didn't go with her up there. She got it and brought it down. I give her a dollar for it.
>
> Whiz Gamble had this one. He lived right down the road there. He was my daddy's brother, too. There was 13 kids in that family. Whiz had that one. Some woman had it and left it there. He took it up to the barn and throwed it in the crib. I said, "What do you want for it?" "Oh," he said, "give me a quarter," so I give him a quarter for it. . . . I didn't give anything for my mammy's, you know. Ever since I was a kid she had it. She could play anything on it.

His mother kept the music box under the bed but pulled it out often to play. When asked what songs his mother played, Lawrence replied, "Anything she would hear. She'd hear one on the radio, and she'd go pick this old box up and play it." She taught Lawrence to play, and he remembers winning one dollar at a local contest about fifty years ago. He tells this story of the contest at Green Hill.

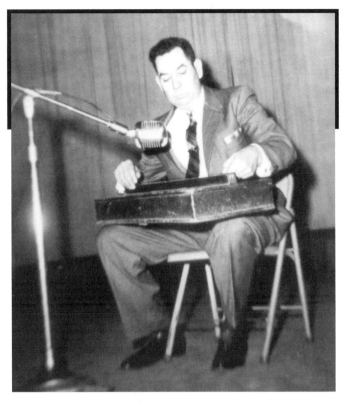

◘ Lawrence Gamble played his music box in a variety show in 1959 in New Prospect, Tennessee. Courtesy of Sandy Conatser.

It's been years ago—way before I ever married. Nadine Williams, my first cousin, she wrote me a letter, a card, and told me, said, "Bring your music box and come over to Green Hill a certain night; we're having a fiddler's contest, and I want you to enter it." Well, I could play a little better then than I can now, and I got it and went down there and started in the door and had it in my hand, sort of like this, you know [carrying it under his arm, against his body]. . . . I don't know what they was charging, but anyhow you had to pay so much to get in. . . . "Nadine Williams wrote me a letter telling me to bring it down here and enter the contest." She said, "Oooooooooooh! You're the one that's got that box." I said, "Yeah, got it in my hand right here." I said, "If you don't believe it, I can set it down over here and sit down on it." I said, "It's just a box." She said, "Stay right there just a minute." She hollered at somebody, and they come up there, and she wanted them to take up the charge, you know, of getting in. She said, "Come on, I want to hear that thing played. Nadine told me all about it, and I couldn't believe." So we went back in there in one of them rooms at the high school in Green Hill, and I sat down and played her a tune. She said, "That beats anything I ever seen." Well, when it come time for me to go on stage, I went on and played mine, and it didn't have nobody to play against . . . and when the thing was over with, they brought me a dollar, a dollar contest. I won a dollar right there. I got to play mine, you know, and the judges called for the other man with a music box, and nobody else had one, so I had to win first prize!

Lawrence is pictured in figure 9.9 playing his music box at a variety night at New Prospect, Tennessee, in 1959. The performance was also recorded, and that recording has now been preserved and archived. The songs he played that night were "Six Months Ain't Long" (the tune we know as "All the Good Times are Past and Gone"), "Red Wing," and "Billy Came across the Wide Ocean." He told the audience that night that the music box came from his grandfather and had been in the family for over seventy-five years.[1]

The memories of Atlas Qualls span three generations. His grandfather built music boxes in the early 1900s, his father built in the 1930s, and he himself built a couple of music boxes in the 1940s. He completed two more boxes in 1996 and 1997. One memory of his father is particularly vivid. When asked about his father and the music boxes, he related this story.

I remember one my daddy made. He made me mad is why I remember it so well. It was an old weight clock—an old one, you know. It was an antique when he tore it up, but it was just about the right size, and it had weights on it to make it run. All he done was took the door off, and took the works out, and just got him a piece of plywood or something, and covered it over, and he had him a music box. . . . That's all my daddy wanted to do. . . . He worked every day, hard work, but when he come home he'd grab up a song book or a music book and study it. And when I got home, I'd have to do all the chores. I should have done it, but back then, it made me angry. You know what I mean. He didn't do nothing, I thought, but play that music. I didn't understand it back then, but I do now.[2]

The Builders

Four of the music boxes are labeled in some way. Louella Pyle of Tullahoma, Tennessee, owns a music box which bears the following label:

The Harmonica
Mfg. & Sold by
Echard & Goodman
No. 239303
Pat. 1881 Imp. 1886

This label has been typed and taped to the side of the box and does not appear to be an original part of the box. The box was purchased at an antique store by her late husband, who was a dulcimer builder and player in Coffee County, Tennessee. There is no additional history on the instrument.

Peggy Baird's music box belonged to her great grandmother. The family lived in Lauderdale County, Alabama, but the box was purchased in Lawrence County, Tennessee. It was catalogued by L. Allen Smith in 1983. A large label affixed to the back is badly worn but reveals this information:

> the harmonica
> Manufactured
> B. Goo
> hel Ma
> oved 18
> THE HARMONICA IS
> most accurate instrument now
> Vocal, Sacred and Instrumental
> This instrument is d ly taki
> nd g perfect
> urchas from the inventor
> to be ie an instrument
> Pric

The "B. Goo" is likely another reference to Goodman, and the "oved 18" is probably a reference to the improved patent from the label on the Pyle dulcimer. Baird's music box also has the word "Harmonica" stenciled on the front.

A third box with similar information originated in Wayne County, Tennessee. This box has been in Reva Loyd's family for over one hundred years. Clearly and neatly stenciled onto the box is the following information:

> New American Music Box
> Pat 1886, Mfg. & Sold by
> T. R. Goodman Mfg. Co.

This box is skillfully decorated with red and black geometric designs. The first two lines of information appear to the left and above the fretboard, and the third line appears on the right of the box below the fretboard.

The fourth label of interest is on a box pictured in Bonnie Carol's instruction book, *Dust Off That Dulcimer and Dance*. Painted directly on the box is the following information:

> THE HARMONACE
> Made by
> Eckard & Goodman of Tennesseey
> . . . . Imp. 1886 350526

All of the labels bear the name Goodman. The Goodman family is one of two families identified in the 1970s by Richard Hulan as builders of the music boxes. In the mid-1800s, this branch of the Goodman family was centered in Lewis and the surrounding counties. W. E. Goodman moved his family to Maury County, where his son Dee (born around 1870) made and sold the music boxes. George Goodman, a cousin of Dee Goodman, traveled in southern Middle Tennessee and sold the boxes which Dee made. George Goodman also lived for a time on Little Beech Creek in Wayne County, just south of White Oak Creek, where John Pevahouse, another builder, lived. Miss Ida Sharp of Savannah, Tennessee, owned a box which her sister bought from George Goodman for four dollars. The Goodman boxes were also called "Harmonicas," and Miss Sharp's box had "The Wonderful Harmonica" lettered on it.[3]

Terrell Robinson (T. R.) Goodman was an earlier Goodman builder. He was born in Perry County in 1840. In 1893 his application for a Confederate soldier's pension was denied, and he reapplied in 1900. In the 1900 application he stated that he "sold music instruments." His marriage records in 1858 place him in Lewis County, the 1860 Census places him in Perry County; the 1893 pension application places him in Henderson County, and the 1900 pension application places him in Lawrence County. He owned no property and listed his occupation as carpenter. His movement throughout southern Middle Tennessee is consistent with the location of many of the boxes.

John Pevahouse of White Oak Creek in Perry County is another music box builder identified by Richard Hulan. Rebecca Pevahouse Murphy says that her father was a carpenter and blacksmith and built square box-like instruments with eight holes, four to each side. His mother, whose maiden name was Scott, had a music box and played it. John wanted to make some, but his father disapproved. John married and left home around 1890 and within a week had made two of the boxes. He sold one each week in the years around 1900. "He made hundreds of them," Mrs. Murphy stated in a 1963 letter to Hulan. "Everybody on White Oak Creek came to him to get a music box, and they came from Linden and Savannah to get one of his models." Pevahouse originally used wooden pegs for tuners but later changed to the eye screws. His boxes were also put together with square nails, probably hand forged due to his skill as a blacksmith.[4]

Henry Steele of Keith Springs, Tennessee, near Belvidere, built similar boxes as late as the 1960s. These dulcimers have many features of the music box but differ in size and hardware. His boxes are approximately 7" wide, 32" long, and 3" deep. His grandfather, Joe Steele, made a music box copied from an instrument owned by Ben Keller. Keller built in the early 1900s. The fretboard on Steele's dulcimer was modified to extend beyond the body of the box to accommodate mechanical tuners. John Putnam collected one of Henry Steele's dulcimers in the 1950s for the Brussels Museum of Musical Instruments in Belgium. Lily Steele, Henry's wife, is pictured playing the music box in *De hommel in de Lage Landen* with one of her sons and two of her daughters. Three of the Steele daughters still live on the mountain at Keith Springs, and two of them have dulcimers which their father made.

The Mysteries

Two of the four labeled music boxes bear the name Eckard/Echard. This connection remains a mystery. Tennessee census records for 1900 list one Eckard and one B. Goodman living in the state. Both lived in Memphis. Henry F. Eckard, age forty-eight, was a barber, and Benjamin Goodman, age thirty-three, was a merchant, and they worked within one block of each other on Main Street. Eva Goodman Quillen of Hohenwald, a great niece of Dee Goodman, remembers her father visiting cousins in Memphis in the 1920s suggesting a possible connection with the Lewis County Goodmans.

The patent numbers which appear on all four boxes are another unexplained feature of the instruments. The 1881 patent (Number 239,303) is for a mechanical music box and was issued to William H. Allen of Washington, Indiana. The improved patent of 1886 (Number 350,256) is also for a mechanical music box and was issued to A. A. Lateulere, a French citizen residing in London. One suggestion is that the soundboxes of some of the instruments were actually shipping boxes used to ship these patented mechanical music boxes. The placement of the lettering on the Loyd box, however, seems to indicate that it was stenciled after the fretboard was positioned. The suggestion may also be made that perhaps the patent numbers were added to deter others from making and selling copies of the instrument. Since the instruments were called music boxes, and the patent was for a music box, anyone checking the patent number could think the patent was genuine.

Some of the boxes are still within the original families. The histories accompanying them have both given insight into their development and created new mysteries. Gerald Young of Giles County states that his grandmother, Mamie Garrett Moore, told him that a music box was purchased for her from the gypsies in 1885 when she was six years old. This may be a reference to the Irish Travellers who traveled through southern Middle Tennessee during that time. The Irish Travellers came to this country from Wales in the early 1800s and settled in New England. They were tinkers who lived a sedentary life during the winter and traveled to trade and sell their wares during the summer. They moved south after the Civil War. While there is no evidence to indicate that the Travellers were builders, their presence throughout the area could easily have put them in contact with the Goodmans and Pevahouses. Their trade practices could have been instrumental in the spread of the boxes throughout

□ Sandy Conatser and David Schnaufer visited with Lawrence Gamble (center) at his home in Iron City, Tennessee, in 1997. Courtesy of Sandy Conatser.

Middle Tennessee. Also, the decoration on several of the boxes is reminiscent of the Irish tinker's trade.

The instrument which Young's grandmother owned was burned in a house fire, but she talked about it so often that Gerald went in search of one to replace it. He found two sisters in Pulaski who had one which he was able to purchase for his grandmother. She played it and assured Gerald that it was almost like the one she had lost. Young still has this box, which is decorated in the tinker style.

Revival

The Tennessee music box has been silent for half a century, collecting dust in barns and corn cribs or under the beds of relatives who hung onto the memories of their grandparents' old tunes. Due to this research and David Schnaufer's career as a recording artist, the music box is enjoying a revival not only in folk music but in popular, rock, and classical music as well. He states,

> In 1996, during the Tennessee Bicentennial, I featured the music box on a solo dulcimer recording that showcased the various styles of playing—fingerpicking, quill and noter, and bowing. This recording begins with "All the Good Times are Past and Gone," the first tune which Lawrence

Gamble played for us. During the time of this recording, I was visited by Cyndi Lauper, also a dulcimer player, who was charmed by the sound of the box and wanted me to play it on a song she was recording for a new album. The bowed music box provided a very ancient bagpipe drone to her dulcimer and vocal rendition of the song "Fearless" on the album *Sisters of Avalon*. Cyndi has a huge following all over the world, and sales of this album are introducing millions to the unique voice of the music box. She will be acquiring a box of her own soon, and the combination of the traditional sounds and her considerable composition skills will provide new music from this instrument for years to come.

In my concerts I usually play at least two numbers on the box, and in 1996, Paul Gambil, conductor of the Nashville Chamber Orchestra, heard the tune "Ten Thousand Charms" and had a vision to use the instrument in a concerto for dulcimer and orchestra. I collaborated with composer Connie Ellisor, and the concerto *Blackberry Winter* was born. The second movement features the music box playing "Ten Thousand Charms" in a setting of twenty-eight other string players. It was recorded with the orchestra for a new Warner Brothers album, *Conversations in Silence,* and was played by my twenty-three-year-old student/duet partner Stephen Seifert. Also, the orchestra has an educational program we perform in schools throughout Tennessee, and the box is always a favorite among the children and teachers alike.

Information about the music box is spreading in many ways. As a part of the Nashville Chamber Orchestra's education program, teachers are provided with historical information and class activities which will introduce a new generation of children to the music box. The music box has been featured on *Prime Time Country* (TNN), and on *Bulger's Backroads* (Nashville's WSMV, channel 4). Also, presentations have been made at music and folk festivals in and outside of Tennessee. Newspaper coverage and presentations in the public libraries of five southern Middle Tennessee counties helped bring several boxes out of hiding. The official historian in each Tennessee county has been sent information about the boxes in an effort to make people aware of the important place this instrument has in the musical and folk history of Tennessee. A new generation of players has begun in at least two of the families. Ellis Truett of Madison County is a dulcimer player, builder, and collector who shares his knowledge of the music boxes in special presentations. He has been instrumental in the discovery of many of the boxes. Henry Beckman, Gerald Young, and Donovan Carpenter have often pointed us in the direction of a new music box and a new discovery. Atlas Qualls of Perry County, who last built a music box in the 1940s, built two more boxes in 1996–97. Other builders are now examining with interest this unique form and sound.

Though the music box has been silent for years, its voice is relevant again. The ease with which it has so quickly moved into pop, country, folk, and classical recordings speaks of the timelessness and purity of its sound and assures it a place in the future of American music.

Notes

1. Lawrence Gamble, interview, November 1995; November 1997.
2. Atlas Qualls, interview, May 1997.
3. Donna Roe Daniell, "The Wonderful Harmonica, Middle Tennessee's Dulcimer," student research project, Vanderbilt University, August 10, 1973.
4. Dr. Richard Hulan, personal correspondence, December 7, 1963.

Further Reading in Folk Music
Instrumental Traditions and Folk Music Collecting

Conway, Cecelia. *African Banjo Echoes in Appalachia: A Study of Folk Traditions.* 1995.

Irwin, John Rice. *Musical Instruments of the Southern Appalachian Mountains.* 1983.

Rosenberg, Neil V. *Bluegrass: A History.* 1993.

Wolfe, Charles K. *The Devil's Box: Masters of Southern Fiddling.* 1997.

———. *Tennessee Strings: The Story of Country Music in Tennessee.* 1977.

Work, John W., Lewis Wade Jones, and Samuel C. Adams Jr. *Lost Delta Found: Rediscovering the Fisk University-Library of Congress Coahoma County Study, 1941–1942.* Ed. by Robert Gordon and Bruce Nemerov. 2005.

PART TEN

Folk Communities

The two articles here illustrate a relatively recent trend within the academic field of folklore to chronicle holistically the full range of folk traditions, that is, the "folklife," within a community. The goal underlying a folklife study is to provide the most complete portrait of a community's diverse traditional culture as possible. The popularity of such studies in the United States is generally traced to the publication of folklorist Don Yoder's edited book *American Folklife* (1976), and it is not a coincidence that four out of the five of these articles from the *Bulletin* were written at the time of, or shortly after, Yoder's book, which communicated the concept of folklife—long a central component of folklore study across Europe—to a large number of American folklorists.

The oldest article, Mildred Haun's "The Traditions of Cocke County," was published in the *Bulletin* in 1967. The article is based partly on her 1937 master's thesis at Vanderbilt University. Best known for her 1940 fictional work *The Hawk's Done Gone and Other Stories,* Haun in her *Bulletin* article focuses on the enduring folk traditions she observed during her early years in Cocke County, long one of the more geographically isolated counties in East Tennessee and thus a place that by the Depression era had not experienced the modernizing influences of industrialization. While more of an impressionistic sketch than a fully representative, analytical folklife study, Haun's article is noteworthy as an early effort to capture a holistic, relatively unromanticized portrayal of Cocke County's folklife.

The community of Free Hill, Tennessee, located in Middle Tennessee in Clay County, was historically an African American community developed by the descendants of freed slaves who in 1830 had been granted a four-hundred-acre tract of land by their former master, a woman with the surname of Hill. Using oral history material gathered during an early 1980s documentary project partly sponsored by the Tennessee Folklore Society, folklorists Elizabeth Peterson and Tom Rankin wrote an illuminating project overview entitled "Free Hill: An Introduction" (1985). The article uncovers the previously uncollected history of this community, exhibiting sensitivity toward the community's collective feelings concerning race relations and family. Beyond its historical revelations, the article provides a fascinating discussion of the process of a community shaping its own "folk history" through the telling of oral narratives and the collective memorization by the community.

Most towns and cities in Tennessee have harbored citizens from a variety of ethnicities, but some communities across the state were intentionally founded by people of the same ethnic background as a means of maintaining a measure of security for its members. The community of Free Hill, as previously noted, offered a group of African Americans a measure of economic and emotional security from the pressures of mainstream white society. A number of other communities across Tennessee have been defined by the ethnic commonality of their members. In East Tennessee, for instance, the town of Rugby was largely settled by English utopians in the mid-nineteenth century, while the towns of Allardt and Wartburg were largely settled by German immigrants during the same period.

The Traditions of Cocke County
[1967]

Mildred Haun

The physiographic features of Cocke County help to keep the economic order of the eastern and northeastern parts almost at a standstill. The high hills make good roads and lines of communication, for the whole county, next to impossible. Modern tools and modern methods of farming are slow to reach the hilly sections. And when they do become known they are not feasible. Tractors, for instance, are not made for steep hillsides.

But even the simplest modern tools do not suit. People have made their own things to suit their own needs for so long that, when they do have access to newer things, they soon discard them for the older. Brooms tied at a factory are not liked as well as those tied at home. And the factory takes half the brooms. So, a person can raise just half as much broom corn and still have the same amount of brooms if he ties his own. Some still use sage brooms, and some of those are made by peeling back thin strips of an elm sapling. Homemade lye soap is preferred to any store-bought soap. And ash-hopper lye is preferred to that one can buy in cans at the country store. So in practically every yard in Hoot Owl section there is an ash-hopper.

Homemade hoe and axe handles and homemade furniture suit the purpose just as well as anything one can buy. And brought-on furniture costs money. Every woman raises her little patch of cotton to seed and card for winter quilts. Frequently one sees small patches of flax. More and more women each year are asking neighbors to save cotton and flax seed for them.

◘ Man tanning a hide in the Great Smoky Mountains. From the Sing Along with Appalachia Collection. Courtesy of the Archives of Appalachia, East Tennessee State University.

Horses and mules are frequently discarded for oxen. A Cocke Countian wants to be up with his brother who lives in Hamblen County. He trades for a team of mules. But even though mules are better than horses, they cannot stand on steep ground as well as oxen. And of course, too, a yoke of oxen is easier kept than a team of mules. They can almost live on roughage, but mules have to have corn.

The social life is no less static than the economic. Folks do not have the opportunity to get together and see each other very often. But when there is a gathering of any sort, everybody within anything like reasonable distance makes use of the opportunity.

Log rollings give a chance for men, and sometimes for women, to get together. Adams starts to clear up a piece of new ground. He sees McMann at the Tumblebug store and tells him about it. He may chop all day the first day by himself. But the next day, when he goes to the woods, he finds just about every man and boy in the whole district there ready to start work. He is not at all surprised. In fact, he would have felt pretty bad if nobody had shown up.

Work, on such occasions, is mixed with the fun of various contests, such as who can tell the biggest tale or who can tell the biggest lie. One man's eyesight is so good that he can see a chigoe sitting on a log on top of Max Patch Mountain, about twenty miles away. That is nothing to another man, for he can see the chigoe's eye.

The women prepare a big dinner, and the men have a long rest period spent in telling tales and jokes and asking old riddles. Most of them are not very proper. Many of the tales are mixed up with the number three or seven or nine. One is told of a man who in order to marry the king's daughter must find three people in the world who are bigger fools than himself. He starts out walking, and the first person he sees is a man rolling a wheelbarrow around his crib. The man says he is trying to roll the sunshine in on his corn so it will dry out quicker. He goes on a little further and finds a man on top of a house tearing off boards. The man says that his wife is sick and that he is doing this to let in fresh air. On down the road a little piece further, he meets a man on a horse, and the man has a sack of corn on his back. By carrying the corn across his shoulder, the man tells him, he makes the load lighter for the horse.

Usually the log rolling crowd stays for supper. After supper they sit around in the yard and sing such songs as "Lord Thomas and Fair Eleanor" and "The Jealous Lover" until everybody has rested enough to dance. Then somebody starts out with "Skip to My Lou," "The Two Sisters," or "Shoot the Buffalo."

The same thing happens at fall wood cuttings, among those who cut enough wood in the fall to last them all winter. Everybody helps everybody else. They cut at one man's house one day and at another's the next. There is usually one especially good tale-teller or riddler or singer in the crowd, and much use is made of his talents.

A "whole bunch" gets together about once during a winter and goes "a-hunting." They hunt till late in the evening. Then they go to the country store and swap their game for plug tobacco, snuff, sardines, and crackers or whatever the crowd is in the mood for at the time. At Tumblebug store there has always been one man in the section who was present on cold, snowy days to make music for the hunters who are likely to come in. He has always been paid in tobacco, sardines, and other things the hunters bought.

The present entertainer spoiled his little game last winter by returning a joke for the many that had been played on him. He told the hunters he just had to have some cash to pay a debt he owed. He needed even more than all their game would bring. And he would not sing unless they cashed their game and gave him all the money. This they did and prepared for an evening of playing and singing. He picked up his fiddle and sang:

Bridle up a rat,
Saddle up a cat,
Hand me down my old straw hat,
And I'll be gone.

And with that, he walked out.

Women have their socials too. All the women of a district get together and help each other do their winter quilting. They haven't seen any fur coats or any shows to talk about, and so, after all the new babies, calves, and pigs have been discussed, they ask riddles, tell witch and ghost and love stories, and sing songs. Everybody knows which woman sings which song best. Cordelia Fletcher is asked to sing "The Three Crows" because she sings that better than anybody else in the crowd. Somebody else sings "Wish I Was a Single Girl Again," and somebody else sings "Forsaken Love." Or each person may be called on to ask all the riddles she knows. Here are a few that are frequently asked:

Within a wall as white as milk
Lined with a skin as soft as silk
Within a fountain crystal clear
A golden apple doth appear,
No doors there are to this strong hold
Yet thieves break in and steal the gold.

Answer: An egg.

Horn eat a horn in a high oak tree
If you can read this riddle, you can hang me.

Answer: A man had done something to make his king mad. The king was going to have him hanged unless he could ask a riddle that the king couldn't answer. This is the riddle that he asked and the king could not solve it. So he told the answer. He said that his name was Horn and that while he was hiding from the king's searchers, in a high oak tree, he had eaten a candy horn.

Fruits of England, flowers of Spain,
Met together in a shower of rain,
Bound with a napkin, tied with a string,
Guess this riddle and I'll give you a ring.

Answer: A sack of flour.

Love I hold, by Love I stand,
Love I hold in my right hand,
Love is blind and he can't see,
Love is in the hollow tree.

Answer: A poor boy loved a rich king's daughter. The king had said the only person that deserved his daughter's love was one who could ask him a question about love that he could not answer. The king thought such a question could not be asked. All the rich boys from everywhere went and asked him questions, and he answered them right off. The poor boy was ashamed to go before the king wearing his shabby clothes. Finally, one day, he saw the king's daughter out walking, and he told her he believed he could win her. She slipped him out a fine green and gold suit to wear. And he went to the king and asked him this riddle. The king could not rede it, so the boy had to tell him the answer. He said he had a little dog whose name was Love. The dog died, and he carried him in his right hand and buried him in a hollow tree. The king got mad and wanted to have the boy hanged. But the daughter would not let him, because she had wanted to marry the poor boy all the time.

When anybody in the district is much sick, a crowd gathers to "set up" with him, cut the wood, and take care of things that need doing around the house. If it is plowing time, they pitch in and do the plowing for him. It is thought necessary for some outsider to stay around and be ready to "carry the word" in case the sick person dies. The sick person, if he thinks he is going to die, from time to time asks those sitting up to sing. He usually calls for a spiritual or religious song such as "Hick's Farewell," or "Can the Circle Be Unbroken?"

And when he does die, a big crowd gathers to "set up" with the dead, help with the cooking, and console the family. The crowd sits around the coffin, which is in the middle of the room. The door is carefully kept ajar so the Spirit can pass out. There are some people who have the ability to see the Spirit, when it leaves the body, and to tell whether it goes up or down. The night is spent in singing. The spirituals, and the songs from *The Sacred Harp* and *The Harp of Columbia,* are thought the most appropriate pieces for such occasions. The ballads of great tragedies like "The New Market Wreck" and "The Orphans," and the sadder love songs, are also appropriate. They are always sung without accompaniment, because the devil likes music instruments. And this is a time when one does not want to invite the devil around.

Sometimes, however, in order to balance the grief and keep the atmosphere from getting too solemn, humorous and nonsense songs are sung. The story is told on Hoot Owl section's old maid that when her beau got killed, the crowd "setting up" with his corpse asked her to lead the singing. She started out with "The Boys Won't Do to Trust."

"Big Parties" are not had very often. But when they are, they begin before dark and last until chickens crow. Practically the whole night is spent in acting out the play songs. "Johnny Was the Miller Boy" and "Love Has Gained the Day" are among the most popular. Some one person leads the songs, and others join in and sing as they act them out. If the leader is a good one, he adds verses of his own or changes the old verses. By doing this he can get the crowd mixed up and get the boys separated from their girls. Everybody that can play an instrument or sing goes to the party to help with the entertainment. Nobody is specially invited. Everybody is welcome and wanted. There is no such thing as social distinction.

All types of songs are sung at corn huskings and pea hullings. Those who are good at making up songs are always called on at such gatherings to show off their abilities. Contests are held to see who can say the most love verses like—

When all the world forsakes you
And lovers love you not,
Then come to me, my darling,
As fast as you can trot.

And

Sailing down the stream of life
in your little bark canoe,
May you have a pleasant trip
With just room enough for two.

Everybody that finds a red ear of corn gets to kiss his girl. Or if he finds a pod with thirteen peas in it he gets to kiss her. And if he fails to kiss her he has a choice either of singing three sweet love songs to her or saying thirteen crazy verses. Here are two examples of what are called crazy verses—

I had a little pony,
His name was Jack,
I rode him of his maw
So's to save his back.

I had a little rooster,
Fed him on dough.
He got so fat
He couldn't crow.

Sometimes he is required to sing a crazy-spelling verse, such as—

H-u—huckle, b-u—buckle,
H-u—huckle, i,
H-u—huckle, b-u—buckle,
Huckleberry pie.

W-x-o-v-e—stove
Unkum, jinjum, y-p-e,
Stove pipe.

□ One-room schoolhouse in the Great Smoky Mountains. From the Sing Along with Appalachia Collection. Courtesy of the Archives of Appalachia, East Tennessee State University.

The satires on love and marriage are the songs usually sung at candy pullings, house raisings, and serenades. "The Ball Headed End of the Broom," "Old Mother-in-Law," "I Wish I Was Single Again," "The Wife Wrapt in Wether's Skin," and "I Wouldn't Marry At All" are some of the favorites.

During the fall months, when there is not a protracted meeting going on, about the only form of entertainment the Hoot Owl section affords is the Saturday night singing. The "singings" held at churches or schoolhouses are, of course, of a different nature from the Saturday night singings. They are all-day affairs with dinner on the ground. Crowds from all the surrounding counties come and join in. Hymns, both old and new, and the best-known spirituals are sung at these gatherings. And occasionally, if the leader knows a new ballad that a number of people have not had an opportunity to learn, he sings it over so they can get it.

The all-day singings are usually held early in the fall, following a singing master's summer circuit. The song leader sings over the notes of the song by himself, then the crowd sings them over with him, then they all join in and sing the song. Only those known to be familiar with the whole crowd are sung. Usually the religious songs that are familiar to one community are familiar to all, because the singing schoolteacher has been to all the communities practicing them up.

The singing teacher holds a two-week school usually, accepting as pay what corn, meat, and chickens the community can give him. He is glad to teach for nothing where he knows people do not have much to spare. He has with him books of all descriptions, from the long- and short-measure books through the four-noted books on up to the shape-noted versions of modern hymnals. And he makes use of all these in his teaching. *The Harp of Columbia* is liked best by most people. The songs are liked. And then it seems simpler, too, to learn that the last note in the bass is always the key-note, that if the note is *do*, the piece is set on the major key, or if it is *la*, it is in the minor key. At least the teacher can make this plainer to the beginner than he can the signatures for sharps and flats, where the lines and spaces of the staff have to be represented by the letters.

Some of the things he tells beginners would sound rather crude to a modern teacher. I will just name a few of the "little things to remember by." When he does forsake *The Harp of Columbia*, he feels he needs something to make it simpler for beginners. So here is something to remember:

> Letters never change their place
> Either on a line or space
> Place for *C* then I know,
> Added line below.

And when one locates *C*, he just goes on up the soprano staff and on down the bass.

And then, too, if beginners have to learn the key by looking at little symbols for sharps and flats, they have to have some easy way of remembering them. So when you see the sign #, just remember the sentence Go Down And Eat Bread. If there is one sign you know it is in the key of G, the letter beginning the first word of your sentence. If there are two signs you know the piece is in the key of D, the letter beginning the second word of your sentence, and so on. There is also a similar sentence for the flats.

Sometimes, when the singing gets to dragging too much, the leader reprimands the group in song,

> Oh, such droning will not do,
> Sing sharp, sing sharp, sing sharp, sing sharp.

Cocke County people are mostly of English, Irish, Scotch, and German descent—about the same as people in any other section of the Appalachians. Few outsiders ever move into the eastern and northeastern sections of the county. And few people that are born there ever move out. People keep on dying and people keep on being born, and the population stays about the same.

Free Hill
An Introduction
[1985]

Elizabeth Peterson and Tom Rankin

At the northeastern edge of the Highland rim abutting the Kentucky line lies Clay County, Tennessee. First settled in the 1790s by men and women from Virginia and North Carolina, Clay County's history is one of small, rural farming communities. The terrain is varied and rugged, encompassing the rich floodplains along the Cumberland River and the steep hills and narrow valleys throughout most of the county. Such topography caused large farms to flourish along the river and small subsistence-type farms to form in the hills and hollows. The jagged landscape also encouraged isolation, making the construction of roads and highways difficult at best and late in coming.[1]

Today, Clay County is a quiet, rural area, though one not unaffected by general national economic and social trends. Like most rural areas throughout the South, Clay County's population has steadily declined since 1910, when young men and women first began migrating north to midwestern industrial cities for employment in steel mills and factories. Although farming is still a primary occupation, its preeminence is diminishing. Many residents now find work as skilled tradesmen or in small garment factories scattered throughout the county, and modern brick houses and mobile homes dot the landscape.

Amidst the hills and hollows of Clay County, high atop a knob overlooking Celina at a point where the Cumberland and Obey Rivers converge, lies Free Hill, Tennessee. Free Hill is a black settlement founded by freed slaves prior to the Civil War. The community's name refers not only to the rugged and isolated hills and hollows that residents call home but also to the families who originally settled the area. Those first families—the Hills—were farmers and landowners, and the legacy of landownership continued after the Civil War as ex-slaves from surrounding counties moved to Free Hill to forge a community based on economic security and self determination.

Historical events, local characters, night rider incidents, blues-style songs, and sacred songs and speech form the basis of a new LP album produced for the Society (cf. announcement elsewhere in this issue). All these are intended to serve as an introductory folk history and sound portrait of Free Hill. The study, consisting of the LP and an accompanying twenty-page booklet, is both descriptive and interpretive in its method and historical in its emphasis. As such, it shares similarities with such varied works as Lynwood Montell's *The Saga of Coe Ridge,* James Borchert's *Alley Life in Washington,* and Elizabeth Rauh Bethel's *Promiseland,* all of which examine the folklife and cultural and social history of diverse Afro-American communities utilizing an integrated historical or sociologically based case-study approach.[2] Although Free Hill never encouraged or enjoyed the outlaw status of Coe Ridge, a neighboring black community whose rise and fall has been chronicled by Lynwood Montell, the particular individuals and the events, the internal relationships and workings of the community are its own, and they are the decided focus on our album. On the other hand, Free Hill's history is emblematic as well. Its themes, concerns, and adaptive strategies portray how one of many similar black communities has struggled to survive in a climate of racial, economic, and social discrimination.

This study of Free Hill, however, is also the study of an Upland South black community and will, we hope, add to the body of scholarship in Afro-American studies that emphasizes almost exclusively the black experience in the Deep South and the urban centers of the north. Through the years, the interplay of certain economic, social, and cultural factors that have served to shape the community differed from those experienced by many rural blacks in the Deep South. Farming in the Upland South, for instance, did not readily lend itself to a plantation-based, slave-holding economy. Thus slavery was not extensive, and the consequent caste and class system it fostered was minimized.[3] There have been few if any mansions in Clay County to loom large over its subjects. In fact, the median income cited in the 1970 census for the entire county is less than eight thousand dollars. Although life in Free Hill has been circumscribed by segregation and economic racism—by Jim Crow laws and night riders—the disparity of income between blacks and whites has not been dramatic, and residents have experienced a degree of economic stability and independence through the years unavailable to many blacks in the Deep South. And not surprisingly, the racial conflict and violence that have

◘ Herbert Plumlee and Herman Burris, Free Hill, Tennessee, 1983. Photo by Tom Rankin.

◘ Brother Norman Hamilton preaching, Free Hill Church of Christ, 1983. Photo by
Tom Rankin.

marked recent decades throughout the United States have been minimal in
Clay County.

Finally, it is significant and appropriate that this study is an album and
not only a book. The underlying assumption here is that folk history, traditional oral narratives, and songs are not merely historical documents, but also

◘ Erie Philpott at home, Free Hill, Tennessee, 1983. Photo by Tom Rankin.

products of the selective and collective imagination at play. They speak to and are informed by the culture, social, and historical values, attitudes, and circumstances from which they emerge. Their truths are as much aesthetic and stylistic as they are historical or factual. As traditional artistic expression, they must be presented and understood as they are spoken, sung, or performed.

Folklorists and ethnomusicologists have long recognized the artistry of Afro-American oral tradition; and the list of Afro-American sound recordings produced by folklorists is voluminous, from the extensive field collections of John and Alan Lomax to the recent efforts of David Evans, Jeff Todd Titon, Christopher Lornell, and others. In most instances, however, recordings have focused on a certain artist, style, genre, or region, with particular emphasis on the Deep South. In contrast, this recording suggests the range of oral and musical traditions found in a single Afro-American community, which is based in the upper Cumberland River Valley and which partakes in the common stock of verbal and musical traditions developed and shared by blacks and whites in the Upland South. Such an approach not only emphasizes the stylistic continuities of oral and musical traditions but the historical continuity of community themes and concerns as well. Thus, the study is organized in two general sections: The first describes the social and cultural history of Free Hill's founding and growth, and the community's traditions are discussed within that context; the second section discusses more specifically the artistic and expressive dimensions of the community's traditions in the contexts of an Afro-American cultural heritage and the regional heritage of the Upland South.

Initial fieldwork in Free Hill was conducted by Elizabeth Peterson in 1981, under the auspices on the Tennessee State Parks Folklife Project. Fieldwork specifically for the recording was undertaken in spring 1983, under the sponsorship of the Tennessee Folklore Society, and was made possible by a grant from the National Endowment for the Arts. For three months, we lived in Clay County and spent most of our days (and many nights) in Free Hill, visiting, photographing, and tape recording church services, musical gatherings, and interviews with various residents. Interviews were generally open-ended, because we hoped to learn as much about people's lives as possible, though our preliminary interests centered upon the origins and early history of the community, preaching, local legends, congregational singing, blues, and other traditional expression. As we began to know people, other topics of community interest emerged in conversation, including kinship and family obligation, race relations, landownership and transfer, and the general business of hustling and making a living. In many cases, information obtained from one person was easy to corroborate through interviews and conversations with other people. Fieldwork was supplemented by additional research with county and federal documents such as census material, wills, and land deeds located in the Tennessee State Archives and Library, the Clay County courthouse, and the Overton County courthouse (a neighboring county which contained the Free Hill settlement until Clay County's formation in 1870).

A few additional problems deserve special mention here. First, it would be foolish to claim that this recording and the accompanying booklet represent more than an introduction to Free Hill, its history, and its traditions. In fact, it is largely due to the patience, cooperation, and graciousness of the Free Hill community and many other county residents that this information was obtained in so brief a stay. Finally, it is difficult to estimate how being white affected the nature and quality of our interactions with community residents. The usual problems of the fieldworker as stranger were compounded by the fact that we were also viewed as representatives of a privileged and dominating race and class.[4] To combat this inevitable situation, we tried to participate as fully as possible in the daily routine of life on Free Hill, hanging out, running errands, exchanging ideas and observations. As former slave Charlie Moore said, "A white man can't tell the history of the Negro."[5] In keeping with his sentiment, we've tried to let the Free Hill community tell their own story. An example of this method follows, in a discussion of the origins of the Free Hill community.

> There's a white, there's a white woman in Virginia. She come here in time of the war where . . . well, when they set the colored people free. And she had some slaves but she didn't treat 'em as slaves. She treated 'em just like, they said just like her own children. They was Hills. So when war ceased, why she come here to Celina and come up in here and bought these hills. That's the reason says, that's the name of it's Free Hills because she come

here and brought, brought them people here. Oh, I don't know how many families there was. And made it over to them. And Uncle Burrell Hill, Uncle Rube Hill, Uncle Josh Hill, and, oh, I don't know, Uncle Josh Lundy, and just a lot of slaves she had. She's a nice white woman.

Erie Philpott

I don't like to tell it but there a white woman that lived across the Cumberland. She had black children. And they didn't allow her to sell her children in slavery. And that's where Free Hill got its name. She had, one of her black children took up over there and they just give him this place, you know. This man, I believe, it was Uncle Bye Hill. That's where Free Hill got its name.

Selma Crawford

You know, way back in the olden days I heard it talked by my father and my older folks that they placed all the black folks up in Free Hill on that rock so they couldn't grow nothing, hopin' they'd stave 'em out. But they finally made it, most of 'em did and lived to be a ripe old age.

Robert "Bud" Garrett

The origins of Free Hill are shrouded in mystery. Oral accounts are often vague and contradictory, and supporting written documents, such as census data, land deeds, and wills, provide inconclusive evidence. This predicament should not be taken as firm proof of the unreliability of oral narratives as historical records. Rather, it is remarkable that so much variety exists in the details and attitudes embodied in the narratives. As Montell states in his preface to *The Saga of Coe Ridge,* "When a people share a common historical experience . . . the events in this experience become a tenacious part of folk memory."[6] What does remain in the legends about Free Hill is a tenacious core of events and not a little ambivalence and indifference.

Any story about Free Hill begins with the Hill family. The few written accounts that exist describe the Hills as a family of freed slaves who were given their freedom and four hundred acres of land prior to the Civil War by their former owner, a Mrs. Hill, from whom they took their name. The most detailed written description is worth presenting here because it effectively encapsulates the essence of the story and is itself based upon oral sources. Written by Clay County resident Walter E. Webb, the following sketch appears in a booklet of local history printed for the county's centennial celebration in 1970.

Before the days of the War between the States, while the Negroes were yet in bondage, an old lady named Hill came to Clay County (then Overton), Tennessee and purchased a tract of land located in the hills just east and north of the town by the Obed (now Obey) River. This body of land is

◘ Sam Page cleaning groundhog, Free Hill, Tennessee, 1983. Photo by Tom Rankin.

composed of hills and hollows and at the time of purchase was covered with virgin timber.

Mrs. Hill brought with her a group of young Negroes, whom she held in bondage in the state of North Carolina, her home state. This family of Negroes consisted of two boys, Rube and Josh, and two girls, Betty and Maria. The tract of 400 acres of land was divided between these four slaves, whom were later given their freedom by Mrs. Hill. They were referred to as the Free Hills. It becomes a coincident because of the name Hill and of the fact this tract of land is very hilly and rough and it is always referred to as the Free Hills.

◘ Herman Burris at home, Free Hill, Tennessee, 1983. Photo by Tom Rankin.

◘ Robert "Bud" Garrett, Herbert Plumlee, and Owen Hamilton, Bud Garrett's junkyard, Free Hill, Tennessee, 1983. Photo by Tom Rankin.

The girl, Betty, became infatuated with a Negro man, named Bye Stone, and later brought him out of bondage and made a down payment on him, but before the final payment was made, the Negroes were set free during the Civil War and the remaining payments were cancelled. After the marriage of Bye Stone to Betty Hill, he became known as Bye Hill, he taking her family name instead of her taking his. They reared a family on a portion of this land. The population of Negroes of Clay County can be traced to this Hill family.[7]

While there is no reason to doubt certain aspects of the above story, time itself has obscured many of the details. The actual year of settlement, for one, may never be determined. Virtually all oral and written accounts simply date the origins of the settlement to a time prior to the beginning of the Civil War. In only one instance were we able to find the year 1831 mentioned as a possible year of settlement, and census data corroborates this assertion.[8] The 1830 census for Overton County lists two black households headed by Hills in the district for Free Hill.[9] In 1850, there were five households, and by 1860, there were eight households of free blacks, all with the surname Hill.[10] Such data provides solid evidence that the free Hill community existed before the Civil War and perhaps as early as 1830. More important, however, are the questions of identity and names raised by the census.

"Uncle Burrell Hill, Uncle Rube Hill, Uncle Josh Hill . . ." so goes the litany of names in Erie Philpott's story printed earlier. Walter Webb, on the other hand, mentions Rube, Josh, Betty, and Maria as the founding ancestors. To add confusion, the heads of households named in the 1850 census are Joshua, Elizabeth, Susan, William, and Ezekial.[11] In 1860, the names of household heads change to Thomas, Anna, Henry, Sooky, Bettsy, Susan, John, William, and Lucinda.[12] Also, the popularity of certain names and the common practice among slaves and free blacks to name offspring after their kin further compound the situation.[13] In any given census before and after the Civil War, there are numerous Joshuas, Rubens, Sarahs, Ezekials, Susans, Johns, and so forth. There is only one Elizabeth (or Betty or Bettsey), however, and it is she and her family that are the most significant "ancestors" in the memories of Free Hill residents.

Several of the older residents of Free Hill speak fondly of Bettsey Hill or "Bettsey Mamie," who was a grown woman at the outbreak of the Civil War. Erie summed it up by saying, "She's the mother of 'em all."[14] In addition, Erie and another Free Hill resident, Bertie Plumlee, both concurred that Bettsey Mamie was married to Bye Hill.[15] Little else is known of her life, and accounts about her siblings are unclear. While she may have had brothers named Ruben, Joshua, and Burrell, it is certain that she had at least seven children, two of whom were Joshua and Ruben. While most of the other Hill families

◘ Bud Garrett's junkyard, 1983. Photo by Tom Rankin.

◘ Fixing a tire in Bud Garrett's junkyard, Free Hill, Tennessee, 1983. Photo by Tom Rankin. Photo by Tom Rankin.

◘ Robert "Bud" Garrett, Free Hill, Tennessee, 1983. Photo by Tom Rankin.

migrated or died out in the decades after the Civil War, Uncle Josh and Uncle
Rube stayed on to raise families and farm. Ruben, who died in 1914 at the age
of sixty-five, had five children of his own, including a son named Joshua. The
few remaining immediate Hill descendants who live in Free Hill claim Josh as
father or grandfather.

The confusion surrounding the actual identities of the original Hills is
matched by the contradictory descriptions of their former owner, Mrs. Hill,
and her relationship to her slaves. In every written or verbal story we've
encountered, she is little more than a vague presence, and we have yet to find

anyone who recalls her first name. According to some, she came from North Carolina, although most people cite Virginia as her home. In versions told by white and black County residents alike, Mrs. Hill was the daughter of a rich Virginia plantation owner who traveled to the area, left her slaves after purchasing land for them, and returned to Virginia. At the very least, the vague descriptions of her suggest that she did not stay long in the area.

The most significant conflicts in several versions, however, center upon Mrs. Hill's motivation and relationship to her slaves and are amply illustrated in the stories by Selma Crawford, Erie Philpott, and Walter Webb. In the most common versions, Mrs. Hill becomes a nice slave owner who freed her slaves. A second variant, however, portrays Mrs. Hill as the mother of mulatto children. According to Oopie Reneau and Landon Anderson, two Celina residents, she brought the children to Celina apparently to ease the scandal and shame her family would have to endure.[16] Curiously, the second variant is more commonly told among whites, whereas Free Hill residents remember Mrs. Hill as a slave owner. In fact, Selma Crawford's version is unique among the people we questioned in Free Hill.

Similarly, no person could account for Mrs. Hill's choice of the Celina area as a place for her mulatto children. At the time of Mrs. Hill's journey, the Upper Cumberland River region would have been sufficiently isolated to preclude easy access. Census data and the land deeds, however, reveal the existence of white slave-owning Hill families who lived and owned land along the Cumberland and Obey rivers near what eventually became Free Hill.[17] If there is credence to this version, it is possible that Mrs. Hill came to the area upon the suggestion of relatives who offered to help her in her plight.

Folk history or the narratives people tell about themselves and their past, states Montell, "articulate the feelings of a group toward the events and persons described."[18] The "official" recorded history reveals little besides confirming the pre–Civil War existence of a sizable free black settlement, an extraordinary feat in itself. No wills remain from the era, and the land deeds show no evidence of any transaction between a Mrs. Hill (or any white Hill) and the freed Hills. Still, the legends persist, though they, too, are becoming vague in their explanatory force. Younger generations in the area seem to recall only a skeletal outline of Free Hill's beginnings. As one man told us, "They tell me that once the slaves were freed that they gave this area up here on top of the Hill to some lady—a Hill I think it was. And then, evidently she had slaves too and she brought some of her slaves here too. And, I don't know, they just turned 'em loose I guess."[19] While the etiological function of the legends lessen, the attitudes are tenacious, particularly among older people in the area.

The narratives are perhaps most important as an interpretation of the intimate but uneasy relationship among white and blacks in the area. The majority of stories told by whites attempt to account for the origins of black and mulatto people in the area. Consequently, they stress the role of Mrs. Hill as a paternalistic benefactor or as a progenitor of mulattoes. On the other hand, the narratives told by blacks exhibit more variety and ambivalence in their interpretations, from Erie's praise of Mrs. Hill as a good white woman to Selma's strong disapproval of miscegenation. The skeptical comments of Bud Garrett, however, are perhaps more to the point with their allusion to the generalized "they" and the motivations of economic racism and isolation. Oopie Reneau's observation about Free Hill's location is apt here. "Have you studied the fact," she said, "that it's practically an island? It lacks just a nick—Obey on the south, Cumberland, then Skinnicky Creek on the north."[20] There is much truth in her observation, but this isolation served the community well as a source of strength in its early days.

Notes

1. Several brief undated local county histories by such Clay County residents as Walter Webb and Landon Anderson have provided invaluable background material, as has Lynwood Montell, *Don't Go Up Kettle Creek* (Knoxville: University of Tennessee Press, 1983).
2. Lynwood Montell, *The Saga of Coe Ridge* (Knoxville: University of Tennessee Press, 1970); James Borchert, *Alley Life in Washington: Family, Community, Religion, and Folklife in the City, 1850–1970* (Chicago: University of Illinois Press, 1980); and Elizabeth Rauh Bethel, *Promiseland: A Century of Life in a Negro Community* (Philadelphia: Temple University Press, 1981).
3. Brett Sutton makes similar observations in his booklet-length study of black and white Primitive Baptist congregational singing traditions, *Primitive Baptist Hymns of the Blue Ridge* (Chapel Hill: University of North Carolina Press, 1982), 3. The booklet accompanies an album of the same title.
4. Carol Stack, *All Our Kin: Strategies for Survival in a Black Community* (New York: Harper Colophon, 1975), xiii–xv.
5. Paul D. Escott, *Slavery Remembered* (Chapel Hill: University of North Carolina Press, 1979), xiii.
6. Montell, *Coe Ridge*, xviii.
7. Walter E. Webb, "Sketches," Clay County Centennial 1870–1970 Commemorative Brochure (Celina, 1970), n.p.
8. Work Projects Administration, Tennessee Clay County Bible and Tombstone Records (Nashville: Historical Records Project 465-44-3-115, 1937), 13.
9. Overton County, Tennessee, manuscript census, 1830, n.p.
10. Overton County, Tennessee, manuscript census, 1860, n.p., and Overton County, Tennessee, manuscript census 1860, n.p.

11. Manuscript census, 1850, n.p.

12. Manuscript census, 1860, n.p.

13. For a detailed discussion of slave-naming practices, see Herbert G. Gutman, *The Black Family in Slavery and Freedom, 1750–1925* (New York: Vintage Books, 1977), 185–229.

14. "Bettsey Mamie" was described by several people in the course of interviews, most notably Erie Philpott, interview, Free Hill, April 29, 1983, and Oopie Reneau, interview, Celina, April 10, 1983.

15. Erie Philpott and Bertie Plumlee, interview, Free Hill, May 2, 1983.

16. Oopie Reneau, April 10, 1983, and Landon Anderson, phone interview, Celina, May 19, 1983.

17. This information was obtained from examining Overton County, Tennessee, land deed records for the years 1806–70.

18. Montell, *Coe Ridge,* xxi.

19. Luke Hamilton, interview, Free Hill, March 12, 1983.

20. Oopie Reneau, April 10, 1983.

Further Reading in Folk Communities

Dunn, Durwood. *Cades Cove: The Life and Death of a Southern Appalachian Community, 1818–1937*. 1989.

Egerton, John. *Visions of Utopia: Nashoba, Rugby, Ruskin, and the "New Communities" in Tennessee's Past*. 1977.

Fike, Rupert. *Voices from the Farm: Adventures in Community Living*. 1998.

Finger, John R. *Tennessee Frontiers: Three Regions in Transition*. 2001.

Olson, Ted. *Blue Ridge Folklife*. 1998.

Williams, Michael Ann. *Great Smoky Mountains Folklife*. 1995.

Epilogue
Current Attitudes toward Folklore
[1940]

Donald Davidson

I have taken the subject "Current Attitudes toward Folklore" because I find myself confused by the mixed results of the vast and far-ranging activity of the devotees of folklore. I number myself among the devotees, but I feel a little concerned to know how to direct my devotion so that it will count. Many others, I imagine, must suffer from a like confusion of mind, and therefore of purpose.

It seems worth while, accordingly, to try to set down the current attitudes, to define them briefly, and to estimate their relative fruitfulness.

It is somewhat difficult to analyze briefly a tradition of study and devotion that, in America, begins, let us say, with the majestic figure of Francis J. Child and surrounds us now with accumulating volumes of balladry and folk song, compiled largely by scholars; with the promotional labors of Mr. Lomax, Miss Jean Thomas, and others; with hill-billy radio singers; with a Negroid popular music emanating chiefly from New York composers and danced to by the season's debutantes. Such phenomena are highly miscellaneous. I can do the job of analysis only by a rather bold attempt at classification. I distinguish at least three prevalent attitudes; and I can imagine, and to some extent define, a fourth attitude, which I would like to see prevailing over and directing the other three.

These attitudes I name as follows: (1) The Historical-Scholarly; (2) The Enthusiastic-Promotional; (3) The Commercial-Exploitative. For the fourth attitude I have no name.

The Historical-Scholarly is of course the most respectable attitude, and naturally is the only one that attracts prestige in the academic world. It is respectable because it views balladry, folk song, and folklore as human cultural phenomena and therefore as inevitably a part of a body of knowledge which may be collected, studied, classified, collated, and annotated. The cultural phenomena bears some relationship—though perhaps a dubious and, it would almost seem, an illicit relationship—to literature. That is the more reason for studying the phenomena and putting them in order—and for rating them worth an occasional (but only an occasional) Ph.D. thesis. The historical scholar is most at ease when he can consider the phenomena as belonging to a culture safely remote in the past. He does not want to be confronted with lively, fluid phenomena, for that kind of phenomena makes him nervous and uncertain of his conclusions, if he has any.

The studies of Child seem to assume that balladry is a dead phenomenon. He moves among his variant versions with the kind of safety enjoyed by an archaeologist moving among his artifacts. Child is in fact a kind of archaeologist, with a mixture of anthropologist. Out of his attitude comes his obsession that he must finally and definitely establish the canon of English and Scottish ballads, fix the exact number to be admitted to the canon, and reject intruders and impostors. His eminent colleagues in the American field, Gummere and Kittredge, follow his lead obediently. They excavate and comment the remains of balladry very much as Schlimann and his successors excavated and commented the ruins of Troy. And so Mr. Kittredge, in 1902, almost triumphantly announced that ballad-making was a "closed account."

The labors of these men to a large degree have determined the course of ballad and folklore study until recent years. We pay tribute to their power when we gather today in the character of a learned society, dutifully presenting papers which embody our researches, which inevitably put great emphasis upon *collecting*. By far the greater number of state and regional collections of balladry follow the model of Child, even to his system of numbers and letters. Apparently the effort of the collectors is first of all to see what "Child ballads" can be recovered, in text and music, in a given region, and to get as many versions as possible—garbled and worthless fragments often being recorded just as dutifully as the best versions.

The enormous conservative value of such work is self-evident and calls for no argument. We owe ballad scholars a considerable debt both for the material that they have preserved and for the insight they give us, through their accompanying studies, into the folk-tradition itself, as a historical and cultural fact. But there, I am afraid, the value stops. The conservation after all is limited, for the ballads are conserved very much as specimens in a museum are conserved. Ballad scholarship, as such, seems to have relatively little impact upon our contemporary culture—nothing like the impact that Bishop Percy's and Walter Scott's collecting had upon the culture of their day. Ballad scholarship may conserve, but it does not *transmit*. And a folklore that is really to count must transmit in other places than graduate seminars. I feel that the Historical-Scholarly attitude, legitimate and valuable though it may be, clearly leads us now to an undue emphasis on collecting per se. It leads to the madness of accumulating, ad nauseam, hundreds of slightly different versions of "Lord Randel" and "Barbara Allen" with which we are familiar to the point of tedium. And worst of all, it diverts the devotees of folklore from other possibilities which might conceivably bear a different fruit from doctoral dissertations.

The Enthusiastic-Promotional attitude is, I suppose, in part a reaction against the excessive frigidities of historical scholarship. I have heard it said that a certain notable professor at an eastern university, who edits ballad collections and directs ballad research, does not himself like ballads; and if one of his students begins to sing a ballad or practice a ballad air on the piano, he makes his excuses and leaves. The Enthusiastic-Promotional attitude is the extreme opposite of this attitude. The devotee of balladry or folk song becomes a zealot who threatens to cheapen the whole subject with too much unrestrained admiration. The mark of the Enthusiastic-Promotional attitude is attempt at popularization, generally through books that drop the paraphernalia of scholarship and deliberately try to win an audience. Of this sort, on the whole, are Mr. Lomax's collection and Carl Sandburg's *The American Songbag*. There is certainly much clear gain here: The enthusiasts are really trying to transmit as well as to conserve, and if they overreach themselves at times, it is the defect of their good qualities; the attempt itself is healthy. But it is still not quite good enough, and the reason why it is not good enough is easy to find.

The popularizations try to win an audience—but what audience? They are aimed at the sophisticated urban audience, the audience with money to buy the books and with a taste jaded enough to welcome for the moment (but only for the moment) the novel bit of antiquity, of local color, of "regional" quaintness. A moment before, the same audience welcome Viennese light opera; tomorrow it will welcome something else, and Lomax and Sandburg will be back numbers.

The situation is more clearly revealed when we turn to the somewhat weaker members of this tribe. Dorothy Scarborough's *On the Trail of Negro Folksong* and *A Song-Catcher in the Southern Mountains* are the romantic adventures of a Columbia professor who happens to be collecting folk songs instead of early American glass. And Jean Thomas's books, it seems to me, deliberately cater to the urban notion of balladry as "quaint." Such works involve a condescending attitude or are willing to come to terms with a condescending attitude. I believe they are dangerous examples. They, too, have relatively little impact upon our culture as a whole; and what impact they do have is specious, inasmuch as they indulge in a theatrical display, and reduce folk song to a kind is parlor vaudeville, a very minor form of entertainment, or at best a fleeting escapism.

The third attitude, the Commercial-Exploitative, needs little definition. At its best it may give us the finished professional performance of folk song, or an occasional appearance of folk song (reformed and furnished with a modern piano accompaniment) upon the noted singer's concert program. And I should certainly concede that, at its very best, it invites us to witness folk song impinging fruitfully upon art-song, in such a way as to give an attitude that might be called the Artistic-Exploitative. On the other hand, at its worst it gives us the hill-billy singer and the hill-billy band, from whom we generally get only the lower levels of folk performance, and very rarely any performance that reflects the genuine worth and dignity of folk song. Radio performance by hill-billy singers notoriously run to sentimental ditties and hardly ever to the true ballad, the really convincing folk song. And what has happened, under the commercial auspices of New York, Harlem, and night club orchestras to the secular or sacred song of the Negro is too obvious to need comment. It is again an exploitation that caters to the passing urban mood and has little to do with folk song as we know it in its traditional haunts. It is a vulgarizing progress.

All these attitudes have one characteristic in common. Their approach is *external* to the tradition and essential being of folk song. They may in one way or another conserve, or at least embalm, the folk-product; they do not transmit it, except at great expense to the object; and even though at times they may, by some rare accident, transmit it, they cannot genuinely cherish it. To transmit the folk-product effectively and to cherish it genuinely, the impetus must come from within the folk itself.

The fourth attitude (which I have spoken of above) would therefore draw its strength from within the folk tradition. It is a real question whether such transmission can be much assisted by a self-conscious effort on our part. Yet I believe it has been done in the past, and may be done again. Why are the Danish ballads available to us in a more fully rounded, less mangled form than the English and Scottish ballads? We are told that the preservation is due to the devotion of certain noble Danish ladies who took care to write down ballads. But these ladies wrote down the ballads that they might be remembered, not that they might be collected; and, still more concretely, that such ballads might be the better performed in Danish households. If we preserve ballads in order to learn them and perform them (as some of us in this very Society are doing today), then we join in the folk process—we become the folk.

And how does it happen that the Confederate song, "I'm a Good Old Rebel," though composed by a known author and indeed published soon after its composition, became a southern folk song rather then a merely literary relic? Aside from its intrinsic appeal and character, it became a folk song because the author let his song go, to whoever would like it, for what it was worth to Confederates, not for what it was worth to a music publisher. We too may become contributors to folk song on one condition: we must be nameless, we must let the song go, we must set up no copyright claim.

The roots of the best attitude toward folk song, it seems to me, lie in such circumstances. And if such views have merit, we ought it become cherishers by participation in at least as much degree as we are cherishers by recording and collecting.

Perhaps we can also do certain other things in a concerted way—things which will do good, or at least work no harm. We can strive to inculcate respect for folk song among those who already posses it naturally. We can strive to see that love of old song is not wholly replaced by love of new song. That means, certainly, that our schools should negatively refrain from some of their customary educational policies—especially their callous assumption that the first duty of the school is to weed out ruthlessly all elements of non-literate culture and replace them by completely literate requirements. And yet I hardly know whether we dare risk the cherishing of folklore by the schools as a planned and definite part of the school program itself. The schools have been so guilty, in the past, of diluting and vulgarizing what they attempt to convey that I am almost ready to say that they should not be trusted. I am tempted to declare that I would rather risk leaving the preservation of folk song to the old, anonymous, accidental process, even under perilous modern conditions, than to risk giving it a place in a curriculum or activities program administered by the certificated products of our higher educational institutions. The point is debatable. But undoubtedly our concern should somehow be directed toward the young folks rather than, as now, exclusively toward the old folks from whom we collect such interesting examples of folk song and folktale. The young folk should have their part in all undertaking—festivals, fairs, entertainments, competitions—which strive to bring folk song into greater respect.

Back of all this lies the soil in which the tradition is to be nurtured. The true cherishers of the folk tradition are, first, the family, in its traditional role, securely established on the land, in occupations not hostile to song and dance and tale; and second, the stable community which is really a community and not a mere real estate development. If we cannot cherish these, we cannot hope to cherish folk song; and probably we cannot long cherish the high forms of art that feed upon folk-tradition; and we may even prove ourselves ignorant of what life really is.

Appendix A

A Brief History of the
Tennessee Folklore Society

T he Tennessee Folklore Society, founded in 1934, has as its primary mission the preservation and interpretation of Tennessee's folk cultural heritage. The *Tennessee Folklore Society Bulletin* was created a year after the society's formation to serve as a mechanism for its members to share their research findings as well as provide information on current trends and perspectives related to the emerging field of folklore studies. Initially, the content of the *Bulletin* consisted of lists of folklore items, such as superstitions, home remedies, riddles, and proverbs; brief commentaries on various folk traditions; and solicitations for information from other members. In recognition of Tennessee's historical and cultural connections with other parts of the South, the *Bulletin's* orientation changed in the 1950s from an essentially Tennessee focus to one more regional in scope. In the 1960s, the *Bulletin* began publishing essays on the folk traditions of cultures from other parts of the world, and later, reflecting the changing cultural landscape of Tennessee, a few articles related to relatively new ethnic groups in the state appeared. The abiding concern of the Tennessee Folklore Society since its inception, however, has been the study and celebration of the folk culture associated with the Volunteer State since its establishment in the late eighteenth century.

It is commonplace among folklorists, anthropologists, and historians these days to dismiss the descriptive-preservationist perspective represented in most of the articles in this anthology. Critics point out, and justifiably so, that folklore is not confined to something antiquated, and it is certainly not disappearing. Nonetheless, the founders of the Tennessee Folklore Society and other state-based folklore societies were more right than wrong in their estimation that many of the folkways associated with early America's agrarian-based way of life would radically change or disappear altogether due to the myriad forces of culture change. The articles in this anthology support the reality of this assertion. Viewed collectively and holistically, the articles offer the reader a portrait of a way of life in Tennessee that in many respects no longer exists. The portrait, however, is delimited in its representation of some genres of folklore and ethnic groups. There is, for example, an abundance of material in the *Bulletin* on verbal lore, notably folk song and folk tale; scant attention was give to material folk culture (e.g., folk architecture, folk art, and foodways) until the early 1970s. African American folklore is poorly represented in early issues of the *Bulletin*. Studies expressly concerned with African Americans did not appear until the 1950s. Unfortunately, virtually nothing on the folklore of Native Americans in Tennessee was published in the *Bulletin*. These shortcomings are best understood within the historical context of the founding of the Tennessee Folklore Society and the history of folklore studies in general.

At the beginning of the twentieth century, academicians and members of a growing and more affluent Euro-American middle class were concerned about the changing cultural landscape of America. From their perspective, the forces of modernization were creating a more homogeneous "national" culture; distinctive regional folk cultural traditions, especially those associated with an agrarian way of life, were rapidly disappearing. The study of folklore for some academicians in both the United States and Europe was tied to an interest in cultural evolution, and their investigations entailed the collection and analysis of cultural survivals (i.e., elements of older culture persisting in the present) useful for reconstructing earlier stages of culture. For others, especially members of the affluent middle class, the folkways of rural Americans, especially those nebulously and often erroneously referred to as "Anglo-Americans" or "Anglo-Saxons," represented the bedrock culture of America. Isolated rural peoples in the South who were previously ridiculed as rude, primitive, and backward came to be viewed as bearers of an antiquated yet exalted folk culture with historical connections traceable to Britain, particularly England. This romanticized view, of course, ignored the fact that the folk culture of rural white southerners was in reality a mosaic of Celtic, Native American, African, German, and French cultural influences.

Several events in the early 1900s led to a folklore preservation movement, but surely a pivotal moment was the discovery of old English ballads canonized by Francis James Child still being sung in southern Appalachia. Hubert Gibson Simpson's article in a 1911 issue of the *Sewanee Review,* "British Ballads in the Cumberland Mountains," was not the first to identify the presence of "Child" ballad survivals in America, but this article, and Simpson's monograph, *Syllabus of Kentucky Folk Songs,* also published in 1911, signified the richness of the folk song tradition in southern Appalachia. Other collections of southern folk songs were published at this time, such as John A. Lomax's *Cowboy Songs and Other Frontier Ballads* (1910), but undoubtedly the most

portions of Georgia and Alabama, and then mostly in
n. The middle-class farmhouses of the Deep South,
ch play the role the two-story I house does in the up-
try, are consistent with the houses of the Southern
water source area: they have one story, generally
d with no loft above. Some successful southern farm-
built dogtrot houses: many frame ones feature jigsaw
and at least one was built solidly of brick;[135] the com-
ble slaveholders Huck Finn encounters in Mark
in's novel live in log dogtrot houses.[136] But the most
home on the big farm and on the right side of the
s in the small towns is a type which arose early on the
lina-Georgia coast (Fig. 32). It has a full classic
gian plan—two rooms on each side of a broad central
which was rarely left open dogtrot style.[137] Typically,
a pair of internal brick chimneys with a tiny shallow
ace for each room; rarely it has four external chim-
two on each gable end. It is a house of one story
high ceilings; the pie-slice shaped area under the roof
generally left unused. Inside, its details (or, the ab-
of the details which tickle the architectural histo-
are typical of the Lowland South: whitewashed

South of Center Point, Howard County, Arkansas (March,

Mark Twain, *The Adventures of Huckleberry Finn*, chapters
2.

Examples: Frederick Doveton Nichols and Francis Benjamin
n, *The Early Architecture of Georgia* (Chapel Hill, 1957), pp.
186; near Sucarnochee, Kemper County, Mississippi (August,

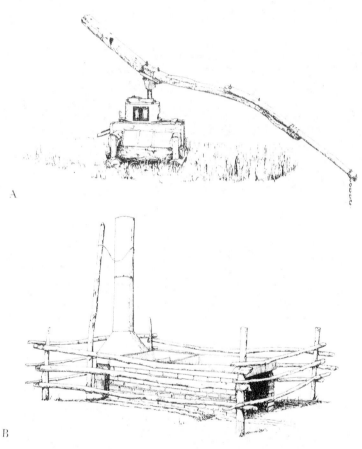

A

B

FIGURE 31

SOUTHERN SYRUP MAKING MACHINERY

A. Cane or syrup mill, west of Allen Gap, Greene County, Tennessee
(May, 1966). The mill proper is usually factory-made; it is set up and
used, however, in a traditional way. B. Evaporator in which the juice is
boiled down to syrup, Pine Hill, near Enterprise, Clarke County, Mississippi (November, 1962).

significant book in terms of giving momentum to the folklore preservation movement in the South was *English Folk Songs from the Southern Appalachians* (1917) by civic leader Olive Dame Campbell and the eminent English scholar of folk song and folk dance, Cecil J. Sharp.

In the early twentieth century, state-based folklore associations were founded in several southern states to promote the systematic collection of folk songs and other folklore that the founders believed were disappearing. The Kentucky Folklore Society and the North Carolina Folklore Society were established in 1912, followed by the Virginia Folklore Society in 1913, the Texas Folklore Society in 1914, and the West Virginia Folklore Society in 1917. The Tennessee Folklore Society was established in 1934 at the suggestion of the famous folk song scholar John A. Lomax, who at the time was serving as honorary consultant and curator of the Archive of American Folk Song (now the Archive of Folk Culture of the American Folklife Center, Library of Congress). In a conversation with J. A. Rickard, professor of history at Tennessee Polytechnic Institute (now Tennessee Technological University), Lomax observed that such an organization was needed in Tennessee, noting that the mountainous sections of the state were "the richest in folklore of any portion of the United States." Rickard sent out invitations with a draft constitution enclosed to individuals who might be interested in "effecting a permanent organization" devoted to the preservation and interpretation of folklore. Upon receiving an invitation, George Pullen Jackson of Vanderbilt University sent a letter to Rickard (dated October 31, 1934) in which he said that he was glad Rickard was taking the lead in creating a society and that he was supportive even though he would not be able to attend. He also offered Rickard some advice. "It would seem wise to me," Jackson wrote, "if you would not depend on the Texas people alone for precedent." He suggested that Rickard consult with Professor Arthur Kyle Davis of the Virginia Folklore Society about how to set up the by-laws. "But whatever you do in the way of organization," he concluded, "please take my advice and have the terms of service (after reelection) of your officers *limited.* The fate of Southern societies has too often been one of ossification under the hand of self-succeeding officers. These 'one man' organizations are never successful in the long run."

A meeting was held on November 10, 1934, in Room 1 of the Administration Building at Tennessee Tech. The fifty Tennesseans who attended, most of whom were educators, succeeded in adopting a constitution and electing officers. Charles S. Pendleton, then chairman of the English Department at George Peabody College for Teachers (now Peabody College of Education at Vanderbilt University), was elected as the Tennessee Folklore Society's first president. The mission of the newly founded organization was set forth by Pendleton in the first issue of the society's regular publication, the *Tennessee Folklore Society Bulletin,* in 1935:

The Society has a serious and worthy purpose. It will endeavor to make an accurate and dependable record of the "natural antiquities" of our state—the bits of unusual speech, of customs and usages, and of songs, dances, and games which are still preserved in Tennessee (and many of them in other states), but which are now being forgotten under changes in education, in frequency of travel, and in manner of living. No material will be dealt with whatever to the detriment of Tennessee, and no material will be released for unworthy exploitation.

Rickard is credited with the founding of the society, but Pendleton was a driving force in its establishment. He was also instrumental in training Tennessee's first generation of folklorists. Under the direction of Pendleton and other faculty at Peabody College from the 1930s to the 1960s, several students wrote theses and dissertations on Tennessee folklore, and many of them subsequently generated interest and research on folklore at other educational institutions. Edwin R. Hunter, professor of English at Maryville College and editor of the *Bulletin* from 1937 to 1942, gave a presentation in 1959 at the Silver Anniversary meeting of the society titled "Reminiscences of the TFS: 1934–1959," in which he observed, "I believe it is fair to say that the major impulse behind the launching of this society was the interest developed in graduate courses at Peabody College in the early thirties, and that Dr. Pendleton was a prime factor in that movement. From this center of interest came such persons as Mr. L. L. McDowell, Bess Alice Owens, E. G. Rogers, Marie Campbell, and Dr. Farr."

At its inception, the Tennessee Folklore Society viewed its mission as one best met through the cooperative efforts of academicians and lay people. The first issue of the *Bulletin* sought to engage all Tennesseans with a serious interest in folklore in the massive effort to collect the state's "natural antiquities," and to this end the first issue provided potential participants with a folklore bibliography and guide to collecting folklore prepared by Rickard. Advised by Rickard that the older generation living in rural areas would be the best repositories of folklore, society members were exhorted to go forth and collect with the minimal tools available: four-by-six-inch cards for recording superstitions, typing paper for documenting stories, and music staff paper (prepared on a typewriter) for notating folk songs. By the spring of 1935, there were eighty-six paid members of the society.

In 1937, T. J. Farr, professor of education at Tennessee Tech, was elected president and Mr. L. L. McDowell the first vice-president. The society announced in the *Bulletin* an ambitious plan for the systematic collection of Tennessee folklore:

The two years of history and experience have done much to outline the scope of the endeavor of the Society and to discover the persons in the

◘ Some of the founding members of the Tennessee Folklore Society. Top row, left to right: J. A. Rickard, T. J. Farr; middle row, left to right: Charles S. Pendleton, Donald Davidson; bottom, George Pullen Jackson. University Archives, Tennessee Technological University, and Vanderbilt University Special Collections and University Archives.

state interested in and qualified to work in the various aspects of folk lore investigation. With this history behind us, we are undertaking to allocate definite responsibilities to persons throughout the state who may act as leaders and organizers in these various areas of study. A number of letters have gone out asking persons to undertake specific work of this sort. So far not all have replied but enough have to encourage greatly our hopes of success for this scheme.

Society members recruited as organizers and their assigned areas of folklore were T. J. Farr, folk remedies; W. A. Redfield, English teacher, Pleasant Hill Academy, riddles and rimes; E. C. Kirkland, professor of English, University of Tennessee, Knoxville, contemporary folk ballads; L. L. McDowell, principal of Dekalb County High School, religious folk song; E. R. Hunter, English professor, Maryville College, proverbs; E. G. Rogers, English professor, Tennessee Wesleyan College, legends and folk stories; Geneva Anderson, English teacher, Maryville High School, traditional ballad survivals; C. H. Mathes, music professor, East Tennessee State University, creative writing on folk themes; Neal Frazier, English professor, Middle Tennessee State University, folk customs; and Hill Shine, English professor, Maryville College, folklore bibliography. While the proposed "scheme" was unsuccessful in generating a coordinated network of folklore collectors, many of the individuals cited above and other society members contributed articles to the *Bulletin* in the following years and later made substantive contributions to the field of folklore studies. In 1933, George Pullen Jackson's landmark scholarly study, *White Spirituals of the Southern Uplands,* was published, while 1937 brought the publication of L. L. McDowell's critically acclaimed collection of religious songs from Middle Tennessee, *Songs of the Old Campground.* In 1938, *Folk Dances in Tennessee,* authored by McDowell and his wife, Flora, was published.

A far more successful strategy of collecting folklore employed by members of the society who were college and high school English and history teachers still used today involved recruiting students to gather folklore in their communities. This approach is well illustrated in a 1937 *Bulletin* article by W. Adelbert Redfield, "Superstitions and Folk Beliefs," which contains materials gathered by students attending Pleasant Hill Academy, a Protestant home mission school located on the Cumberland Plateau between Crossville and Sparta. The editor of the *Bulletin,* E. R. Hunter, included the following introductory note to the article which reveals much about who the society members had in mind as the ideal folklore informant: someone (more often than not white) residing in a relatively isolated agrarian community who had little or no formal education:

[This study] is a collection of superstitions and folk beliefs made by Mr. Redfield through his first-year classes. Since these students are all attending a boarding school in which they have to earn all of their way, it becomes

clear that their social and economic backgrounds of home life are pecu-
liarly of the sort into which this type of folklore is most deeply rooted.

In 1938, J. A. Rickard left Tennessee Tech for a teaching position at Texas
A&M. In an issue of *Bulletin* that year, the editor noted a problem related to
statewide involvement in the society's mission: "As our work has gone forward
in the four years of our life as a Society we have had splendid interest in Middle
and East Tennessee but the fact that there has been relatively slight interest
from the western end of the state has been to a large degree the omission of our
organization to make contacts in that section rather than lack of interest." To
improve the participation of West Tennessee residents in the society's mission,
former society president C. S. Pendleton gave a presentation to the English
section of the West Tennessee Education Association that year. His effort met
with some success, but the eastern and middle sections of Tennessee, especially East Tennessee because of its association with the "culturally retarded"
world of Appalachia, are better represented in the articles published in early
issues of the *Bulletin*.

At a meeting of the society in Nashville in 1940, member Donald Davidson
delivered a provocative paper subsequently published in the *Bulletin*, "Current
Attitudes Toward Folklore," that in essence called into question the motivations of those whom he politely referred to as "devotees" of folklore. Born in
Campbellsville, Tennessee, Davidson is best known for his association with the
Agrarian movement at Vanderbilt University. He was one of the "Twelve Southerners" (authors) of *I'll Take My Stand: The South and the Agrarian Tradition*
(1931), a treatise that argued for the preservation of the distinctive, agrarian
cultural traditions of the South considered under threat of obliteration by mass
commercial-industrial forces of change. Unfortunately, his notion of cultural
preservation also embraced racial segregation. To Davidson's credit, however,
was his interest in preserving the folk traditions of the South with the ultimate
intent of keeping them alive in a genuine folk matrix of citizen performance. As
he says in his essay:

> The true cherishers of folk traditions are, first, the family, in its traditional
> role, securely established on the land, in occupations not hostile to song
> and dance and tale, and second, the stable community which is really a
> community and not a mere real estate development. If we cannot cherish
> these, we cannot hope to cherish folk song; and probably we cannot long
> cherish the high forms of art that feed upon folk traditions; and we may
> even prove ourselves ignorant of what life really is.

The attitudes toward folklore discussed in Davidson's paper include the
"historical-scholarly," "enthusiastic-promotional," "commercial-exploitative,"
and a fourth that he advocated but did not name. In a footnote to the article,

the editor of the *Bulletin,* Edwin Hunter, suggested calling it "participating-propagative."

Davidson expressed concern about the corruption of folklore through the formal educational process, but other members of the society believed that folklore should be an integral part of the secondary school curriculum. In an article, "Folklore as an Aid to the Teachers of History," published in a 1939 issue of the *Bulletin,* J. A. Rickard wrote,

> There have been complaints that history deals only with the great, tells only of vast movements, of decisive changes, and outstanding leaders; that it ignores the common man as an individual. Folklore, in a measure at least, fills that lack. Folklore is the embroidery of a people's history. It is often a better clue to the character and psychology of a country than is the cold and factual account of its history.

Rickard's article examined how folklore can be used to broaden the scope of history in ways that historians today recognize as "social history." In "The Teacher and Folk Arts" (1943), Susan B. Riley, a professor of English at Peabody College, dismissed Davidson's purist position about the legitimacy of folklore promulgated through formal instruction:

> Their attitude is like that of all of us who enjoin an outsider not to handle or blow his breath upon a magnolia lest its petals blight and turn brown. They feel that a natural art can not flourish in the unnatural setting of a school house; that when folk materials become conscious, they cease to exist.

Another article published in the *Bulletin,* "Folklore as a Foundation in Public School Education" (1950), by C. S. Pendleton, endorses Rickard's and Riley's position that folklore materials have an essential place in humanities courses. Many early members of the society, mostly English teachers, were already involving students in the collection of folklore and were using folk tales, legends, riddles, and proverbs published in the *Bulletin* as teaching aids to introduce students to the folk "literature" of Tennessee. Pendleton, Rickard, and Riley, however, were seeking an official imprimatur. A major step toward that goal occurred in 1946, when two society members, George Pullen Jackson and Charles F. Bryan, a professor of music at Tennessee Tech who later moved to Peabody College, coauthored the first public school textbook devoted to American folk music, *American Folk Music for High Schools and Other Choral Groups.*

Following the precedent of other classical music composers, Bryan, supported by a Guggenheim Fellowship, drew upon a well-known Tennessee folk legend and elements of traditional music in crafting his composition, *Bell Witch Cantata,* which premiered at Carnegie Hall in 1949. Two years later a performance of that composition was given in Nashville. In an issue of the *Bulletin* that year, Bryan reflected on his creative motivation:

The enthusiasm of the sophisticates who write, arrange, and concertize will have great influence on the "folk," and will help them re-discover that which for centuries was theirs alone. Perhaps, most of all, the real folk music will return because there is no substitute for the genuine. The pseudo may sparkle, but the genuine satisfies.

Though they differed in their perspective on including folklore in school curricula, Bryan and Donald Davidson had a mutual interest in promoting among the public a greater appreciation of "genuine" folk music, and the two men worked together on a "folk" opera, *Singin' Billy*, that premiered in Nashville in 1952. Bryan composed the musical score and Davidson conceived the plot and lyrics. They never stated in print the context of their position on "genuine" folk music, but it is reasonable to infer that they were reacting to what they perceived as the negative consequences of the commercialization of folk music by an emerging country music industry in Nashville.

In a 1939 issue of the *Bulletin*, editor E. R. Hunter announced that the society would not be able to cover the cost of printing four issues of the journal. Partial support for the journal from the National Youth Administration during the Depression had been withdrawn, and the society had to depend solely on modest annual membership dues of $1.00. That amounted to $112.00, just enough to sustain the *Bulletin*, but several society members were delinquent in paying their dues. "Two immediate conclusions seem clear," Hunter wrote. "1) We must have more members. 2) Those who have not paid for 1940 must pay if we are to hold our ground." Fortunately, membership increased significantly from 1940 to 1947 from 112 to over 200. More important, library subscriptions, altogether representing twenty-nine states, increased dramatically from six in 1937 to seventy-two in 1947. The society was now exchanging journals with several state, regional, and international folklore associations and numerous other professional associations.

Edwin C. Kirkland of the University of Tennessee at Knoxville became editor of the *Bulletin* in 1942, a position he held for less than a year due to military service. Dorothy Horne, professor of music at Maryville College, assumed editorship that year and continued in that role until 1947. E. G. Rogers of Tennessee Wesleyan College served as editor from 1947 to 1952, and William Griffin, professor of English at Peabody College, was editor from 1952 to 1966.

In 1966, production of the *Bulletin* moved from Peabody College to Middle Tennessee State University in Murfreesboro, where it remained until 2007. A succession of MTSU professors served as editor. Ralph W. Hyde was editor from 1966 to 1979, with MTSU's Ann Farris, William H. Holland, and Charles K. Wolfe serving as assistant editors. Wolfe served as editor from 1979 to 2004, with the assistance of Guy F. Anderson for much of that time. The *Bulletin* is currently headquartered at the Jubilee Community Arts Center in Knoxville and edited by Brent Cantrell.

The *Bulletin* today is the longest continuously published regional folklore journal in the United States. Throughout its long history, the journal has published articles by many of America's leading folklore scholars, including Henry Glassie, Alan Dundes, Richard Dorson, Stith Thompson, Joseph S. Hall, Archie Green, Wayland Hand, Dorothy Horne, and D. K. Wilgus. Over the years, several articles published in the *Bulletin* have been reprinted in textbooks and anthologies, thereby greatly expanding its visibility. One standard and very popular folklore textbook, Jan Harold Brunvand's *Study of American Folklore,* includes references to numerous articles from the *Bulletin.*

During the society's "golden era," the period of its largest membership and widest influence, arguably 1947 to 1985, the society could boast of a number of accomplishments. In the 1960s, the organization cosponsored its first recording project for public release: a seven-inch disc containing play-party songs recorded by Tennessee singer Billy Jack McDowell. In 1967, the society played a role in influencing Governor Ellington to declare November 4, 1967, Tennessee Folklore Day. The next year the society contributed to the implementation of the Tennessee Arts Commission's Folk Arts Advisory Panel.

During the 1970s, the society spearheaded several efforts to promote the study and preservation of folklore in Tennessee and across the nation. In 1973, the society cosponsored the American Folklore Society's annual meeting, which was held that year in Nashville. Also that year, the influence of the society on Tennessee's legislators ensured that Tennessee was the first state in the nation to witness its full congressional delegation supporting the American Folklore Preservation Act (Senate Bill 1844). By the mid-1970s, the society was working with the Tennessee Arts Commission to create the position of director of folk arts/state folklorist. Concurrently, responding to the need for obtaining funding from state and federal sources to support its projects, the society applied for and attained not-for-profit status.

In 1976, the society issued its first LP recording, a collection of field recordings of Uncle Dave Macon made in 1950 by Charles Bryan, George Boswell, and David Cobb. Also at this time, the organization supported the production of a series of newer documentary field recordings, including such projects as a collection of historical ballads from the Tennessee Valley, recordings of performances of traditional material by the Hicks Family, and an oral history of the Free Hill community. In the 1980s, the society supported television documentary productions such as the regional Emmy Award–winning *Uncle Dave Macon Show.* Recent society-sponsored productions include recordings of two important African American musicians: one featuring rare performances by former Grand Ole Opry harmonica player DeFord Bailey and the other containing performances of banjo songs by Will Slayden, a musician from West Tennessee.

The society reached its peak of membership and influence at approximately the time of its fiftieth anniversary celebration in 1984. The annual meeting that year was a widely publicized gala event held at the place where it all began, Tennessee Tech. One later accomplishment of the society was the nationally renowned Tennessee Banjo Institute, a series of events celebrating the folk heritage of the banjo initiated by society member Bobby Fulcher in the early 1990s.

Folklorists continued to recognize the *Bulletin*'s more traditional role of publishing descriptive studies. In 1984, prominent folklorist Herbert Halpert, long associated with the folklore program at Memorial University of New-foundland and author/mentor of several articles published in the *Bulletin*, wrote a general letter to the society in which he said, "Keep on doing what you're doing. Too many of the journals feel they have to be theory oriented. Those are fine, but you are making an important contribution by reporting the folklore, folk tales, and folk music of your area." Over the years, other scholars have echoed Halpert's endorsement of the *Bulletin*.

In 2009, the Tennessee Folklore Society marks its seventy-fifth anniversary. In the future, the society must endeavor to adjust to evolving notions of the purpose and meaning of folklore studies in a postmodern society seemingly more interested in popular rather than traditional culture. Much work remains to be done on preserving and interpreting the old folk culture of Tennessee and the South, but the society and its journal must also recognize and embrace a much more diverse cultural landscape. These challenges can be met only if the society continues do what it has done since its inception: cultivate a strong working relationship between the academic community and the public it serves.

Appendix B
Past Presidents of the
Tennessee Folklore Society

1935–36	Charles S. Pendleton	George Peabody College
1937–38	T. J. Farr	Tennessee Technological University
1939–40	L. L. McDowell	Dekalb County Schools
1941	Edwin C. Kirkland	University of Tennessee, Knoxville
1942	George Pullen Jackson	Vanderbilt University
1943–44	Susan B. Riley	George Peabody College
1945–48	Ms. L. L. McDowell	Smithville
1949–50	Charles F. Bryan	George Peabody College
1951–52	Freida Johnson	George Peabody College
1953–54	George Boswell	Austin Peay State University
1955–56	E. G. Rogers	Tennessee Wesleyan College
1957–58	George C. Grise	Austin Peay State University
1959–60	Mildred Hatcher	Clarksville
1961–62	Gordon Wood	University of Chattanooga
1963–64	Ambrose Manning	East Tennessee State University
1965–66	Thomas G. Burton	East Tennessee State University
1966–67	Mildred Payne	University of Tennessee, Martin
1968–69	C. P. Snelgrove	Tennessee Technological University
1970–71	Walter Haden	University of Tennessee, Martin

1972–73	Robert S. Whitman	George Peabody College
1974–75	Mary Manning	East Tennessee State University
1976–77	Stephen F. Davis	Austin Peay State University
1978–79	James E. Spears	University of Tennessee, Martin
1980–81	Graham S. Kash	Tennessee Technological University
1982–83	Michael Lofaro	University of Tennessee, Knoxville
1984–85	Bobby Fulcher	Tennessee State Parks
1986–87	Richard Blaustein	East Tennessee State University
1988	Homer Kemp	Tennessee Technological University
1988–89	Charles H. Seeman	Country Music Foundation
1990–91	Anthony Cavender	East Tennessee State University
1992–93	Bettye C. Kash	Tennessee Technological University
1994–95	Laura C. Jarmon	Middle Tennessee State University
1996–97	James Akenson	Tennessee Technological University
1998–1999	Patricia Wells	Middle Tennessee State University
2000–1	Richard Blaustein	East Tennessee State University
2002–3	Brent Cantrell	Jubilee Community Arts , Knoxville
2004–5	Ted Olson	East Tennessee State University
2006–7	Walter Haden	University of Tennessee, Martin
2008–9	Evan Hatch	Arts Center of Cannon County

Index

414   INDEX

Honeycutt, D. H., 287–88
Hopkins, Lewis, 89, 92
Horne, Dorothy, 405–6
horse, 61, 67–69, 88–89, 145, 368; ghostlore, 97
"House Carpenter," 302
House of Representatives, 253
Houston, Sam, 254
Houston, Texas, 279, 284
"How Many Times," 294
Howard University, 315, 325
Howell, Benita, xv
Hubbard, Clarence T., 137n15
Hubbard, Elizabeth Wheeler, 155, 159
Huddelson, Stokley, 228
Hudson, Palmer, 155
Hughes, Washington, 137n11
Hugo Worch instruments, 311–12
Hulan, Richard, 278–79, 287, 358
Hull, Billy, 229
Hull, Cordell, 229
Hull, Mrs. Cordell, xii
Hunter, Edwin R., 400, 402, 404–5
hunting, 30, 369–70; bear hunts, 96
Huntsman, Adam, 253
Hurston, Zora Neale, xxiii
Hurt, John, 324
Hyde, Ralph, xix, 279, 281–83, 405
Hyde, Thomas, 117
hymn, 295, 324, 349, 373

I

"I Love Thy Kingdom," 319
"I Want to be Ready," 323
"I Wish I Was Single Again," 373
"I Would if I Could," 328
"I Wouldn't Marry At All," 373
I'll Take My Stand: The South and the Agrarian Tradition, 403
"I'm a Good Old Rebel," 394

"I'm Going Back Home," 335n7
"I'm Working on a Building," 324
identity, xi, xvii, xxi, xxiv, 109, 124, 203, 212; individualism, 9
"If I Had My Way," 329
Illinois, 132; Fairbury, 132; Monmouth, 30
Illinois Traditional Country Music Festival, 261
immigration, xxiii, 12, 87, 299, 366, 374
"In the Jailhouse Now," 269–70
Independence Day, See Fourth of July
India, 25
Indiana, 123, 129–30, 132, 359
industrialization, 365, 375; food production, 45; Tennessee, xvii
Institute of Musical Art, 316
instrument manufacturers: Gibson, 336, 342; Martin, 336, 342
instrument, collection, 311–13, 358, 316; drone basses, 311–13, 350; folk, 308, 310, 312; homemade, 336, 348–49; novelty, 325; string gauge, 350
instrumental music, 307, 319, 322; folk music, xxv
International Storytelling Center, xiii, 217
Ireland, 43, 156–57
Irish Travellers, 359–60
Iron Men, 134, 138n26
Iron Mountain, 110, 114
Irwin, John Rice, xiii
Irwin, Ned, xv
Isle of Man, 156–57, 159
Ives, Burl, 159
Ivey, Bill, xii

J

Jack Daniel distillery, 279–80
Jackson, Andrew, 234, 239, 249–50, 253–55

Jackson, Ewing, 175, 177
Jackson, George Pullen, xii, 317, 324, 399, 402, 404, 409
Jackson, Mahalia, 296
James, Henry, 334
James, William, 325
"James Harris (The Daemon Lover)," 299, 302
Jarmon, Laura C., 410
jazz music, 322, 332
"Jealous Lover, The," 369
Jefferson, Blind Lemon, 335n8
Jefferson, Jesse James "Preacher," 322
"Jesus, Jesus," 292
"Jim Bobo's Fatal Ride," 278–79, 283–91; author, 282–83, 28–88; text, 282–83; textual analysis, 283, 286, 288, 290; variations, 288–91; witness account, 285–86
Jim Crow laws, 376
Jimmie Rodgers Memorial Festival Talent Contest, 262
"Jimmy Randall," 302
"John Henry," 315, 324
"John the Revelator," 329
John W. Work III: Recording Black Culture, xiv
"Johnny Was the Miller Boy," 372
Johnson City Comet, 219–20
Johnson City Press Chronicle, 226
Johnson City Staff, 220–21, 226
Johnson, Andrew, 202
Johnson, Charles S., 323, 326, 330
Johnson, Freida, 409
Johnson, Guy B., 317
Johnson, Hall, 316
Johnson, James Weldon, 319, 333
Johnson, Lyndon B., 132
Johnston, Jack, 235
Jones, Benjamin Franklin, 302–3
Jones, Bud, 219, 221–24, 226–27